MW01115000

Bomber Pilot

A Time for Love and a Time for War

10 March 01

Bomber Pilot

A Time for Love and a Time for War

a novel by

William Wheeler

*To Nick Berger,
Hope enjoy my story

Sincerely,
Bill Wheeler*

Rutledge Books, Inc. Danbury, CT

The names of several individuals have been changed at the discretion of the author in order to protect their privacy.

Front cover photo by Joseph Harlick, photographer, 91st Bomb Group.

Rutledge Books, Inc.
107 Mill Plain Road, Danbury, Ct. 06811
1-800-278-8533

Manufactured in the United States of America

Cataloging in Publication Data
Wheeler, William

   Bomber Pilot

   ISBN: 1-58244-080-8

   1. Fiction.

Library of Congress Catalog Card Number: 00-103214

Dedicated to:

Mary, a truly remarkable young woman
...And the young men of Aviation Cadet Class 42G
who gave their lives in the air war over Europe.

Acknowledgements:

James Parton's book *Air Force Spoken Here*
General Ira Eaker and the Command of the Air.

Jospeh Harlick, 91st Bomb Group photographer for the jacket
cover, *Contrails*.

John Gillespie Magee poem: *High Flight*

High Flight

Oh, I have slipped the surly bonds of earth
And danced the skies on laughter-silvered wings:
Sunward I've climbed, and joined the tumbling mirth
Of sun-split clouds—and done a hundred things
You have not dreamed of—wheeled and
soared and swung
High in sunlit silence, Hov'ring there,
I've chased the shouting wind along, and flung
My eager craft through footless halls of air.
Up, up the long delirious, burning blue
I've topped the windswept heights with easy grace
Where never lark, or even eagle flew.
And, while the silent, lifting mind I've trod
The high untrespassed sancity of space
Put out my hand, and touched the face of God.

John Gillespie Magee

Prologue

Doris Carlton was nineteen years old when she arrived at the Anderson's estate in Oxfordshire, England. It was a warm sunny day in October 1918. She was employed as a nanny for the Anderson's four-year-old grandson, Matthew. Their daughter Martha was abroad with her husband, a member of the foreign service assigned to the embassy in Cairo. Although Doris wasn't a trained nanny, she obtained the job through a mutual friend of her mother's.

Doris left her home in Holywood, Northern Ireland, when her mother decided to remarry. Her father David was a major in the medical corps and had served with the Royal Ulster Brigade. He was killed in a forward aid station during the battle of the Somme in August 1916. Two years after his death her mother decided to remarry Michael O'Leary, a man whom she'd recently met. He was dark and handsome, but to Doris he was a coarse brute of a man, completely different from her father. She saw him as an uncouth braggart and could not imagine what her mother saw in him. Doris told her mother she would not live in the same house with O'Leary. Her mother would not alter her marital plans and finally agreed to let Doris go to England.

Doris's father was a kind and gentle man who had been born in County Armagh. His father, Squire Charles Richard Carlton, inherited a large landholding in Armagh and emigrated from England to claim the estate in 1886. David elected to practice medicine while his twin brother Charles assumed his father's title and landholdings. Before the war, Doctor Carlton had a medical practice in nearby Belfast where he willingly served all his patients regardless of their faith. Most of them admired and respected him. He was a Protestant, but not a pious one.

Doris's mother Mary was a beautiful, fiery, and vivacious woman from Grogheda in southern Ireland. She was a casual Catholic who attended Mass infrequently, ignoring the wrath of her parish priest. Doris was educated in a Catholic school and attended Mass with her mother, but there was never any pressure placed on her to swear an allegiance to any religion.

The Anderson's son, Captain Frank Anderson, was released from a hospital near Le Havre, France, and returned home to Shipton six months after Doris arrived. He was an infantry officer and had served with the British Fourth Army in France. He was seriously wounded in the last major battle of the Great War.

Captain Anderson was reassigned to duty at a British Army installation in the Midlands in December 1919. During subsequent visits home from his duty station, Frank and Doris became romantically involved. By autumn of the following year, Frank's attraction to Doris manifested itself into a deep and ardent affection and she, in turn, fell madly in love with him. His parents and the household staff were unaware of their relationship.

On January 4, 1921, Captain Anderson received orders for duty in Dublin, Ireland. He wrote to Doris from his duty station and begged her to come to see him before he left England. She readily agreed and journeyed by train to Northampton, a short distance from his duty station. The trip was Doris' first venture away from the Anderson's household and she went with great anticipation and a throbbing heart. There she and Frank spent the better part of her three-day holiday in bed at the small inn where she was staying.

The morning after their last night together, Frank saw Doris off at the rail station for her return trip to Shipton. Before boarding the train, he held her close, reaffirmed his love for her, and promised they would marry on his first leave from duty in Ireland. Ninety-two days after reporting for duty, on April 10, 1921, Captain Anderson was shot in the back and killed by an eleven-year-old Irish boy.

Mrs. Coughan, the Anderson's housekeeper, was the first to notice Doris's pregnancy and managed to extract the truth from her. When the Andersons were informed, they dismissed Doris. They would not consider the possibility that their son was the father of her unborn child. Doris refused to go home to Ireland because of her fear of and dislike for Michael O'Leary. Mrs. Coughan found accommodations for her in London.

Doris left the Andersons in May 1921, and moved to Paddington, London, where she rented a small flat from Mrs. Maryann Chambers. Although the Andersons wouldn't acknowledge their son's involvement, they did make arrangements for Doris's financial support.

The baby was named Mary, after Doris's mother, and was born on October 7, 1921. Doris died two months later from complications suffered during childbirth. Mrs. Chambers, through arrangements made with Mrs. Coughan, agreed to care for the baby. Chambers received a suitable financial settlement from the Andersons for Mary's continued care and support. No formal adoption action was taken.

Chapter 1

On November 24, 1942 thirty second lieutenants stepped off a Pullman into an early morning chill and a dampness that threatened snow. As airmen will, their first glance was skyward to the low, moisture-laden clouds. They were a grubby lot in their wrinkled uniforms and unshaven faces. There was the usual amount of bitching after a long, tiresome, and uncomfortable train ride. But for the most part they were a happy group and their eager expressions reflected adventurous anticipation. They left Rapid City, South Dakota, the previous day and rode a day coach through the night. The hard, stuffed, wicket-covered bench seats offered little comfort and less chance for sleep.

The airmen dropped their B-4 bags and gathered around an army captain and a sergeant who were standing on the deserted end of the railroad station platform. The captain was slight of build, probably 5' 7", and his dark mustache and glasses gave him a prim appearance. He was dressed in a short army overcoat, freshly pressed pink trousers, and highly polished brown shoes. His black-rimmed glasses and neat attire, and especially his stiff-rimmed garrison cap, marked him as a nonrated officer. When the arriving group of officers settled down around the captain, he spoke to them in a soft Georgian accent.

"Good morning, gentlemen. Welcome to Pocatello, Idaho. I'm Captain Kramer, adjutant of the Harris Provisional Group. The best transport I could get for you all were four GI trucks." He pointed to the canvas-topped, two-and-a-half-ton trucks behind him. "Sorry, but that's all I could get from base motor pool. Sergeant Williams and his men will help you load your gear in one truck. Then climb aboard the others. We'll drop you off at the base mess hall where you can get breakfast. Your gear will be left at the transit BOQ. You'll bunk there until permanent quarters are assigned. There's no scheduled activity for today, but I suggest you all start clearing in. Be sure to check in with personnel and finance."

The sergeant passed around base clearance sheets listing all the base functions they would be required to report to. The captain added, "You may not have a hell of a lot of time to clear in later. The colonel's got a pretty rigid schedule set up for you all-starting at 0700 hours tomorrow in the mess hall where you'll meet the man. Your air crew assignments will be made right after the briefing. Any questions?"

"Yeah, what about the officer's club?" one of the guys shouted.

"There is one, but it's not finished. There's a bar, but no mess. It's a new base. The permanent party, the air base group, arrived here just two weeks ago in time to receive our complement of B-17s. You guys should be accustomed to moving into new bases by now. This one's no different."

Lieutenant Ed McMann looked up at the trench-coated officer beside him and said, "He's got that right, Bill. That's all we've seen since we left Boise. Remember they didn't have runway lights at Rapid City when we finished our phase training at Walla Walla and had to divert back to Boise." McMann bore a remarkable resemblance to the Walt Disney character, Dopey, and had a disposition to complement his likable personality. His large, innocent-looking, and wide-set eyes were set in a round, youthful face.

"Yeah, I remember, Dopey, but I didn't mind it a bit and I wasn't the only one. Most of the group found some reason to delay leaving so we could have another run at Boise. That was a great town," responded Bill Weyland, recalling the racy blonde, Helen, he'd met there. She was all right and Bill enjoyed the couple of dates he had with her. But she was apparently interested in someone with a higher rank than he had.

Bill Weyland was a tall, slender young man with light brown hair and blue eyes. He was a soft-spoken New Yorker who grew up in Scarsdale, a suburb of the city. Although he appeared reserved and aloof, his slow smile and the reckless glint in his eyes seemed to contradict that impression. He had a casual, confident demeanor that men as well as women found attractive and likable.

Weyland had been a restless young man. He left college early to roam the country, convinced that worldly experience was more important than a formal education. Fortunately, he found his niche in the army where he settled down and earned his silver wings and a commission. He was part of the pilot training class that graduated the previous July at Columbus, Mississippi. The class of two hundred pilots-much to their disappointment, as most had visions of becoming fighter pilots-was assigned to Second Air Force at Salt Lake City to be trained in heavy bombardment aircraft. There they were disbursed to several newly formed bombardment groups throughout the Rocky Mountain states. Weyland and twenty-nine classmates joined the Ninety-sixth Bomb Group stationed at Boise, Idaho, as B-17 copilots.

In October, the Ninety-sixth Bomb Group was scheduled to take off from Walla Walla at 1100 hours to arrive at their new base, Rapid City, before dark. But at 1300, nineteen of the group's B-17s were still on the ramp faking some mechanical malfunction. They finally got off at 1500 and were forced to divert back to their former base at Boise for one more hell-raising night in a very hospitable city.

The Ninety-sixth was scheduled to deploy overseas in November after completing their phase training; however, the airbases in the United Kingdom were not ready to receive new groups. America was organizing and training bombardment units faster than airfields in the UK could be built. This was a great break for Weyland and his classmates. They were upgraded to first pilots and transferred to Pocatello,

Idaho, as aircraft commanders, leaving the Ninety-sixth at Rapid City.

The experience of the new pilots left much to be desired, but they eagerly accepted their new roles as B-17 pilots. Bill, in particular, dreaded the thought of being sent overseas as a copilot. Above all, he wanted his own crew and all the recognition and responsibility that went with the position. Stick time for a B-17 copilot was based strictly on the generosity of the pilot he flew with. Bill's pilot would occasionally, but reluctantly, relinquish the left seat so his copilot could shoot some touch-and-go landings. Weyland had 248 hours of four-engine time, most of which was in the right seat, and very little actual instrument time. He had about thirty takeoffs and landings and felt confident that he could get the bomber off the ground and back down again. The rest, he reasoned, would come as he acquired more time in the left seat. Bill grinned inwardly when he recalled his upgrade flight. It was a dark, starless, November night over western South Dakota when he and his classmate, Larry Wilcox, got checked out. They were scheduled to fly with an instructor pilot, Lieutenant Sheldon.

Shortly after takeoff the IP climbed out of the left seat and told Larry and Bill to stay in the local area and shoot some landings. He then went down in the crawl space beneath the cockpit and sacked out. After four landings each and about an hour and a half later, Sheldon came back up, got in the left seat, and landed the Seventeen. He silently filled out Form 1, dropped down to the ramp and, without a word, headed for Base Operations. Wilcox and Weyland followed him wondering, "What's with this guy? He's sure not very talkative." Just before entering the Ops building, Sheldon stopped and turned to the anxious young flyers and said, "Well, you guys didn't kill me so I guess you passed your check ride. "Congratulations. Consider yourselves B-17 aircraft commanders."

Captain Kramer said, "Okay, men, if there's no more questions load up and get some chow. I'll see you at 0700 tomorrow morning."

The pilots handed their bags up to a private in the back of one truck and then climbed into the three remaining trucks and dropped their butts on the hardwood benches and headed for the greatest adventure of their lives.

Shortly before seven o'clock the following morning, some three hundred souls had finished breakfast, cleared the tables, and sat patiently waiting for their new commander.

Lieutenant Colonel Hunter Harris arrived at precisely 0700 hours. Captain Kramer, a major, and three captains accompanied him. The colonel had a ruddy complexion and thinning hair, but was trim and handsome in his well-cut green air force uniform. He was not a tall man, but was sturdily built, probably not more than 5′ 7″, but when he spoke he had the aura of a much taller person. There was a commanding presence about him. He spoke firmly and with authority. However, there was something about his manner that made him appear friendly and approachable.

"Welcome to Pocatello and your new organization. Our mission is to train thirty combat-ready aircrews in three months. A pretty tall order, but I know we can do it. We've set up a twenty-four-hour schedule to fully utilize our complement of B-17s. You'll fly eight hours and spend eight hours in ground school and I suggest you try to get some sleep in the remaining eight hours. That will be our routine six days a week. We've set you up in three flights of ten crews each. Captains Evans, Slater, and Todd here will be your flight commanders. Major Kirkland is my exec and he'll double as your training officer. Captain Kramer will take care of your personnel and administration needs. Not much of a staff, but there's an airbase group here, the 417th, that will support us in all the other essential base functions. It's a tough schedule, but I know you men can handle it and get through your training by 1 March. And like all young Americans, I'm sure you're anxious to get overseas and into combat.

"Some of you might be concerned about your limited flying time and training, but we'll start you off with the basics and you'll be well supervised. I am particularly concerned about safety and I want you to conform to all the flight safety regulations and requirements we've established. You'll be trained systematically and effectively to prevent any problems or accidents. Flying and being a part of a B-17 aircrew is a demanding and a serious challenge, but a really rewarding one. It is extremely important that each crew member develops the essential skills required to ensure the safety and survival of the whole crew. And this is particularly important and necessary in combat. It's a team effort. So let's get the job done and do it right.

"Captain Kramer will call out the crew assignments. He'll assign each pilot a crew number from H-2 to H-31, and fill in the crew members from the roster of officers and men here. The official designation of our thirty aircrews will be the Harris Provisional Group. After crew assignments, Major Kirkland will brief you on your flight training schedules and assign you to one of the three flights. Captains Evans, Slater, and Todd, our flight leaders, will check you all out initially and fly with you occasionally to check your progress.

"That's it men. Welcome aboard. You'll soon be well-qualified combat replacement crews ready for any assignment your country demands of you. Thank you.

At the adjutant's sharp command, all men present stood erect and watched Colonel Harris leave the building. When they settled down, Kramer opened a folder with a stack of orders containing a list of 270 aircrew members who had recently arrived at Pocatello to be assigned to each pilot's crew. Weyland's was crew H-29.

The newly arrived crew members were fresh out of their specialized training courses in pilot, navigation, bombardment, flight engineering, radio, and gunnery. Some had less than six months of military service and most had never before seen or been in a B-17.

After the adjutant assigned each pilot his crew designation, he arbitrarily called out the names of the men to fill the crew positions in the numbered crew: Andrews, crew H-2, Hamilton, crew H-17, Scurlock, crew H-29, Thompson, crew H-27, Toner, crew H-28.

Weyland looked each man over carefully as they joined him to become a member of his crew. They were a diverse group-all sizes and shapes, ages from eighteen to twenty-eight-but he was generally pleased and impressed by the look of them. However, now that he faced his new crew for the first time, Bill was suddenly struck with the awesome responsibility he'd just assumed. He realized that these men came under his command by the luck of the draw. They had volunteered and were willingly putting themselves in his hands. Every decision he made as aircraft commander would impact all of them. Did he have the necessary experience and skill to be trusted with their lives? Second Lieutenant Weyland had his silent doubts, but reasoned that the army apparently thought he could do the job, and he was determined to prove them right.

The crews gathered in groups around their pilots. Weyland stood before his team and gave them a brief sketch of his background. Bill's overly modest remarks about his qualifications and experience did not go over well at all. Their expressions clearly reflected the anxiety and concern they had about his ability. They had all volunteered for aircrew duty as he had, but he realized that the reality suddenly became apparent and they must be thinking, "Here's the guy we've got to fly with. How good is he?" They would learn of his ability much sooner than he or his crew expected.

Their first flight together as a crew with their assigned flight leader, Captain Todd, went well. Todd sat in the right seat, paying particular attention to pilot's performance. The flight was primarily to assess the pilot's ability and familiarize the crew with the terrain and the local flying area. After three reasonably good landings, Todd was satisfied that Weyland was capable of handling the B-17. As they gathered after the flight, Bill was particularly pleased to note the crew's reaction, reflecting perhaps some confidence in his ability.

On the third day after Weyland's crew was formed, they were scheduled to practice takeoffs and landings in the immediate area of the airfield. However, an aircraft mechanical problem delayed their takeoff and it was dusk before they lifted off their B-17. All went well until they were climbing out after their third touch-and-go. Suddenly the aircraft was completely engulfed in thick clouds. There was little warning and the pilot failed to notice that a fast-moving weather system had quickly moved down the valley and settled over the field.

The ceiling dropped instantly, and Bill found himself immersed in the thickest fog he had ever encountered. As he desperately searched for the ground while trying to control his growing panic, he was startled by the voice in his headset.

"Seven zero six niner. This is the tower. Do you read me?"

Bill quickly replied, hoping that help was close at hand. "Seven zero six niner, go ahead tower."

"Ah, seven zero six niner, be advised that the field is below minimums. Maintain your downwind leg heading and advise tower of your intentions."

The response from the tower stunned Bill. What intentions? He had none. He hadn't the foggiest idea what to do. With less than twenty hours of actual instrument time, all of which had been with an experienced pilot in the cockpit with him, Bill was now completely on his own. His fear was beyond anything he'd ever experienced. He had absolutely no vision outside the aircraft.

"Seven zero six niner, did you copy?"

Bill glanced hurriedly at his copilot, who was sitting with his hands clenched in his lap, looking out the side window as though he was sightseeing and hadn't heard the tower. Bill realized he'd get no help from him. Close to panic, Bill resisted the temptation to stare into the black void in front of the windshield and forced his eyes back to the lighted instrument gauges. He saw that the aircraft had slipped to the left in a descending turn. Rejecting his initial panicked reaction to haul back on the control column, he eased the left wing up, then gently raised the nose and added power until he regained the lost altitude and slowly banked the aircraft back to its original heading.

He steadied himself, and in the calmest voice he could muster said, "Tower this is seven zero six niner. I'm running out of downwind leg. If I can't land, request immediate clearance out of the area."

To his surprise, his commander answered, "Bill, this is Colonel Harris. I don't want you to attempt a landing in this stuff. Climb out of it in a shallow turn to your left. Start turning now and begin climbing. Keep your rate of climb to five hundred feet a minute and hold your turn to one half needles width. Circle the field until you break out. The tops of the clouds are estimated at eleven thousand feet. Wind is out of the northwest at twenty knots. Tune in to our radio beacon here and try to stay within a ten-mile radius of the field. I'll get an alternate for you. In the meantime, I'm here in the tower if you need me."

Hearing the calm, confident voice of his CO had an immediate and positive effect on Weyland. With a sense of renewed strength, he replied anxiously, "Seven zero six niner, yes, sir. Wilco." He turned to his copilot and said, "Hal, give me twenty-three hundred RPM and thirty-five inches and let's get the hell out of this stuff."

Hal DeBolt was a healthy-looking six footer, with brown hair and light gray eyes set in a pleasant, open face. A typical American lad, he was eager and enthusiastic about being part of a B-17 crew. He had been a postal worker in Holister, California, where he spent most of his life, except for two years at a state college. Hal was assigned to Weyland's crew fresh out of flying school with a total of two hundred flying hours. His eagerness and enthusiasm more than made up for his lack of experience.

"Roger, Bill," Hal replied as he advanced the throttles and prop controls. "Damn, that stuff really rolled in fast. Looks like it's pretty thick, too." He hesitated, forced a smile, and added, "You're doing great, Bill."

With his eyes glued to the flight instruments, Bill started climbing over what he believed was the airfield. When Hal tried to tune in the radio compass to the local beacon, Bill said, "That thing is no damn good. The ball turret gunner on an earlier flight shot off the antenna. It was written up as a discrepancy in the Form 1 and I signed off on it. Didn't think we'd need it shooting touch-and-go's." That's one mistake I won't make again, he swore.

Prior to takeoff, the pilot is required to check the discrepancies written on the aircraft maintenance forms. If a fault hasn't been repaired and the pilot feels it will not jeopardize the flight, he may initial it and fly the plane.

To further complicate matters, the radio range station for

Pocatello hadn't been activated. The lack of these essential navigational aids did little to ease Weyland's apprehension. His confidence was further shattered when chunks of ice off the props were thrown with great force onto the fuselage. After the initial shock, he regained some sense of control but realized that surface ice was a real danger. As it built up, the aircraft became noticeably sluggish, and the rate of climb dropped to less than three hundred feet a minute. Silence replaced the usual chatter on the intercom as the crew heard for the first time ice being hurled at them from the propellers.

Bill turned to the anxious, white-faced flight engineer standing behind the two pilots and said, "Bayne, keep an eye on the manifold pressure for any sign of carburetor ice." The manifold pressure instruments measured the amount of power output of each engine. The first indication of carburetor ice, a condition that would choke off the fuel supply to the engines, would be a rise in manifold pressure.

"Yes, sir. I've been watching them, lieutenant," he replied in a shaky voice.

Sergeant Bayne Scurlock was a Texan and a mighty proud one: self-assured, direct, and quick to exalt the greatness of his state. His chiseled, attractive features complemented an imposing physical appearance and precise military manner. He was a technical sergeant with more military experience than most of the other enlisted crew members, and Bill was fortunate to have him in his crew.

Bill muttered to no one in particular, "I sure hope we're over the damn airfield." The most frightening and unsettling aspect to Weyland was not knowing exactly where he was. His crew could do nothing to help him. He was completely on his own and their lives were in his hands. The airfield was located in a valley surrounded by some of the highest mountains in the Rockies. Try as he might to concentrate on the instruments, it was impossible to dispel the vision of the aircraft slamming into the side of a mountain. He feared not so much for himself as he regained some sense of steadfastness, but his fear and agonizing concern for the crew weighed heavily on him. Bill heard the crew's fear in their voices when each one responded to his order to put on their oxygen masks as they slowly climbed through eight thousand feet.

As hard as Bill tried to concentrate on the flight instruments, he couldn't resist the temptation to look out into dark gray night sky. The magnetism of the dense clouds that surrounded the aircraft was more appealing than the green, subdued, fluorescent lights of the instrument panel. The drone of the aircraft engines and its rotating beacon reflecting off the clouds did little to block out his fascination for the scene outside the cockpit. He sat for several minutes staring into the void, gripping the control column, and willing the clouds to dissipate and vanish. But the tense presence of Bayne and Hal close to him in the cockpit, leaning forward and staring into the emptiness, forced him back to reality and to the instruments he knew he must trust.

Climbing up through the thick clouds, the aircraft suddenly shook with an intensity beyond anything Bill had ever experienced. It felt like a huge force was determined to tear the wings off the bomber and wrench the control column from his hands. The turbulence was so severe that Bill knew they couldn't possibly survive the night. The B-17 abruptly plunged several hundred feet in an air pocket. It felt as though the bottom fell out from under him and he could do nothing to stop it. He heard Scurlock cry out behind him and Bill shouted to the copilot, "Check the crew, Hal! Get them strapped down."

The flight engineer pulled himself up groaning, but appeared to be okay. Without any effort on his part, the bomber ascended sharply regaining the lost altitude of seven hundred feet.

"The guys are all right, Bill. A little banged up and scared, but okay."

Finally, they mercifully climbed out of the rough air and the pilot regained a share of confidence. In the cockpit, as cold as it was at their altitude, Bill had difficulty maintaining a good grip on the sweat-slicked control column. He kept rotating his hands between the yoke and his thighs, pressing the palms of his hands against the fabric of his flying suit in an effort to wipe them dry. If only a little of that moisture could relieve the dryness in his throat. His tension eased each time he heard the confident and encouraging voice of his commander. They'd been in the clouds for less than thirty minutes, but to the pilot it was an eternity.

Suddenly, as if he'd abruptly awakened from a nightmare, the B-17 broke out into a beautiful, clear, night sky. The snow-covered peaks rising out of the clouds seemed close enough to touch. The brilliant moon illuminated the sky so brightly they could see the shadow of the aircraft racing along on the clouds beneath them. It was unquestionably the most spectacular sight he had ever seen. The relief was spontaneous as the crew released their tension in a chorus of exclamations. Although overwhelmed by relief and the sheer beauty of the night, Weyland looked at the solid undercast beneath them. It wasn't time to relax.

"Tower this is seven zero six niner in the clear at 11,500 feet, request alternate field, over."

"Well done, Bill. Your alternate is Salt Lake City. Current weather there is five hundred feet, five tenths cloud cover, and ten miles visibility. They expect the present conditions to hold for an hour, so you shouldn't have any trouble getting in there. Call me when you put down."

"Roger, sir. Leaving your frequency for air traffic control en route to Salt Lake City."

With Colonel Harris's praise ringing in his ear, Bill confidently switched to air traffic control and received permission to proceed to his destination. He called the navigator for a heading, and he responded with his first contribution as a crew member. Their destination was a little less than two hundred miles to the south and they estimated fifty minutes en route.

Without a radio compass, Weyland tuned in to Salt Lake City radio range station and turned to intercept the north leg. Letting down on a radio range station was difficult under the best circumstances, particularly for a pilot with limited experience. He finally recognized static sound where the A and N quadrant's signal overlaps and started his erratic flight down the beam toward his alternate.

The undercast beneath them remained solid and Bill knew that the frontal system was rapidly moving toward his destination. He said a little prayer, trusting more in the Lord than the weatherman.

Approximately thirty miles from their destination breaks began to appear in the clouds below. Soon the partially obscured lights of the city were visible through the clouds. A sigh of relief escaped Bill as he realized that they'd won the race with the weather front.

"Landing checklist, Hal!" he almost shouted.

"Yes, sir," came the equally enthusiastic response as Hal turned and grinned at the pilot.

The engineer behind them anxiously reported in a voice that also was a bit too loud. "All systems in the green, lieutenant."

Bill hauled back the throttles, pushed the nose down, and headed for the largest hole in the clouds. He contacted the tower and was cleared to land. He was told to expedite his landing as the field was expected to go below minimums in a matter of minutes.

"Not before we get there," Weyland murmured.

He steepened his descent and rolled the B-17 over in a near vertical bank. As the aircraft approached, the opening in the undercast seemed to get smaller, but Bill slid the bomber through and leveled off just beneath the base of the clouds.

"Jesus, lieutenant," Bayne choked out behind him, "You've couldn't have done better with a P-40. Nice flying."

Bill silently accepted Scurlock's spontaneous compliment but didn't have time to acknowledge it because immediately in front of them, just west of the city, was the airfield.

Weyland grabbed the mike, "Salt Lake tower this is Army Air Force seven zero six niner. Request straight-in on runway 27."

The radio crackled in his ear, "Roger, army air force seven zero six niner. You're cleared for a straight-in on Runway 27."

Bill called, "Check gear down, Hal."

Hal replied instantly, "Gear down, locked, and in the green. One half flaps coming down, 2,300 RPM."

The resonance of increased power and the lowered pitch of the propeller rumbled though the cockpit, the latter giving the pilot more responsive acceleration in the event of a missed approach. Bill approached the runway in a nice gentle descent, but leveled off about twenty feet too high and dropped the fort down onto the hardtop. He was so relieved to be on the ground that the rough landing didn't bother him at all. He did, however, proudly and silently accept the expressions of relief and complimentary wisecracks from the crew as he taxied to the parking ramp. Before he cut the switches, the tower announced that the field was closed.

Weyland remained in the pilot's seat for a short time after the crew had anxiously deplaned and thought how lucky he was. With the grace of God, he'd landed them safely. Two B-17's from Second Air Force were lost that night. One crew bailed out and was eventually picked up after being scattered over a wide area of Wyoming.

On Christmas Eve 1942, the thirty pilots of the Harris Provisional Group were promoted to first lieutenant. What a glorious day it was. However, because of the scheduled activity, Weyland had to wait until New Year's Eve to celebrate-and celebrate he did. He and three classmates thoroughly enjoyed the gracious hospitality of the wonderful people of Pocatello.

Throughout the course of the evening, Bill met a cool brunette who was far from the country bumpkin one might expect in Idaho. She was great fun and they had a ball. He vaguely remembered her putting him in a taxi that got him back to the base and dumped him off at Base Operations. He managed to get a couple of hours sleep, lying on the floor on top of his parachute.

"Hey, Bill, let's go." Weyland woke and looked up to see Hal leaning over him.

"What's up, Hal?" Bill replied, rubbing his eyes and trying to focus on his copilot.

"We're scheduled to take off in an hour. What happened to you? You look like hell. Where have you been? You weren't in your sack."

"I'm okay. Just thought I'd get some sack time here instead of going back to the BOQ."

"You sure you're okay to fly? The crew's on their way out to the Seventeen."

"I'm fine, Hal. I got my gear right here. Let me wash up a bit," Bill said as he stood up, brushed his uniform off, and ran his hand through his hair. He opened his parachute bag and pulled out his flight suit and headed for the men's room.

"I'll start the clearance, Bill. Get yourself some coffee. There's a pot in the weather office."

After Bill signed off on the clearance and they both sat in on the weather briefing, they picked up their chutes and headed across the ramp. Bill, suffering from a violent hangover, said to Hal, "The weather looks real good. Should be a good flight."

The crew was onboard when Bill and Hall reached the bomber. After the walkaround inspection, Bill threw his chute up in the forward hatch and then tried to chin himself up. After three failed attempts, Hal said, "Here, let me give you a boost up."

As soon as Bill got into the left seat, he put on his oxygen mask and turned the regulator to one hundred percent. They went through the checklist, cranked the engines, and taxied to the runway. Bill turned to the centerline of the runway and pushed down on the brake pedals. Before advancing the throttles, he turned to his copilot and said, "All set?"

Hal looked at Bill for a moment before responding. "I'm all set. How 'bout you?"

Weyland pushed the throttles full forward, released the breaks, and off they went. It was a wonderful flight and he felt that he could do just about anything with that big old Fort. He zoomed down through the valleys and soared up over the mountains, skimming the tops by a mere hundred feet. They played in and around the big white fluffy clouds and the crew loved it, but Hal, knowing Bill's condition, at times looked a little tense and concerned. Bill's landing after the six-hour flight was flawless. But the minute he dropped down through the hatch and hit the tarmac, his hangover returned with a vengeance. Later, when he sobered, he realized what a stupid and irresponsible stunt it was to endanger the lives of his crew and faithfully promised himself that he'd never do it again.

Chapter 2

In their short time together, Weyland's crew developed a closeness and camaraderie that would probably never be equaled again in their lives. They had an elitist feeling about themselves, and their pride and loyalty were matched only by the confidence they had in each other, and particularly in their pilot. Their trust in his ability was difficult to comprehend since he was as inexperienced as any member of his crew. For his part, Bill was well aware of his limitations and mindful of the grave responsibility that he alone had for the lives of the nine men who flew with him. Yet he flew with a certain bravado and daring that bordered on recklessness. However, the men in his crew never showed any reluctance to fly with him. Most bomber pilots, and Bill was certainly among them, were frustrated fighter jocks and flew the Seventeen like it was a hot, single-engine aircraft.

The crew would fly under the worst possible conditions, and more often than not be scared to death during the flight. Together they had survived several harrowing experiences flying over and through the Rocky Mountains in the foulest weather conditions.

Early one morning, returning from a long flight to Little Rock, Arkansas, they bumped into a fierce snow squall over Kansas. The radio compass spun around like the pointed needle on a roulette wheel. Stunned for a moment, Bill wondered, "What now?" The radio compass was used religiously by pilots as the primary navigational aid even though there was a navigator aboard. He picked up his mike and called the navigator, "Joe, our compass is out. Can you give me some idea where we are?"

"Hold on a second, Bill."

Lieutenant Joseph Newberry was a tall, stocky, and gentle-looking young man from Crookston, Minnesota. He had three years of college at the University of Minnesota before joining the army. He was an amicable and congenial fellow and the guys in the crew really liked him. Although an affable and accommodating person, he was particularly serious and conscientious about his assigned duty.

"Bill, we're about one hundred and twenty miles west of Wichita."

"Joe, I don't want to fly into the Rockies with no compass. Can you find some place where we can put down? Looks like we're flying right into this stuff."

"Right, Bill. According to the weather reports it should still be clear to the south of us. I can give you a heading to Amarillo. It's 220 degrees magnetic-about three hundred miles."

"Sounds good, Joe. I'll clear with traffic control and head for Texas." He switched over to the intercom call button. "Okay, guys, it looks like we're going to ROM at Amarillo Air Force Base. Hope you've got your toothbrushes."

Weyland was pleasantly surprised by Newberry's quick response to what could have been a serious problem. Bill thought, "I've got a navigator aboard-a real good one and I should damn well use him."

All the crew members, officers, and enlisted men ate and slept together in the same barracks, something frowned on by the army. But no doubt, some bright young psychologist reasoned that if they had to fight together, they should live together. Whatever the rationale, it worked. They managed to find fun and laughter in the monotony of ground school, eating unsavory GI food, or while trying to keep warm in cold barracks.

BOMBER PILOT

No crew members were spared from the unrelenting and constant pranks that followed them through their endless hours of training. They used humor to relieve the tension that came as they prepared for and flew in the weary and overworked bombers. Generally the crew's practical jokes were directed at the pilot and the officers in the crew. When Bill attempted to grow a mustache, the crew gave him an ultimatum: Shave it off or we won't fly with you. He had to admit it was kind of scraggy, but he refused. He then suffered the indignity of being held down by the entire crew while Scurlock shaved it off.

Despite the closeness and familiarity between the officers and enlisted men, no one took advantage of his position or rank. There was no morale problem with this crew. They were eager and ready for war. They found the sleepy Western towns different, but the local people welcomed them with open arms and treated them as if they were their own sons. The young girls were eager to show their patriotism by pleasing and accommodating the glamorous airmen while the local young men were away in the armed services.

Lieutenant Woodward, their bombardier, and DeBolt met twin girls in Pocatello. They were beautiful brunettes. It turned out to be serious and both Hal and Woody promised to return after the war and marry them.

The group had eighteen old B-17E models, and to fully utilize the aircraft, the thirty crews were equally divided into three flights and put on three eight-hour alternating shifts. Most of the sleeping was done while flying or during ground school, while the eight-hour period for sleeping was spent bullshitting or horsing around.

The flight training amounted to little more than staying airborne for eight hours and accomplishing a navigational exercise at most. Aside from the navigator and the pilots accumulating flying and instrument time, the other crew members accomplished little or no training. They could normally plan their own flights over a large area of the West. The only limitation was the eight-hour fuel range of the aircraft.

On one occasion they flew to Crookston, Minnesota, to Joe Newberry's hometown. The sun was just rising over the little

Midwestern town when their bomber arrived overhead. Half joking, Bill asked Joe if he wanted to wake up his neighbors.

"Well, we wouldn't want anyone to oversleep and be late for work. So I guess we better go down and shake them up a little," responded the navigator.

"Okay, Joe," Bill grinned as he dropped down from their cruising altitude of six thousand feet to two hundred feet, increasing the airspeed to 210 knots, and made a pass over the town and climbed out in an abrupt vertical bank to the left.

After Joe completed navigation school and before reporting for crew duty at Pocatello, he went home and married his high-school sweetheart. He called up, "Hey, Bill, can't you get a little lower? I'd like a closer look. Martha's house is north of town on the main drag. I might get to see her."

Over the intercom, the entire crew shouted their support in vociferous unison.

"Sure can, Joe. We've heard a lot about that gal of yours, so I think we better see if she's as beautiful as you claim."

He nosed the bomber down to treetop level and headed for downtown. The bomber roared directly over the main street of the town. They were so low that Bill had to lift the right wing over the church steeple. As they pulled up, Hal pushed the props up to 2,600 RPM and the Seventeen climbed out in a thunderous, window-rattling roar. Looking back, Bill watched the people rushing out of their houses and looking up in shock at the huge bomber flying just above them. He saw an engineer stop a locomotive in railroad yard and jump down to get a better look. The little town came to life quickly.

Unknown to Bill, Joe dropped a note to his wife out of a small hatch in the Plexiglas nose. Fortunately, the ammo canister cover used as a weight tore through the paper bag in the slip stream and the note blew away. Two weeks later Joe got a copy of his hometown newspaper displaying a huge headline and a story describing the terrifying mock attack on their town by a giant bomber. Luckily no one there thought of taking the tail number of the aircraft. If they had, Weyland may have ended up a ground pounder in the infantry. And no one in the crew, including Joe, got to see Martha.

On the first of February, the group was moved to a new base at Casper, Wyoming, where bulldozers had cut away all the vegetation leaving only loose sand, tar-papered buildings, and a concrete runway and ramp. With a constant thirty-knot wind, a mixture of sand and snow cut exposed skin like a sandblaster. The tar-papered barracks had four open bays, each with one small potbellied stove. The bays had four two-man cubicles each separated by six-foot partitions. They were bitterly cold and some of the crew slept in their clothes, including their sheepskin flying suits. To make matters worse, Weyland insisted on sleeping with the windows open.

"Woody" Woodward, their bombardier, objected vigorously, "Come on, Bill, we'll freeze our balls off in here. Christ, it's minus twenty degrees outside and with the windchill factor it must be down around minus sixty."

Lieutenant Denver Woodward was from Portsmouth, Ohio. He was a big raw-boned man with the complexion and classic features of an American Indian. His accent was a mixture of a Kentucky drawl and an Ohio twang, and he had a down-home sense of humor that matched his rugged appearance. Having washed out of pilot training, Woody ended up in bombardier school, but didn't seem overly upset about not being a pilot. He said he just wanted to drop bombs on Hitler's Deutschland.

"Look, Woody. I've slept with my window open all my life and I'm not going to change now. My mom always said fresh air is the best thing for you and it stops you from getting colds," Bill responded stubbornly.

"That's bullshit, Bill, and you know it. Shut the damn windows. You'll be sorry when your whole crew comes down with pneumonia and we're all grounded." The crew supported Woody.

The crew finally conceded when they realized there were double windows on the barracks and Weyland hadn't noticed and was just opening the inside ones. He didn't realize the difference because the wintry wind whistled through the many cracks in the buildings and he got all the fresh air he wanted.

Second Air Force finally set up a gunnery range near their base so the gunners could use live ammunition. There was a lot of excitement about it when the crews were told that they could finally fire their fifty-caliber machine guns. Bill was briefed to fly the figure-eight course at five hundred feet so the waist gunners on both sides would have an opportunity to fire at the target. His gunners insisted that he fly lower to give them a more realistic target. It turned out to be a pretty hairy experience flying at less than two hundred feet above rough terrain while the gunners fired at a shed in the middle of the course. It got much worse when two other Seventeens entered the course and started firing. Bill had a hard time trying to concentrate on the terrain he was flying over while in his peripheral vision he could see tracer slugs from adjacent bombers ricocheting off the ground toward him. They found several bullet holes in the fuselage after the gunnery mission. Shooting at stationary targets on the ground did little to prepare the gunners for air combat, but it was fun if not a little scary.

Before they left Casper, the crews were told they had to drop two hundred one-hundred-pound practice bombs. This unwelcome news came two days before they were scheduled to complete their phase training and leave Casper.

Weyland looked at their bombardier and asked, "Can we do it in two days, Woody?"

No one, including Woody, had any desire to stay in Casper a minute longer than necessary. Without any hesitation, he replied, "No problem. On each run, I'll salvo the load of blue dummies and have ordnance guys waiting to load another twenty when we land."

"Okay. It'll take us at least forty minutes to climb 12,000 feet and fly to the bombing range. If we drop at the minimum altitude with one bomb run, we should be able to get back in an hour and ten minutes. If we land, load up, and take off in thirty minutes, we can drop the two hundred bombs in two eight-hour flights and finish up tomorrow. How about it, guys?"

The response from his crew was a resounding, "Let's do it."

They dropped the two hundred bombs in ten flights. The exercise did little to improve the proficiency of the bombardier, but it got them through the last phase of training and out of Wyoming-and hopefully on their way to England. They had to wait two additional days for all the crews to finish.

When the thirty crews of the Harris Provisional Group finished their phase training at Casper, they entrained to an airfield at Salinas, Kansas, where they picked up their brand new B-17Fs. At the time, it was the most modern and formidable aircraft in the world. Representatives from Boeing Aircraft briefed the crews on its advanced features, and after twenty hours of familiarization flights, they flew to their embarkation base at West Palm Beach.

In Florida, Bill and several others pilots decided to hit the town for their last fling in the States. After numerous bars, his friends left him when he insisted there were many more night spots to check out. He went solo and finally turned himself in at the police station for fear of doing something stupid. He got a few hours sleep there before returning to the base.

Weyland arrived late the following morning for a scheduled meeting with Colonel Harris, well hung over and looking like hell. In retribution for his tardiness, the colonel appointed him the group supply officer. The remainder of his Florida stay was spent chasing down everything from chemical toilets to watches and sextants for the crews, while his friends lounged around the pool in the sun. He personally signed for over $50,000 worth of supplies. Every time he turned around someone handed him a scrap of paper with more demands.

Bill got little sleep the night before they left. With the help of three enlisted men, he unloaded three trucks filled with supplies. They sorted and stacked the equipment in front of thirty planes lined up on the ramp. He was so tired when they took off the following morning that he forgot to uncage his gyros and almost augered in when climbing out through the clouds. "Nice start," he thought.

They were finally on their way to Puerto Rico, the first leg of their journey overseas and, hopefully, to England and the air war over Europe. Everything else seemed insignificant. His tiredness soon dissipated and was replaced by a strong feeling of satisfaction as they left the clouds over the Florida coast and flew into a brilliant blue sky. He was exhilarated and his body pulsed with excitement in anticipation of the adventurous events ahead. From their lofty height of six thousand feet, he gazed down on the sparkling blue waters of the Caribbean. Suddenly, the color of the sea changed and he realized they were flying over the Gulf Stream. The emerald green river flowing through the azure sea was a magnificent sight. The remarkable change in color of the sea was a picture he would long remember.

They landed at Borinquen Field, a base located on a raised plateau overlooking the sea. That evening at the officer's club bar, Bill heard a familiar laugh. He turned and not five feet away was his old home-town buddy, Johnny O'Shea. Johnny was a cargo supervisor with American Airlines and was returning from South America. They hadn't seen each other in over two years, so they spent the rest of the night talking about old times over a bottle of scotch.

Bill suffered from another hangover when they took off the next day for Trinidad. Fortunately, they had an excellent autopilot onboard and that helped a lot. The following day the Harris crews went on to Belém in Brazil, at the mouth of the Amazon River. After landing, Bill left the crew to unload while he checked in at Base Ops.

When he returned, he said, "Looks like we might be here for a few days. The German subs are sinking our tankers bringing fuel here from the States."

They got transport and dropped the enlisted crew off at their billets. Bill told them, "If we don't see you guys later, take it easy and stay out of trouble. I don't want to leave any of you behind. I hear Brazil is very protective toward their young señoritas. So be careful."

"Yes, sir. We'll be real careful. We almost lost a pilot in West Palm," grinned McGovern. Sergeant Jim McGovern was one of the waist gunners and he was from New Haven, Connecticut. He was a little guy, slight of frame, but had a certain arrogant swagger about him. He had a mobile and expressive face that constantly seemed to conceal something humorous or witty.

The fiesta was in full swing at the time so the layover was not too unpleasant. Colonel Harris had been to BelÈm before the war on a goodwill tour and led the willing crew members to all the interesting places from the finest restaurants to the best whorehouses. The men quickly fell into the spirit of the celebration marking the beginning of Lent, joining young and old women in long conga lines that danced through hotel lobbies and across city parks.

After five days of celebration, the crews left for NATAL, the most easterly point of land in Brazil, where they remained overnight. The following day they made the long over-water flight to Ascension Island. It was a good navigational exercise to find the tiny mile-long island in the south Atlantic, which boasted a radio beacon with a range of just 150 miles.

As they approached the island, Captain Todd, a flight leader riding with Weyland's crew, left the nose compartment and came up to the cockpit. The three flight leaders in the group alternately flew a leg of each flight with different crews. It was Bill's turn to have Todd aboard.

Todd said to Bill, "Let me up there. I want to make the landing here."

Bill shook his head and said, "Hell no. I've been looking forward to this landing."

"Come on, Weyland, out of the seat and that's an order."

"Sorry, sir. It's my damn airplane and I'm going to set it down."
The argument continued onto the final approach; and when Weyland turned and glanced at his instruments, he realized that he was coming in too fast. He retarded the throttles, looked ahead, and noticed that the runway threshold was immediately at the edge of a cliff and it then sloped upward. Bill came over the boundary too hot and floated about a thousand feet down the runway. He hauled back on the yoke and dropped the plane in tail first. The landing was the worst he'd ever

made, and when the Fort started to wobble violently, he realized the tail wheel tire had blown when the plane hit the runway. The airfield was built on a small volcanic island and the runway followed the contour of the land over a fair-sized hill so that Bill couldn't see the far end when the plane touched down. They rolled over the crest of the hill at a pretty good clip and he was startled to see that the end of the runway was no more than a thousand feet away.

"Damn," Bill shouted. "Pull the emergency hand brake, Hal. Quick!"

The pilot stood on the brakes and hauled the yoke back to his chest. Fortunately, the blown tail wheel tire caused enough drag to slow the Fort down and they stopped at the very end of the runway. A short distance beyond was the edge of a cliff that dropped off to the ocean sixty feet below.

Todd, who was standing behind Bill, said angrily, "Well, Weyland, you damn near killed us. I ought to ground your ass, lieutenant." He left the cockpit through the bomb bay to collect his gear.

Hal grinned, looked at the pilot, and said, "Pretty close, Bill. Let's not do that again."

"Any landing that you can walk away from is a good one," Bayne laughed nervously, looking a little shaken from the near miss, "but I'm with Lieutenant DeBolt on this one, sir."

The serious nature of the incident hadn't been lost on Bill and he felt like a fool. "Sorry about that guys. I guess I should've gone around. Promise it won't happen again. I'll taxi off the runway and call for a tug to tow us in."

Weyland took a lot of abuse from his crew and other pilots when they heard about his landing. Bill was mad at himself for acting so foolishly and he hoped he'd seen the last of Captain Todd. As mad as Todd was, Bill half expected he'd try to court-martial him for insubordination.

The embarrassment was compounded when the crew learned it would take days, perhaps weeks, to get a replacement tail wheel. The following morning Bill was forced to watch the remaining crews, now only nineteen of the original thirty, take off for Africa on the next leg of their journey. Later that morning, Bill, thoroughly disheartened, went out to check on their plane. When he arrived he found his crew hard at work replacing the tail wheel.

"Where did you find that, sergeant?"

Suppressing a grin, flight engineer Bayne casually replied, "We found one on base."

Bill immediately dropped the subject when everyone appeared overly innocent and sheepishly silent. He realized that it wasn't wise for him to question the honesty of his crew and knowingly dropped the subject.

"How long do you estimate it'll take to get the wheel on, sergeant?"

"She'll be ready to go in a half hour, lieutenant."

"Good, then we'll head out for Dakar immediately."

"That would probably be a good idea, sir."

A short time later as they were taxiing out to take off, Bill noticed a B-17 parked next to the hangar with the aft end of the fuselage resting on blocks, minus a tail wheel.

"You guys do a little midnight requisitioning?" he asked Bayne.

"Now, you know I wouldn't do anything like that, lieutenant," Scurlock replied in mock innocence. "I believe that would be against regulations."

"That Seventeen one of ours?"

"No, sir. It belongs to some other outfit. They've been here for a couple of weeks. Lost an engine on the flight over and they're waiting

Bill looked at Hal, who shrugged his shoulders and said, "Probably blew that tire when they landed. This strip is real hard on tail wheels."

"Let's get the hell out of here," Bill said.

"Yes, sir, let's do that! The sooner the better," Bayne urged the pilot as he watched a jeep approaching them with a sergeant standing up in the front next to the driver. The sergeant was holding onto the windshield with one hand while waving frantically with the other for them to stop. With that, Bill turned onto the runway, pushed the throttles full forward, and let her roll. "Tower, this is

Army Air Force four seven seven niner clearing your frequency en route to Dakar."

The tower responded, "Roger, you're cleared." Behind them they heard Scurlock sigh loudly with relief.

They landed at an airfield near Dakar just before dark and were directed to taxi to an isolated dispersal area. There they were greeted by a group of painted black men armed with spears and shields. Under the circumstances, the crew was reluctant to deplane.

Bill called down to the bombardier, "You're not going to let a few cannibals scare you, are you, Woody? Go on out there and have a little powwow with them."

Woody responded, "Hell no, but I think I'll load up my .45 and take it with me just in case. You guys coming?"

"Yeah, we'll be right behind you, Woody. As soon as I finish filling out the Form 1." He turned and added, "Why don't you go along with them, Bayne."

After the three crew members disappeared through the bomb bay, they deplaned by the rear waist door with the rest of the crew. Bill looked out his side window as they came around the tail to the left side of the plane where the natives were grouped together. Woody held up his right arm in the traditional sign of peace and Bill expected to hear him to say, "We come in peace."

A tall, fierce-looking black man stepped up to Woody, held out his hand, and in passable English asked, "You got chocolate and cigarettes, yes?"

They proved to be very friendly after receiving generous amounts of candy and cigarettes. With smiles all around, they disappeared back into the bush to await the next American plane. The crew later learned that the fierce war paint and weapons were just their way of adding a little pizzazz to the reception in the hope of receiving gifts from the rich Americans.

Weyland's crew missed joining the other crews who were in town enjoying an erotic floor show at a French nightclub. Bill was awakened around midnight by the noisy gang of airmen returning from town. He could hear the guys in the next room taking about the sex show they'd seen. From what he heard, the acts were pretty damn explicit and obscene. He was glad that he hadn't gone. Not that he was prudish, but it would've been embarrassing, in the company of friends, watching what he considered to be something personal between two people.

At the takeoff briefing the next morning, the crew learned that two more aircraft in their group had been lost. One ditched off the coast of Africa, but the crew members were picked up. The other B-17, flown by Bill's good friend, Dopey McMann, with Colonel Harris aboard, made a forced landing in Portuguese Guinea. The plane and crew were detained because Portugal was a neutral country. The crew could possibly be held there for the duration.

Marrakesh, located at the foot of the Atlas Mountains in Morocco was their next stop. After landing and engine shutdown, Bill asked Bayne to hand him his briefcase.

"Okay, guys, listen up. I'm going to open our sealed orders. Keep your fingers crossed."

He pulled out the manila envelope marked SECRET in big red letters and tore it open, silently praying it wouldn't be Africa or the Pacific. The relief on Bill's face was unmistakable, and in a rare display of excitement, he shouted, "It's the UK. We're going to England. Hot damn!"

He heard the guys in the back cheering and shouting. Smiling broadly, Hal grabbed Bill's arm and Bayne broke out in a wild rebel yell. Woody popped up through the hatch between the pilots grinning from ear to ear.

Thirty combat replacement crews of the Harris Provisional Group had taken off from West Palm Beach on March 7, 1943, in their brand-new B-17s. Only seventeen reached Marrakesh on schedule. The others were lost, dropped out along the way with mechanical troubles, or ditched crossing the south Atlantic.

After a two-day weather delay, the remaining crews took off on their final leg for England, but only sixteen would reach their planned destination.

Shortly before reaching cruising altitude, Weyland was forced to shut down the number two engine when the oil pressure dropped. With a blackout in force, it took them a harrowing twenty minutes to get back and locate the airfield while trying to maintain a safe distance from the nearby Atlas Mountains. They circled the field for another agonizing thirty minutes before the ground crew got a few smudge pots lit so the pilot could line up the plane with the runway. The prospect of landing a fully loaded aircraft on a poorly lit, dirt runway just five thousand feet long brought many disturbing thoughts to Bill's mind.

When they were finally cleared to land, Weyland lined up the Seventeen and as they started down the final approach Sergeant Scurlock, standing between the two pilots, put his hand on the pilot's shoulder and said, "Put it in there, Bill, I know you can do it."

That being the first time that Bayne had called the pilot anything but sir or lieutenant provided just the added incentive Bill needed. It wasn't a pretty landing, dropping the plane in over the airfield boundary, but after a couple of severe bounces he managed to stop it just short of the runway's end. As disappointed as the crew was at turning back, they all felt relieved to be safe on the ground.

It took two days to get a replacement engine from Casablanca installed. After it was installed, Bill took the Seventeen up for the required test hop. Immediately after takeoff he had to shut down the new engine for loss of oil pressure. They waited two weeks for another engine, and it also failed shortly after takeoff. Each time the oil pump cover was removed they found it full of brass shavings. The possibility that someone had sabotaged the engines was considered. But eager to get to England, Bill wanted no part of a lengthy investigation and didn't press the matter.

Weyland said to Hal, "Let's find the base ops officer. I'm going to fly this bird to Casablanca."

Hal stopped and grabbed Bill's arm said anxiously, "You mean on three engines?"

"Yup," Bill replied.

They found the operations officer and Bill made his pitch.

"At the rate we're going through engines, we might be here for the duration. So what I'm going to do is off-load everything that's not essential and Hal and I, and my flight engineer, are going to fly our Seventeen to Casablanca and get an engine installed there. All you have to do is to give me a clearance and I'll be out of here."

The ops officer looked at Bill in amazement and said, "Are you nuts? No way would I clear you to fly there on three engines."

"Look, it'll be perfectly safe with just the three of us and the reduced weight," Bill argued.

"Absolutely not. They'd damn well court-martial me if I authorized your flight. Forget it."

The argument became intense, but ended when the ops officer threatened to call the base commander. Weyland reluctantly abandoned his flight of desperation and decided to go to Casablanca and get an engine. He found one, had it loaded aboard the C-47 shuttle, and accompanied it back to Marrakesh. The engine checked out and, finally, after an agonizing three-week delay, the frustrated crew departed for the United Kingdom. Weyland, impatient to leave and anxious to get to England, was not too attentive during the four preflight briefings he'd sat through and probably missed several essential elements of the presentation. Unfortunately, this inattentiveness would cause him considerable grief later.

Chapter 3

Seven and a half hours after takeoff they were flying east between a high overcast that screened the early morning sun and a darker undercast that covered the north Atlantic. The three airmen sat in the cockpit silently staring at the cloud-filled sky. They sat listening to the synchronized rumble of the four Wright Cyclone engines that loudly penetrated their metal and Plexiglas enclosure. It was a satisfying and secure sound and to the flyers it was the difference between being above the Atlantic and not in the frigid waters below.

The crew was anxiously awaiting their first glimpse of the British Isles. The pilot leaned forward over the control column and stared intently through the windshield as if willing the sky to clear so he might be the first to sight land. However, the high stratus and the clouds beneath them appeared to merge in an indistinct, gray void that extended far ahead of the aircraft. Bill turned to his copilot beside him studying a radio functional chart.

"Well, Hal, it looks like we're finally going to make it. I thought for a while we'd never get out of Marrakesh."

DeBolt replied hesitantly and with some concern, quite unusual from his normal upbeat attitude, "Yeah, it shouldn't be long now. But I don't like the look of that undercast. According to our weather briefing, there's supposed to be broken clouds over southwest England, but it looks pretty solid to me. I'd feel a lot better if we saw a few breaks in it."

"Roger that, Hal, but merry old England is up ahead somewhere and we'll damn well find it. You can take that to the bank. I've looked forward to this day for a hell of a long time and I'll be damned if we miss our final destination."

Bill looked out his side window at the ragged tops of the sea of clouds below them. He glanced back at the instrument panel and to the mounted clock for the fifth time in the last two minutes. Their estimated time of arrival was 0630 hours, nine minutes to Lands End. After a short pause, he said, "Let see how they're doing up front."

He picked up the hand mike, "How about it, Joe, where are we?"

"Give me a couple of minutes, Bill. I'm getting a fix now."

"Roger, but let me know as soon as you have it," Bill replied as he wondered what Joe was getting a fix on. There was no sun or stars. Maintaining a course by dead reckoning and celestial navigation while sustaining radio silence was a demanding exercise for even the best navigator.

Bill turned to the flight engineer, Sergeant Scurlock, who was standing just behind the copilot, "How are we doing on fuel, Bayne. Think we can suck any more out of the wing tanks?"

Bayne quickly but carefully scanned the fuel gauges, then turned to check the fuel transfer valves. "Got every last drop out of them, lieutenant. Less than two hundred gallons left in the mains, no more than thirty minutes flying time."

Bill thought his flight engineer's response lacked the confidence he normally conveyed. "Yeah, that's about right," the pilot agreed as he reached over and eased back the fuel mixture controls. "We've been airborne seven hours and thirty minutes. Guess I better lean out the mixture a little more. I sure don't want to ditch her short of England."

Their planned route from North Africa to the United Kingdom was designed to avoid overflying the neutral countries of Spain and

Portugal, and more importantly, to stay well clear of occupied France. They flew west from Africa to a turning point over the Atlantic Ocean, then directly north to fifty-one degrees north by fifteen degrees west where they turned again to an easterly heading toward Europe and their destination, England. Their time en route was estimated at seven hours and thirty minutes. Their flight had been uneventful, except for seeing the lights of Lisbon and some apprehension about meeting a German JU-88 night fighter over the Bay of Biscay. Most of the way, they flew through a dark but star-filled sky until they were within a few hundred miles of England, then the clouds materialized above and beneath them.

Now wide awake after a drowsy and sleepless night, their anticipation and excitement grew as they stared anxiously out of their Plexiglas ports at the cloud-filled sky. They were joining the Eighth Air Force in the United Kingdom, considered the roughest combat theater of operations in the world. At the time, there were only four operational B-17 groups in England. The American airmen were tasked to prove that daylight bombing against a formidable German Air Force was not only feasible, but effective.

Bill Weyland, more than any member of the crew, found it extremely difficult to control his excitement as they approached their destination. Getting to England had been his obsession for nearly three years. Now, as he sat in the left seat with his feet up on the rudder bar contemplating their arrival, he realized his dream had been fulfilled beyond his most optimistic expectations. He was in command of a Flying Fortress and its crew, and he was joining the courageous people of England in their fight against Hitler.

Weyland's thoughts were abruptly brought back to the present when the number four engine started to sputter. He quickly eased the mixture control forward until the engine smoothed out. He turned to his flight engineer standing behind him.

"Must've gotten a little too much air in the mix. The other engines seem okay. We'll just keep this setting. Okay with you, Bayne?"

"Not many other options, sir," Scurlock replied.

Bill looked out ahead. There were still no breaks in the clouds.

"Hal, give Joe a call. See if he's got that fix yet. I'd like to know where the hell we are."

The navigator called back, "Give me another minute. I'm working on it."

Bill's anxiety grew as they exceeded their estimated time of arrival over the coast of England. The possibility of overflying the British Isles and mistakenly thinking the Brest Peninsula in occupied France was the Cornwall coast was a real possibility. The similarity of the two coastlines on the navigational charts was striking. That would be a hell of a way to end his war.

With a measure of concern, he turned to the copilot. "How you doing with the radio compass, Hal? Identify anything yet? We should be able to pick up a station in England by now."

The radio compass was the most advanced navigational aid on the aircraft. Tuning the frequency to a known radio station at a specific location, the needle on the instrument would point to the station giving the pilot the compass heading to fly.

"Can't seem to interpret the facility charts and identify the frequencies in the listings they gave us. It's not set up like it is back in the States."

Glancing at the radio facility charts, Bill said, "Yeah, I see what you mean. I guess being in the war zone makes a difference. Can't publish everything so openly as we do back home. Just keep trying. I wonder if we missed something about radio aids at the preflight briefing last night."

Weyland took his headset and cap off, rubbed his eyes, and stretched out his arms. He turned to see Sergeant Thomas standing behind him next to Bayne and said, "Hi, Lloyd. How are the guys in the back room doing?"

Staff Sergeant Lloyd Thomas was a redheaded, ruddy-faced youngster from Joplin, Missouri, whom Bill probably admired more than other crew member. He was clean-cut-the perfect example of a wholesome Midwestern farm boy. He was also a brave and courageous young man, having elected to fly as the ball turret gunner, the most dangerous position in a B-17 crew.

Lloyd smiled and replied, "Fine, sir. But they're gettin' a mite anxious, so I came up to see how we're gettin' on."

The pilot grinned and in an effort to conceal his doubts said optimistically, "Doing great, Lloyd. Just about there. Joe's checking our position right now. I'll have a better fix on our e.t.a. in a few moments and let you all know."

"Okay, lieutenant. Guess we're all gettin' a little antsy and anxious to get to a place where we can settle in for more than a couple of days. Seems like a real long times since we left Florida."

"Yeah. Just about a month ago," Bill responded, thinking about their long and tiresome flight from the States.

After waiting several minutes and getting no response from the navigator, the pilot called again, "Hey, Joe, where are we?"

There was a prolonged silence and finally the navigator answered in a somewhat resigned and frustrated voice, "Hell, Bill, I don't know."

As surprising and alarming as the navigator's announcement was, and despite his anxiety, Weyland couldn't help but grin. "Now that was the most positively negative response I've ever heard." Shaking his head, he added, "That's not like Joe."

Hal forced a smile that failed to conceal his uneasiness. "It sure doesn't sound like our navigator. He must have some idea where we are."

"He better," replied Bill. Then into the mike, he said, "Come on, Joe, you gotta be kidding. Give me some idea where we are. Our e.t.a. is up and we should be close to the coast of England by now."

Joe replied reticently, "My last check on the winds indicated that we were bucking a stronger head wind than they forecasted."

Weyland hesitated for a moment, then announced to the crew, "Okay, I'm going down through this mess and take a look. I'll be damned if we're going to overfly England. Hold on and keep your eyes peeled."

Making the necessary prop and throttle adjustments, Bill cautiously nosed the aircraft down in a shallow glide into the clouds, trusting

God that the altimeter setting was not too far off and that they were over the ocean and not the hills of western England. Luckily, they broke out at six hundred feet, above water, but directly over a British cruiser and two destroyers. The ship's signal lights immediately started flashing, no doubt demanding the identification of the strange bomber overhead.

Bill shouted, "Give me the flare pistol, Bayne!" Quickly, he turned to the copilot, "Colors-of-the-day, Hal, what are they?"

Scurlock handed the pilot the flare gun, grabbed the box of flares, and held them up between the pilots. Hal looked at them and said,

"Damned if I know which ones to use, Bill."

"How about it, Joe. What colors?" Bill snapped into the mike as he watched men running to their gun positions aboard the ships preparing to fire on the unknown intruder.

"I'm not sure. Let me look."

"I need to know now!" Before Joe could respond, Weyland shouted, "Hell, I'm getting out of here. Give me some power, Hal, we're going back upstairs."

He shoved the throttles forward as the copilot adjusted the props. Bill visualized the gun crews aboard the ships anxiously waiting for the command to fire at the unidentified bomber. He decided to get the hell out of there as quickly as possible knowing discretion was far better in this instance than confrontation. No one would blame the ships' captains if they shot down the threatening aircraft rather than risk a sneak attack. After much confusion in the cockpit, everyone surmised that the colors-of-the-day was no doubt one of the essential elements they had missed during last night's briefing. As they disappeared into the clouds, Bill expected any minute to hear and feel the crash of cannon fire. He realized the clouds offered no real protection, only a sense of safety. Fortunately, the Royal Navy took no aggressive action and he slowly regained control of himself and leveled off the aircraft just above the cloud layer.

Ray Gillet, the waist gunner on the port side, called, "Sir, I saw a coastline to the north when we broke out under the clouds."

Sergeant Raymond Gillet was the assistant flight engineer and the other waist gunner. Ray was a dark, curly-haired, brown-eyed, handsome kid from Stockton, California. He looked Italian, like some of the young friends Bill grew up with. He was an unassuming and quiet guy, but he got along well and appeared to enjoy his relationship with the other men on the crew.

Woody called from the nose to confirm that he too had seen land to the north.

Bill, with obvious relief in his voice, responded, "Okay, Ray, Woody. Good. What do you think, Joe? Was it Ireland or England?"

"According to our e.t.a., it's gotta be England."

"Roger, Joe, I'm going to come around to the left and head in that direction, and I want everyone to keep their eyes open for any breaks in the clouds."

He turned to Hal. "Damn, I knew we should've paid more attention to those frequencies at the briefing. Just keep working that radio compass and see if you can find some station that we can identify and lock onto. I'll try to contact someone on VHF."

"Wilco," replied Hal.

After flipping through several ground control frequencies and getting no response, Bill began to wonder if he was, indeed, over England. He desperately punched through the VHF channels calling for assistance. Thinking the set was malfunctioning, Bayne changed crystals in the radio and the pilot went through the sequence again. Still no response.

Bill asked the radio operator, "Jim, who are you in contact with on the command set?"

Staff Sergeant James Cobb, the radio operator, was from Cove Creek, North Carolina. He was a good old southern boy with a drawl to match his quite and gentle manner. He was a tall, heavy-set, cigar-smoking man, and, though a bit untidy, he was a damn good radioman.

"Preswick, sir. What do you want me to tell them?"

"Never mind, Jim, they can't help us. Too far away. Just stay in contact in case we need them." Bill hoped they wouldn't run out of fuel and have to ditch or bail out and be forced to radio Preswick to alert search and rescue.

He got no response from repeated calls on VHF, just a lot of static. "What the hell am I gonna do now?" he wondered. All the fuel gauges were reading empty and the solid undercast remained beneath them. Just as he was about to broadcast a Mayday, the silence was broken by a perfectly delightful feminine voice that was so clear and distinct she sounded as if she were beside him in the cockpit.

"Army Air Force four seven seven niner, this is Red Ruth Control. Can I help you?"

Momentarily speechless, Bill turned to Hal, recovered and replied, "You sure can, ma'am. Can you give me a steer to the nearest airfield?"

"Roger, Army Air Force four seven seven niner. Give me a sixty-second transmission and I'll plot a fix on your aircraft." There was a slight hesitation and then, "Begin transmitting . . . now!"

The pilot slowly counted off the seconds, released the mike button, and waited. A minute later, the delightfully buoyant voice was back in his headset. "Roger, Army Air Force four seven seven niner, one minute please."

Bill said to Hal, "Boy, how about that? I sure love that English accent. She's got to be beautiful with a voice like that."

"She sure sounds good to me. Why don't we have controllers like that back in the States?"

"Army Air Force four seven seven niner, this is Red Ruth Control. I have you approximately fifty-five miles north northeast of Saint Eval Airdrome. Steer two two four degrees. Met reports ceiling six hundred feet, broken clouds, five miles visibility. Switch to tower frequency 247.7 megacycles for landing instructions. Welcome to England, over."

"Four seven seven niner to Red Ruth. Steering two two four degrees. Thank you! Thank you! You're a doll, and we're mighty happy to be here."

Bill switched to intercom and cheerfully announced, "Pilot to crew. Okay, you guys settle down and stop drooling over the body behind the beautiful voice. We've gotta get this bird on the ground before we run out of fuel."

The procedure of locating aircraft by radar was new to Weyland and the crew. "I sure like the way she got a fix on us. Didn't take her more than a few minutes. As far as I know we have nothing like that stateside. Hal, it's really great being here. They sure seem well organized. To say nothing of the delightful way these gals speak. I'm really going to like it here."

After turning to their new heading and letting down, a few breaks appeared in the undercast. Bill made a quick check of the navigational chart and found that Saint Eval was on the northern Cornwall coast near the town of Newquay. There were some fairly high hills to the east of the field, so Weyland let down rather cautiously and leveled off just under the cloud base. Eyes straining, he stared anxiously through the windshield trying desperately to penetrate the early morning mist to see the airfield. His first view of the English countryside was disappointing-nothing but drab, grayish-green, rolling hills. The only structure he saw was a small church completely isolated in what appeared to be uncultivated fields. Ah, but there just beyond it-almost invisible-was the runway. Bill thought the church was a good omen. It was an ancient Gothic structure with narrow stained-glass windows and a half finished steeple, as he watched it disappear beneath his right wing. The airbase beyond the church was almost obscured in the surrounding area with its camouflage buildings and painted runway.

"Oh, boy, what a beautiful sight," sighed Bill, after releasing great quantities of air from his lungs. "I don't think there's anything more satisfying after a long, nerve-racking flight than to break out of the clouds and there in front of you is that good old strip of blacktop. I feel like I've added five years to my life in the past hour."

"We've been airborne for eight hours and twenty-eight minutes. I'd say that's pretty good range on eight hours of fuel," replied Hal, as he reached forward to tap the fuel gauges with his knuckle.

"Not even a flutter," added Scurlock. "We're operating on empty, lieutenant. Can't cut the fuel mixture back any more 'cause we're running on fumes now. I'll feel a lot better when we get this bird on the ground. The engines must be just about ready to konk out."

Bill grinned, "We'll make it just fine, Bayne. I'll play it safe and keep my altitude until I get within gliding range of the runway."

The tower cleared them for a straight-in approach and after completing the landing checklist, Weyland finally relaxed when he reached the point where a dead-stick landing was possible. Bill looked to his left and saw a large, twin-engine aircraft turning onto a short base leg. He sat and watched in disbelief as the plane came straight across and turned directly in front of them for a landing.

"Jesus Christ!" he shouted, hauled back on the control column, and pulled the bomber up sharply while pushing the throttles full forward. "Goddamn idiot. What the hell is he doing? That was too damn close."

He grabbed the mike, but before he could transmit, the tower controller said, "Go around Army Air Force four seven seven niner."

"Roger," snapped Bill through clenched teeth. "Request immediate clearance to land. Low fuel, extremely low."

"Army Air Force four seven seven niner, you're cleared to pancake, number two after aircraft on downwind leg," replied the tower operator in a precise British accent.

Bill looked to his left and saw one aircraft on the downwind and another about to enter it. "What the hell does he mean, pancake? I'm going to land now." He flicked the mike button, "Tower, four seven seven niner, this is an emergency! I'm landing on 22, now! Over."

When directly over the field, he pushed the plane's nose down abruptly and turned sharply to the left in a near vertical bank. He made a tight 360-degree turn and just managed to level his wings about one hundred feet above the approach end of the runway. From there, he greased it in for the prettiest landing he ever made, much to the crew's surprise as well as his.

The incident didn't pass without several heated and disparaging remarks from the crew in the aircraft behind him and from the tower operator. Bill felt completely justified as he taxied to the parking ramp and his two outboard engines quit from fuel starvation. It was not the most unpretentious arrival to a nation known for being polite and proper, but purely a matter of necessity. The possibility of ditching the airplane a few miles from their destination sent shivers through his body.

They later learned that Saint Eval was used primarily as a submarine patrol base and the RAF pilots flying the old twin-engine Wimpies were not a happy lot. After a long, tiresome, and cold patrol they felt they'd earned the right to land when they wanted and certainly before a bloody Yank in a Fortress.

The American liaison officer met them with a big grin, remarked about the fighter approach and landing, then added, "Pretty nice touchdown. Welcome to the UK."

Bill, relieved, merely nodded, and said, "Sorry about that."

At debriefing, special mention was made of the incident involving an unidentified Fortress buzzing three Royal Navy ships. Bill acknowledged that they were the culprits and said they failed to respond because of radio and flare gun problems.

When Bill and Hal returned to their aircraft they found it secured and the crew standing by with all their B-4 bags lined up on the tarmac. Bayne stepped forward and in a very military manner said, "We've got your bags and the Seventeen is all buttoned up, lieutenant."

"Good, I've arranged for quarters and transport. It should be along soon."

Fifteen minutes later a small canvas cover van driven by an elderly Englishman arrived. He welcomed them aboard his lorry and they crowded into it.

On their way to quarters, they passed a group of big, rugged-looking women marching in loose formation carrying assorted farm tools. They were dressed in heavy brown wool knickers, sweaters, and socks and wore heavy shod boots. They were singing robustly, "Lay me down in the clover, Oh lay me down, roll me over, and do it again..." They raised their voices even higher when they saw the American and waved eagerly as the truck passed.

Bill, in front, heard McGovern holler, "Let me at 'em." And he made an attempt to jump off the moving truck. Bill also heard Bayne shout, "Hold it, little man. They'll tear you apart. Those gals are big-real big."

Bill asked the driver who the women were. The driver replied, "They're British Land Army young women. A good lot, they are. Do their part replacing the men that had to leave the farms for military service."

By the time they reached the officer's billet the guys in the back had settled down. The four officers got off, unloaded their gear, and thanked the driver. Bill walked to the rear of the truck and told the crew, "Get some chow and sack time." He looked at his watch and added, "We're going into town later. If you want to come along, meet us here at 1645. The bus leaves for town on the hour."

"Yes, sir!" they all responded enthusiastically.

Bayne got up in the front seat and Bill watched them drive off. He felt a sense of relief and pride knowing that they finally made it to England.

Chapter 4

Mary Carlton rushed out of her London apartment building on that morning in early April. It was obvious to those who knew her that she was at the moment not her usual self. Dressed in a stylish, dark-green suit that accented a stunningly mature body that belied her twenty-one years, her stride was purposeful. Her face, framed by shoulder-length, deep-brown hair that glistened auburn in the early morning sun, was notable for the angry set of her mouth and jaw. She looked neither right nor left to acknowledge the pleasantries of the concierge, or the haltingly suggestive remarks of young uniformed servicemen she passed, few of whom would have dared interpose themselves in front of what they perceived was a dauntingly self-assured and self-possessed woman.

As she reached the corner, Mary saw the number 73 bus pulling away from the stop across Park Road. The conductor, standing on the rear platform, called out to her, "Come along, luv. You can make it."

With a burst of speed, she caught the handhold and the busman grabbed her other arm to help her aboard. She smiled up at him and said breathlessly, "Thank you, Ralph. Don't know what I'd do without you. I'd be late for work most every morning. Poor Mr. Chalmers."

"Ere, don't you worry that pretty 'ead of yours, luv. I wouldn't leave without you."

Mary thanked him again and sat inside for the twenty-minute ride to Oxford Circus. Her face once again took on a troubled expression. She had a fitful night's sleep. The air raid sirens had aroused her on three different occasions. She'd also had a troubling experience at dinner the previous night.

Mary had met Anthony Hamilton a fortnight ago while modeling coats for Mr. Chalmers. After the showing, Hamilton asked her out to dinner that evening and she accepted. He was probably twenty-eight or so and wore a well-tailored civilian suit, which surprised her. But a number of young men had service deferments and she dismissed any objection she had to a man not in uniform. Mary was not one to pass up a dinner invitation when good food was so scarce during the wartime rationing, particularly when it was with a handsome, well-mannered, young man. His accent was distinctly upper-middle class, and he had a personable and charming way of talking to her, not at all stuffy like some Englishmen.

During the evening he scarcely mentioned her job or Chalmers's business. Afterward, he dropped her at her flat, held her hand, and brushed a good night kiss on her cheek. Mary had thoroughly enjoyed her evening with him and when he called her yesterday, she willingly accepted a dinner invitation and looked forward to an enjoyable evening.

After a delicious meal of Dover sole, Hamilton suggested they go to the Café de Paris. Shortly after they were seated, a gorgeous Eurasian girl approached their table and greeted Mary's companion very amicably and with a certain possessive familiarity.

"Hello, Tony, how are you?" She gave Mary a studied glance then turned to Hamilton, "If you have a moment later, I'd like to talk to you."

Hamilton stood, took her hand, and said, "Hello, Chinky. You're looking very beautiful tonight." He put his hand on Mary's shoulder and added, "I'd like you to meet Mary Carlton."

She looked at Mary, bowed slightly, and smiled reticently. She reminded Mary of an Oriental doll with beautiful dark, but lifeless, eyes. When Mary acknowledged the introduction, he added, "I'll stop by and chat before we leave."

Mary had seen the woman before. Of the many beautiful hostesses employed by the club, Chinky was certainly the most glamorous. She had a magnificent body, olive-colored skin, almond-shaped eyes and long sleek black hair that gave her a mysterious and exotic appearance. Quite obviously, she and Hamilton were more than just passing acquaintances. Mary was somewhat flattered to think that Hamilton was her escort when he could be with this magnificent creature.

When the girl left, Hamilton turned to Mary and said, "Lovely girl, isn't she?"

"Yes, she's very beautiful."

"I've known her for some time now. In fact, I helped her to get the position here. She does very well. As you might imagine." He stopped and smiled. A serious look crossed his face and he added, "How long have you been with Chalmers?"

"A bit less than a year."

"Do you enjoy your work there? I should think a girl with your ability would be doing something more demanding and interesting." He paused as if to gauge her reaction. "But, of course, the most important thing is that you're happy with your job. Chalmers seems rather a good chap. I imagine he pays well."

"Yes, I do like working there very much and Mr. Chalmers has been awfully good to me. In addition to my salary, he helps with my wardrobe. He made two lovely suits for me which I couldn't possibly buy with the few clothing coupons we're allotted." She hesitated and then went on to say, "I make enough to pay the rent and put a bit away each week."

Hamilton seemed satisfied with her response, but his expression changed as though he considered saying something but wasn't sure how to approach it.

Finally, he asked, "You had rather a long relationship with Georges Lavanas. What happened?"

"Yes, I did," Mary replied. "I left him about a year ago." She was surprised that he knew about her affair and added. "Do you know Georges?"

"No, Karas Peteros. I believe he's a friend of Lavanas. I know him quite well."

Peteros, as she recalled, had quite a reputation in London as a womanizer while his wife was stranded in occupied Greece. Mary wasn't comfortable with the direction the conversation was taking. To change the subject she asked, "What do you do, Tony?"

"I sometimes advise Joe Harris, the buyer I was with, on women's clothes. He's an old chum. I also do a bit of modeling menswear. But, I'm more interested in what you do. You know, you're a very beautiful girl, and I know you could do much better than you are working for Chalmers. I have a friend I'd like you meet. She's a lovely girl. I think you'd have a lot in common with her. I introduced her to a client of mine and she's doing very well. She has a delightful little flat on Mount Street in Mayfair."

"Really," Mary replied, impressed with the address. "Awfully good of you, Tony. But, I'm quite happy working for Mr. Chalmers. If I do decide to change employers in the future, I'll call you. I promise." They continued to talk and in his charming way he made Mary feel that he was sincere in wanting to help her. However, the hour was late and finally she said, "I must leave, Tony. I've enjoyed being with you very much but I have a work day tomorrow. Will you excuse me?" He stood when she left the table to go to the ladies' room.

While freshening her makeup, she overheard two women talking and when one mentioned Hamilton's name, her curiosity immediately drew her in.

"Oh, I hear he does rather well. Has several girls on the game. That Asian girl is one of his." They were quite involved in the discussion and didn't notice Mary among the other women there.

The woman's companion responded, "Quite. And I see he has a

new one with him tonight. She looks a bit young, but apparently that's the way he fancies them. I just can't imagine how a man can live off of women like that. He must be a real rotter. Paid someone to serve in the army for him as well."

Mary stood for a moment, stunned and trembling. After getting hold of herself she hurried from the powder room. Hamilton was not at the table, but over talking to Chinky when she returned. She picked up her fur coat and fled, hailed a taxi, and didn't stop shaking until she got home.

Mary had difficulty dismissing the unpleasant experience. What a fool she'd been! How could she have been so naive? It was difficult for her to believe that she had actually liked the man. All the while he'd been attempting to encourage her to become a prostitute. The busman call at Oxford Circus shut out Mary's thoughts about last night, and that man, Hamilton.

Mr. Chalmers's place of business was located on the first floor of a large building a few doors beyond Great Castle on Regent Street. Mary rushed up the stairs and into the showroom to be greeted by a cheerful, "Good morning, Miss Chapman." He stopped and looked closer and continued, "I can see you're not your happy cheerful self this morning? Anything wrong? Can I help?"

"No, thank you, Mr. Chalmers. Just had a bad night, a horrid dream."

Chalmers was a short, stout, bald-headed Jewish man who, along with his wife Paula had managed to escape Poland just before the Germans invaded the country. Within a short period of time, he'd established himself as a successful designer of women's outerwear. His greatest asset was an ability to design the garment and cut material with the least amount of waste. Given the wartime shortage of yard goods for clothing, he held a considerable advantage over his competitors in the trade.

Mary began working for Chalmers just under a year ago. In the short time with him she assumed many tasks beyond her principle role of modeling his coats. He was a very astute and shrewd businessman, but he had limited knowledge of London, and an Englishwoman's preference in clothing. Mary's fashion sense, pleasant personality, and natural talent for dealing with people made her a valuable assistant. She became his initial contact for new and potential buyers and an important asset to him in building a successful business. In addition to being his girl Friday, he was fond of Mary and treated her much like a daughter. He was a fine gentleman and would do anything for her. However, when it came to raising her salary, he did so reluctantly, saying with a grin that it wasn't consistent with his Jewish faith.

Mary modeled his sample suits and coats and he provided the clothing manufacturers with the patterns used to fabricate the styles they selected. They were medium-priced garments sold to large retailers. Although Mary wasn't involved in selling, Mr. Chalmers never discouraged her from influencing the buyers into purchasing a particular item she liked. She enjoyed her work and liked the people working there in the pleasant atmosphere of the small shop.

That day, Mary left work at the usual time and planned to spend a quiet evening at home. "No date tonight, thank you very much," she thought. During the day, she had actually come to think of the episode with Hamilton the pimp as quite amusing.

After her dinner of bangers and mashed potatoes, she settled down in her lounge chair to listen to BBC and the music of Jack Hilton. However, the music couldn't erase the humiliation of the night before and that turned to anger when she remembered dancing with Hamilton. Not surprisingly, her thoughts turned to her mother, thinking how similar her characteristics were to Hamilton's. Her mother was a strikingly handsome woman whose stylish clothes and elegant appearance distinguished her as a woman of culture. Hamilton, too, was well-bred and appeared to be a gentleman, but beneath that veneer they were depraved. A chill swept through her at the thought of anyone being that deceptive and morally corrupt.

On her own since she was seventeen, Mary Carlton rarely saw her mother now. She had an unpleasant childhood and wasn't close to her family. She knew nothing of her father, having been told that he died before she was born. Her half brother and half sister were much older and married with their own families.

When Mary was born, her forty-four-year-old mother was not overly thrilled with the prospect of raising another child, and she took it out on Mary, who became more a servant than a family member. One of her most lucid childhood memories was of a slate on the kitchen wall on which were listed her weekly tasks. She had to scrub the front steps and entryway, clean the silver and brass and polish the hardwood floors and furniture. Failure to perform any of the assigned chores resulted in harsh punishment.

Although Mary's life within the home was one of abusiveness and frequent punishment, outside her mother was obsessive about presenting a picture of upper-class, domestic tranquillity. She constantly reminded her daughter of the importance of good manners, proper diction, and the need to be fastidious about her appearance. When she accompanied her mother away from home, Mary was always dressed in expensive and stylish clothes, and her pageboy hairstyle was carefully groomed to complement her oval face and beautiful eyes. The impression her mother intended proved to be rewarding.

When Mary was six years old, her mother took her to Pontings, a large and popular department store on Queensway. On the main floor there was a crowd of children, Mary's age, gathered around a small stage set. Mary was wearing a green velvet dress trimmed with ermine. She attracted the attention of a man in charge and he asked Mary if she would like to join the other children in a screening contest sponsored by the store. Mary hesitated, but her mother did not. Mary was selected among the first group of twelve children, and following three days of tedious elimination, she was chosen the winner. The prize was an invitation to meet Henry Wilcox, the prominent film director, who offered Mary a part in a motion picture he was making. Mary later learned that her mother had prior knowledge of the screen tests and she'd taken special care in preparing her daughter for the occasion.

Mary's mother enrolled her in singing, dancing, drama classes, and numerous other courses that would enhance her acting potential.

She insisted that her daughter was capable and ready to accept any acting part that came along. She forced the child to one studio after another auditioning for any film in which the script called for a child actress.

Mary remembered with some fondness and embarrassment her first attempt at performing on the stage. While working on a film, she met Gracie Fields, the most popular musical comedy star in England. Gracie was immediately attracted to Mary and took considerable time offering her suggestions on how better to play particular scenes. A short time later, Miss Fields asked Mary to join her onstage at the Palladium where she was the featured performer. Mary explained she couldn't sing and dance, but her mother insisted she could. Within two weeks, Mary was taught a tap dance and song routine. Her performance was not one that she was proud of, but the audience and Gracie Fields liked it very much. Mary, however, as young as she was, realized song and dance were not her forte and she never attempted them again. Her mother reluctantly agreed and devoted her energy to Mary's motion picture career.

By the time Mary was nine years old, she'd acted in a number of films and was professionally recognized as a talented child actress. Her mother was completely enraptured by the film sets and the people. She became a person of importance through her daughter's acting ability. Mary became an entree into the theatrical scene that her mother used to satisfy her own interests. She drove Mary to complete exhaustion and if Mary rebelled she was harshly treated and most often beaten. Even with her frantic schedule of normal schooling, dramatic exercises, and auditions, Mary was still required to be the household drudge. Consequently, she became quite disenchanted with her acting career as she approached adolescence.

Mary dismissed the unpleasant memories of the obscene similarities of her mother and Hamilton and found herself thinking back to meeting and falling in love with Georges two and a half years ago. Their relationship ended last year and their breakup had left her emotionally distressed and lonely. Since then, she hadn't become seriously involved with anyone. She did meet an American major, Ernest (Tex)

BOMBER PILOT

Lee, an aide to General Eisenhower. Major Lee was an amicable and accommodating person. His rugged facial features and gentle manner made him attractively appealing. He told Mary he was married, loved his wife, and had every intention of remaining faithful to her.

Mary respected and accepted his candid declaration, as she had no real desire to become romantically involved with anyone. They dated regularly and she enjoyed being with him. He was an excellent dancer and they usually dined at a restaurant or club where there was music. Tex was an accomplished storyteller and entertained Mary with many wonderful anecdotes about America, but most generally about Texas, which he dearly loved. Their friendship ended when he left with the general for North Africa prior to the invasion in November 1942. Since then she'd met several Americans, most of whom wanted to jump in bed with her immediately after buying her dinner. After several close calls, Mary had become quite leery of Americans. Meeting the right person did concern her, though not too much, since she was still young. At times she regretted leaving Georges and the wonderful warm and loving relationship they shared together. Would she ever meet the man of her dreams and fall in love?

Mary's thoughts were interrupted by the telephone and the cheerful voice of her friend, Dorothy Shepard. "Mary, darling, Stephanos just walked in and handed me three tickets to New Faces at the Prince of Wales Theatre. Knowing how much you like Sid Fields, he just knew you would love to see the show. It's this Saturday night, darling. You will come?"

Mary gratefully accepted, saying she would love to join them. After the harrowing experience she had the night before, she looked forward to an evening with Dorothy and Stephanos and to seeing London's most talked about new musical.

Chapter 5

Weyland's crew met at five o'clock that afternoon all clean and bright-eyed and looking sharp in their class A uniforms. They boarded the bus and with much anticipation headed for the town of Newquay (pronounced "Nooky"). But, unfortunately, it failed to live up to their expectations. It was a quiet town, more so because it was early spring and tourism was not encouraged, particularly along the coast, while England was at war. Bill, however, was pleased by the quaint seacoast village situated on a slight rise that overlooked the Irish Sea. It was a picture-perfect postcard setting. The houses and shops were crowded together along the high street. Most of the buildings were whitewashed brick or bleached limestone with exposed wood beams. Some of the buildings were old and leaned to one side, appearing to be held up by the buildings beside them. To Bill, the town was very picturesque, much as he'd envisioned England.

Their first priority, however, was an English pub and a glass of beer. Finding one was no problem-there was one on almost every corner. They settled on the Golden Boar and cautiously made their way to the uncrowded bar. They were greeted with a big smile by a plump redheaded barmaid saying, "Evenin' luvs, what'll it be?"

WILLIAM WHEELER

After a slight hesitation, Bill replied, "We'll have half-and-half, ma'am." He had heard that it was the standard English drink and felt good about showing off his knowledge of their beer.

The flamboyant barmaid grinned, "Right you are, darlings."
They were served large mugs filled with dark foamy fluid. They looked at it skeptically, but grinned when Bill raised his glass and said, "Cheers. Well, we finally made it. Here's to merry ol' England."

They raised their glasses and together took a big slug. Their jubilant expressions suddenly changed to sheer astonishment. Only Bill managed to conceal his shock after boasting of his knowledge of English beer.

He looked at them, then grinned and watched McGovern turn away looking for a place to spit it out. He finally swallowed it, "Lieutenant, this taste like horse s . . ." He stopped, looked at his pilot, and added, "Sorry, sir."

Woody shook his head and said, "How could anyone do this to beer! It sure does. It's so bitter, flat . . . ugh . . . and warm."

The barmaid watched them and grinned. " 'ere, try our lager. You'll find it more to your liking. No charge, gents."

The lager was somewhat better.

Despite the warm brew, they resolved to enjoy themselves. However, the few patrons in the pub and the lack of activity were disappointing. Bill turned to the Englishman beside him and asked, "Sir, how far is Plymouth from here and can we get there by train?"

He responded, "It's a lovely train ride. No more than an hour there. The last train back leaves at eleven."

Bill thanked him and after getting directions to the rail station they boarded the train for Plymouth. There they found a large crowded pub where, after several lagers, the beer began to taste better. They ate a variety of meat pies, cold cuts, cheeses, and other strange-looking food. But it was good. They were enjoying themselves among the boisterous patrons when a short, stout man approached them and introduced himself. He was dressed in a pea jacket and navy bell bottom trousers. He appeared to be middle aged, but because of his ruddy complexion it was hard to tell exactly how old he was. He spoke a language completely foreign to them although they knew it must be some form of English. He later explained it was a true West Country, or Welsh, dialect. And although they had difficulty understanding him, they enjoyed his sea stories.

He had been torpedoed four times while on convoy duty with the British merchant marine. The last time, he said, he had spent six days alone in a lifeboat without food or water. But happily had a thirty-six man/five-day rum ration aboard.

He insisted on taking them up to the Hoe, a huge park that overlooked the harbor. On the top of the hill there were several beautifully kept bowling greens. There he pantomimed Sir Francis Drake playing a game of boles on the green when he was told that the Spanish Armada was off the coast threatening to invade England. Drake insisted on finishing the game before he went out to meet the Spaniards and defeat them. And to prove his point the Englishman introduced the Americans to a magnificent bronze statue of Drake sitting high on the hill beside the greens guarding the harbor below.

They barely made the last train back to Newquay. Bill was pleasantly surprised by the people he had met. They were friendly and helpful. England so far had lived up to his every expectation. He knew now that the wait had been worth it and being here would be the most important time of his life.

After an overnight stay at the Saint Eval, the Weyland crew flew on to Burtonwood, near Liverpool, an army air force depot where B-17s were serviced and prepared for combat. The crew thought they'd keep their brand-new Seventeen and be assigned with it to a tactical bomb group. They were disappointed and watched a crew chief taxi it to a hangar to be made combat ready.

The following day, after a short indoctrination, Bill was assigned to ferry a B-17 to Bovington, an air base near London. With two other B-17s, they flew a three-ship formation. The lead plane was flown by a veteran from one of the operational groups. The other B-17 was flown by Lieutenant Harry Lay, pilot of a new crew that had just arrived in the UK via the North Atlantic route. Before takeoff, Weyland and Lay were told to leave the power set at 2,300 RPM and thirty-two inches of manifold pressure-a power setting for cruising that was unheard of during training back in the United States.

The lead pilot never flew higher than five hundred feet above the ground and kept urging the two wingmen to fly closer to him in a tight formation. This was Bill's first experience flying in formation, perhaps the most important requirement for combat. He soon stopped his erratic throttle adjustments and began making slight changes. His grip on the control column slackened as well, but his eyes remained glued on the lead bomber.

When the tension eased, he shouted to Hal, "Boy, this is really flying. Just wait until you try it, Hal. It's not that hard once you get the hang of it. If this is the way they fly here I'm going to love it."

The sensation of flying close to another plane and just above the treetops where Bill could feel the true speed of flight was beyond any thrill he had ever experienced.

Hal and Bayne stared at the lead plane in a near-hypnotic state, not sure whether the nearness of the two planes was good or bad. Woody and Joe were silent in the nose compartment, but the guys back in the waist were having a ball, encouraging Bill over the intercom, shouting, "Stick it in there, lieutenant."

The flight to Bovington seemed to take a matter of minutes. After landing, Bill taxied to Base Ops and as he pulled up to park, standing on the ramp grinning broadly up at him was Dopey McMann. Surprised, Weyland shut down the engines, slid the side window back, and shouted down at the extraordinarily young officer standing on the tarmac, looking much too young to be commanding a Flying Fortress. Everyone liked and admired McMann and his comrades were disturbed by the thought of him stuck in Africa for the duration.

"Dopey, boy am I glad to see you! Hold it right there, I'll be down in a minute." He unbuckled, got out of his seat and told his copilot, "Finish up for me, Hal. Bring the Form 1 and we'll sign her off in Base Ops. I gotta hear what happened to Dopey's crew and Colonel Harris."

BOMBER PILOT

Bill dropped down through the forward hatch and grabbed his friend. "Dopey, how the hell did you get out of Guinea? I thought you'd be there for the duration."

"We were damn lucky, Bill, and the fact that we had a little rank on board certainly didn't hurt. The attaché there wasn't much help so Colonel Harris went right to the top and got through to Hap Arnold by phone. General Arnold apparently got the State Department off their asses, who then jacked up the ambassador there. A deal apparently was cut on the q.t. to turn us loose, but the Seventeen had to stay. The colonel was mad as hell when he heard that; but, hey, it was more important to get us out. Besides, that aircraft needed at least one new engine. God only knows when it would have arrived.

"The embassy types drove us across the border to British Guinea after dark in the back of a closed truck. From there we got an air transport flight to the UK."

"Is Colonel Harris here with you?"

"No. He headed right back to the States. He's anxious to get his own bomb group and come back to England."

"What's the scoop on this place, Dopey? How long are we going to be here?"

"Two weeks. This is the Combat Crew Replacement Center. No flying, just more ground school. Two weeks of courses on how we should behave ourselves in the U K and all about the ETO—that's the European Theater of Operations."

"Damn. I thought we'd be assigned directly to a combat group."

"No such luck."

"How long have you been here? Have you heard from Norm or George? They should have gotten here three weeks ago."

"I arrived two days ago, and talked to Norm by phone yesterday. He's assigned to the 91st Bomb Group at Bassingbourn and George is at Molesworth with the 303rd. I plan to meet them at Watford train station tomorrow and go to London. How about it, Bill? Up to going to London tomorrow?"

"You bet. I'm ready," he replied enthusiastically.

Chapter 6

Weyland and McMann met Norman Richards and George Perry on Saturday afternoon at Watford Rail Station. They were all classmates, having been together since March 1942, at the start of basic flight training at Greenville, Mississippi.

Norman Richards was a sophisticated young Jewish man from Chicago with a marvelous sense of humor and an outstanding personality. He was married and had been a successful advertising executive with the most prestigious ad company in that city. Norm was envied for his strikingly beautiful wife, and equally important, for his late-model Ford convertible. Norm's wife, along with a few other wives, followed her husband from base to base during their phase training. With the exception of one night a week, all the men were restricted to quarters. However, the married guys, not satisfied with one night, found many ingenious ways to sneak off base. One night, an MP caught Norm hiding in the closed rumble seat of their convertible. He, like many young Americans, left his family and profession and volunteered for combat duty.

George Perry, a handsome, dark-haired young man from Atlanta, left Georgia Tech in his third year to join the air force. He was a quiet, well-mannered southerner who'd been an outstanding halfback for the university.

"We bombed the GM Works at Antwerp on Monday, my first raid," Norm explained. "Boy, it was really something. Enemy fighters were waiting for us right at the Dutch coast. I'm telling you, the first time you see those cannons blasting away at you, it scares the living hell out of you. And the flak over Antwerp was unbelievable. You could almost reach out and touch it. You gotta fly your first couple of missions as copilot with an experienced crew."

George added, "Next week, I'm sure we'll get to take our own crew on a raid. They're as anxious to go as I am."

Both Norm and George went on at great length about the raids, much to Bill's envy. He had another two weeks at Bovington before he'd see any combat. But their enthusiasm made him realize how lucky he was to be here in England and in the Eighth Air Force. He soon overcame his resentment and looked forward to the exciting times ahead.

Norm had been to London twice and seemed to know all about the city. On the way in they passed a lot of bomb damage to the factories and warehouses on the outskirts of London. But that did not prepare Weyland for the devastation he'd see in the city. As the train flashed by the bombed-out structures, it was like seeing the war-ravaged and gutted buildings in the newsreels.

They arrived at Euston Station, one of the many railroad stations servicing the great city of London. They left the terminal and walked down Woburn Road to Russell Square, where they had rooms reserved at the Lincoln Hotel. The bomb damage here was shocking and it brought home to Bill the real horror of war. There were so many vacant lots where buildings had once stood. Now most of the debris had been cleared away, but the skeletons and burned-out remains of buildings left standing looked depressingly desolate. The people they passed looked well-kept and well-fed, but were dressed plainly. The men, if not in uniform, wore dark-gray suits and black derbies and most carried an umbrella. The women's clothes appeared to be more durable than stylish. Although most of the people they passed walked with a determined stride and there was a seriousness about them, they all had a ready smile and a cheerful greeting for the Americans. Bill was impressed by the people he saw considering the horrors they'd been through the past few years.

After dropping off their kit bags in their rooms, they hurried out of the hotel to hail a taxi. Before they could give the cabbie their destination, he turned around and said, "Where to gents? Piccadilly?"

They looked surprised, then laughed, and in unison replied, "You bet."

Their first stop was the American Bar at the Regency Palace Hotel just off Piccadilly Circus. The first scotch, not much more then a thimbleful, was weak and warm. They soon remedied that by ordering doubles and triples and forgot about the ice. To Bill, the atmosphere of the noisy crowded bar, the variety of uniforms and the attractive women were more stimulating then the liquor. The exhilaration he felt was beyond his wildest dreams. There was a certain similarity about the bar that reminded Bill of the Commodore Hotel in New York, but it was older and more decorative. The patrons were three deep at the bar and their conversations were in a multitude of dialects and languages. The laughter was loud and boisterous and most of it was, as far as Bill could determine, from the few Americans there.

After several drinks and much talk of flying, fighting, and Englishwomen, they left the bar. Out on the sidewalk, they bumped into three Irish girls in uniform. They stopped and said hello and the girls responded in a friendly manner. The tall black-haired one was very comely and Bill raised the beam of his flashlight to see if she had blue eyes. His dream girl was a blue-eyed brunette. He instantly felt a heavy hand on his shoulder and heard an authoritative voice proclaim in his ear, "Put that bloody torch down, Yank!" Bill turned to see the ruddy stern face of a big London bobby. Bill later learned that everyone in England carried a flashlight that they used to find their way, but it was never pointed skyward. The popular farewell expression in England was, "Got your torchlight and gas mask. Well, goodnight then."

Norm wasn't interested in the Irish girls and said, "Come on, Bill. Let's go." He led them across blacked-out Piccadilly, down Shaftsbury Avenue to Wardour Street, and into a small Greek restaurant, formerly Italian, but renamed for obvious reasons. The head-waiter met them with great enthusiasm and led them to a small table in a crowded room. He suggested veal with a side order of spaghetti, to which they readily agreed. When served, the unusual taste of the veal led them to speculate that, because of the shortage of meat in England, they were probably eating cat, and the more they joked about it, the more convinced they were that it was not veal. However, it didn't thwart their appetite or high spirits.

They left the restaurant and went on to the Astor, a bottle club just off St. James Street. Norm had been raving about the club all evening. He and George were members and although it was a private club, anyone in uniform, particularly Americans with ready cash, were immediately welcome to join.

Ed and Bill became instant members after meeting the club manager, reputed to be a former RAF pilot. The club was formerly a spacious townhouse, which still reflected all the glory and glitter of the Victorian period. The foyer was dominated by a massive crystal chandelier that hung from the second-floor ceiling thirty feet above. A large marble staircase and balusters curved up to the first floor. The walls were done in gray and gold flock, set off by a lavish display of gold-leaf decorative molding. It was truly magnificent and with his modest background, Bill was hard-pressed to imagine a single family living in such opulence and splendor.

They were given an excellent table just off the dance floor in the main ballroom. A waiter arrived with a bottle of scotch and seltzer water and left a check for £10 ($40), which the pilots considered reasonable. The evening progressed with a robust discussion about combat flying, accompanied by an occasional comment about an attractive woman as the bottle was consumed.

There were a number of unattached women in the club, but the four Americans didn't venture onto the dance floor. However, Bill did notice a dark-haired, stunningly attractive young woman sitting across the dance floor in the company of a well-dressed couple. Although he tried to keep his mind on their discussion, his glance and thoughts kept returning to the girl. She had the most magnificent eyes-large and set well apart in a truly beautiful face. Bill became enamored with her. She was in an animated conversation with the man and woman with her. Bill admired how expressively she used her long, slender fingers to enunciate her spoken words. Occasionally, she'd glance at couples dancing with a look that seemed to indicate she would prefer participating to watching. When she listened to her companions, she had a way of holding her head slightly tilted that accentuated her long and elegant neck.

Bill became so entranced that he failed to respond to a question put to him.

George followed Bill's gaze, grinned, and said, "Very nice, William. Very nice, indeed. Why don't you ask her to dance?"

"I don't know. She might say no," he replied hesitantly. "She doesn't seem to be interested."

"Go on. How could she refuse a serviceman in uniform about to do battle for her country?" teased Norm.

"All right, you guys, hold it down. How could I possibly leave such stimulating company?"

While they were badgering him, the young woman looked up and glanced over at them in what seemed an amused, amiable way, as though she knew what they were talking about. Having caught her look, the guys intensified the pressure on Bill, and he finally made his way slowly across the room where, once again, she was involved in a lively conversation with her friends. He stood behind her, glaring at his friends across the room. She turned, looked up at him, and smiled. Her pleasant expression revealed the slightest suggestion of expectancy, but he wasn't certain how to interpret its meaning. When he found himself looking directly into those gorgeous green eyes, he forgot his prepared opening, and had to settle for, "Hi, would you care to? I'm not interrupting anything am I?"

"No...no, we were discussing Sid Fields and how much we enjoyed the wonderful musical we saw this evening." She hesitated, looked at him closely, then added, "Yes, leftenant, I would very much like to dance but please sit down and meet my friends."

She introduced her friends as Dorothy Shepard and Stephanos Pateras. Dorothy was a close friend and Stephanos was a Greek civilian. Bill later learned that he was a shipowner living in London while his ships were being used in Allied convoys to and from America.

Her name was Mary Carlton and her eyes were like polished jade, a shade of green that reminded Bill of the color of the Gulf Stream when he flew over the Caribbean Sea. Her brilliant violet irises sparkled when she looked at him. Her eyes were even more beautiful close up-so expressive and warm. But her most remarkable feature, aside from her eyes, was her pristine complexion. Her skin, the color of fresh cream, had the finest texture and looked as smooth as Dresden china. The skillful application of cosmetics dramatically enhanced her exquisite face and sparkling eyes. Her dark-brown hair was parted in the middle and fell below her shoulders in soft waves. From her high forehead to the pronounced cleavage of her full breasts, her pale flesh made a striking contrast against her dark hair and the plain black décolleté dress she wore. She had a slightly crooked nose that gave character to an otherwise perfect face. Her voice was exceptionally appealing to Bill and although her diction was impeccably British, it was more cosmopolitan and not overly affected. Her cultured voice, long slender fingers, and graceful, swanlike neck, gave the distinct impression that she was a person of exceptionally good breeding.

He acknowledged the introductions and said, "I'm Bill Weyland and I'd like to dance with you. That is, if your friends don't mind."

Mary replied, "I'm certain Dorothy and Stephanos will excuse me."

Dorothy quickly said, "Oh, please do leftenant, I know Mary would enjoy dancing with you." She looked to Stephanos, who nodded.

He thanked them, got up, and followed her as she moved between the tables to the dance floor. She wasn't quite as tall as she appeared to be sitting at the table, but she was well endowed with a tiny waist and a petite but curvaceous body. She was about six inches shorter than his six foot frame, but when she came into his arms, they fit perfectly together. The press of her body against his sent shivers through him, and his first steps were rather awkward.

They danced silently, each enjoying the pleasure of the other's closeness. He gradually overcame his awkwardness but her nearness was disturbing, and he found it difficult to think of something to say.

She looked up at him. "How long have you been in England, left-enant?"

"Three days. We landed in Cornwall Wednesday and flew to Bovington yesterday. It's just half an hour from London."

"Really," she replied. "My, but you've covered a lot of ground in such a short time."

He quickly replied, "Not as much as I would've liked. They've put me back in ground school when I should be flying and fighting. But not to worry, it won't be long now that we're here to take care of the Germans." He was surprised at how the words came out. He hadn't intended to sound so pompous.

She looked up at him, her eyes flashing with anger. and said, "We've done rather well without you. Why don't you go back where you came from, Yank!" With that she pushed herself away from him, lost her balance, and fell backward onto the trumpet player's lap. The orchestra was located slightly below the raised dance floor.

She sat there glaring at him and said, "Why you bloody . . . !"

Bill looked down at her, grinned sheepishly, and said inanely, "What are you doing down there?"

She didn't seem a bit embarrassed, but the poor trumpet player was. Bill reached down to help her up. She was furious and he thought she'd lash out at him again. But she took his hand and allowed him to pull her up. She turned around and apologized to the trumpet player, who blushed and smiled up at her forgivingly. Other couples on the dance floor seemed oblivious to the little drama that had taken place. After a rather stilted effort to resume dancing, she suggested that they return to the table. Once there, he didn't know whether to stay or leave.

Dorothy conveniently solved his dilemma by saying, "If your friends can spare you for a few minutes, please have a drink with us." He looked at Mary who said sarcastically, "Please do, leftenant. We'd love to hear how you plan to win the war."

He answered, "Look, I'm sorry. I didn't mean to sound that way."

Bill sat down as Dorothy motioned to a chair beside her. After several uncomfortable minutes Bill relaxed and responded to Dorothy's many questions about the States. Mary remained relatively silent, watching him in a critical and skeptical way as he talked with Dorothy and Stephanos. After responding to their questions, he'd look to her for some form of acceptance. However, she made no effort to be amicable, remaining taciturn, and seemingly indifferent to his presence.

Eventually, when Mary's silence became awkward, Stephanos picked up his cigarettes and said, "I have an early train to Southampton in the morning. If you'll excuse us, leftenant, I think we should be leaving."

Bill stood and quickly turned to Mary, his eyes imploring her to stay. "Must you leave, too?" He turned to Dorothy, "I'll see Miss Carlton home safely. I promise."

Dorothy appeared hesitant, "I don't think Mary . . . " She stopped when she caught her friend's eye.

To Bill's surprise, Mary replied, "I'll be fine, Dorothy. Please don't worry. I'm certain Leftenant Weyland will see me home."

Bill was pleasantly surprised when she agreed to stay. Dorothy appeared to be satisfied, gave Mary a maternal look, and kissed her cheek, then turned to Bill and said, "Next time you're in London, leftenant, please have dinner with us." She gave him a card. "That's Stephanos's business card, but our home number is there too. You will call?"

Bill said he'd like that very much and after shaking hands, Dorothy and Stephanos left. For a moment, Mary and Bill stood quietly watching them go. Bill finally asked, "Would you like to meet my friends?"

She responded affirmatively, but didn't appear to be overly anxious. As they moved over to his table, he was troubled. She certainly didn't appear to like him and yet she stayed when her friends left. How complicated can a person be, or was it just that he couldn't figure out how a woman's mind worked?

His friends stood to be introduced, and while waiting for the waiter to bring a chair, Bill reached for his cigarettes on the table and accidentally knocked over a drink. At that moment, Mary turned to the waiter, who just arrived, and said something to him. Bill thought she said, "These clumsy Americans." He glared at her but said nothing, thinking, "Boy, she's really had it with me."

They sat down and she immediately fell into a lively conversation with his friends. They were completely captivated by her and when she admitted being a Londoner, they deluged her with questions about the city, the people, and the Blitz. She was thoroughly enjoying herself while Bill sat sulking.

After several attempts he finally got her attention, and she agreed to dance with him saying, "I'll dance with you if you promise not to push me into the orchestra again."

Although she smiled when she said it, he remained skeptical. He tried to suppress his feelings about her because as attracted to her as he was, he was not sure she felt the same toward him. His perplexed state of mind quickly vanished when she came into his arms and he was suddenly overcome by a very pleasant sensation. When they danced it became one of those magical moments when the music is perfect, the tempo just right, and two people move together as one. Never before had he felt so confident or moved so smoothly as he did to the appropriate rendition of "It Had to be You" played superbly by the orchestra. They danced without speaking, each experiencing a strange and exciting awareness of the other and that extraordinary feeling of being completely alone on a crowded dance floor.

When the music stopped, they stood holding onto each other, their eyes locked in a warm embrace. When they realized they were alone in the center of the dance floor, they quickly moved apart and walked back to the table holding hands.

She became much quieter when they rejoined his friends, who seemed to sense that the two of them wanted to be alone.

Dopey, with a knowing look, turned to Norm and said, "I've about had it. I'm ready for the sack. George, how about you, what say we leave these two?"

Bill could have hugged Dopey for being so understanding. "If you guys must, but I think I'll stay a while if it's okay with you, Mary."

"All right, I don't mind staying a bit longer. No work day tomorrow, " Mary replied.

When his friends got up to leave, Bill said, "I'll meet you all in the morning at the Jules Club. Will I have any trouble finding it?"

Norm replied, "No. It's just down the road on Jermyn Street. Just tell the cabbie. He'll know where it is." Then jokingly he turned to Mary, "Take good care of him, Mary. Don't let him wander off and get lost. He doesn't speak the language very well."

Mary laughingly replied, "Don't worry, Norman, I'll see that he gets back to his hotel safely. I've enjoyed meeting you." She then turned to Dopey and George, took their hands, and added, "Good night, I'm sure you're going to love England. Hope to see you all again. Please, do be careful and take care of yourselves."

Dopey added, "Bye, Mary, been great talking to you." And with a wink at Bill, "You behave yourself."

Bill and Mary stayed until the club was almost empty. As they got up to leave, Bill realized how unusually talkative and effusive he'd been. There was something about her, an openness, that made it so easy to talk freely and candidly.

He retrieved his trench coat and her ermine coat, which surprised and impressed him. They left the club and Mary suggested that they walk, even though it was very dark in the blackout and quite cold. He heard distant sirens as they walked away from the building but when Mary ignored them, he didn't mention them. She led him through some narrow streets to Queens Walk and out to Piccadilly Road where they walked beside Green Park toward Hyde Park Corner. There seemed to be no one about and in the total darkness they felt completely alone. It was difficult to believe a city as large as London could be so quiet and still.

Bill thought, "It is absolutely inconceivable to think that here I am in London, it's past midnight, and I'm walking with an incredibly attractive English girl whom I just met a few hours ago on my first night in this fascinating city." He was completely overcome by a most exhilarating feeling of pure happiness. The damp, fragrant smell of spring coming from the park conspired to heighten the thrill and infatuation he felt for this extraordinary and exciting young woman beside him.

Suddenly, he was stunned by an ear-shattering sound of thundering guns exploding so close he could feel the heat. He turned quickly to his left and there, not thirty yards away in the park, was a battery of anticraft guns illuminated by the flashing flames erupting from their muzzles as they hammered skyward in rapid fire.

He stood mesmerized watching the gun crew hurriedly feed the canisters into the gun's breeches. Now the loud shrill sound of air raid sirens were all about him. Mary's response to the instant panic that seized him was a slight tightening of her grip on his arm, "I'm sorry," she said. "I guess we should've gone to the shelter when we first heard the air raid alarm." She paused, looked up at him, and added, "I'm sure we'll be all right. There hasn't been a serious raid on London in some time. If you prefer, there's a shelter in the underpass just up the road a bit."

"No . . . No, I'm fine. I didn't realize there was an air raid in progress."

Despite hearing the sirens early, the shocking reality suddenly hit him. He now understood why the city was so quiet and realized with some anxiety that he was actually in his first air raid. Between the bursts of gunfire, he could hear aircraft droning overhead and see searchlight beams swinging across the sky. Apparently to Mary this was no big deal. After all, she'd stayed in London through the Blitz, and an occasional nuisance raid wasn't going to frighten her into a shelter.

After the "all clear," they found a taxi at Hyde Park Corner and

Mary gave the driver her address on Gloucester Place. Immediately after settling in the backseat, they were in each other arms as though they'd been waiting all evening for this moment. Both had the same intense desire to devour the other in deep breathless kisses. In what seemed to be but a few fleeting minutes later, they came apart reluctantly when the cab stopped and the driver reached back and opened the door. Aroused by their intense and passionate embrace, Bill grudgingly relinquished his hold on Mary and got out of the cab. When he reached into his pocket to pay the driver, she stopped him with a hand on his arm.

"You'll not find another cab this late. Tell him to wait."

Confused and disappointed after their heated coupling, he was caught off balance and gave her a questioning look. She appeared not to notice, took his hand, and led him through the foyer of a large apartment block and down the hall to her flat. After opening her door, he took her in his arms and kissed her. She returned his kiss eagerly and held him close. For a moment, he thought she had changed her mind and would ask him in. But she gently pushed him away.

"Good night, Bill. Call me in the morning, first thing. I've enjoyed our evening together very much. Thank you for seeing me home."

Mary stood in the hall and watched Bill walk away. When he reached the lobby, he turned, hesitated, waved, and left. She waited until she heard the taxi depart, then went inside wondering why she didn't invite him in. She wanted the passion and desire she felt in his embrace to continue.

Mary got to bed knowing she'd probably spend a restless night thinking about the young American pilot. He was rather tall, slender, and very good-looking in his well-tailored green uniform. Although his military dress was proper, there was a certain casual look about him that made him stand out among all the other military men in the club. She recalled the exciting and pleasant emotion that flowed through her body when she looked up and caught him watching her. When their eyes met, he smiled a boyish shy smile, certainly not cocky like some Americans she'd met. She had very much wanted to meet him. And, as if he had read her thoughts, he got up and came directly toward her table. To cover her anxiety, she quickly became involved in a conversation with Dorothy and Stephanos.

A moment later, he stood beside her looking down into her eyes and asking rather hesitantly if she'd like to dance. His eyes were very blue and well-set in a handsome face, accentuated by a full and sensual mouth and a dimpled chin. He appeared to be bashful, yet self-confident. He was well-scrubbed and his unruly light-brown hair looked freshly washed. He truly was a man who could set her heart pounding. Somehow she managed to control her outward emotions and greeted him discreetly. She had never felt like that before, neither had she experienced the tingling sensation that raged through her body when they danced or the uncontrollable passion when he kissed her.

Bill seemed to be sincerely attracted to her. But her recent experiences had taught her that there was no way she could be certain. They'd been together fewer than four hours. You simply don't fall in love with a stranger that quickly. He'd just arrived in England, his first night in London, and she no doubt was the first British girl he'd met. She must be mad, she thought, wanting to invite him into her bed. Ridiculous. How could she be so foolish? Remember Hamilton-handsome, well-mannered-and a charlatan. You'll probably never see this fellow again and be all the better for it. Savior of we poor English folk. Indeed!

But sleep wouldn't come so easily. Mary sat up in bed pushing and punching the pillows behind her, wide awake, wondering whether she'd finally met that special person. It seemed that her relationships always ended tragically, leaving her alone and brokenhearted. Could Bill Weyland be the man for her? Would she see him again? Why did she feel so unsure about him?

When Bill returned to the cab, he sat trembling uncontrollably. Was it the thought of making love to her or was it something more complex that caused the strange sensation he felt? Completely overcome and somewhat perplexed, he mumbled, "God, what's happened to me? I've never felt like this before. Never."

WILLIAM WHEELER

The driver was an old man beyond military age who'd probably seen more than his share of amorous young men with a little too much to drink turned away by a young woman. In his wisdom of years he felt qualified to say, "Ah, you'll think better of it after you've had a good night's sleep, lad. Where to?"

At his hotel, Bill managed to wake the night porter, who unlocked the door and let him in. When the porter asked him what time he'd like to be knocked up, he was so stunned by the remark that he stood still for an awkward moment, and finally said, "Hell, anytime it's convenient." Immediately afterward he thought, "Norman was right, I guess I don't speak the language."

In his room, he pulled off his clothes, fell on the bed, and realized he'd consumed a hell of a lot of liquor through the course of the evening. Although he felt completely sober, he wasn't surprised when he laid back and the room started to rotate. Just before losing consciousness he thought about the beautiful and desirable English girl he'd just met. And amazingly, for the first time that evening, he thought about the girl back in Arizona he'd promised to marry.

Chapter 7

Bill was awakened by the sensation that someone had entered his room. He rolled over and realized that someone had been there and left a tray on his bedside table. On it was a plate with a piece of fish floating in some milk, two slices of toast, milk, and coffee. At the sight of food, particularly the fish, he felt his stomach rumble and dashed to the bathroom where he left his previous night's dinner.

Avoiding the floating fish, he settled for the cold dry toast and a strange-tasting coffee that he realized after the first unsavory sip was a poor substitute used because of wartime shortages. He showered, shaved, dressed and, after two aborted attempts, found the courage to call Mary.

Her throaty, sleepy, "hello" sounded so provocative and sensual that he was hard-pressed to keep the excitement out of his voice. "I'd really like to see you today. Can I pick you up at three o'clock?"

"I'd be delighted, Bill."

He was instantly relieved and more relaxed at her affirmative response. "Do you do want to go to the Regency Palace, as Norm suggested last night?"

"If you want to," she replied indifferently.

"Great, see you at three." He hesitated, then continued with a mischievous grin, "Say, when I got back to the hotel, the night porter asked me when I'd like to be knocked up. What do you suppose he meant by that?"

She laughed and answered, "Silly, he meant what time did you want to be awakened. What did you think it meant?"

Bill had a feeling that she knew what he meant but said, "Oh, we have a different meaning for it back in the States."

"Yes, I'm sure you have. See you here at three. Ta Ta, Bill."

The Jules Club was run by the American Red Cross for servicemen in London. Bill found a breakfast of good coffee, donuts, beer, and cold cuts more to his liking. He struggled through a battery of good-natured questions about the previous night trying to evade inquiries about their romantic interlude. Failing that, in response to Dopey's direct question he announced, "No, gentlemen, I do not have carnal knowledge of the lady."

They had several beers while they played billiards and an unfamiliar game on a circular, green felt-covered table with six pockets, each one guarded by a rubber syringe. The object of the game was to get a small ball in your opponent's pocket. It was an unbelievably silly game, but they roared with laughter when they'd alternately gang up on one and force the ball at him while he fought desperately to keep it out of his pocket. Each one had an opportunity to stand against three opponents.

Laughter came easily to these young men, and even though Bill and Dopey had not yet experienced combat, their emotional high and bravado of other two were infectious. Bill became so involved in the game that he forgot about the time and suddenly realized it was after three and he'd be late for the tea dance at the Regency Palace Hotel in Piccadilly with Mary. He rushed out of the club and, luckily, into a taxi that had just discharged three American officers.

He arrived at Ivor Court about forty-five minutes late and buzzed her apartment. She didn't greet him over the intercom or buzz the door open. He waited several minutes and finally saw her through the glass partition walking down the hall toward him.

When she met him in the lobby, he said, "Hi, sorry I'm late."

Mary's look was stern and unforgiving. "You're nearly an hour late. Perhaps we should call off our date."

"Please forgive me. I was at the Jules Club playing this silly game and I completely forgot about the time. Let's not allow a little thing like this spoil our afternoon. I promise you it'll never happen again."

"I really don't consider it a little thing, Bill. I simply do not like to be kept waiting."

She was dressed in a tweed suit with matching hat and low-heeled shoes. She looked smaller and younger, and it was difficult for him to believe that anyone as young as she could be so determined and unyielding about anything. Mary was five years his junior. He had two kid sisters, one a year older and the other a year younger than Mary, and Bill was having difficulty taking her seriously.

Mary watched him while he silently scrutinized her. Finally, she smiled and said, "I know what you're thinking. But believe me, I mean it. I won't forgive you again, you can count on it." She then added, "I hope you don't mind if we don't go to the Regency Palace. I don't think you'd enjoy the crowd and the types of people there. Let's just spend the afternoon together."

He was happy just to be there and relieved that she forgave him for being late. "Sounds great," he replied with obvious relief.

When she refused to let him hail a taxi, they took a bus up Baker Street to Oxford Street. They got off at Marble Arch and crossed over to the entrance to Hyde Park where several groups of people surrounded four speakers. Bill stopped to listen.

"This is Speakers' Corner," Mary explained. "It's a place where anyone can speak openly, say anything they want for or against England, the government, even the royal family, without fear of being prosecuted. It started many years ago, probably as far back as the Magna Carta."

There were three men and a woman standing on homemade wooden platforms. The woman was dressed dottily, much like a charwoman, but spoke with a crisp upper-class English accent. This surprised Bill, but Mary told him that she was actually a titled person and was known as Lady Ann. After her husband Lord Ashford died, she turned over his land holdings and their manor house to the armed forces. She now lives in a small flat in Belgravia. When Germany invaded Russia she joined the Communist Party. She was praising Marxism, demanding that the rich share their wealth with the poor.

One of the three men was dressed in black and was preaching a sermon much like a southern Baptist-all fire and brimstone. Of the other two, one was dressed in bright-colored checks and stripes, his cockney accent was so outrageous it was impossible for Bill to understand a word he said. The third apparently was an advocate of national socialism.

"Well, from the little I've heard, most of them would be arrested or run out of town if they tried that in America. Particularly when we're at war."

They found little worth listening to and left. The early April day was beautiful but cool with all the magnificent signs of spring so evident in the park. Everything seemed to be in harmony with their mood as they walked together, somewhat uncertain about their feeling toward one another, each recalling the passion experienced in that short taxi ride last night. But now in the daylight, the interlude seemed more a fantasy than the real thing. A shyness came over him and when she took his arm and held it against her breast, a sensation shivered through him much like the one he felt the first time he held a girl close.

Mary's mood was just the opposite, very loquacious, cheerfully finding humor in just about everything-particularly the people around them in the park. He had to admit there were some really strange characters there. One couple was so outrageously overdressed they looked like characters out of the 1920s. And the red-faced joggers, loudly puffing down the paths in their long droopy shorts and socks, were really comical.

They walked through the park along the Ring and crossed over the

Serpentine. She turned Bill to the right into Kensington Gardens. There they stopped to admire the magnificent display of tulips and other spring flowers. The war hadn't dampened the English spirit, nor the effort to keep these beautiful gardens at their best. However, the reality of war was obvious by the number of antiaircraft batteries scattered throughout the park, as well as several anchored barrage balloons. Their presence brought back the shocking experience of last night's air raid and the fact that the serene beauty of the park could be so quickly disrupted by falling bombs.

Mary and Bill stopped at Prince Albert's memorial as they were leaving the gardens. She told him of Queen Victoria's love for her consort and the long period of mourning she endured after his death and remarked, "That was truly real love."

They then turned down South Carriage Drive and as they passed the Prince of Wales Gate, Mary had a few disparaging remarks to make about the infamous Mrs. Simpson. The prince was apparently adored by the English people prior to the arrival of "that woman," as Mary referred to her.

Bill was smitten with Mary's voice. Aside from her delightful British accent, she had a buoyant and animated way of expressing herself. She was an excellent mimic and skillfully used cockney expressions to emphasize a point. She certainly had all the attributes of a fine actress. He also realized that he was walking through some interesting English history and listened to her intently.

They left the park at Edinburgh Gate and crossed over into Knightsbridge. As they walked down Brompton Road, Mary asked Bill, "Would you like to stop for tea? It's nearly five o'clock. Tea time in England is very important. If you want to enjoy our country you must learn to like tea."

Not all that keen about the thought of tea in the afternoon as opposed to a beer or a drink, he replied hesitantly, "Okay, it's fine with me."

Mary led him into a tea shop behind Harrods. It was a small Tudor-style building wedged between two larger structures. The little restaurant was surprisingly elegant and quite crowded. Mary's friendly smile was rewarded by being offered the last small table there.

Once seated she said to Bill, "As you can see, afternoon tea is a very popular English pastime. Everything stops for tea in England. I hope you enjoy it."

Bill was pleasantly surprised by the tearoom's quaint coziness and the marvelous aroma of baked goods. Mary ordered tea and toasted scones, then led Bill to a table covered with a surprising variety of wonderful little cakes and thin sandwiches.

"The cakes aren't nearly as good as they were before the war," Mary whispered. "Fresh cream is very scarce. Most bake shops must use a synthetic substitute."

"They look mighty good to me and smell even better. I think I'll try one of those, and that one, too," Bill replied eagerly, putting two large creamy pastries on his plate.

Shortly after they were seated, Mary smiled up at the young waitress and thanked her when she placed a steaming pot of tea and a small pitcher of warm milk on their table. The ambience of the tearoom had a soothing effect on Bill. The tea and scones were excellent, as were the cakes. They talked openly about themselves, each eager to know about the other. Mary began talking about her childhood.

"When I was nearly six years old," Mary said, "my mother entered me in a contest. I won and received a small part in a film. It wasn't much of a part but the director and some of the players said that I was very good. I didn't think too much about it. At age six, playing make-believe comes naturally to most children. However, my mother was convinced that I had talent. From then on, I was either working in a film, waiting in a casting room, or taking lessons in some form that would enhance my career. She enrolled me in a variety of classes: dancing, music, fencing, and elocution. My drama teacher was the composer Ivor Novello's mother, Madam Clara Davis Novello. She was a lovely lady, but quite a character and very strict. Instead of attending regular classes, I was tutored by Reverend Leslie Saul. He was not a very nice person." She made a face of disdain and added, "In fact, he was lecherous old man whom

I disliked intensely."

Mary paused and Bill saw a vague sadness reflected in her eyes. She smiled to conceal the unpleasant memory and continued, "I guess I missed attending school and having friends my age. It was quite a difficult and rather lonely existence, but at the time I didn't think too much about it."

"Sounds like you didn't have a very normal childhood. I guess I was pretty lucky. My brother Andy and I grew up in a neighborhood with lots of kids our age. We never had any trouble getting enough guys together for a scratch game of baseball or football. We had a lot of good times together, but all I seem to remember was wishing I could grow up faster."

"You were fortunate to have been brought up in a wholesome family with many friends about. I know I missed having a normal childhood and I envied the children I saw playing together. I expect they envied me being in films. There were times when I would've gladly exchanged places. Of course, it was exciting at times, particularly when I had a good part and worked with a prominent film star. But for the most part, my life seemed nothing more than waiting for interviews, reading scripts, and tryouts. I was under constant pressure. I remember my mother saying repeatedly, "Speak up, sound your vowels, enunciate clearly, keep your head up, and smile." My career became rather an obsession with her. I sometimes believe she was trying to relive her life through mine, or perhaps she was searching for her own recognition, I'm not certain which."

Mary hesitated a moment, finished her scone, and continued, "It wasn't for the money. Not really. Because she spent a great deal on me. My clothes were very expensive-coats trimmed with fur, velvet suits, and fancy silk dresses-all to impress. She drove me to the point where I came to dislike it terribly and frequently rebelled." She hesitated again as her eyes seemed to fill. "When I did, her punishment was often . . . It was quite severe."

Mary stopped, sipped her tea, put the cup back in the saucer, and looked down pensively at it for a moment and added, "My acting career continued until I was thirteen. At that age, I began to develop rather quickly and could no longer play child parts. After several unpleasant incidents she packed me off to the Ursuline convent near Brussels where I stayed for nearly two years."

When Mary paused, Bill interjected, "We're not Catholics, but my mother sent my two younger sisters to a Catholic day school. She thought it would be a better environment for them."

Mary looked at Bill with an amused, knowing expression, and said with a grin, "We weren't Catholic either. And my mother's intentions were certainly not the same as your mother's. She jolly well sent me to the convent to discipline and punish me. While I was there, I rarely heard from her. She never sent me presents or gifts like most other girls received. I was there alone during Christmas and other holidays. When the other girls received candy and sweets, I'd steal them more out of spite than desire. My punishments doing penance are probably the most vivid memory I have of the time I spent at the convent. It was a very lonely and unhappy time in my life."

"Where were you when England declared war on Germany?" Bill asked.

"My best friend Muriel and I were living with my mother in her house on George Street when the war started. It was a Sunday at eleven o'clock. I remember it clearly. We rushed to the window when the sirens started. Our house was not that far from Marble Arch and we could see the people running in that direction, probably to the tube station. They all carried gas masks and the loudspeakers were blaring, "England is at war with Germany!" We quickly turned on the wireless and listened to Prime Minister Chamberlain. We were told to report to our designated shelters and bring our identity cards and gas masks. Our shelter was a church just around the corner on Seymour Place.

"The following month when I became eighteen, I was required to report to the registry for conscripted war work. Joining a women's army auxiliary force was not appealing to Muriel and me because we didn't want to leave London. We were initially assigned to work in a munitions factory. Fortunately, we were both found unsuitable for the work and were released after two weeks. The work there was repetitive, boring, and tedious, and we were happy to leave. When we reported for reassignment we were interviewed by a very understanding elderly gentlemen, not the usual officious civil servant, and he graciously accepted our preferences. I was sent to driver's training and Muriel went to cooking school. After several weeks of rigorous training, I was posted to a part-time job driving a Red Cross van. Negotiating the bombed-out streets of London after a raid was difficult and quite frightening, but I felt good about doing my part.

"In May 1940, my mother gave up her house on George Street and moved back to Hampstead. I didn't want to move back there with her, so Muriel and I decided to find a place in London. We were lucky to find a magnificent flat in Maida Vale. The couple who owned the flat wanted to get out of London and away from the bombs they believed would inevitably rain down on them. They let us have it more as caretakers for just four pounds a week. We were happy and content to live in such a spacious and well-furnished flat even though it was on the top floor of the building. And we didn't seem to mind dashing up and down the eight flights of stairs during the bombings when the power was off."

Bill sat entranced, fascinated by the way she described her experiences. His face glowed with admiration for this remarkable and fascinating girl. Finally he said, "God, how in the world did you live here in London through the Blitz? From what we saw in the newsreels it looked like the whole of London was burning. And to hear Edward Murrow on the radio describing the terror of the bombing-it was absolutely awesome."

"It was awful and scary, but it's amazing how you can adjust and live with danger even during the terrible bombing. War is horrible, but most English people shared the hardships and discomfort with good spirits and rarely complained," she replied.

Conceit was certainly not one of Mary's vices. She played down her screen successes and her experiences during the Blitz. The exciting events she spoke of were recounted with a fine sense of humor and often belittled or downplayed her part.

WILLIAM WHEELER

Bill recounted how much he had wanted to come to England. He told her it started over two years ago. "One instance, in particular, forced the issue," he said. "It was a scene in a newsreel showing a small child, alone and crying on a street curb in England while fire and bombing raged around her. The next day, I left my job in Connecticut and went to Montreal to enlist in the Royal Canadian Air Force. That was the summer of 1940 and because the large number of Americans had the same idea, the RCAF couldn't handle the number of volunteers. Most of us were told to go home and wait until they notified us to report for duty. I waited several months and when I received no word from Canada, I got so angry that I enlisted in the U.S. Army. Just before I left for overseas last February, my father wrote and told me that a letter had arrived from Canada five days after I came home from Montreal. The RCAF had accepted me, but there was no assurance that I'd be trained as a pilot. So in the end it all worked out for the best. But I..."

"Go on, Bill. You must've been very angry with your parents, although I'm certain they did it for your own good."

"I was angry and amazed when my dad told me he opened my mail and decided not to show the letter to me. Dad said he and my mother spent many months agonizing over their decision, but felt they were doing the right thing. The reported losses in the RAF were very high and they just didn't want me in a war that America wasn't involved in. That was before Pearl Harbor, of course, and Americans who volunteered to serve in a foreign military service forfeited their citizenship. That was obviously another reason they didn't want me to join the Canadian Air Force. When my Dad told me, I was on my way overseas and hopefully to England, so I forgave them."

Bill now felt particularly forgiving as he sat in this cozy English tearoom with a vibrant and attractive young Englishwoman. The contrast between the feeling he'd experienced last night and the quiet tranquil afternoon they had spent together left him quite mellow and content.

She offered to see him off to Bovington and they taxied together to Euston Station with a stop at the Jules Club to pick up his kit bag. When they reached the platform where the train to Watford waited, he found it hard to believe they'd been together for six hours and holding hands was the extent of any physical affection between them. Just before boarding the train they embraced rather awkwardly and he promised to call her.

Mary left the rail station and hailed a cab to take her home. On the way, her taxi stopped at the corner of Euston and Tottenham Court Road for a traffic light. Sitting back thinking of Bill and looking out the side window, Mary noticed two women standing at the curb just a few feet away. Even in the blackout she recognized them as prostitutes. They were heavily made up and dressed in short skirts and tight sweaters. One looked to be in her mid-thirties; the other was quite young-probably not more than eighteen. Mary's mind reeled back to a frightening experience she had not too far from where these two women stood.

When Mary was fourteen she left home on one of her many ventures to find a job and a place of her own away from her mother. She rented a cheap room in Soho hoping to find a job at one of the stores in Piccadilly. Living across the hall from her was a rather attractive young woman. Her name was Mavis. She was a friendly person with a pronounced cockney accent who seemed sincere in wanting to help Mary. The love and maternal care that Mary lacked as a child made her vulnerable to anyone who was friendly and pleasant to her. One evening, Mavis asked Mary if she wanted to go out for a bite to eat. Mary, considering it a friendly gesture, agreed to go with her. They left their building and walked down Shaftesbury Road toward Piccadilly Circus. Mary assumed they were going to Lyons Corner House down the road. They hadn't gone far when two men in an automobile stopped at the curbside. Mary stood back while Mavis walked over to the car and spoke to the passenger in the front seat. After a short conversation, he got out of the car.

Mavis turned to Mary. "Dearie, this is John, a friend of mine. Get in the back seat with him."

Somewhat uncertain, Mary nevertheless did as she was told and the man got into the car after her. Mavis joined the driver in the front seat and they drove off. John put one arm around Mary and the other hand on her leg.

Pushing away from him she cried out, "Oh, no! Please don't do that."

She tried to get out of the car, but he grabbed her arm, pulled her back against his chest, and looked at her closely. After a frightening interval of no more than ten or fifteen seconds, he shouted to the driver, "Stop the car, mate." He then pushed her away and for a moment stared at the terrified girl beside him. " 'Ow old are you?" he asked her gruffly.

Subverting the truth she unwittingly murmured, "Eighteen."

He made a dismissive gesture and shook his head, "Bloody 'ell you're 'eyeteen." He took out his wallet, and pulled a £5 note from it. "Ere, take it and go 'ome. Go 'ome to your mum."

Mary quickly got out of the car and ran to the corner where she caught a bus as it was moving away from the curb and hurried back to her mother in Hampstead. She realized that something horrible could've happened to her. She had no idea her friend was a prostitute and was eager to get Mary started in the profession. Once again, someone "up there" was watching over her. Had the man been of a different character, the outcome might've been painfully tragic.

Inside her flat, Mary put the kettle on, made tea, and sat back in her lounge chair. She dismissed the thoughts about the prostitutes and tried to concentrate on the afternoon she'd spent with Bill. She wasn't quite sure how she felt about him. It wasn't that the desire she felt when he first kissed her was gone. The passion was simply restrained.

After some silent contemplation she said to herself, "Perhaps I am truly in love and my feeling today was more a reaction to his demeanor during our afternoon together. He seemed more sincere and real than he had been the night before when I'm sure he had a bit too much to drink, which probably reinforced and heightened his desire and impulsiveness." But today she thought he seemed a bit shy, rather hesitant, and he was obviously trying to impress and please her. Mary Carlton liked those characteristics in a man and she hoped with all her heart that the American lieutenant would call her again-and soon.

Chapter 8

Weyland's first week at the Combat Crew Replacement Center at Bovington passed slowly. No flying, just endless lectures-indoctrination courses on the European theater of operation taught by RAF and American instructors. They covered everything about the customs of the English people and the differences between the two nationalities. Most importantly, the Americans were urged to recognize and be considerate of the Brits' courage for going it alone against Hitler. During that class, Bill realized how awful his remarks sounded to Mary when they first met.

Orientation courses were given on air-traffic control and navigational aids in the British Isles, aircraft identification, German air tactics, and the importance of formation flying and air discipline. Lectures followed on the dangers of frostbite, loss of oxygen, first aid to wounded crew members, combat fatigue, and escape and evasion. Bill was singled out to be taught a secret code to be used in the event he was taken prisoner. It was a method of sending messages by code in his personal letters. He hoped it wasn't an indication of things to come.

Weyland's nights were spent agonizing over Mary Carlton, the most extraordinary girl he'd ever met, and whether he should continue seeing her. Bill realized it would be easy to fall in love with her, but he had made a commitment to marry Clare Beatty, a wealthy and attractive brunette he had met more than two years ago.

By the late summer of 1940, with no word from the RCAF, Bill became angry and embittered. Having left his job, and not particularly anxious to find another, he found himself living from day to day in a void. A friend's bar became his favorite haunt. He drank too much and became a willing partner to any woman who was attracted to him. Before long, he had run up a sizable bar tab. Fortunately, his friend offered him the opportunity to work off his debt as a temporary bartender and he took it.

Near the end of August while working the bar at the Red Door, a tall, attractive brunette came into the bar with another woman, whom he later learned was her maid. The brunette greeted the owner, Pete Reilly, cordially and ordered two martinis, which Bill prepared. She scrutinized Bill openly and then started a conversation. She introduced herself as Clare Beatty and began asking him some personal questions. Where did he live? Was he married? Why was he working as a bartender? He responded willingly and was amused at her precocious advances. It was obvious that she was interested in him and he wasn't about to discourage her. When she stood to leave, Clare said she had a dinner engagement, but she would like to meet him later. He agreed and she said she would pick him up when he finished work.

When she left, Pete told Bill that she was tobacco heiress, married but separated from her second husband who was in a sanitarium in upstate New York. Her father made a fortune in marketing two of the most popular cigars sold in America.

Clare arrived in her Lincoln Continental convertible at eleven that night and took Bill home to bed. From that point, he was hooked. She restored his torn ego and provided a stimulating sexual relationship and an extravagant lifestyle to which he was most certainly not accustomed. Ensconced in a magnificent home in one of Scarsdale's better neighborhoods, she owned two expensive cars, had several servants, and an infinite line of credit. Her hobbies were raising pedigreed miniature schnauzers and show horses. Most weekends were spent at dog shows or horse shows where her handlers worked and rode her cherished pets. Reservations were always made at the finest inns, hotels, and restaurants. She also had a townhouse on East 63rd Street in New York. When they were in the city there was always a table for her at Twenty One or the Stock Club.

She was considerate and discreet in taking care of the charges they accumulated. The bills were handled judiciously and without embarrassing Bill, who rarely paid and couldn't have if he tried. He did, however, develop a strong sense of guilt and uneasiness. But, try as he often did, he could not break away from her. He was extremely vulnerable and allowed himself to be submissive and influenced by her strong personality. He was surprised at his weakness and ashamed, as well. But the sexual attraction, more than the extravagant living, was too compelling to forgo.

Before long, Bill immersed himself in self-pity and blamed it on the fact that Canada had rejected him. His self-esteem was at a low level, and he wasn't proud of himself. His frustration was difficult to control and he was desperate to find some way to end the relationship without hurting Clare.

The Selective Service Act had become law in September and Bill hoped that he would be drafted. But when his number was among the highest drawn, he was upset and realized he might never be called up.

Finally, out of desperation and with parental encouragement, Bill enlisted in the Army Air Corp in December 1940. He prayed that the army would send him to some faraway base where he might regain some self-respect and distance himself from Clare. Once again, he was thoroughly disappointed when he was assigned to Mitchell Field on Long Island, a little more than an hour's drive from his home in Scarsdale.

The second weekend at Bovington, Bill didn't call Mary as he had promised. Instead, he and Dopey met Norm and George for another Saturday night in London. He'd reasoned that another meeting with Mary would be the beginning of a serious affair, and he felt an obligation to Clare.

WILLIAM WHEELER

The evening in London progressed much like the last one, from the American Bar to a Soho restaurant, and then to the Astor. There he chanced to meet an attractive Greek blond, Sylvia Catapopolos, who thought Americans were marvelous. She was a very accommodating young woman.

The train ride back to Bovington the next day was made with a rough hangover and a certain amount of guilt for not calling Mary. He had little success convincing himself that he had done the right thing. But in no way could he compare this weekend to the one before.

During the second week at the Combat Crew Replacement Center the crews were told of the planned buildup of American combat units in England and how essential it was to prove that daylight bombing was not only feasible, but also extremely effective. The young and aggressive air force planners in Washington were determined to prove their theory. They had developed their tactics around an airplane designed and built in the 1930s, convinced that B-17s flying in a "combat box" formation, with its massive firepower of ten fifty-caliber machine guns, could successfully penetrate the German defenses without fighter escort.

On Friday, April 23, Weyland and his crew received orders to report to the 91st Bomb Group at Bassingbourn, Norm Richard's group.

After considerable deliberation and soul-searching, Bill called Mary and asked her if he could see her that weekend. He planned to tell her about his commitment to Clare, certain that it would end any relationship between them. He wasn't sure how she felt about him, but realized that he could easily become serious about her. He arranged to meet her at one o'clock Saturday afternoon.

Bill went to London that morning with Dopey and met George and Norm at the Regency Palace Hotel. They opened the bar at eleven and decided to have whiskey sours to start the weekend. The barmaid, under their direction, mixed them with scotch and lemon quash. The drinks were so good they had several.

As was Bill's fate previously, the time slipped by unnoticed until he heard the barmaid call, "time gentlemen," and realized, "Oh my God, it's two o'clock and the bar is closing!" Bill dashed out to look for a cab, but he wasn't so fortunate this time. While he stood waiting he saw an elderly woman on the corner selling large bunches of sprigs with tiny blue blossoms. Bill didn't recognize the flowers and asked what they were.

"Heather, ducks," she replied. "Three bob a bunch."

He gave her £2. "I'll take the lot."

"Right you are, luv," she answered with a pleasant smile. "I fancy the lady must be quite something."

"Actually," Bill answered after a moment's pause, "you're right about that. She's quite a woman."

They loaded the heather aboard a taxi and off he went at least an hour and a half late. Unable to think of a plausible excuse when he arrived at Ivor Court, he told the driver to wait and called Mary on the house phone in the lobby.

"What's your excuse this time, leftenant."

"Please come outside," he implored. "I want to show you something."

She hesitated before agreeing. "Oh, very well, but it best be good."

As he was paying the driver, she stepped out to the sidewalk and watched him unload the heather. "What's that?" she asked.

"It's heather, Mary. I flew to Scotland just to get some for you."

Mary was hard-pressed to keep from smiling as she said, "Now that's not true and you know it."

Unable to continue with the farce, Bill said, "Please forgive me. I got carried away and stayed too long with the guys. I promise you it won't happen again."

"This is the second time. And you're half-bombed already. How can you possibly start drinking this early?"

He looked so dejected and unhappy she finally added, "Fine, but not again, Bill. Please wait a minute while I get my coat, and you'd better bring that heather indoors. I'll try to find something to put it in."

The flat looked a bit like a Scottish moor when she finished.

"I thought we might go to St. James Park and perhaps Westminster Abbey, if you'd like," Mary suggested.

They spent a quiet afternoon with little serious conversation, both engrossed in their own thoughts, each trying to analyze their feelings toward the other. They wandered through the park feeding the ducks and geese and they never did get to the Abbey.

They got on a bus at Parliament Square and as they rode passed Downing Street, Mary pointed to the prime minister's residence and mentioned the horse guards when they passed the mounted guards.

They arrived back at Ivor Court just before six and after entering her flat, Mary remarked teasingly, "I bought a half bottle of scotch. But after all you had this morning I don't think you need any more. You'll turn into an old sot." Then she added, "But go ahead and have a drink while I bathe and change."

"Thank you. You certainly know the way to a man's heart," he quipped.

"Don't give me that malarkey. If you ever arrive here half-bombed again, Leftenant Weyland, you'll never get another bottle from me."

Bill poured a good measure of scotch in a glass, added a splash of soda, and sat back in a lounge chair, completely relaxed and grateful that Mary had forgiven him.

He was pleasantly surprised to see how comfortable and nicely furnished her flat was. The entryway consisted of a small closet and an alcove that served as a kitchen with a small, two-burner stove and oven, a tiny fridge, and a cabinet for silverware, china, and cooking utensils. Beyond that was a large bathroom. The main living/dining area where Bill now sat was modestly furnished and attractively decorated. The walls were papered in a soft off-white material that complemented the cream-colored, painted woodwork. There were three large bay windows on one side of the room and a mantled fireplace centered between two bookcases on the inside wall. A small highly polished mahogany dining table and two chairs were placed to the right of the entryway. The room consisted of two upholstered lounge chairs covered in ivory brocade, a three-quarter bed that served as a sofa, a chest of drawers, a dressing table, and a large oak wardrobe. A thick white Turkish rug covered the floor, accented by the colorful English chintz drapes and matching spread that covered the daybed. The apartment was not only attractively decorated but it was spotlessly clean, bright, and cheerful. Bill was impressed and thought how easy it would be to fall in love with this beautiful English girl and spend his time away from the war here in this pleasant home of hers.

He got up and walked over to the bookcase to get a closer look at several signed photographs, two of which he recognized: David Niven, the actor and Richard Lleywellen, the author. The other two pictures, signed by Cecil Beaton and Jack Profumo, featured men who were unknown to him.

Mary finally appeared, looking more beautiful than ever, while Bill was on his second scotch. She'd changed into a dark-green sheath dress, which accentuated her slim waist and exquisite breasts.

She looked at Bill and smiled demurely when she noted his pleased reaction and said, "You're welcome to freshen up before we leave. Where would you like to go? We might try to get a table at Hacketts. The food is quite good there and they have a small orchestra. Shall I ring for a reservation?"

"Sounds fine. I'll just wash up a bit." He took his tunic off and went into the bathroom.

Mary remained subdued and quiet throughout dinner, sipping her wine and observing him intently while he tried to make conversation. If she was still upset with him about being late, he thought she was being a little unreasonable. Something was bothering her, but instead of trying to understand the cause, he became defensive and drank more. She said nothing, but her expression failed to conceal her displeasure when fresh drinks arrived for him. After dinner he insisted on going to the Astor, thinking that might change her mood. However, the more he drank there, the quieter she became. When they returned to her flat, she surprised him by saying, "If you'd like to come in, let the taxi go."

He went in with her, but was determined to leave as soon as possible because she quite obviously wasn't happy being with him. Inside, after several awkward moments, he asserted himself and said, "What's bothering you, Mary? What have I done to make you so quiet?"

"I'm sorry. It's not you." She paused before saying quietly, "I visited my mother this morning and it wasn't at all pleasant. In fact, it was quite depressing and I'd rather not talk about it. If you'd like another drink, help yourself. I'm going to make some coffee."

"No, coffee will be fine. But then I'd better leave."

Their conversation was stilted and awkward as they sat together on her daybed drinking coffee. He finally stood up and said, "I better be going."

She replied, "If you must, but I believe you've missed the last train to Watford. Stay here if you like."

Bill hesitated. He wanted to stay, but knowing it was wrong he was determined to resist the temptation. The train was of no consequence. There was no need to return to Bovington because he had a room at the Lincoln Hotel. He realized it would be a simple matter to put aside his good intentions and take advantage of her as he had done numerous times before with other women. But for some reason Mary was different. Yes, he wanted her; but, for the first time in Bill Weyland's life, his physical need was overcome by a strong sense of righteousness. In his mind, he was committed to Clare and knew he should simply tell Mary why he couldn't see her anymore, and then leave.

However, he sat back down, and when she moved closer to him, he put his arm around her. She turned to him and he kissed her gently on the lips. She came into his arms and returned his kiss with an intensity reminiscent of their first meeting, but as his passion grew, he became riddled with guilt and indecision. Something intuitively held back the words that he'd vowed to tell her about his commitment to another woman. He just couldn't, not with this beautiful and desirable young woman so close to him. They kissed again, but he simply was unable to respond to her passion. The emotional uncertainty of desperately wanting her and knowing it was not right made him hesitate and left him completely incapable of physical love. He just could not, in good conscience, take advantage of her.

Mary also became tentative and uncertain about his intentions and withdrew. Sensing his unwillingness to make love, she moved away and lay back on the bed.

Confused and angry with himself, he finally lay down beside her and took her hand. Fully clothed, they held hands lying silently side by side.

After several uncomfortable moments she said quietly, "I told you how persistent and determined my mother was for me to become an actress." She stopped as though trying to decide whether or not to continue. She looked away from him and then went on. "She would become very difficult and angry, particularly so when I made mistakes or failed to get a part in a film. She drank quite a lot. Actually, she was an alcoholic, and when drunk she became a sadist." Mary stopped, sat up quickly, and pushed herself up against the wall. Bill reached over and pushed a cushion behind her.

"On many occasions she physically beat and abused me. I know it was because of the liquor. She drank gin and port. Every time I smell either of them my stomach reacts violently. It's difficult to explain how I feel but that's why I get frightened when someone I care for drinks too much. It happened to my best friend."

Mary was silent for several minutes and then sighed audibly and continued to talk about her childhood.

"I was sixteen when I was sent home from the Ursuline convent. After being away for nearly two years, I'd hoped that my mother had changed and would be more caring and understanding toward me. But I soon found she was even more abusive. Particularly when I told her I was no longer interested in film work and that I was going to find a job.

"The sisters at the convent were very strict and almost as menacing as my mother. But I accepted their harsh treatment and discipline. I believe it made me a stronger person capable of standing up to my mother. When I did, her reaction amazed me. She just quietly backed down when I told her what I intended to do. I guess she was just a bully at heart and backed off when I faced up to her.

WILLIAM WHEELER

"I heard that a new nightclub, the Lido, was opening on Kingley Street in the West End and they were looking for hostesses. I wasn't quite certain what a hostess did, but I applied. The club manager wouldn't hire me as a hostess but he did offer me the job of cigarette girl. I told him I was eighteen. He apparently liked what he saw when I put on the cigarette girl's costume and didn't bother to ask for proof of my age. He hired me. After a few nervous nights, I found the job interesting and exciting. I really felt free and independent. The job not only gave me self-confidence, but strengthened my resolve to stand up to my mother.

"I worked from eleven o'clock at night until two or three in the morning. I'd take the bus home to Hampstead, get to bed about four o'clock, and sleep until eleven or twelve. On Sunday, my day off, I stayed home and rested, and cooked dinner for my mother if she was home and not drunk at the local pub.

"My mother's attitude toward me changed. I paid her £4 a week for board and she treated me more like an adult. However, she frequently made derogatory remarks about working in a cheap nightclub, telling me that I could've become a great actress had I followed her advice and guidance. She wouldn't let me forget the amount of money and effort she'd spent on me."   Mary stopped and looked at Bill for some reaction.

He just tightened his arm around her and said, "Please go on. I'd like to hear about your job. Sounds like a gutsy thing to do at your age."

"It wasn't really. I had no training or experience beyond what I had as a child actress. I studied for a year at the Royal Academy of Dramatic Arts. But that did nothing to help me find a decent job. After working at the Lido for seven months, I heard that the cigarette girl at The Cabaret was leaving. The Cabaret was considered the most prestigious nightclub in London, far more respectable than the Lido. I was determined to get the job. The club manager, Mr. Murray, was skeptical about hiring me because I was so young. But I persuaded him to give me an opportunity to prove myself. And in two weeks, he hired me.

BOMBER PILOT

"I loved working at The Cabaret. Everything was absolutely wonderful. I worked on commission and enjoyed the challenge of selling. I developed a real talent for conning the patrons into buying. One scheme was to match male customers double or nothing. I rarely lost, and when I did, usually the tip was more than enough to cover my loss. On many occasions, a man would end up with ten or more packs of cigarettes. It was a very lucrative and satisfying job. I was making more money than I ever dreamed possible.

"For the first time in my life I could shop and buy the clothes I liked and not the ones my mother selected. I loved beautiful things and extravagantly indulged myself to the point that when one of the showgirls offered to sell me her ermine coat, I bought that too. Wearing it made me feel important and self-confident."

"It certainly sounds like an exciting place to work. Is it still there? The only club I'm familiar with is the Astor," Bill commented.

"I'm sure it's still a very popular night spot. But I left the club two and a half years ago and haven't been back since.

"I know getting the job at The Cabaret and breaking away from my mother was an important turning point in my life. It was a maturing experience and I really enjoyed working there. I was not allowed to sit with the customers. Margot, the former cigarette girl, was married and never dated the patrons. Whereas the showgirls and hostesses could socialize with the customers, the cigarette girl could not. I rarely dated, but as I became better acquainted with some of the patrons, I accepted invitations. Generally, it was with a person who was known to Mr. Murray. Richard Lleywellen, the author of How Green Was My Valley, was a regular at the club and I went out to dinner with him on several occasions. He was a sweet man. Said he just loved to sit and listen to me talk. I also dated David Niven when he was in London. That, of course, was before he became a popular actor in America. However, I rarely went out after work. I was usually too tired. If I dated it was on my evening off."

Mary hesitated again when she saw Bill turn and look at the autographed photos he had noticed earlier. But he said nothing.

"Muriel Elton, my best friend, worked at the club as a showgirl. I had known her from my earlier film work. Muriel was a beautiful blond from a small village in Yorkshire. She had a strong, Midlands accent and a matching sense of humor. She came from a working-class family and sometimes her slang and down-to-earth attitude shocked me. But any faults she had were overshadowed by a spirited vitality and a fun-loving disposition.

"Muriel came to London for a screening, but got no further than being a stand-in for Madeleine Carroll. She became disenchanted and impatient with film work and got a job as a showgirl at The Cabaret. I was surprised when my mother agreed to let Muriel move in with us as a boarder. More surprising was the fact that my mother didn't object to me having a friend. When I was younger she'd discouraged any relationships I attempted to have.

"I was two years younger than Muriel and completely in awe of her beauty and worldly knowledge. In a short time, we formed a close relationship. It was my first experience at having a friend, one who seemed to understand and respond to my many questions about life. I loved being with Muriel. We laughed a lot and enjoyed doing things together. We whispered and giggled about people we'd see riding the bus. I enjoyed the intimate and risquÈ conversations we had about men and women we saw at the club.

"I found Muriel to be a person I could trust, one who'd listen and respond to my most troubling thoughts. I'm sure that the openness between us helped me to mature in many ways. In fact, I arranged a trip to Paris for us. We went on a Cook's tour during the Christmas holiday in 1938 while my mother was on a Mediterranean cruise. I also went to Monte Carlo by myself in August, the month before the war was declared.

"Muriel and I were living in a beautiful flat in Maida Vale. I told you about the apartment there. I was very happy living with her and working at The Cabaret. Everything was wonderful until the man Muriel was dating, a German named Werner Schmit, left her. He was a handsome man, well-mannered, and quite wealthy. She fell madly in love with him. He became a regular patron at the club and Muriel spent much of her free time with him. I thought he was an exceptionally fine person and was sure that he loved Muriel. Suddenly, he disappeared and Muriel never saw him again. It happened the day after the Blitz began in September 1940. Muriel and I tried desperately to find him, but no one seemed to know what happen to him. His flat was locked and his concierge told us he left the night before with three men and hadn't returned. His manservant lived in Lambeth and he, too, was gone. Werner just vanished. It was rumored that he might've been a German spy and was picked up by English authorities.

"I'm not completely obsessed about drinking. I enjoy a glass of wine or champagne occasionally, but after Werner's disappearance, Muriel became completely distraught and buried herself in grief, self-pity, and scotch whiskey. Her personality changed dramatically when she drank and she became aggressive and argumentative. Our relationship became tense and difficult. I was wretched and unhappy watching this beautiful girl ruin her life. It was like living with my mother again and I couldn't bear that, not ever again. Finally, I told her that I would move out and leave the flat to her. The following day when I returned to our flat, I found Muriel packing. She simply said she was leaving, said goodbye, and moved out.

"It was a crushing blow. Muriel was the first and only real friend I'd had. We broke up in October 1940, just after my nineteenth birthday. After Muriel left, I moved to a smaller flat on Stanhope Terrace. The bombing of London had been raging for weeks and many nights I was too tired and depressed to go to a shelter. I just stayed in my flat and prayed. It was a lonely and unhappy time for me. My job at The Cabaret became my only haven and salvation."

Bill could hardly hear Mary as her voice drifted off. He remained quiet. She started to speak again, but in a tired and subdued voice. "I was very lonely and I . . . I met . . ." She stopped talking, slid off of Bill's shoulder, and settled her head on his chest.

He held her close and finally she fell asleep. For some time, Bill lay beside her thinking about this young woman and the unusual and difficult life she'd had. He realized he was being drawn to her not just physically, but emotionally. It was a benevolent feeling he often had toward anyone who wasn't as lucky as he'd been-particularly a young person who hadn't been brought up in a normal two-parent family. He probably inherited his sensitivity from his mother. She was orphaned at a young age when her mother died and her father deserted his family to seek gold in Alaska and never returned. Bill's mother was brought up by two older malicious sisters who treated her like a sully maid. She was later taken away from her abusive sisters and placed in an adoptive home. Bill's mother always had a soft spot in her heart for less fortunate people. Thinking of her, Bill thought, "Boy, my mom was the best-really the best."

Bill first experienced this sensitivity toward others when he was nine years old. He was new in the neighborhood and one day he came upon three large boys pushing and punching a smaller one. The little guy was in there slugging away, but was no match for his tormentors. Without questioning who was right or wrong, Bill waded in with both fists flying. His surprise attack broke up the fight and the three antagonists hurried away. Bill later learned that the youngster, Johnny O'Shea, had three strikes against him: He was Irish, Catholic, and an orphan. And that, living in a Protestant neighborhood in the 1920s, was unforgivable. Johnny became Bill's closest and lifelong friend.

In high school, Bill's first serious relationship was with a young girl, Joanne Desci. She, too, lived alone. The girl's father had deserted her mother, who worked in a hospital in New Haven, Connecticut. Joanne boarded with a family in White Plains where she attended school and rarely saw her mother. So it was not surprising that Bill felt the way he did toward Mary.

Weyland wanted this lovely young woman beside him. He wanted her very much. Wake her, he thought, and make love to her. It would be such a simple matter. But he knew it was wrong. He was in the middle of a serious dilemma and he damn well better do something about it. Either break away from her completely or write to Clare and tell her he was in love with someone else. After many soul-searching and brooding thoughts he, too, finally fell asleep.

Bill woke and watched the cold light of dawn creep into the room through the bay window of Mary's flat. And with it came reality. He thought, "As much as I wanted Mary, thank God I didn't make love to her last night. The remorse now would be unbearable." He knew he was right. He mustn't see her again. The next time he might not be so reticent because she was so damn desirable. He had to get away, break it off, and leave. He tried to disengage himself without waking her. When he got off the bed, he turned and looked down at her. She was awake, looking so vulnerable and beautiful with her rumpled hair and those huge magnificent eyes. He thought, "Damn, what a fool I am."

"Good morning, Bill. What time is it?"

"A little after six, and I better be going." He hesitated before adding, "I'm sorry about last night. I just . . . well, I gotta go."

"Let me get you some breakfast. Some coffee? It's so early. Must you leave now?"

"Yes, I really should."

He went into the bathroom, splashed cold water on his face and straightened his shirt and tie, came back in the room, put his tunic on, and picked up his cap and trench coat.

She looked up at him, searching his face for some sign of understanding. But she saw only dismay and uncertainty. She knew that she'd never see him again.

Finally, he said, "Mary, I'll call you. I'm being transferred to a tactical unit on Monday and I haven't any idea what my schedule will be or when I'll be able to get to London. But, I'll call you. Okay?"

Mary got up, walked over to him, and kissed him softly on the lips. "Please call me. I'd like to see you again." She waited for his response and when he didn't answer her, she said, "Goodbye. Take care of yourself."

She opened the door for him. He held her for a moment, said goodbye, and walked away cursing himself for being such a stupid, tongue-tied jerk. He felt guilty and cowardly for not telling her that he would not see her again. He left London more confused and distraught than ever vowing to follow through on his promise.

When Bill left, Mary turned from the door and instinctively turned on the kettle as she passed the stove. She stood for a moment trying to rationalize the thoughts that crowded her mind. Why did Bill leave the way he did? It was obvious that she would never see him again and she wondered why.

She moved into her room, stopped, and stared at the ruffled bed for a moment and suddenly realized that it was Sunday morning and it was just six-thirty. She undressed, slipped into a nightgown, and drew the cover off the daybed. She made a cup of tea, brought it to the nightstand, bunched up the pillows, and got back in bed.

Mary sat back, sipping her tea thinking about the past fifteen or sixteen hours she had been with Bill. She knew that she was in love with him. She was quite certain of that and wanted so much for him to make love to her. Why hadn't he? Was it something she did or said? Everything went wrong. To begin with, she was depressed after seeing her mother and then got mad at him for being late. She had looked forward with great anticipation to seeing Bill again and it turned out to be a complete disaster. He seemed so sincere and lovable the last time they met and she was sure that he truly liked her. What had changed? Perhaps it was her reaction to the way he was drinking. He started at eleven o'clock and continued to drink right through the evening. It was difficult for her to conceal her annoyance toward someone who drank excessively. Was it that obvious? If that was the cause of his change of heart, then so be it. Maybe it was just as well that she didn't get involved with him. No more drunks. Not again. Not ever. Not after Muriel and particularly her mother.

Mary hadn't seen her mother, Maryann Chambers, for nearly two months. She rarely visited her mother after the scene they had just after Mary's twenty-first birthday, when Mary asked her mother to release the money that was held in trust for her. It was a distasteful scene, but her mother finally relinquished some of her earnings. Her visit yesterday was no exception. Her mother was maliciously intoxicated and treated

Mary with the usual contempt. Mary's mother was an alcoholic and under the influence she was a pervert as well as a sadist.

As a child, Mary lived in constant fear of her mother. Every day when she came home from her lessons she would pray that her mother was alone and sober. Her young mind was fearful of finding her mother in a depraved and spiteful mood. The slightest provocation, particularly when drunk, would be sufficient cause to physically abuse her daughter.

Mary tried to forgive and understand her mother's behavior, but there were times when she hated her so much that the thought of doing her bodily harm flashed through Mary's mind. Her mother seemed to find perverted pleasure in beating her daughter's naked body. On one occasion when her mother knelt in front of the fireplace to undress and whip her, Mary was tempted to pick up the heavy brass poker and strike her. Fortunately, she realized the consequences and resisted the temptation.

At age twelve, Mary's adolescence arrived rather abruptly when her breasts began to develop. She literally outgrew children's acting roles. When her mother tried to bind her breasts, a director, Carol Reed, told her that her daughter had excellent potential, but to wait until she outgrew the awkward age. Forcing her into unsuitable roles could be harmful.

When Mary's acting career ended she was enrolled in the Royal Academy of Dramatic Arts. Without the glamour and esteem of the film sets, her mother became more abusive to her daughter. The beatings became more violent and frequent. Mary could not hold back the screams of pain when the strap cut her bare bottom, but she stoically held back the tears and resolved that one day she would escape her mother's tyranny and find a life of her own. With each beating her defiance strengthened, and although it provoked her mother's anger, she endured the consequences with silent determination.

As Mary grew older, she devised various schemes to avoid her mother. She spent hours away from home wandering about London or hiding in cinemas watching the same film over and over.

Inevitably, she would be found and brutally whipped for causing her mother to worry.

At age thirteen she found a street vendor who, for ten shillings, provided her with a new identity card that falsified her age so she could get a work permit. She accepted any type of work just to find a place away from her mother.

On one occasion, she sought refuge working for a Mrs. Furgeson, who owned a pub. She hired Mary to take care of her children, but demanded much more. Mary was not old enough to work in the pub. But she was required to scrub the floors and clean the tables and glasses when the pub was closed. As demanding as the woman was, and as hard as Mary worked, she was happy. She had a small, bare, but clean room and got her meals and four shillings a day in return for fourteen hours of work. But that ended when the woman's husband attempted to rape Mary. Her screams brought Mrs. Furgeson to the scene. In a blind rage, the woman cursed Mary and told her to get out.

Instead of going home, Mary found a job working in a doss-house cleaning up the kitchen and serving food to the inmates. Here, again, she was completely content to live in a small cell-like room instead of living at home with her mother. She worked there for a fortnight before she was found by the police. When she was brought home her mother bound her to the bedpost and beat her unmercifully. Mary's half brother Harry, who never challenged his mother's authority or treatment of her daughter, finally stopped her. Not satisfied with the beating, her mother rubbed salt into her scarred and bleeding back. She was untied and left alone, naked. Crying hysterically, Mary climbed out of her dormer window to the roof ledge three stories above the ground. She was found there by a neighbor, who called the police. On arrival, the constable quickly assessed the situation and invited Mrs. Chambers to accompany him to the police station. Her mother was detained overnight and Mary was placed in the care of the Salvation Army. When her mother was released the following morning and her daughter was brought home, she swore that Mary would pay for the shame and discomfort she had caused her.

Chapter 9

Weyland and his crew arrived at Bassingbourn in Cambridgeshire on Monday morning and were assigned to the 401st squadron, one of four in the 91st Bomb Group. Two other B-17 replacement crews piloted by Lieutenants Harry Lay and Frank Brown arrived with them from Bovington. The three crews were pleasantly surprised to see that Bassingbourn was a permanent prewar Royal Air Force base. All the camouflage buildings were good brick structures and each squadron had a large concrete hangar on the flight line. The grounds were well-kept, with plush green lawns and an abundance of shrubs and trees. All the streets were paved. Each squadron was allotted four houses, formerly used as family quarters, to house separately the pilots, copilots, navigators, and bombardiers. The enlisted aircrews were billeted in large brick barracks.

The base was vastly different from most American bases in England, particularly the new rapidly constructed ones, where everyone lived in Quonset huts and most roads were unpaved and muddy. Bassigbourn was a base Eighth Air Force liked to show off, and being so accessible to London, most war correspondents favored it and portrayed it as the typical way American bomber crews lived. Several celebrities made it the base of their operations, as John Steinbeck did.

He bunked with the enlisted aircrew to get the real sense of their fears, anxieties, and emotions.

After a welcoming pep talk by the group commander, Colonel Stanley Wray, Hal and Bill along with Lay and Brown and their copilots, checked in at squadron operations in the 401st hangar. There they met Major Clyde Gilford, the squadron commander, and captains Dave Eames and John Carroll, the squadron operations officer and flight leader, respectively, and several officers lounging in the ready room. They all appeared to be subdued and quiet, and an atmosphere of gloom hung heavily about them. Hal and Bill soon learned the reason for the oppressiveness.

Weyland's and the other crews from Bovington were in part replacements for six crews in the squadron who were shot down on April 17. One whole flight of six Fortress crews was lost from the 401st squadron on a bombing raid on Bremen. The flight leader, Captain Oscar O'Neill, was on his twenty-fourth mission. He was obviously admired and his courage and leadership had made him a legend in the squadron. His loss was deeply felt by his comrades. The sudden realization that they were in a shooting war with the possibility of being killed had a profound and sobering effect on the new crews.

Bill had a room to himself in the pilot's house. Most of the officers preferred sharing a room, but not him. He was issued a bicycle and inherited a black cocker spaniel, Duke, left by the previous unfortunate occupant of the room. After settling in, he met Hal, Joe, and Woody at the club. The officer's mess was a large brick building with all the amenities of a fine stateside club. It had a large ornate bar and a well-equipped game room. An active and robust craps game was in progress on one of the snooker tables. Bill was amazed to see the large amount of pound notes staked out on the table. The rate of exchange was $4 to £1 and they were tossed around like a dollar. It was not uncommon to see $1,000 in pounds being bet on one throw of the dice.

Finally, all of Bill's dreams had materialized and were proving to be far better than he had ever hoped. A flyer's alternative to being in the United Kingdom was either the jungles of southeast Asia or the desert of North Africa. The Eighth Air Force was the most active and dangerous of all the American combat theaters of operations. The losses were high, but being in the United Kingdom had its advantages, foremost being the city of London less than an hour by train from the town of Royston, a few miles from the base.

On Wednesday, Captain Carroll took Lay and Weyland up on a short formation training flight. They climbed to 8,000 feet and leveled off. Carroll kept urging them to fly closer. He was patient, encouraging them to keep their throttle adjustments to a minimum. In less than an hour, he had them holding steady and staying within a wingspan of his aircraft. They flew for another hour making turns, ascents, and descents, followed by some modest evasive maneuvers and gradually descended to 5,000 feet. Without warning, Carroll pushed the nose of his plane down sharply. Lay and Weyland were quick to react, but were unable to reform on Carroll's wings until he leveled of at fifty feet above the ground. They flew at that altitude with maximum power settings.

Weyland's adrenaline was really boiling as he flew with his eyes glued to the lead plane, seeing in his peripheral vision the trees and fields rushing by beneath them. He had no idea where he was or how long they'd been flying when suddenly Carroll pulled up and directly beneath them was their base. They peeled off and landed in one-minute intervals. As he turned the Seventeen off the runway, Bill shouted uncharacteristically, "Boy, that's what I call flying. Whattayou think, Hal? How did I do?"

The copilot gave him the thumbs up and Bayne yelled vigorously, "Yes, sir, that's what I call flying."

The three other squadrons of the Ninety-first were alerted for a mission on Thursday, but it was scrubbed. Weyland's crew flew a practice mission later that day in a two-flight formation. The group was alerted for a mission on Saturday and as the 401st was standing down, they were left behind. Norm Richards in the 326th squadron was on the mission. How Bill envied him as he watched the formation leave for a mission to Saint Nazaire to bomb the submarine shipyards. These more commonly called subpens were constructed inland with access to them by walled canals that led to the underground shelters. The side-walls of the subpens were eight feet thick and the roofs were eleven-foot-thick reinforced concrete. Once in the pens the submarines were well protected and bombing had little effect on the fortified bunkers.

Bill again put off a confrontation with Mary by telling her that he couldn't leave the base and he wouldn't be able to see her this weekend.

On Saturday night, he and his crew visited a local pub in the village of Bassingbourn. The village patrons were friendly and hospitable. Their attitudes surprised Bill considering how close they lived to the base and the noise of the aircraft. If not on a high-altitude training mission, most flights at that time were made on the deck. He wondered how the people in the countryside, particularly the farmers, withstood the noise and terror of those monstrous aircraft roaring over their lands at treetop level.

On Monday, the group was alerted for a mission over Belgium. Bill was scheduled to fly with Lieutenant Donald Frank, but the sortie was scrubbed due to bad weather. Daylight precision bombing required visual sighting of the target. This was particularly necessary when bombing targets in the occupied countries of Europe, where the Americans made every effort to minimize civilian casualties.

On Tuesday morning, the mission to Antwerp was rescheduled and the excitement Weyland felt was impossible to control. Lieutenant Frank's crew were all veterans and they appeared quite relaxed. He tried to emulate them but felt he failed miserably. It was as though a low-voltage electric current were running through his body.

The formation consisted of fifty-four B-17s from three bomb groups, the 91st, 303d, and the 306th. Seeing such a large number of Fortresses for the first time was a spectacularly thrilling sight. Bill was amazed at how well the groups formed over the English coast, and then headed out over the North Sea. The day was beautifully clear except for a slight haze that obscured the coastline of Europe. Once over water the crew was ordered to clear their guns and immediately the sharp test bursts of the fifty-caliber machine guns vibrated through the plane. Each gunner called in an affirmative response when his guns were cleared. The navigator called to say they were on track and on time. The bombardier announced to the pilot that the bombs were armed and ready.

Bill strained to get his first glimpse of occupied Europe through the Plexiglas windshield. Finally, there it was, more than four miles beneath them. Most conspicuous were the inundated tributaries of the great continental river meandering through Holland to the sea.

As the formation crossed over the outer islands, several antiaircraft barrages greeted them. Floating in grayish clouds through the formation, the exploding flak looked harmless, but Bill suddenly realized that this was what he had been looking forward to. Now that it was happening, he wondered what his reactions would be under fire. The tail gunner called to report that the covering Spitfires of the Royal Air Force were approaching and no enemy aircraft were sighted.

The bomber formation made good uncontested progress up the Western Scheldt over Holland and on to the target. Then, as if by some prearranged signal, just as the bombardier called "bomb bay doors open," the aircraft rocked with the thunderous sound of machine guns being fired in rapid succession. The shouts of "bandits" were repeated from several crew members. Searching the skies around him for an enemy, Bill cranked his head around wildly until he spotted the gray enemy fighters with their distinctive black crosses concentrating their attacks on the lead group below him.

An excited call from the waist gunner, "Two bogeys, three o'clock," forced Bill to turn quickly to his right. He heard the top turret swivel behind him and above his head.

"Got 'em. 109s setting up for a frontal. How about it Nav, see 'em?" shouted the flight engineer.

"Yeah, I see them. We're all set here," responded the navigator.

"Okay guys, watch them," warned Frank. "They'll be turning in on us in a couple of minutes. Hold your fire until they're in range."

Bill watched the two fighters intently as they flew passed them off to the right, just out of effective range for the bomber's guns. He looked at Frank and saw the pilot tighten his grip on the control column. Bill felt completely helpless sitting there. With nothing to do with his hands, he grabbed his knees and held tight in a futile effort to stop them from shaking.

A little more than a mile ahead of them the two ME-109s made an abrupt, 180-degree turn and headed directly for their bomber. The action quickly blurred as the German fighters sped toward the bomber. In a matter of seconds, their wing cannons started to blink and Bill came to the shocking revelation that they were shooting at him with every intention to kill him. He involuntarily hunched his back and momentarily tried to duck down behind the instrument panel in front of him, but instantly realized the metal would be no protection from a direct hit by the enemy cannon fire.

All the Fort's forward guns were now returning fire, and the aircraft shook so violently that Bill thought they'd surely been hit. The acrid smell of cordite filled the cockpit as small quantities of exploding gunpowder escaped from the breaches of the guns each time a round was fired and a new one chambered. Bill found it impossible to stop shaking, whether from excitement or fear. Probably both. He realized that as copilot he could do nothing more than sit and watch-a horrible, helpless feeling. If only he had something to hold onto, a gun or a control column. He wanted to fight back. Flying copilot, as far as he was concerned, was undoubtedly the worst possible crew position.

The top turret guns, just above Bill, continued firing long angry bursts. Bill watched the tracers flying out over his head toward the two German fighters. The guns in the nose of the bomber were flashing and the fiery red tracer rounds converged on the enemy aircraft, falling about them like burnt-out sparklers. So intense was the crew's effort to blast the two fighters out of the sky that with the exception of several verbal expletives, the usual chatter on the intercom ceased when the firing started.

Occasionally, directions were shouted from one gunner to another. "Sons of bitches are comin' at ya, Al," the top gunner shouted to the ball turret gunner, hoping he could get off a quick shot at the Germans as they dove beneath the bomber.

"All set here," came the excited reply.

Undaunted, the Germans pressed on through a mass of fifty-caliber slugs coming from the Fortress, as well as others in the flight. They came so close that Bill felt sure they intended to crash head-on into their B-17. But just a few hundred yards from the bomber, the German pilots, in perfect unison, suddenly snapped their fighters in a half roll and disappeared in a steep dive beneath the bomber.

"Low right, Al!" came a scream from the top turret.

"Okay, I got them!" replied the ball turret gunner as his guns were heard for the first time.

The closing speed of the two enemy aircraft was so fast and the action so quick that their attack was over in a matter of seconds, leaving Bill feeling amazingly calm and unafraid. He quickly realized that the fear of anticipating danger was far greater than actually facing it. Beyond the enormous relief he felt, his solemn thoughts were of the courage and awesome daring of both the Germans and the crew of the Fortress. Each desperately intent on destroy their adversary.

A frantic dogfight continued around them as the Spitfires joined the action. Ignoring the guns of the Fortresses, the British fighters sped through the formation in hot pursuit of the Germans. Bill later learned that the Spits were flown by Polish volunteers who had every reason to hate the Germans. The necessity to fly through streams of bomber bullets was no deterrent to them.

The flak over the target area was heavy and concentrated, but their flight seemed to be above most of it. After what seemed to be an infinite period of time, the words "Bombs away" were heard loud and clear over the intercom. As quickly as the enemy fighters appeared, they departed and the maddening sound of the guns ceased. Except for the drone of the engines, an eerie quiet filled the aircraft. The silence lasted for a minute or so and then with the sudden realization that the action was over, the excited voices of the crew vibrated loudly in Bill's headset.

"Everyone okay?" the pilot questioned. "Give me a damage report."

The aircraft had somehow escaped being hit. When the bomb bay doors closed, the formation turned west and headed home. The group came together in perfect formation after being partially separated during the attack. With the exception of a few aircraft that aborted, the formation looked fairly well-intact. Several B-17s had engines shut down and one in the lead flight had smoke streaming from an outboard engine. Bill also settled down, wondering whether anyone noticed how badly he shook before the first attack. He hoped not. Would it be different with his own crew? How would he handle it? Would he be able to control the fear he felt when the action started? He faced some pretty serious questions on the return flight, but felt confident he could overcome any doubts. The closer the formation got to the English coast the more self-assured he became. And when his group reached the airfield and peeled off to land, he felt absolutely confident in his ability to lead his crew into combat.

The elation of returning alive was beyond any sensation he had ever experienced. He had a tremendous feeling of relief. When they pulled into their dispersal area, his entire crew was there to greet him. The minute he dropped out of the forward hatch, they surrounded him and bombarded him with questions. These were the men he had grown so close to and if they were lucky, they'd be coming back as he had today feeling the way he did.

On Thursday, they flew a training mission. The 351st Bomb Group had just arrived from the States and the 91st, along with the 306th, were showing the new unit how to form in a combat wing formation. Bill glanced up and saw the new group moving into position. They looked good flying in a relatively tight formation when a plane in the low flight pulled up suddenly and hit the bomber above. It immediately burst into flames and broke apart while the other plane went into a wild tailspin. Large chunks of debris from the exploding aircraft hit a third B-17, forcing it out of control into a crazy earthward spiral. It was a tragic and deadly end for three crews who had not yet seen combat. With little or no formation training before arriving overseas, such accidents happened. The sky was full of eager young pilots and the mark of a good combat flyer was how close and how tight he could stay on the wing of another Seventeen. Midair crashes occurred all too frequently, especially in combat, where inexperience, coupled with prop wash, weather, enemy action, and fear, made formation flying extraordinarily dangerous.

Chapter 10

Bill called Mary Friday night and told her that his squadron was confined to the base. He'd decided not to see her again, and felt confident the conflict he'd been wrestling with was settled. He vowed to tell her the next time he spoke to her. At the Officers Club that evening, Norm Richards suggested that they visit London the following day. Bill agreed, and to further strengthen his determination not to see Mary, he called Sylvia, who promised to meet him at the Astor.

Norm and Bill arrived at the club a little after nine and met Sylvia in the lobby. While Bill was signing the members' register, Mary and Dorothy came down the stairs from the first-floor powder room. He didn't see her, but sensing someone behind him, he turned to find her standing five feet away glaring at him.

"Well, hello. Fancy meeting you here," she said abrasively.

When he finally found his voice, he replied, "Hi. You know, I just knew you would be here tonight." Before she could respond, he added, "Hello, Dorothy, how nice to see you again."

He turned to introduce Sylvia, but Mary cut him off by saying, "Hello, Sylvia, how nice to see you. Is your husband still in Greece?" She then turned to Norm and said, "Bill told me you were all confined to the base. How did you manage to get away?"

Norm, enjoying Bill's discomfort, answered, "Did Bill say that? I guess he must have got a reprieve."

Mary turned to Sylvia, "I didn't know that you knew Bill."

Bill picked it up quickly by saying, "Oh, Sylvia's with Norm."

Sylvia looked at him strangely.

Mary caught the look and responded, "Oh, really," and after several silent and uncomfortable seconds Mary turned to Dorothy and said, "Come along, Dorothy, we'd best return to Stephanos." She gave Bill a scathing look, turned, and left.

Bill had little luck explaining to Sylvia what he meant and Norm was no help at all. He then thought, "Why am I being so defensive? I don't have any commitment to Mary. Damn it. I'm acting like I did something wrong."

They finally got seated. When Bill looked up, there across the floor was Mary, sitting between Dorothy and Stephanos, glaring at them. She reached for the bottle of scotch, half filled a highball glass, took a deep swallow, recovered with a shocking grimace, and picked up a cigarette. After some confusion, Stephanos lit it for her, and she sat back puffing away in a cloud of smoke.

Bill had not seen her drink whiskey or smoke and realized the extent of her anger. She raised the glass of scotch to her lips again, apparently decided against it, and put it down. Bill felt completely helpless and very uncomfortable, not knowing which way to turn. He didn't want to leave and yet he didn't want to stay. He could almost feel the daggers being hurled across the room at him. About ten minutes after they were seated, Mary got up and walked casually over to their table.

Bill jumped up as she asked, "May I sit down?"

"Of course." He quickly replied and pulled up a chair, wondering what she was up to.

To his complete surprise she was amiable and pleasant and asked sweetly, "How's Duke?" Before he could answer, she turned to Sylvia, "Did Bill tell you that we have a little black cocker spaniel back at Bassingbourn?"

He'd mentioned to Mary over the phone that he had inherited the cocker. The conversation became one-sided with Mary telling Sylvia all about Bill and herself. This was all a big surprise to him and he sat there looking bewildered, first at Sylvia, then at Norm. Sylvia looked uncomfortable and Norm was thoroughly enjoying himself, sitting there with a smirk on his face. They sat listening to a number of Mary's fabricated stories inferring that she and Bill were lovers. Finally, Sylvia excused herself and walked away from the table.

Glaring at Mary, Bill got up and said, "I'll be back." He caught up to Sylvia in the lobby, but failed miserably to explain what was going on.

At that point, Norm arrived and Sylvia asked him, "Will you take me home, Norman?"

He eagerly agreed and turned to Bill, "Bye-bye, lover."

Sylvia stalked out without a word.

Mary had rejoined Dorothy and Stephanos by the time Bill returned. Mary watched him hesitate for a moment and then walk to their table.

When he arrived, she greeted him teasingly, "How is dear, lonely Sylvia? Did she forgive you?"

"No, she left madder than hell. I hope you're satisfied. Where in the world did you dream up all those stories about us?"

"Actually, it was rather easy, and I'd just begun to warm up when she marched off. Poor thing looked a bit cross." Mary looked at Bill with an expression of mock concern. "I can't for the life of me fathom why. After all, she was with Norm." She stopped and her expression suddenly changed and became serious, "Or was that the second lie you told me? The first being that you were confined to the base."

He started to respond but thought better of it. "Look, Mary, I'm sure Dorothy and Stephanos are not interested in this. Why can't we talk about something else?"

Happily, Dorothy picked up the suggestion. "Come sit down, Bill, and tell us how you like your new duty station."

They talked, but the conversation continued rather lamely with Mary looking at him as if he were some low form of animal life. When Bill asked, they danced, somewhat apart and silently, and returned to the table to find Dorothy and Stephanos waiting to say good night. Dorothy made Bill promise to let her know the next time he came to London so he and Mary could have dinner with them.

When they left, Mary sat while he stood with a hand on the back of his chair looking uncomfortable. After several long minutes, Mary said quietly, "Please take me home."

Not a word was spoken as they sat together in the taxi on the way to Ivor Court. He got out of the cab with her and said, "Good night, Mary."

She took his hand, "Tell the driver to go, Bill, and come in."

In the flat, she disappeared into the bathroom after lighting the gas fire. He slumped in her lounge chair and lit a cigarette. Now, alone and inwardly seething, he became contentious and angry. He'd been apologizing all night and, damn it, what for? He'd made no commitment to her. So why did he feel guilty? It was time to change all that. He would tell her to get the hell out of his life. So he sat sulking, wrapping himself in righteous self-pity.

Mary eventually came out of the bathroom in her nightgown and got into bed. He lit another cigarette and sat brooding, not wanting to look at her. She asked him if he was coming to bed. He mumbled something that sounded like, "Okay, in a while." He was seriously thinking about leaving. He reckoned he'd better make the move now or he never would.

They were silent for several minutes and finally she said so softly that he could hardly hear her, "Please, Bill, come to bed and hold me."

He got up, crushed out his cigarette, silently undressed down to his shorts, got in bed, and took her in his arms. When their bodies came together, suddenly all the hurt, frustration, and unpleasant remarks were forgotten. They confessed their love for each other and promised never to do or say such hateful things to one another again. The first time they made love it was quick and urgent as if they both had a desperate need to consummate their new love. The second time they patiently savored each act of lovemaking with an unrelenting lust and desire. There was no apprehension on his part and she responded to each touch and taste with a sensual intensity. They were insatiable, waking each other throughout the night to make love again and again.

It was late morning when Bill awoke. He was momentarily perplexed, but quickly recalled the night of sexual ecstasy with the exciting and passionate woman beside him. He was lying on his side with one arm draped over her waist. She slept soundly curled up with her back to him. The sensual feel of her nakedness soon aroused him. He moved closer to her curved body forcing his groin against her smooth bottom. She stirred, sighed softly at the feel of him, and snuggled against his hardness. He found her moist and entered her gently.

They finally relinquished their hold on each other and decided that if they wanted to pursue their arduous lovemaking, they'd need nourishment. Mary insisted that he stay in bed while she prepared breakfast. She slipped on fitted trousers and a sweater, dashed out, and returned within fifteen minutes with a newspaper and a small bag of groceries. In minutes, he heard bacon sizzling and the aroma of coffee filled the flat. He sat up in bed amazed, watching her move about the tiny stove preparing the food. When it was ready, she brought the tray to him and he held it while she undressed and got back into bed. They shared two fresh eggs, which he had not seen since leaving the States, the best bacon he'd ever tasted, marvelous fried potatoes, broiled tomatoes, and surprisingly good coffee. After the meal they shoved the tray aside, lay back, held onto each other, and made love again.

Later, they walked across the street to Regent Park. Arm in arm they strolled, a couple obviously in love. She looked like a woman who had made love that morning with her man and couldn't wait to make love to him again. His expression was a mirror image of her thoughts. They were completely oblivious to the people around them, some of whom stopped and watched them as they passed, recalling perhaps their own memories of past love affairs.

They spent about an hour in the park until a cold drizzle settled down on them. Mary hurried him to the bus stop and they rode to the local cinema. There they saw the popular screen couple, Spencer Tracy and Katherine Hepburn, in Woman of the Year. It was an excellent movie and they tried to concentrate on the film, but they failed miserably. Holding hands wasn't what he wanted. He wanted her in his arms again and felt certain she wanted to be there. They left before the film ended and hurried back to her flat for what Mary called a "little lie down."

The moment she closed the door they were in each other's arms. Unwilling to part they struggled, with their mouths fused together, to undress each other. When completely disrobed, he drew her toward the bed. She held back and said, "Let's bathe first. We are only allowed four inches of water, but together we can fill it to eight. It'll be wonderfully extravagant. Would you fancy that, Bill?"

"You bet. Sounds great."

When the water reached the allowable level, they washed and caressed each other. She made him lie back while she made love to him. Her pleasure was reflected in her enlarged violet pupils as she held him in a state of ecstatic helplessness.

When the water cooled, they got out and dried each other. He then picked her up, carried her to her bed and said, "My turn."

She looked up at him and smiled, not quite sure what he intended so soon after she'd made love to him. "Please close the curtains, Bill, and come lie down and hold me," she said, patting the bed beside her.

He closed the drapes, returned to the bed, spread her legs, and knelt between them. "I want to make love to you," and he did, touching and kissing every bit of her. Never before had she been loved so tenderly and unselfishly-and yet so wickedly delicious. Finally, they slept, locked in each other's arms.

Later, they walked to the corner of Park and Baker streets to the local pub, the Volunteer, for Sunday night supper. Being among such friendly and pleasant people was a refreshing experience for Bill. They were all anxious to meet Mary's Yank, shake his hand, and buy them a drink. Mary and Bill left before the pub closed and they arrived at Kings Cross Station just in time for him to catch the last train to Royston. On the platform, they clung to each other completely indifferent to the people around them. They held on until the last possible minute before he was forced to climb into his compartment as the train pulled out of the station. Bill leaned out of the compartment window and waved until the train disappeared around the curve and they lost sight of each other.

In the taxi on the way back to her flat, Mary smiled when she recalled the events at the Astor last night and her reaction to seeing Bill with Sylvia. There had been no question in her mind that Norman wasn't Sylvia's date, and her first impulse was "If that's the type of woman he likes, she can bloody well have him." But the more she thought about it, the angrier she became. And yes, jealous. She realized that Bill had made no commitment to her, but she wasn't going to let him off that easy, certainly not without an effort on her part, and particularly after he told her he couldn't leave the base. So she decided to cause him a little unpleasantness and embarrassment, which, if it upset Sylvia, so much the better.

Of all people, it was ironic that Bill had met Sylvia Catapopolis. Mary knew her and had every reason to dislike her. Although married with a husband back in Greece, Sylvia enjoyed male companionship. She was quite wealthy and lived comfortably in a luxury flat just off Bayswater Road. Two years ago, Sylvia tried desperately to break up the relationship Mary had with Georges Lavanas. She wasn't successful then, and she certainly wasn't going to interfere with her relationship with Bill.

Mary was amazed at her own audacity, joining their table and then brazenly inferring that she and Bill were lovers. It was great fun seeing Bill's shocked expression and watching him squirm, but it was much more satisfying to see Sylvia's obvious discomfort. Yes, she did exaggerate horribly, but her mischief was effective and quickly ended any further threat from Mrs. Catapopolis.

Thank God she didn't follow her initial instinct. She may have never seen Bill again and regretted it all her life. Now, in her heart, Mary felt that Bill really cared for her and she was truly his girl.

Mary was completely exhausted when she got home. She was tired and sore from an overindulgence in lovemaking, but it was a marvelous kind of hurt and exhaustion. She felt excruciatingly alive, happier than she had ever been, and quite sure she was truly in love. She stripped off her clothes and fell wearily into her bed thinking she should change the sheets, but the smell of him and their sex felt so wonderful and sensual that she wanted the memory of their loving to last. So she settled between the warm sheets to savor his scent.

Bill was not her first affair and she wondered why this time it was so different. With Bill, her behavior had been completely wanton, reckless, and unrestrained. Never before had she been so eager and willing. She just wanted to give every bit of herself to him, engulf him deep inside her body, and keep him there. Before, there had always been a nervousness and uncertainty about sex that she associated with the horrible and painful experiences she'd suffered during childhood.

As a young girl, sex and all its ramifications had never been explained to Mary by her mother or any other relative. Since she was allowed no friends her own age, she knew nothing about the male and female relationships that most children picked up from more knowing companions. In later years, Mary realized that her mother seemed to get an obscene pleasure in exposing herself. At home, she openly engaged in sex with men, never attempting to conceal the acts from her daughter. At times, she'd force Mary to watch. One vivid recollection Mary had was seeing her mother astride a man, moaning in the throes of intercourse. She was neither young nor svelte, and the sight of her ample breasts flopping clumsy about as she impaled herself again and again on the man's swollen member became a repulsive nightmare that Mary lived with for years. Mary was too young at the time to understand, but she knew somehow that her mother's sexual exhibitions were shameful, wrong, and disgusting.

Not only was Mary forced to watch these copulations, but at times she was compelled to enter the same bed while her mother entertained a man. She was told these men were "uncles" who loved her. They touched and caressed her to show their "love." Usually, they never did more than fondle her. Nonetheless, Mary found the experience terrifying and traumatic. She left the bed as soon as she could, feeling bewildered, unclean, and close to hysteria.

BOMBER PILOT

When she was fourteen years old, Mary experienced a most terrifying and savage assault by a lecher while her mother slept. One afternoon, returning from her classes, she heard her mother talking to a man in her bedroom. Fearing what might happen, Mary tried to slip quietly to her own room, but was stopped by her mother's slurred order, "Mary, come in here."

Mary entered hesitantly, saw her mother in bed with the man, and turned to leave.

"Take your clothes off and get into bed. This is your Uncle Jack. He's a very nice man and he loves you." Her mother's demanding, harsh words left her no alternative.

Tearful and trembling, Mary obeyed. Jack smiled lasciviously, but did nothing until her mother had fallen into a drunken stupor and Mary tried to leave. He grabbed her and pulled her back against his naked torso. She struggled and cried out, "Please, let me go," but he held her close. She screamed when be forced his hand between her legs and pushed a finger inside her. He clamped his hand over her mouth and stifled her screams. When she bit his hand, he slapped her hard across the face and for a moment she lost consciousness. When she regained her senses and begged him to stop, he told her to be quiet or he'd strike her again. He mounted her and forced her legs apart with his knee while his finger viciously probed her vagina. She cried out for her mother, but her muffled pleas went unheard. The man withdrew his finger and brutally thrust a larger part of him into her, intensifying a terrible pain that racked her body. His foul breath, smelling of stale food and whiskey, caused waves of nausea to sweep through her. She couldn't breathe with his hand clamped over her mouth or move under the crushing weight of his large, sweaty body. A fear of suffocating gripped her. She fought desperately to pull his hand away from her mouth, but couldn't. In stark terror, her enlarged eyes filled with tears, but he continued to tear her apart by ramming himself into her innocent young body. She sobbed uncontrollably until the pain was washed away as panic seized her and she fainted.

When Mary regained consciousness, her mother was still asleep beside her. For a moment, she couldn't remember what had happened until the pain in her groin revived the horrible memory. The man was gone, but the repulsive odor of him and the pungent unfamiliar smell of semen remained. She couldn't understand why he wanted to hurt her. She wanted to tell her mother, but decided not to wake her. She was over-wrought by shame and guilt and felt dirty and gruesomely violated.

She quietly got out of the bed, filled the bathtub, and gingerly low-ered herself into the scalding water. Once again, she was seized by nau-sea and panic when the water turned pink. She covered her mouth, held back the urge to cry out, and lay back trying desperately to clear her mind of the horrible hurt she experienced. She knew if she told her mother what happened, she'd be blamed and beaten, so she resolved to suffer in silence and somehow purge herself of the repulsive memory.

Three and a half months later, Mary woke one morning feeling sick and nauseous. She told her mother, who had noticed that her daughter had gained weight. When her mother questioned Mary about her menstrual period, with some uncertainty she told her that she no longer menstruated. Her mother looked alarmed and said angrily, "You stupid girl. You must be pregnant."

Shocked and bewildered, Mary frantically asked, "What do you mean?"

"You're going to have a baby. But I'll take care of it."

Mary had never been told how babies were born. In her mind, only married people had babies.

The following day her mother took her to a clinic where she was examined by a woman who confirmed the pregnancy. Her mother made her drink a vile liquid and held her down while the woman inserted something into Mary's vagina. She shrieked in pain when the woman pierced her uterus and then forced a syringe of scalding liquid into her.

Afterward, they left her on a small bed in a locked room where she screamed and fought the severe spasmodic cramps for nearly ten hours. Several times during the period of living hell her mother came into the room, looked at her unsympathetically, and told her to be quiet. Finally, when the pain reached an intolerable level, the two women returned. The nurse explained that the only way Mary could stop the pain was to push down hard on her stomach and force the hurt out. She cried out as she pushed, and suddenly she felt a lump of flesh and fluid gush out of her. Her mother wrapped the bloody mess in a towel and took it out of the room. The pain had eased, but the terror of the rape remained.

Days later, when her mother still hadn't questioned her about how she became pregnant, Mary realized she must've known what happened that dreadful day she'd forced her daughter to get into her bed. Sick, painfully sore, and desperately unhappy, Mary took several pounds from her mother's purse and left home. Instead of going to her classes, she went to Paddington Station and boarded a train to Bodwin in Cornwall. There, the station manager directed her to the home of Hazel Chambers, the wife of Mary's half brother Fred. When Mary was very young, Fred died from wounds he received during the Great War. Mary remembered his wife as a kind and caring person. When she arrived, Hazel Chambers welcomed her and for the first time in Mary's life she found what it was like to live in a home with a normal family. Mary's sister-in-law had two young children, and she felt secure there. But her happiness was short-lived.

A few days after Mary arrived, she was about to enter her newfound home when she heard her mother's voice inside. Terrified, Mary turned and ran back to the street. When her mother came out of the house, Mary desperately looked for a way to escape. A man's bicycle was leaning against the neighbor's fence. Mary grabbed it and managed to get up on the high seat and turn the bicycle down the hill. As it gathered speed, she realized she couldn't reach the pedals or the hand brake. Fear of her mother overcame any anxiety she had about the danger of speeding toward the village. She looked back and saw her mother standing in the road. When she turned to look forward, a huge lorry was crossing the intersection in front of her. She closed her eyes and screamed.

Mary regained consciousness in a hospital with her arm in a cast and numerous cuts and bruises over her body. Her nose was broken and her wrist was fractured in several places. The doctor said it would have to be reset again or she'd suffer a permanent deformity.

Days later when she was brought home, her mother, in a sober and somewhat regretful state of mind, decided to send her daughter off to school. She enrolled Mary in a convent in Belgium. Mary had little knowledge of French, a language she was forced to use, and was deprived of many things, including food, when she failed to make the proper response. It was a lonely and depressing time for her. She was sent home when she was caught stealing candy from other children.

Mary set aside the horrible memories and finally drifted off to sleep, snug in the security of the bed she had shared so passionately with Bill.

Chapter 11

On Monday, the weather at Bassingbourn turned miserable and Bill's group stood down. Finally, on Wednesday night, the alert came down. At the briefing the following morning, Bill saw that he was scheduled to fly with his own crew and that gave him few uneasy moments.

Hal appeared pleased and grinned when they announced the crew loading lists. "Hey, Bill, we're all going together."

There had been some concern among his crew that they might have to fly their first mission with another pilot who had more combat experience

"Damn right. If we're going down, let's go together. I sure don't want to fly with another crew. How about it, Joe?" replied Woody, the eternal pessimist, constantly reminding anyone who'd listen of the slim chance they had of making it through twenty-five missions.

"Nope," Joe Newberry replied. "I'm all for staying together. That's what we've been training for. So the sooner we get started, the better, as far as I'm concerned."

The officers felt better about taking their chances with Bill than with another pilot even though he had no combat experience. Weyland would have to wait to see the reaction of the enlisted crew members when they all met at the personal equipment shack. He was sure they had the same anxious feeling of fluttering butterflies in the pit of their stomachs as he had before his first mission.

The planned mission was to bomb the Avions-Potez aircraft factory at Meaulte in France. After the general and specialized briefings, Bill, Hal, Joe, and Woody met the other crew members checking out their flight gear. Bill noticed a strange uneasiness when he met his crew.

Bayne Scurlock didn't look like the self-assured Texan he'd been. He was unusually quiet and tried to appear unconcerned and casual about the mission, but his nervousness was apparent.

Sergeant Ray Gillet, assistant flight engineer and waist gunner, attempted to look nonchalant and indifferent. However, it was evident he, too, had difficulty concealing his true feelings. Quite often while in training, Bill would let Ray come up front and get into the pilot seat and fly the airplane, particularly during long, monotonous training flights and especially when the autopilot was inoperative. Ray could hold a course heading and altitude better than the pilot. Bill had once overheard Scurlock boasting to the crew that if anything happened to the pilot and copilot on a bombing mission he'd fly the plane and get the crew back safely. Bill had his doubts, but if anyone could get the crew back, it would be Ray Gillet.

This morning Gillet seemed overly preoccupied with checking his parachute and just nodded and quietly responded, "Yes, sir," when the pilot asked if he had all his gear.

Jim Cobb, the radio operator, looked up at Bill but quickly turned back to his radio folder and attempted to relight his cigar, which was already lit. Bill didn't expect much of Jim as a gunner but he was a good reliable radio operator. He was the only direct contact the pilot would have with the other ships in the formation and, most important, the formation leaders.

When Bill asked Lloyd Thomas if he was ready, he grinned and replied, "Yes, sir. All set." He didn't seem a bit nervous. The pilot had absolutely no doubts about this young man. He flew curled up in a fetal position, hanging from the belly of the bomber, enclosed in a steel-and-Plexiglas ball less than a four feet in diameter, his legs jammed in between twin fifty-caliber machine guns and a gunsight. The turret could turn 360 degrees horizontally and 180 degrees in azimuth. It was the most dangerous and gutsy position on the bomber and Lloyd relished every minute of it.

Sergeant Jim McBride grinned at his pilot. Bill had little doubt about Jim's ability and readiness to fight. McBride was a former dirt-track race car driver, a happy-go-lucky, fun-loving, twenty year old who got along with everyone and rarely bitched about anything. He would do well as the tail gunner or, as the crew put it, "protecting our ass."

Jim McGovern, the wise-cracking, raunchy, second waist gunner, didn't look happy about the prospect of being shot at, but he grinned when Bill asked him if he was ready, "I guess I'm as ready as I'll ever be, lieutenant. But I'm sure not looking forward to it." For once, he had nothing flippant to say.

Bayne walked out of the equipment shack alongside Bill and, with a slight tremor, said, "Smithy in Carroll's crew said this is going to be a milk run. What do you think, lieutenant?"

"I figure it shouldn't be too bad. But, you can never tell."

They all crowded into a weapons carrier and headed for the biggest adventure of their lives. From the front seat, Bill heard them horsing around and joking in the back. The tension seemed to leave them as they rode out to the dispersal area a good half-mile from the flight line. They drove around a group of trees, through a large opening in a stone wall and into a field of newly planted crops. The truck brought them up to a circular hardstand, just large enough for a B-17 to make a 180-degree turn. The forty dispersed and camouflaged aircraft parking sites were scattered over a wide area away from the airfield itself.

They unloaded their gear in front of the brand new B-17F.

She was a beauty without a scratch on her slender brown-and-green camouflage body. The early morning sun sparkled on the Plexiglas nose and top turret. With the plane's cigar-shaped fuselage and its high dorsallike vertical stabilizer, the Flying Fortress was the sleekest, sturdiest, and most modern bomber in the world. The B-17 was seventy-five feet long with a wingspan of 104 feet. The largest section of the fuselage measured less than nine feet high and seven feet wide. Mounted on the bomber were eleven fifty-caliber machine guns covering every possible angle of attack. The B-17F was indeed a mighty fortress.

Someone had already christened the plane Eager Beaver. The crew muttered several disparaging remarks about the name. Bayne said they would change it when they got back if it was going to be their permanently assigned bomber.

The crew left their gear on the tarmac and headed for the rear entryway. Hal and Bill made a thorough walkaround, carefully checking the exterior of the bomber. When they finished, Hal chinned himself up through the forward hatch to the cockpit. Bill walked around and entered through the rear door on the right side of the fuselage. He crawled back into the tail of the plane and squeezed in behind McBride, who was checking his position. Jim was caressing the grips of the twin fifties and admiring their long perforated barrels that projected out beyond the tail. It was a snug little area and McBride felt right at home there. Bill noticed the armor plate they'd added to protect the tail gunner. As he backed out, Bill tapped Jim on the shoulder. Jim turned and raised his hand touching his index finger to his thumb.

Weyland extracted himself from the narrow confines of the tail, turned, and stood upright in the rear section of the fuselage once he had sufficient headroom. He moved forward to where Gillet and McGovern were checking their gun positions in the waist of the bomber. The two flexible guns, one on each side, were swivel-mounted on sturdy stanchions bolted to the deck. The linked ammunition was fed to guns from large ammo canisters secured to the deck. When in combat, the gunners slid the Plexiglas ports back and fired through the opening. Deflectors protected the gunners from the slipstream, but not the bitter cold. Temperatures above twenty thousand feet ranged from minus thirty to minus forty degrees centigrade.

With a rudimentary bead sight, the weapons were not too effective, but the waist gunners swore by them. You had to lead the enemy fighter like you would when shooting a running deer and hope the target flew into the stream of lead. Ray and Jim seemed satisfied after checking the limited equipment at their gun stations and they, too, gave Bill the okay sign when he asked them if everything was all right.

A short distance forward, Bill stopped and looked down at Sergeant Thomas stuffed into his ball turret. He was lying on his back with his knees bent between the two fifty-caliber machine guns. His feet rested on foot pedals that turned and operated the turret while his hands were free to hold the gun grips. He looked up from his gun sight directly in front of his face and grinned, "Looks real good, lieutenant. All shining and new. Just hope I can hit something."

While in training, all the crew members were required to shoot skeet. Lloyd consistently beat everyone, hitting sixteen to eighteen clay pigeons out of twenty. Weyland had no doubt about his marksmanship. The gunners, however, had very little gunnery practice and had never shot at a live target and Bill was sure they were all a little squeamish about trying to kill someone.

Weyland grinned down at him, "You'll do all right down there, Lloyd. Just be sure your oxygen regulator is working."

Bill moved a few spaces forward and opened the door to the radio compartment. Cobb turned, the stub of a dead cigar in his mouth, and said, "Got everything I need here, sir. Nothing new from what we had on the one we flew over on."

"Okay, Jim, as soon as we get the power on you can check it all out," replied Bill.

The compartment was stuffed full of radio equipment. There was a fifty-caliber gun mounted on a sliding bar in the open hatch at the top of the compartment. The opening was also used for ditching after the gun was tossed overboard. The overwater ditching position for all the crew, except the pilot and copilot, was in the radio compartment. They sat toboggan-style on the floor, braced against the bulkhead, and exited through the top hatch-hopefully before the plane sank. The pilot and copilot got out through the side windows in the cockpit.

Weyland opened the hatch, entered the bomb bay, and stepped onto the catwalk that ran the length of the bay. He patted the five-hundred pounders as he moved forward. Four of them were shackled on each side of the bay. The bomb load varied based on the bombing altitude, distance to, and type of target. The bomb bay doors were open and he could look down to the ground just several feet below. The forward hatch to the cockpit was so small Bill had to bend down to get through it. The top turret was immediately on the other side of the bulkhead and he had to crawl through it before he could stand upright in the cockpit. This was Sergeant Scurlock's gun position. He stood upright with his head in the enclosed Plexiglas dome that was elevated above the fuselage. From his position, he had a clear unobstructed view of 360 degrees. The electrically operated turret had twin fifties and a good Sperry gun sight. Scurlock's guns were the most effective ones on the B-17.

The flight engineer was standing behind the pilot's seat talking to DeBolt in the right seat when Bill came through the turret and stood up behind the pilots' seats. Hal had his hand up on the cowling above the instrument panel and grinned broadly at Bill. Bayne, too, looked pleased and said, "Pretty nice-looking Seventeen, lieutenant."

"Yup. She sure is. Everything okay here?"

When both Hal and Bayne replied affirmatively, Bill continued. "Okay, let's pick up our gear and load up."

Weyland stood back while the engineer and copilot went down through the hatch between the pilots' seats and out the forward opening on the left underside of the nose compartment. Bill stayed in the cockpit for a few minutes admiring the symmetry and orderliness of the pilot and copilot's positions. The aluminum, hydraulic fluid, and oil, combined with the newness of the aircraft, gave the cockpit a familiar metallic smell. Bill's eyes settled on the throttles mounted prominently on the center console between the pilots' seats. They were to him the most important and essential pieces of hardware in the cockpit. Made of sturdy forged aluminum, the throttles resembled two F's facing each other. Using one hand, the pilot could control each engine separately or all four together. The sensation of holding the power of four engines, over 4,000 horsepower, in his fist was really awesome.

The B-17 without a doubt was a magnificent machine, and Bill considered himself the luckiest guy in the world to be the commander of such a formidable aircraft. For a moment, he thought about the mission and wondered whether he and his crew were ready to face such a challenge. But he quickly dismissed any doubts, sighed audibly, and dropped down between the seats to the crawl space below the cockpit.

Woodward and Newberry were still in the nose compartment talking. Bill sat down on the deck with his legs dangling out of the forward hatch and said to them, "Everything okay?"

"Mighty fine," replied Woody, patting the fifty-caliber gun mounted in the Plexiglas nose. "Nice setup. Two fifties up here." He then went on to say, "If I can't use a bomb sight, the guns will do fine."

Norton bomb sights were installed only in the flight leader's aircraft. The other bombardiers salvoed their bombs on the leaders. Another machine gun was mounted on the port side window in the nose for the navigator.

"How about it, Joe?" Bill asked.

"Got all I need, Bill. Everything is new and top notch. I'm as ready as I'll ever be," Joe responded quiescently.

"Okay," Bill replied, just before he dropped down to the tarmac, "let's saddle up."

Bill walked over to the crew gathered in front of the Seventeen and waited for Joe and Woody to join them. He looked his crew over, stopping an instant to make eye contact with each man. They all seemed flushed with excitement and ready, if not eager, to go. He had thought about this moment many times and about what he'd say to his crew. But for the life of him, he couldn't think of anything profound or humorous to say so he simply offered, "This is what we've been waiting for so let's make it good."

The takeoff of twenty B-17s at one-minute intervals was made with flawless proficiency and all went well during the assembly.

A tactical group formation was comprised of three flights of six B-17s, a total of eighteen aircraft. Two spare B-17s were normally launched to replace aircraft that may abort. Each of the three flights consisted of two elements of three aircraft. Each element had a leader and two wingmen flying in a close V formation with the second element flying slightly below and behind the first. The low flight flew a distance of two wingspans to the left, behind and below the lead flight, while the high flight held the same separation to the right, behind and above the lead flight. The formation was called a combat box and was designed to provide maximum defensive firepower and a high concentrated impact of bombs on the target.

Only the bombardiers in the flight leader's aircraft had the Norden bombsight installed. The other bombardiers in the group formation toggled their bombs the instant they saw the leader release his bombs. The bombardiers in the lead aircraft in high and low flights had a bomb sight to back up the group leader in the event his bomber was shot down, aborted, or disabled.

A tactical wing formation consisted of three groups totaling fifty-four B-17s. Each group is separated vertically by five hundred feet. They, too, are staggered in the same manner as the groups. The high group flies above, behind, and to the right of the lead group while the low group is positioned below and to the left of the lead group. In a wing formation, each group bombed independently.

Bill was flying on John Carroll's right wing, which gave him a good measure of confidence. He, like most men in the squadron, admired Captain Carroll. Johnny was a handsome, dark-haired young man probably no older than Bill, but his experience gave him a respected maturity. He was a quiet, modest young man with all the attributes that Bill admired in a person. He had flown more combat missions than anyone in the squadron. That was the most revered accomplishment.

The formation looked great as it crossed the Suffolk coast of England. Over the North Sea, Bill saw puffs of smoke coming from the other planes and realized that he hadn't told the crew to test fire their guns. After ordering them to clear their guns, he heard a short burst from the top turret, nothing from the nose, and a few sporadic rounds from the rear of the aircraft. He got a couple of hesitant "Rogers" from the rear gunners. Woody called to say that he couldn't clear his or Joe's gun. He was followed immediately by Bayne, who shouted that his turret guns had jammed.

Bill angrily called back to the crew, "Come on you guys, let's get those damn guns working!" He hesitated before saying, "If you think I'm turning back on our first mission, you're nuts. So you better start praying that we don't run into the Luftwaffe."

He heard Scurlock behind him cursing and trying to chamber shells into his turret guns. The gunners in the rear were silent. Bill wasn't completely confident about the condition of their guns, but decided not to press them for fear that they, too, would admit to having problems.

The day was clear and beautiful with unlimited visibility, perfect for visual bombing. When they crossed the enemy coast, they picked up several persistent fighter attacks. Fortunately, they were directed at the lead flight, but shortly more Germans joined the attack, seeking out any likely target. The bombers were about ten minutes from the Initial Point when eight enemy fighters made a wide sweeping left turn and came charging toward Carroll's flight in a head-on attack. Every gun in the formation was concentrating on the approaching fighters and as Bill watched the tracers converging on German planes, he suddenly realized that not one of the eleven guns on board his plane was firing. He felt completely helpless, but knew his gunners felt worse, sitting there and not being able to fire back. He nudged the Fortress in as close as he could to the flight leader's wing for all the protection he could get and hung there with the tenacity of a drowning man.

Just before turning onto the IP, the enemy aircraft returned to concentrate on the lead squadron, much to Bill's relief. As they approached the target, he called the bombardier, "Woody, let's damn well get those bombs out."

"No problem. I'm toggling on the lead plane and if they don't come out I'll go back and kick them out," Woody shouted back. "I'd feel a hell of a lot better if I could get these damn guns working. I feel naked down here."

Bill said, "I bet you do, and I'd like to know what the hell's wrong with them-or you for that matter-and that goes for the rest of you guys. What a sorry lot we are."

He got no response from the crew, just an unusual silence. The bombs went out without any problem, and as they turned away from the target, Bill said sarcastically, "Thank God something works on this plane."

He looked down and could see the Luftwaffe slugging away at the group beneath them.

The return trip, with the exception of some flak, went without incident. Although the pilot chewed the crew out unmercifully, he knew that he must carry most of the blame for not checking to see that his crew had properly cleaned and prepared the guns for high altitude. When they landed and deplaned, Weyland got the crew together and told them angrily, "I want all the guns removed and taken to the armament shop. I want you all to stay there, find out why they jammed, clean them, and put them back together. You better put your names on your guns because you're going to use the same ones on every mission. You're going to download your guns when we land, take them to the shop, clean them, and be damn sure they're ready to go for the next mission. Any questions?"

He got a subdued but affirmative response from all of them. "I know I'm as much to blame." He paused, then continued, "But god-dammit, they're your guns and you'll damn well better see that they operate properly." Again he paused, "I say again, as I did on the way back, the next guy that screws up better look for another crew or a job on the ground because he's not going to be part of this crew."

When he was satisfied they all got his meaning, he got in the weapons carrier, leaned out, and looked at Hal, who appeared uncertain whether or not to join Bill. Weyland said, "Hal, stay with them. You just got promoted to gunnery officer for the crew and you'll be responsible to see that guys do exactly what I just told them." After receiving an affirmative reply, Bill added, "I'll send transport out to help you get your guns to the ordnance shop. See you at debriefing."

At the debriefing, Bill learned that two B-17s from their group were shot down. Fortunately, no one else in the group noticed the silent guns of the Eager Beaver. Again, the lack of training was coming back to haunt them. Bill could recall but two gunnery missions they had while training in the Second Air Force. Both of those were low-level flights firing at stationary ground targets. Either the instructors failed to teach the gunners how to prepare the weapons for high-altitude flights, or that may have been one of the many ground school classes that the crew had slept through.

The following morning the group was briefed to bomb the sub-pens and shipyard at Kiel. This would be Bill's first mission into Germany, and it would be a tough one. Again, he was fortunate to get an inside wing position, but he was in the low flight of the lead group, the one that usually took a beating.

The group got off as briefed and formed up with the others at the assembly point. It was another beautiful clear day with unlimited visibility. When they were over the North Sea, Bill ordered the crew to clear their guns. Apparently to impress the pilot, Bayne laid his twin fifties right above the pilots' heads on top of the cockpit canopy and blasted away. Hearing Scurlock's guns for the first time scared the living hell out of Bill and Hal. The aircraft shook violently as dust and dirt flew around the cockpit like a small twister.

After the firing stopped, Hal called to the crew, "Report by position the status of your guns." And they did, from Jim in the tail to Woody in the nose. All guns were operational.

The pilot replied, "Thank God for that, now let's see if you can hit anything."

At the coast, they picked up much more flak than Bill had seen on his previous missions. He had heard how deadly the flak was over Germany and was now convinced of it. Almost immediately, they were surrounded by German fighters. Forty to fifty enemy aircraft sped in and out of the formation. The excessive evasive action taken by some of the flight leaders caused some separation of bombers, exactly what the Germans wanted. After a harsh command from the group leader, they closed the formation, but several gaps had appeared. They were either shot down or weren't able to reform in their proper position.

The first frontal attack came as two FW-190s turned just beyond the range of the B-17 guns and headed directly at Carroll's flight. Bayne started firing his twin fifties from the top turret. Bill could see the tracers falling far short and cautioned the crew about firing too soon. Woody responded quickly, "We may not hit anything out there, but we sure as hell are scaring the crap out of them."

To Bill, it didn't look like they were scaring anyone, but he said nothing. Literally thousands of rounds, indicated by the number of tracers, were converging on the enemy fighters. One couldn't help but admire the German pilots. When the Focke Wolfes got within range, their wing cannons resembled a signal light rapidly flashing a series of dots in Morse code. Woody was pouring out a steady stream of lead from the nose gun. Just as the two enemy fighters appeared to be within the gun range of the Eager Beaver, they made a perfectly coordinated half-roll, their guns still flashing and dove to complete the split S maneuver as they closed within a few hundred yards of the bombers.

They came so close the fighter's image filled the windshield and Bill could clearly see the German pilots. At a closing rate of over 600 MPH, the action occurred so quickly it was over before the crew had a chance to react. The top turret was the best defense against such an attack and it was only effective when the bomber was in a slight descent. However, in the nose, Woody had a straight shot at the fighters. Bayne started firing too soon, then failed to fire when the German fighter got in range. He froze momentarily when, for the first time, he faced the cannon fire from the FW-190 blasting directly at him. Lloyd in the ball turret got off a short but ineffective burst as the fighters flashed by beneath the Fort. The rear gunners had no opportunity to fire.

"They're going to have to do better than that," Bill thought.

The frontal attack was a frightening experience, particularly for those in the nose or the cockpit of the B-17. Watching the guns flashing directly at them and thinking any minute a 20-millimeter round would tear into them or explode in the cockpit was definitely a nerve-wracking nightmare.

Bill hardly noticed the evasive action they'd taken as he followed Carroll in a shallow descent during the attack. It wasn't much, but it deflected the enemy fire. When the bomber was in a slight descent, the fighter pilot had to fire ahead of and below it. If the bomber pilot maintained level flight, the enemy had an easy straight shot at him and didn't have to lead his target in deflection. The evasive action gave the pilot the feeling he was combating the terror of the attack, as well as giving the top turret operator a better shot at the incoming fighter.

In the cockpit, Bill could hear the rattle of the ball turret and could picture Lloyd jerking the turret around to a point where he was literally shooting upside down and thought, "Talk about guts, there's one guy with enough for the whole crew." Bill did see two fighters diving away trailing heavy black smoke. On the second frontal attack one ME-109 was hit and disintegrated before them with its debris tumbling through the formation.

Moments later from the tail position, Jim called, "I got that son of a bitch."

Some German fighters were attacking from the rear, which Bill couldn't see, but he was relieved to know that McBride was back there holding up his end. Bill told Joe to mark the time and position for confirmation of Jim's kill. This was the crew's truly bloody debut to combat and, except for the moment of hesitation during the first attack, they were performing well. No question about their guns functioning this time. There was no shouting or screaming over the intercom, although the excitement in their voices was apparent as they called out the location of enemy aircraft.

They got better at waiting for the Germans to close within range before firing. On the second frontal attack there was no hesitation from Bayne-his short bursts of fifty-caliber rounds were right on target, causing one fighter to break off. He was also warning Lloyd, giving him a better opportunity to fire at the fighters as they passed beneath the bomber in a high-speed inverted dive.

They took one more frontal attack before they reached the IP and then the Luftwaffe attacks slacked off, but as Bill suddenly realized, this was only to give the German antiaircraft batteries a turn at the formations. Up the ugly puffs came in angry dark-gray bursts. They filled the sky around them so thick, it looked impossible to fly over the area without being hit. It was hard to dispel the horror and fear, thinking any minute an 88-mm antiaircraft slug would tear through the thin skin of the aircraft and explode with deadly force. The thought of Lloyd hanging so exposed in the ball turret was terrifying.

Even with the intense fear they all felt, there was a great sense of pride seeing the bombers in the lead squadron press on to the target. The three-minute bomb run seemed an eternity but when Woody finally called, "Bombs away," it was the greatest sense of relief Bill had ever experienced. Now they'd tighten the formation and head for home. "And let the bloody Hun try to stop us!" he mumbled to himself.

The group leader slowed the formation to let the damaged stragglers catch up. Then, back came the German fighters, and this time the attacks were made mainly from behind. Bill could hear them being called out from the four o'clock through the eight o'clock positions to the rear. He didn't feel the fear he felt from the frontal attacks. He was either getting used to being shot at, or what he couldn't see didn't frighten him quite as much. Probably the latter, he thought.

The German coast was now in sight and that gave them a sense of relief. When they finally reached the North Sea, the attacks ended abruptly when the German fighters concentrated on the American groups behind them. The German pilots became less aggressive out over the North Sea. If they had to bail out, their flimsy dinghies provided little protection against the bitter cold waters of the North Sea.

BOMBER PILOT

The tension and fear the crew had lived with for the past one hundred and ten minutes dissipated quickly. In the excitement of their unharmed deliverance, they all tried to talk at once over the intercom. This was their first real test and Weyland was proud of them. With the exception of a few panic calls, they handled themselves well.

In sight of the English coast, the formation started to let down. To Bill, this would become the most exhilarating and satisfying time of the mission, when they descended through ten thousand feet and he could call the crew and tell them to "take off your oxygen masks and light up." He sat back and let Hal fly while he deeply inhaled great quantities of smoke from a Lucky Strike. What a great feeling to survive and feel so completely alive! Bill discarded the practiced discipline and let the crew talk back and forth over intercom as much as they wanted.

After landing, the pilots went though the shutdown checklist and after signing off on the Form 1, Bill dropped to the ground through the forward hatch. Waiting there were Ray Gillet and Jim McGovern, machine guns slung over their shoulders. Bill grinned and said, "Well, it didn't take you guys long to download your guns. Guess I made an impression."

"We had them off the mounts before you touched down. Mine worked a hell of a lot better than the first time out," McGovern grinned.

"I bet it did," Bill replied. As he started to walk away, he stopped and added, "Good show, Jim, Ray. You all did real great today, real fine shooting."

He glanced over his shoulder and saw Woody and the other guys hauling their guns off of the bomber. He climbed up in the weapons carrier and watched them, smiling contentedly.

Later that afternoon at the officer's club, Bill received the shocking news from Norm Richards that Dopey had been shot down on the raid to Kiel. He was flying with the 306th Bomb Group on his second mission with his own crew. McMann's squadron commander told Norm he saw Dopey's plane go down on fire, but saw no chutes. Dopey was married and their baby was due in June. The first thing to come to Bill's mind was their meeting at Bovington and how happy

Ed was about getting to England and out of that neutral country in Africa, only to be shot down-and probably killed-less than four weeks later.

Bill and Norm tried in vain to console each other over the loss of their friend. For some time, they sat silently staring at their beer, experiencing a deep sadness for Dopey and his wife. But they'd learn quickly to set aside their grief and not dwell on death.

The second disturbing piece of news came from Woody, who called to tell Bill he'd taken Hal to the base dispensary because of severe abdominal pains.

"The doc thinks it's probably appendicitis. They're going to take him to the hospital at Brampton. Looks like we'll be without a copilot for a while, Bill."

"I'll be right there," Bill replied as he put his beer glass down. To Norm he said, "See you later. Gotta go."

He rushed to the base dispensary just in time to see Hal before they took him away in a field ambulance to Brampton Grange Hospital for a possible appendectomy. He wished Hal well and told him they'd be up to see him. Weyland would be looking for a new copilot and that certainly didn't register well with him. Hal was a good reliable pilot.

To further complicate matters, Mary was on her way to Cambridge to spend the weekend with Bill and the group had been alerted for a mission on Saturday, which meant that Bill couldn't leave the base.

Chapter 12

Mary left work early on Friday afternoon excited about going to Cambridge to see Bill. At her flat, she gathered her things and was disappointed to discover she had no alluring nightgown to take with her. Realistically, she knew Bill wouldn't let her keep it on long regardless of how attractive it was. So she threw a prewar nightie, some undergarments, the last pair of silk stockings she owned, and her best dress into a suitcase, and rushed off to Kings Cross Station.

On the train, she settled back alone in a first-class compartment. Just before the train left the station, a dark-haired man accompanied by an exceptionally attractive blonde entered the compartment. He removed his hat, bowed slightly, and said, "May we, miss?"

Mary responded, "Yes, of course." She was impressed and liked the show of good manners.

They sat across from Mary. The man was handsome, distinguished-looking, and immaculately dressed in civilian clothes, which was odd because he couldn't have been more than forty years old. Most men his age were in uniform. The woman, somewhat younger, was beautiful and elegantly attired in a lightweight pale-gray flannel suit.

He unfolded the Times and she opened Harpers magazine and they settled back absorbed in their reading material. She reminded

Mary of Muriel, strikingly attractive but not as beautiful or voluptuous. Whether it was the civilian clothes or the dark hair, she wasn't sure, but the man reminded her of Georges. He was obviously British while Georges was very much a southern European. He occasionally glanced at Mary and his companion would immediately look up and smile pleasantly at her.

When the train moved out of the station, Mary turned to look out and caught the couple's reflection in the window. As the train gathered speed, she watched the scenery glide by behind their images and it brought back bittersweet memories of Muriel and Georges.

With the exception of a few unpleasant memories, Mary realized that getting the job at The Cabaret and breaking away from her mother was an important turning point in her life. It was a maturing experience. It was also a happy and pleasant time. All the emotions and endearing qualities that had been bottled up inside her for so long by her mother were finally freed. The atmosphere of the club and the diversity of people she met there were the perfect setting for her personality. She gained an extraordinary amount of self-confidence and was completely at ease with all the club patrons regardless of their social standing. Her quick wit, sense of humor, charm, and candid innocence earned her the admiration and respect among all that she came in contact with. It was also an exciting place to work, particularly after the declaration of war with Germany. The club was patronized by a large group of international dignitaries, celebrities, and military men, and Mary flourished in the cosmopolitan surroundings.

However, after her breakup with Muriel the enjoyment of working there lost a certain amount of its appeal. Mary stayed at the club because it was all she had. Aside from Muriel, the only relationships she had were with the people she worked with. It was her sole refuge and a lonely existence when she was not working.

One night, shortly after Muriel left, Mary was asked to join a small party of men and women. The club manager, Mr. Murray, asked Mary to join the group. He made exceptions when the patrons were wealthy and generous. Georges Lavanas, the youngest man in the party, acknowledged that he had initiated the invitation and said that he wanted to meet her. Mary had noticed him when the group arrived and how he watched her as she moved about the club. He was attractive, and she became aware of his attentiveness and the emotional effect it was having on her.

After the introductions, Lavanas took her cigarette tray, set it aside, tucked a £100 note under a cigar box, and said, "That should cover your lost sales for the evening."

Mary refused the money. "Thank you very much, but I can't possibly accept that much money."

He insisted, saying he wanted her to keep it and wouldn't be denied. He was of medium height and build, with dark hair and brown eyes, probably in his early thirties. He wore a dark suit, a cream-colored silk shirt, and a blue-and-red tie. He had the dark and suavely handsome features of a southern European.

Initially, Mary felt a little stilted. The four men at the table were Greeks and although they spoke perfect, but accented, English, they were foreigners and she was somewhat uncomfortable in their presence. Particularly when, in their native language, they were obviously discussing her and their young friend. Georges was solicitous and charming to her. It was embarrassing and yet flattering. Dorothy Shepard, a woman in the party, was exceptionally warm and friendly and made Mary feel welcome. The only hostility toward Mary came from Sylvia Catapopolos, who was openly resentful of the attention the young Greek was lavishing on Mary.

After a glass of champagne and the gracious compliments directed at her, Mary relaxed and enjoyed their company. She was flattered by Georges's attentiveness and the affectionate way he looked at and spoke to her.

After their initial meeting, Georges Lavanas became a regular customer at the club. He would arrive late and wait patiently for Mary to join him at his table. They'd leave the club together and usually stop for breakfast at another club. Georges would then drop Mary off at her flat and leave her after a long and warm embrace.

Mary was experiencing a strangely exciting and emotional feeling when he held her and kissed her, and realized that she was falling in love. Their after-work rendezvous went on for two weeks during which time he made no sexual advances toward her.

When Georges asked Mary to dinner, she accepted and took the night off, wanting it to be different from their early-morning encounters. She looked forward with great enthusiasm to their first real date. Georges took her to the Hungarian restaurant where Mary indulged in several glasses of champagne during a marvelous meal. Most of the evening they were surrounded by gypsy violinists and by dinner's end she knew she was desperately in love.

Mary wasn't certain about a physical relationship with Georges, but she admittedly found that she had to repress the passion she felt when he embraced her. It was a wonderfully sensual feeling. Although she couldn't forget the distasteful scenes of sex as a child, she knew in her heart that it must be different when a person is in love.

When Mary and Georges left the Hungarian restaurant, they were greeted by the shrill sounds of air-raid sirens and were forced to take shelter. There they could feel the concussion of the falling bombs above them. This time the West End was receiving the full force of one of the most destructive bombings of central London during the first months of the Blitz. After the raid, Mary and Georges left the shelter in Piccadilly and he finally found a taxi to take Mary to her flat on Stanhope Terrace.

The taxi driver pulled up at the corner of Bayswater Road. A barrier prevented him from entering Westbourne Street and he told Georges he couldn't go any further. They left the cab and walked to the corner of Stanhope Terrace and were stopped by a scene that had become commonplace in London—angry flames flaring from the windows of wrecked buildings, the eerie sight of flashing red lights on the emergency vehicles, and the futile attempt made by the firemen to put the fires out. The stretcher bearers treading their way over sidewalks littered with building debris and tangled water hoses carrying the wounded to overloaded ambulances were an all-too-familiar sight. Worst of all were the screams, shouts, and cries.

BOMBER PILOT

Mary stood beside Georges in shocked disbelief looking at her bombed-out building. In London, where there was the constant fear and awareness of the surrounding devastation caused by the bombing, one went on believing that it happened to others, but not to oneself. Everything that Mary owned was gone. But when she thought of the consequences of being in her flat during the bombing, she thanked God she was with Georges.

He held her close and said, "Come home with me, Mary."

She looked up at him, fighting back the tears and simply replied, "Yes, Georges. Please take me away from this."

They made love that night. In their short relationship, he had recognized her anxieties toward physical love and through gentleness, understanding, and patience helped her to overcome her fear of sex. She found that sex could be beautiful, and that she was able to shed the ugly memories of her childhood.

Mary came out of her daydream when the train stopped and the couple across from her started to leave. She looked out and saw that they'd arrived at Cambridge.

As she got up and reached for her bag, the man said, "Here, allow me to help you." He got her bag down, stepped out onto the platform, and helped his companion and Mary off the train. "May I give you a hand with your bag?"

"No, thank you. I can manage." She took her bag, smiled at the blonde woman and said, "Goodbye and thank you," and hurried off to the cab stand. She was anxious to see what the accommodations were like that she'd booked at the inn and was excited to see Bill.

There was a message from Bill when she arrived. Disappointed, she read that he couldn't leave the base and meet her in Cambridge as they'd planned. After Mary registered and got settled, she returned Bill's call. She insisted she come out to the base to see him, particularly after hearing about Dopey. He told her where to get the base bus in Cambridge and said he'd met her at the main gate.

Bill met her but had little to say as they walked to the officers club. Mary accepted his silence and tried to keep a one-sided conversation going. She seemed satisfied with Bill's brief responses. There was little activity at the club because of a standby alert for the following day. With the exception of a few ground officers playing cards, the bar was quiet.

It was after serving time, but Bill managed to get some cold cuts from an accommodating mess sergeant. They sat at a table in a far corner of the club. Bill hadn't eaten since breakfast and as appetizing as the food was, he couldn't get anything down. He felt bad about Dopey but there was something else that made him particularly pensive. He wasn't sure why he felt that way. He pushed his food aside and looked into Mary's eyes. They were moist, large, and beautiful, full of warmth and sympathy.

Mary said, "Please try to talk to me. You've lost a good friend and I know it must be very painful but there's nothing you can do about it. And it's possible that he may have gotten out of the plane and used his parachute."

"No, I'm sure he didn't make it. Dopey's dead, I know it. And I should be sad and I think I am. But it's not that. I just can't explain how I feel. I've always felt that the death of a friend would be more devastating, and that I'd feel greater sorrow. Is there something wrong with me?"

"Certainly not, Bill, I can see the hurt and sadness in your face."

Bill shook his head slightly, "It was just the way Norm and I were talking about Dopey here earlier. We just didn't seem to understand that we'd never see him again." Bill looked away from Mary and was silent for some time. He turned back to her and continued, "I met Dopey's wife, June, at West Palm Beach just before we left for overseas. She was very attractive, really lovely-and so nice. She came down to stay with Ed. Several wives did. We were there just three days. They were at the hotel swimming pool when I met June. She was pregnant and just starting to show. Boy, was Dopey happy and proud of her. Her happiness just glowed and . . . gosh, she really was pretty and . . ." Bill's faltering speech caused him to stop and he looked down in an attempt to hide his emotion.

Mary reached across the table and took Bill's hand. "Look at me, Bill." When he looked up, she said, "Please go on, I think it'll help."

BOMBER PILOT

"I met Dopey when I landed at Bovington. Both of us were three weeks late getting to England. I got hung up in Marrakesh and Dopey was forced to land in Portuguese Guinea on his flight from Ascension Island to Dakar. He could've been interned there for the duration because Portugal's a neutral country. But he was flying with Colonel Harris on that leg of the flight and the colonel pulled some strings in Washington and they got out of the country. Damn, Dopey was so happy. You should've seen his face when I met him. I remember he said, 'Thank God, Colonel Harris was with us. I might have been stuck there for the duration.' Oh, how I wish he was still down there, stuck in that awful country." Bill sighed, "Damn, why Dopey?"

Mary thought she had better change her approach and said, "Bill, I understand. Please let's talk about something else." She hesitated, watching him for an angry reaction. When there was none she continued, "Do you think you can come to Cambridge tomorrow night? Mrs. Graves, the woman who manages the inn, was very disappointed when I told her you wouldn't be there tonight for dinner. She said she had a special meal planned for us. She's such a sweet person and I don't think she'll mind if you stay there with me tomorrow night. It's a delightful inn-comfortable and quiet. I don't believe anyone else is staying there. We'll have it all to ourselves. It'll be wonderful being there with you, darling." She held his hands tightly and forced him to look up.

"Okay, Mary. Sorry I've been such a gloomy bore. I'm sure I'll be able to leave the base and see you tomorrow night. But I won't know until I get back from the mission tomorrow. If there isn't another one planned for Sunday, I promise we'll be together tomorrow in Cambridge."

They sat holding hands and looking into each other's eyes, hers so warm and inviting, his reflecting a compelling desire to hold her and make love to her. He was sure that she felt the same way and he seriously considered taking her to his room in the pilot's house. But at the time it didn't seem the right thing to do. After a long and warm embrace, he put her on the late bus for Cambridge promising to be with her the following night.

Chapter 13

The most dramatic part of the pre-mission briefing came the moment the operations officer, standing in front of a large screen, drew the curtain aside revealing a large map of Europe. It was covered with a clear plastic overlay that displayed red areas of flak concentrations and other essential bits of enemy intelligence. But the most important object that caught the airmen's eyes was the red ribbon that showed the planned route of the bombers to their target. The parting of the curtain brought different reactions. Raids to France or Belgium and Holland were usually accepted with a sigh or loud applause. When the ribbon stretched across the occupied countries into Germany, however, the reaction was quite different. This morning was no exception. The target was Wilhelmshaven, a formidable city and one of the best guarded in Germany. Not surprising was the rumble of agony and displeasure that came from the crews' lips as the curtains parted. This noisy reaction seemed to break the tension and after the few minutes it took the briefing officer to quiet the crews down, they became serious and ready to listen.

Bill hadn't fully recovered from the excitement of the previous day's mission. He had mixed feelings about going back to Germany so soon and wondered about his crew as well. With Hal DeBolt hospitalized, he was assigned a newly arrived pilot to fly as his copilot,

Lieutenant Maurice Berg, a young Germanic type who looked capable and eager. He had the flushed and excited look of one anticipating his first raid and during the briefing watched attentively, taking copious notes.

After the general comments concerning the target and the German order of battle estimates, Joe and Woody would break away from the general briefing to get their specialized instructions in navigation and bombing. Later, the entire crew would meet and ride out to the hardstand together where their Seventeen stood waiting-a proud warrior, but more like an elephant than a race horse, especially when it moved on the ground. The loud groaning of the bomber's brakes as the group moved out, nose to tail, to takeoff position, sounded like a herd of horny male elephants.

By the time Bill reached their plane he had quickly set aside any bad premonitions and was anxious to get on with the mission. When he was making his walk-around prior to entering the bomber, he noticed the plane was still named the Eager Beaver, and he asked Bayne why they hadn't changed it. After all, there were many other more scintillating and glamorous monikers. Particularly those adorned with sexy unclad women.

Bayne responded, "Sir, she's been good to us so far. So we decided not to press our luck. Besides, from what I've seen of this crew, the name fits her well."

"That's okay with me unless anyone else has an objection," Bill answered. "Woody, Joe, how about you guys?"

They had no objections, so he let the name stand. He later learned that it was considered bad luck to change a plane's original name.

As the formation of Fortresses approached the enemy coast, they were confronted with a solid mass of clouds beneath and above them. Bill thought the met officer had certainly goofed on this one and couldn't believe that they'd try to bomb under such conditions, even over Germany. He was flying in the high flight of the high group, which was just scraping the bottom of the clouds overhead.

BOMBER PILOT

The lead group beneath them, the 306th, was taking the brunt of the German fighter attacks that had come up from the airfields in the occupied countries of Belgium and Holland. The high clouds provided the Ninety-first some limited protection. However, if they were forced to fly into the overcast at their altitude, the possibility of a midair collision could be as dangerous as facing enemy fighters.

They didn't entirely escape enemy action. Several tenacious head-on attacks were made by the Germans. However, the American bombers pressed on to the IP above the solid undercast.

When the German fighters left to concentrate on the low group, heavy flak came up through the clouds searching for the American bomber force. At the IP, a yellow flare blossomed from the group leader's plane, signaling an abort, and the formation started a wide turn to the left instead of the planned right turn. For a moment, Bill thought they were going back to base, but the leader rolled out on a northerly heading. Cobb came on the intercom to advise the pilot that he'd received a transmission that the formation would strike the pre-planned secondary target instead. Although notified over the radio, the name of the target was not given so the Germans wouldn't be alerted. The secondary target was the naval base on the island of Helgoland off the coast of Holland. As they approached the island, the base was partially visible through broken clouds. The lead bombardier made an excellent run and as a result the German naval base received the full fury of the Eighth Air Force.

They arrived back over Bassingbourn at mid-afternoon where Bill anxiously awaited his turn to land. Now that the raid was over, he was eager to get to Cambridge. When on the ground, he motored rapidly to the dispersal area and by the time he made his 180 on the hardstand to park, he had the post-flight checklist complete, and the number four engine died as the Seventeen came to rest. He quickly cut the switches, unlatched his seat belt, got up, and moved out hurriedly between the seats.

Lieutenant Berg said, "What's the hurry, Bill? Got a heavy date?"

"Yup."

WILLIAM WHEELER

The rest of the crew were in no hurry, wanting to relish the pleasure of finishing another sortie, so Bill rode back with his ops officer while his crew gathered around the Eager Beaver and talked, waiting for their transport. At debriefing, they learned that the 305th lost three B-17s and two from the 306th were shot down.

Bill arrived in Cambridge about five o'clock. He had difficulty finding the inn amid the crooked ancient streets, but he got overwhelming help from anyone he stopped to ask. The only trouble was they would inevitably say, "You can't miss it," but he always did. Finally, an elderly couple insisted on showing him the way and walked almost a mile with him to the entrance of the inn.

He had called Mary shortly after landing, so she was expecting him. He found her in the kitchen helping Mrs. Graves who was, in her own words, "sorting out his dinner." He was pushed out of the kitchen and into the lounge where he found a small bottle of scotch and seltzer water, but no ice. He sat back contentedly sipping the weak wartime whiskey while listening to the BBC on the wireless.

Later, he was ceremonially ushered into a small dining room. There, near the window, was a small table set for two with candles and flowers. Mary and Bill had the dining room to themselves. There were no other guests in residence at the time, or if there were, they weren't hungry.

Their dinner consisted of one smoked trout that they shared, a thick, floury pea soup, baked stuffed chicken, three vegetables, and lots of potatoes. What a feast, Bill thought. A bottle of white, Portuguese wine was placed on the table. Mrs. Graves said she was sure the owner would want them to have it with his compliments. It was not the best meal he'd ever had. But, for wartime England, it certainly was most enjoyable because he was sitting across from an exceptionally beautiful girl in a charming and delightful English inn. Mary liked touching, something Bill had never been comfortable with, but now, with her, it was a sensual and pleasant experience.

There was little conversation. Most of the time was spent holding hands, caressing, or just looking at each other. Bill thought life could not possibly be any better than this.

Mrs. Graves seemed overly anxious to get them into Mary's room and said when they finally finished their coffee, "Now you two loves go upstairs and have a nice long rest."

Bill was certain that there was a strong conspiracy by the whole of England to foster his relationship with Mary. The English people were the most gracious, helpful, and friendly individuals he'd ever met.

They had purposely lingered over their coffee, keeping their desire in check to prolong the more lavish desserts that would come when they were alone. When they finally left, they went like two newly married people, a little nervous in their expectations, yet knowing exactly what the night held for them. When they reached Mary's room, she suggested that they have what she called, "a little wash up." She did have an affinity for being clean before sex. She went to the little bathroom at the end of the hall and when she came back she handed Bill a bottle saying, "Here, use this. It'll make you smell nice and clean."

After bathing and in anticipation of Mary's mouth caressing him, Bill took the bottle and splashed it lavishly over himself-specifically on his private parts. He silently screamed in agony as it burned him unmercifully.

Back in the room he told her what he did and she laughed unsympathetically saying, "Dummy, that's Dettol. It's a disinfectant, not cologne. You just put a few drops in the bath water."

He said, "It's a hell of a time to tell me. I've burned all the skin off it."

It was obvious that they'd have to postpone any immediate amorous acts, but they made up for it later.

Mrs. Graves greeted them the following morning with a big knowing smile and said she'd have breakfast ready in a jiffy. Bill sat in the kitchen watching her and Mary busy themselves over breakfast. He was shocked watching Mrs. Graves make coffee. She dumped coffee grounds, milk, and sugar all together into the pot of boiling water and let it cook for a few minutes. But it was a wonderful meal: one egg each, two strips of bacon, potatoes, broiled tomatoes, toast, and coffee. Mrs. Graves fussed over them like a mother hen.

After breakfast, they took a long walk through the winding cobblestone streets of Cambridge, a beautiful old city with quaint buildings and lovely gardens. There was not much bomb damage here compared to London.

They stopped on a hunchbacked bridge to watch families and lovers punt on the River Cam. Later, they wandered into to the ancient cathedral at Kings College in time to enjoy a solemn and impressive religious service. Back at the inn, they had a rather unappetizing boiled English dinner, after which Mary suggested they have "a little lie down." They slept amazingly well after some gentle loving.

Bill saw Mary off at the Cambridge rail station and returned to the base to find an alert in place for a mission in the morning.

The mission on Monday, May 17, to Keroman, France, was relatively easy with moderate-to-heavy flak in the target area. The Memphis Belle, in the 324th squadron, piloted by Frank Morgan, completed its twenty-fifth mission on that raid. They were the first of the original crews in the Ninety-first, and for that matter in the Eighth Air Force, to complete twenty-five missions. A UPI correspondent, Dixie Tighe, had a crush on Morgan. She'd meet his plane after each mission to get his interpretation of what happened and release it to the wire service. Most pilots in the group thought the stories were slanted a little too much in Frank's favor.

While the Ninety-first crews were unloading their gear after the mission to Keroman, several American P-47s broke from their formation and made a low pass over Bassingbourn. Since they weren't yet operational, the fighters were probably returning from a practice mission. The bomber crews felt this was obnoxious of them inasmuch as they hadn't as yet seen combat. The following morning as several of the pilots and other crew members were sitting around Squadron Ops, Johnny Carroll brought up yesterday's buzz job by the fighter jocks. The more they talked about it, the madder they got.

Finally, Johnny said, "Let's see if engineering has any Seventeens ready to fly. I'd like to go over and check out Duxbury."

The squadron had four operational B-17s, so Carroll, Lay, Lockhart, and Weyland picked up some assorted crew members, fired up the Forts, and took off. They formed up in a four-ship diamond with Johnny leading, Weyland in the slot, and Lay and Lockhart in the wing positions. They circled Bassingbourn once and then roared down over the fighter base at Duxbury, pulled up, and came around again, this time right over their ramp, less than fifty feet above the ground. Bill was so low he tore the antennae off of their control tower. On the next pass it seemed that everyone on the fighter base came out onto the flight line and was looking up at them. Some threw anything they could find at the Forts as they flew down and over the ramp-stones, wrenches, even flares were shot up at them.

Carroll made one more pass, and after feeling satisfied they'd made their point, returned to base. There, they found a reception party waiting for them, and most prominent among them was their group commander. The ass chewing they got was impressive by any standard. Apparently, the fighter group commander at Duxbury called their commander, Colonel Lawrence, and raised hell, saying he had to divert a flight of P-47s to another base because they were low on fuel and couldn't land because of the commotion over his field.

The biggest problem facing the American fighters at that time was their limited range. When the P-47s first arrived in the UK, they'd take off, climb to forty thousand feet, and have only twenty minutes of fuel left-just enough to land.

The four crews got hell, but felt it was worth it. However, the event was reported to higher headquarters, and that resulted in a directive prohibiting buzzing, except for crews returning from their twenty-fifth and last mission.

On Wednesday, the group was briefed to go back to Kiel. Captain Weitzenfeld had just arrived with a new crew and Bill was checking him out on his first combat mission. Shortly after they reached the coast of Germany, the turbo supercharger on the number three engine came apart and the buckets from the turbine flew around like the slugs from a fifty-caliber machine gun. Fortunately, no one was hit, but one slug must've pierced an oil line on the number four engine and Bill had to shut it down. Without an operable turbo on the number three engine, he couldn't maintain their altitude and was forced to turn back.

Weyland called his crew, "We're going to leave the formation and get down where I can get some power out of number three. Keep a sharp lookout for fighters."

This was the most vulnerable time for an enemy attack. The Germans thoroughly enjoyed taking on a lonely cripple. Weyland wanted to unload the bombs and reduce the weight in the aircraft so he could maintain a reasonable speed to get back to Bassingbourn. Only in the case of a severe emergency could they drop their bombs over occupied countries and then they'd disarm them.

"Joe, give me a heading back to base and I want you and Woody to be on the lookout for a target of opportunity. If you can't find one we'll drop the bombs in the North Sea. Okay, Woody?"

"Got ya, Bill. We'll find something," replied the bombardier optimistically.

Weyland pushed the nose over in a steep dive and headed for the deck. When the airspeed indicator redlined, he pulled back power. They saw no fighters on the way down and leveled off just above the treetops. With number three producing good power they were able to maintain a fairly reasonable airspeed, but he was anxious to dump the bombs. Joe had plotted the course back and told Bill that it would take them directly over a German air base on the coast of Holland.

Bill called, "Woody, I know you don't have a bombsight. Can you hit the airfield without spreading the bombs all over the Dutch countryside?"

Woody came back on the intercom, "Don't worry, Bill, I'll use the old broomstick handle procedure. It never fails. You get me over the field and I'll hit it."

Weyland wasn't quite sure what Woody meant, but told him, "Have at it, Woody, but be sure the camera's on."

Sure enough there was an airfield directly ahead of them. They were only doing 140 MPH, so Bill figured Woody should have sufficient time to get a good look at his target. He heard the bomb doors open and waited.

"Bombs away," Woody announced as he salvoed out the eight five-hundred pounders.

Almost immediately, Lloyd called from the ball turret, "Bingo! Good show, lieutenant. Your bombs landed right on the ramp and one hit a hangar. Sure made a hell of a mess."

Bill pushed the throttles forward nosing the plane down further and headed out over the water. Although they took some light fire from a flak ship, they got back safely and received credit for a sortie. Not a bad day, considering it could've been a disaster. Shortly after he left the formation, his group took a severe mauling following bomb release. Lieutenant Bakely, a classmate of Bill's also in the 401st squadron, did not return.

Chapter 14

The briefing on Friday morning, May 21, was a repeat perform-ance of last Saturday's-another try at Wilhelmshaven. This would be Bill's seventh mission and he was beginning to feel like a veteran: confident and ready. His crew was eager to get on with the show as well. Another new copilot, Lieutenant Andrew Wieneth, a young good-looking lad who had just arrived from the States, was assigned. His crew had been broken up and used to fill crew vacancies caused by enemy action.

The Ninety-first was leading the newly designated First Combat Wing, the first of two wings each consisting of fifty-four B-17s. Only a few enemy fighters were seen until the formation was a short dis-tance from the IP. At that point, some forty to sixty FW-190s and ME-109s arrived and took up positions on each side of the bomber force. Just as they reached the IP, their Luftwaffe escort peeled off in waves of four, six, or eight aircraft and attacked. Seven or eight attacks were made before bomb release. The enemy pilots were intent on breaking up the formation. The arrival of the new American groups was no secret to the Germans. Their intelligence knew when they arrived, where they were stationed in the UK, and the name and rank of the officers down to the aircraft commanders. With this knowledge, the

Luftwaffe concentrated its attacks on those new inexperienced units in an effort to break up the formation and disrupt the bomb run.

Although the new groups were experiencing their first enemy action and the formation appeared ragged and spread out, they hung in and pressed on. Bill was holding his position on Carroll's wing. When Woody called "Bombs away," Bill tauntingly shouted, "Hiel, Hitler!" At that point, a rapidly descending B-17 suddenly appeared directly in front of the Eager Beaver. Bill was forced to pull up sharply and away from his flight to avoid a collision. In the few minutes that he was separated from his element leader, their aircraft immediately came under heavy enemy attack. Bill could hear the shells ripping through the plane. One 20-mm round burst through the instrument panel and into the cockpit. It entered on the copilot's side at an angle, crossing in front of Bill, blasting a chunk out of the control column he was holding and exited through the fuselage beside him. He quickly turned to look to his copilot who had covered his face with his blood-stained hands.

Bill pressed his throat mike button, "Joe, get up here. Andy's been hit. Get him out of the seat and take care of him."

At that point, Bayne called out, "Bandits nine o'clock, coming at us."

McBride followed immediately with, "Two more turning in, five o'clock."

Isolated as they were, it wouldn't take the Germans long to finish them off. Bill rolled the right wing down and saw Carroll's flight slightly ahead and beneath him. While cursing the damn pilot that cut him out of formation, he shoved the control column and throttles forward in a frantic effort to reach the protection of his flight. He pulled up tight on Carroll's wing with a tremendous feeling of relief. As soon as he got back in position the enemy fighters appeared to lose interest in him. By then, Joe had helped Wieneth out of the seat and got him down to the crawl space.

After a short interval Joe called, "He's cut pretty badly around the eyes, Bill. Can't tell whether his eyes are injured. He seems to think he's okay. I'll get him settled down here and then I'll be up to give you a hand."

Bill responded, "Thanks, Joe. I can use you up here. Everyone else stay on your guns. We're not out of this yet."

Fortunately, the 20-mm round failed to explode and Andy's cuts were caused by the shattered glass and metal from the instrument panel. Had it exploded, the cockpit would've been torn apart along with everyone forward of the bomb bay, leaving little chance of survival for those in the rear.

Most of the activity was now concentrated on the combat wing behind them and their exit from Germany went without further incident. When they were about halfway across the North Sea, Bill broke from the formation, put the plane in a shallow dive, advanced the throttles, and headed for Bassingbourn. Bayne changed places with Joe to assist in landing. When they were within radio range, Bill called the tower and alerted the medics. They were cleared for a straight approach to Bassingbourn and an ambulance was waiting for them as they pulled off the end of the runway.

As the medics helped Wieneth out through the forward hatch, Bill called down, "Take care, Andy. We'll be by to see you later."

With another sortie behind them, debriefing was normally an exhilarating time for the crews-a time to relax, joke, and release pent-up emotion. But not always. Bill would normally participate half-heartedly, letting Woody and Joe respond to the intelligence officer's questions. Bill was more interested in the returning crews. He knew they lost four aircraft from the group and he watched intently as the crews filed in and sat down at their assigned tables. When all the crews had reported to the briefing room, Bill saw that there were two empty tables in the 323rd, Norm's squadron, and he wasn't among the assembled crews. Bill sat for a moment, overcome by an oppressive feeling of loss and condemnation. He then got up and went over to Norm's flight leader, "What happened to Norm?"

"He went down with number three on fire just after we left the target. We saw several chutes. But I don't know if they all got out. Damn shame. Norm was a hell of a nice guy. You two were classmates?"

"Yeah. We were. Thanks." Bill couldn't think of anything else to say so he returned to his crew.

Woody had watched Bill talking to Norm's flight leader. When Bill came back to their table, Woody asked, "Richards's crew go down?"

When Bill nodded, Woodward added, "Did they all get out?"

Norman's bombardier, Brinkley, was Woody's roommate and his friend. He was a hell of a nice young kid who couldn't have been more than eighteen years old.

"I don't know. Bishop said they saw six chutes."

"You know we're all operating on borrowed time, Bill. Damn well hope that we're not next."

Weyland started to respond, but thought better of it and shrugged his shoulders.

Bill later heard that the pilot who cut him out of formation was Jack Ford, the first B-17 pilot he'd flown with in the 96th Bomb Group as a copilot. Jack Ford was flying with his group, one of the new units that had just arrived. Ford had apparently gotten off late, didn't want to miss the raid, and when he couldn't find his group, tried to join the 91st.

Later that afternoon, Bill borrowed a jeep and drove out to the hospital at Brampton Grange. He found Wieneth in a ward with about thirty wounded airmen. Andy appeared to be in good spirits, and although his face was heavily bandaged, he told Bill that his goggles had saved his eyes. Fourteen stitches were needed to patch him up, but according to the doctor he'd be out of the hospital and back on flying status in a couple of weeks. Bill also visited Hal and found that he wasn't doing well at all. In fact, the doctor wasn't sure when he'd be released. He had picked up an infection after surgery and it was causing serious complications.

The following morning, Bill went to their hangar to check the damage to their Seventeen. A six-man crew was hard at work on the battered bomber. The crew chief of the Eager Beaver, technical sergeant Joe Blaylock, was unquestionably the most conscientious and dedicated mechanic, sergeant, soldier, airman, or whatever, in the entire U.S. Army. It seemed that he never slept. No matter what time of day or night, when Bill or any other crew member went to check their plane, Blaylock was there. Regardless of the damage, whether it was an engine change or extensive sheet metal work, the bomber would be ready to fly when required. The B-17 was his and no one in the air crew disputed that.

After Joe cleared the Eager Beaver out of the dispersal pad on a mission, he'd join the other ground crews in front of the control tower, watch it take off, and wait until the bomber returned. They may have worked all night, but when their Fort left on a raid, they'd wait and "sweat out" its return.

Sergeant Blaylock would be on the hardstand to guide Bill to the exact spot Blaylock wanted him to park the Seventeen. As soon as Weyland shut down the number two engine, Joe had the forward hatch open and was on the flight deck with the same three questions, "How did it go, lieutenant? Was she okay? Any problems?" It was possible that there were other crew chiefs as good as Joe, but no one in Weyland's crew would ever concede to that.

Unlike the aircrew, the ground crews got no glory, but as far as their contributions and dedication were concerned, they deserved more credit than most aircrews. They didn't go home after twenty-five missions. They were there for the duration.

This morning, Bill greeted his crew chief, who was under the wing supervising a fuel tank replacement. "How you doing, Sergeant Blaylock?"

"Morning, sir. Not too bad. We found twenty-two fifty-caliber holes in her. Looks like some of our guys shot you up pretty good."

"Yeah. We got cut from the formation and I guess we got in the way of some of our gunners. Damn lucky no one was hit."

"You took six 20-mm hits and I think there's still one in this fuel cell."

Bill watched as they carefully removed the tank. Blaylock continued, "Yeah, the round is still in there. I'll call ordnance and have them pick the tank up. I'm not going to take it out. You were mighty lucky that slug didn't explode." Knowing there was an unexploded round in the tank, they carefully loaded it on a dolly and eased it away from the bomber.

"I'm gonna change number two engine. It was hit and she's running pretty rough. They're cleaning up the cockpit now. She'll be ready for a test hop at 1500 hours. How's Lieutenant Wieneth?"

"He's okay. Should be back to duty in a couple of weeks."

Weyland chinned himself up through the forward hatch and entered the cockpit where two mechanics were replacing the instrument panel. He greeted them, looked on for a couple of minutes, then went back through the bomb bay and out the rear exit. He walked around the bomber and back to Blaylock. "A few sheet metal patches makes her look more like a veteran. Good job, Joe. See you at three."

He returned Blaylock's salute and walked through the hangar to the squadron ready room thinking that someone "upstairs" was watching over him. "There must be some truth in the rumor that the forced laborers are passing duds by the inspectors in German munitions factories," he thought. Had the 20-mm round exploded in the fuel cell, it would've blown the plane to bits.

There were no missions scheduled for the weekend, so Bill headed for London. At Mary's suggestion, he picked up his weekly candy ration, which he never used. Food rationing in England forced an English person to subsist on a weekly ration of one egg, four ounces of meat, three ounces of sugar, and a half pound of tea, in addition to the many shortages like fuel and clothing. Most children in England hadn't tasted candy since 1939. Mary's butcher had three young ones, and she knew he'd appreciated Bill's candy ration. In fact, he was so appreciative that he brought out a fine joint of beef from the back of his shop and insisted that Mary have it. Secretly, she had hoped he would show his appreciation in some tangible way and accepted the gift graciously.

Knowing the end of the month was near and Bill was probably close to being broke, Mary suggested that they have a lazy loving weekend. She knew of a small Greek restaurant in Soho where they could get an inexpensive meal and Sunday she planned to prepare dinner.

After a hectic and emotionally draining week, Bill was only too happy to agree. They had a ten-shilling dinner, went to the local cinema, and then to bed for the most marvelous loving imaginable.

BOMBER PILOT

The dinner on Sunday was unbelievable. Bill hadn't had a meal like that since he left home. It was his introduction to savory Yorkshire pudding, complementing the succulent, rare roast beef. The batter for the pudding, Mary explained, required a week's egg ration, plus flour and water. Baked separately in the meat drippings, it was served with crisp potatoes that were also cooked in the drippings. The gravy, another product of the drippings, was made with an English ingredient called Bisto, and Bill thought the meal was truly scrumptious. How Mary prepared such a palatable dinner on that tiny stove of hers was absolutely miraculous. Bill vowed that his candy ration would forever go to her butcher. Mary promised if she could get a bigger joint, she'd invite his whole crew to dinner and she did a few weeks later.

Not wanting to spoil the weekend, Bill didn't tell Mary about Norm going down until after dinner on Sunday. Mary's moist eyes reflected the sadness she felt for Norm and Bill as she held him close. He found himself harboring a deep feeling of loss. That sorrow was tempered only when Bill recalled that he and Norm felt they were doing something really worthwhile for the first time in their lives. But for Bill to have such a wonderful young woman to share this most exciting adventure was beyond his wildest dreams. Like everyone else, he wanted the war to end, but if it had to go on, he wanted to stay right here in England doing exactly what he was doing. He was happier than he'd ever been in his life.

Chapter 15

As was often the case, the weather turned foul the following week and grounded all scheduled missions through Thursday. On Friday, an anticipated break in the weather had them standing by their loaded aircraft for two hours waiting for the word to fly a planned mission to Bremen that was eventually scrubbed. The most frustrating and nerve-racking time for the crews was spent waiting to leave. Once airborne, the jitters left and they settled down to the job at hand. By actual count, the crews of the Ninety-first attended sixty-five preflight briefings, but had actually flown just fifteen accredited missions.

The group went back to the sub pens at Saint Nazaire on Saturday. Some crews considered it a milk run because of its location on the Brest Peninsula just across the channel. But it could be a rough one. The heavy loss of Allied shipping in 1943 made the sub pens the most frequently visited targets. The Germans, on the other hand, fortified their shipyards with the best flak units and a large concentration of guns. To the bomber crews, Saint Nazaire was known as Flak City. Their anti-aircraft gunners were good-they had a lot of practice.

Over one hundred Flying Fortresses were sent airborne to bomb the sub pens at Saint Nazaire. The bombers had an American fighter escort and for the first time the crew of the Eager Beaver saw their "little friends," and they sure looked good! However, the Luftwaffe had its own priorities and tactics. They stayed ahead of the formation until the American fighters had to turn back, then the Germans attacked. And attack they did-viciously. Weyland's crew reported two Forts going down and they later learned that six were lost.

The flak over the target was deadly. Flak was probably the most disconcerting and frightening of all the German countermeasures. At a distance, it looked rather harmless, bursting in dark-gray benign clusters, usually with two streamers projecting downward like legs. But when it was close and the men could see the angry orange center and hear it explode above the roar of the engines, it was terrifying. Most crews feared it more than enemy fighters even though the fighters actually brought down more American bombers. With fighters, one could shoot back or take some evasive action. Not so with flak. You sat there trying to convince yourself that the sky was a mighty big place and the odds of one burst hitting you was remote. It still scared the living hell out of the average airman, particularly after seeing what it could do to a Fortress. During briefings, the intelligence people tried to make as little as possible of its danger by saying, "We've routed you around the worst flak positions" or "Alter your speed and altitude to fool the gunners." As far as Weyland's crew was concerned they weren't fooling anyone, and especially not the Germans.

After landing and debriefing, Bill hurried to his quarters to find his room spotless, bed made, clothes hung, shoes shined and a snack waiting for him in the kitchen. Each house had a charge of quarters (CQ) or striker, who was an American GI. He was similar to an English batman, not normally permitted in the American army, but a custom favored by their former group commander, Colonel Wray. The quarters that housed the 401st pilots had one of the best, Private Fred Simmons. Fred was in his mid-forties, well educated and the most accommodating soul you'd ever meet. Doing everything he could for the pilots in his house was his mission in life. He had seen many pilots come and go. In fact, not one of the pilots from his house had finished his tour since the group's arrival in September 1942. Bill thought Fred might have been a conscientious objector. Whatever he was, Fred certainly made life for the pilots pleasant and comfortable. Surprisingly, the task didn't seem to be demeaning to him. He seemed to enjoy his job and made it his contribution to the war effort.

For Bill, to come back from a raid to a clean and comfortable room, bathe, dress, and, in a little more than an hour, be in London with Mary, how could life be any sweeter? Under such conditions, it was not a hard way to fight a war. Certainly far better than the miserable Quonset hut or tent that most airmen called their home away from home.

Mary and Bill had dinner with Dorothy and Stephanos on Saturday night-and what a sumptuous dinner it was. Stephanos, and for that matter Dorothy, did not suffer from any of the typical wartime shortages. Being the owner of a fleet of ships doing convoy duty back and forth to America had the advantage of bringing back scarce delicacies that enabled the fine steak dinner to be topped off with thick black Turkish coffee and a fine French brandy.

Dorothy fussed over Mary. She was caring and motherly. Bill was amazed by the way she adored Mary. She was ten or twelve years older than Mary and treated her like a daughter. There was probably a more affectionate relationship between them than Mary had with her own mother. This affinity was warmly accepted by Mary and she responded equally toward Dorothy. Stephanos, too, in his way, was fond of Mary. He was dark, sleek, and dapper. His slicked-down black hair, long cigarette holder, pointed black shoes, and Italian-cut suits gave him a sinister look. As generous as he was, Bill couldn't dismiss the thought of how perfectly he could portray the part of a Hollywood villain. He was married and had a family back in Greece.

Stephanos and Dorothy lived in a magnificently furnished and spacious apartment on Bayswater Road. Dorothy seemed to accept the fact that Stephanos would leave her and return to Greece after the war. It was difficult to picture Dorothy as a mistress. She was such a refined, sweet, and gentle person. Her appearance and mannerisms bordered on prissiness. The arrangement was unusual, but Bill had no problem with it. They were amicable and hospitable toward Bill, graciously accepting him because of their devotion to Mary. He was constantly surprised to find how good people were to her. Mary loved people, and they returned her friendly openness with an affection that bordered on reverence. She seemed to have a hypnotic power over everyone with whom she came in contact.

At times, she could be quite demanding of her friends and Bill was often amazed to see them respond so graciously. She had a personality and a sincerity that attracted people in a most uncanny way. And Bill was among her most ardent worshipers.

That evening when they got back to Mary's flat, Bill asked her how she'd met their evening's hosts. Mary took a deep breath and nervously told Bill about her affair with Georges.

"I told you about the job I had at The Cabaret and my friendship with Muriel and how it ended. And about the German Muriel met in July 1940 and fell in love with and then he disappeared in September.

"It was a few weeks after my nineteenth birthday." Mary stopped recalling what a miserable and lonely day that was. There was a bombing the night of her birthday and she stayed in her flat instead of going to the smelly tube station for shelter. She lay on her bed in the darkness with her face buried in her pillow shaking with uncontrollable fear. She didn't seem to mind the bombings when she was living with Muriel. But alone it was terribly frightening.

After a short pause, Mary continued. "Yes, it was just after my birthday, I was working at The Cabaret and was asked to join a small group of people at their table. The manager, Mr. Murray, made an exception because one of the men, Mr. Karapolas, was very rich and an exceptionally good customer at the club. So I was allowed to sit with the party. There were four men and three women in the group. That's where I first met Dorothy and Stephanos. I also met Georges Lavanas. He initiated the invitation to have me join them. Your friend Mrs. Catapopolos was also there. It was our first meeting and she took an instant dislike to me because of Georges's interest toward me. After meeting Georges that evening, he came to the club quite frequently and when he asked me out to dinner, I accepted. We dated after that and I enjiyed being with him.

"About three weeks after I met Georges, he took me to the Hungarian restaurant for dinner. When we left the restaurant we were caught in a fierce German raid. After the raid, when we arrived at Stanhope Terrace, my building had taken a direct hit and my flat was completely destroyed. Everything I owned was gone in the crumbled remains of the apartment building."

Mary stopped again and buried her face in Bill's chest. "I was probably very vulnerable at the time, and . . . well . . . when Georges asked me to come home with him, I did. The following day Georges said he wanted me to stay with him so he could take care of me and I agreed. He took me out that day to a very exclusive salon and bought me a completely new wardrobe. The ration coupons he relinquished for my clothes impressed me more than the cost.

"Georges had a large apartment on Queens Way across from Hyde Park. His apartment had a small separate suite that he offered to me so that I could have as much privacy as I wanted. He had a housekeeper, a charwoman, and a car hire and driver on call. Although I had my own living space, he made me feel it was my home to share and encouraged me to assume the household duties of supervising his housekeeper and hosting his guests. He taught me many of the social graces that I had missed growing up. He insisted that I quit my job at The Cabaret and prompted me to enroll in the university.

"Georges was about thirty-two. He was a soft-spoken and well-mannered person and very generous. He got immense pleasure in giving me beautiful gifts. He was a gentle and loving man who never lost his temper. He always appeared to be in complete control of his emotions. It was a new experience for me, living with a person who made no demands, and didn't pressure or threaten me in any way.

"I was completely happy and content. I no longer had the pressure of working long hours at The Cabaret or the persistent and suggestive advances of male customers. I had no financial worries, no fear of loneliness and, most importantly, Georges loved and cared for me in a way I'd never known before.

"I continued to serve as a Red Cross driver and became more conscientious and active in the war work. I volunteered for air-raid warden and took a turn at watch duty on the roof of our apartment block.

"Our social life was generally limited to his group of friends and associates, most of whom were involved in shipping. They formed a small Greek community in London and lived mainly in the Bayswater area. The nightclubs of London, most of them were located in cellars, were popular during the Blitz. The affluent Londoners preferred them to air-raid shelters. The public shelters, mainly in the underground stations, were overcrowded, with limited sanitary facilities. For the families who lost their homes in bombing raids, the shelters were the only place they had to stay.

Generally, during a period of intense bombing, Georges and I would dine out and then retire to a bottle club just before the Germans arrived overhead. There we could sit comfortably in relative safety, sip champagne, talk, or dance to the music of a fine orchestra and socialize with Georges's friends and people who could afford such pleasant surroundings.

"With the exception of Dorothy Shepard, I had little in common with the women companions of Georges's friends. For reasons I never really tried to define, I found them to be pretentious and self-serving.

"Dorothy and I developed a warm and friendly relationship. One that proved to be more stable and sincere than my friendship with Muriel. Dorothy was a person I could confide in and relate to. She counseled me in many ways, helping me to accept and enjoy the relationship I shared with Georges."

Mary stopped and drew in a ragged breath. She realized she was trembling inside and was terribly worried about her confession and how Bill would react to it. "I did love him, or at least I thought I did," she continued. "I know better now, because what I felt for Georges was nothing like the love I have for you.

"Our affair lasted for a year and a half. I know he loved me very much, but I came to realize that he would never marry me. He wasn't married and was free in that respect, but being from a prominent, Greek family his marriage had been arranged. It's customary for Greeks to marry Greeks, particularly when it is financially beneficial to a business arrangement. I was later told that his marriage would bring together two of the largest shipping companies in Greece. When I realized that he'd go back home after the war and marry a Greek woman, I left him. I didn't want to hang on like Dorothy and the other English girls who were living with Georges's friends. So one day, as much as I loved him, I packed up and left. I know I hurt him deeply, but I couldn't continue our relationship."

She moved away from Bill when she realized he no longer had his arm around her. She looked at him and tried to read the expression on his face. When she failed to see any understanding, she went on to say, "After I left Georges, I was recommended to Mr. Chalmers by an acquaintance and he hired me."

Bill accepted her explanation with mixed emotions. His initial reaction was one of jealousy and resentment of the time she'd spent with Lavanas. However, when he thought about her affair and tried to be honest and reasonable, hers was no different from the relationship he had with Clare. When Mary realized there was no future for her living with Lavanas, even though she loved him, she had the strength and determination to leave. Giving up a secure and pleasant living arrangement to return to a lonely and uncertain life took a great deal of willpower and courage. That was an admirable trait. It was one Bill could relate to and respect.

He realized that it was time to tell Mary of his affair with Clare Beatty and of his proposal to her before leaving the States.

"You know I was reluctant to start a relationship with you when we first met. Well, it was because I was involved with a woman back home. A person I'd been seeing off and on for more than two years."

Mary got off the bed, walked across the room, came back, and stared at Bill. Finally she sat down in her lounge chair and in a cold grim voice said, "Go on."

"I told you how disappointed I was when I hadn't heard from Canada. I lived from day to day waiting to hear from the RCAF. I became frustrated and bitter. I had left my job in Connecticut and I wasn't particularly anxious to find another. With nothing but time on my hands, a friend's bar became my favorite hangout. I drank too much and before long I'd run up a considerable bar tab. Fortunately, my friend offered me a job as bartender to work off my debt.

"The bar, called the Red Door, was a small restaurant owned by two brothers, Pete and Joe Reilly. It was a real nice place that catered to a group of people who lived in an exclusive area of our town. It was quite an education for me working there, listening to the patrons unload their troubles while drinking.

"I found some solace in being patronized by some of the women who frequented the bar looking for more than conversation. The more aggressive they were the better."

"What do you mean by that?" Mary asked angrily.

"Just that I was a willing partner to any woman who wanted to play around."

"That's a horrible expression," Mary responded bitterly.

"I know. My self-esteem wasn't what I recall with a great amount of pride."

Bill stopped and pushed himself up so his back was against the wall. From the angry look on Mary's face, he was concerned about going on.

Finally, Mary said in a clipped voice, "Well, go on."

"Her name is Clare Beatty. I met her while I was working at the Red Door in August 1940. She and a companion came in and ordered two martinis. She introduced herself and started a conversation, asking me some personal questions. I wasn't particularly offended by her directness. I had encountered it before. In fact, I was flattered by her interest. She was attractive and I enjoyed the flirtation.

"After two drinks, they got up and before leaving she asked me what time I finished working. I told her and she said she'd pick me up. She arrived at eleven o'clock and took me to her home. And that was the beginning.

"Clare helped me get over the anger and animosity I felt toward a country that rejected my offer to serve. She also introduced me to an extravagant lifestyle. She was loaded. Her father had left her a large inheritance, which she spent lavishly. She indulged herself in just about anything she wanted-including men. She had been married twice and was separated from her second husband. He was a former riding master and was in an upstate sanitarium.

"I met her mother once. She lived in a suite of rooms in the Waldorf Hotel on Park Avenue. She was very much the lady, quite regal and superior. She appeared indifferent to the way her daughter lived, who she liked, and how she spent her money. I guess she just wanted her daughter to be happy as long as it didn't interfere with her life. She was very gracious, but I don't think she really approved of me.

"Initially, I enjoyed the extravagance and exhilarating ride into a lifestyle that I wasn't accustomed to, but eventually it all seemed kind of frivolous. Her friends who we associated with were financially and intellectually far above my modest means. And I often felt inadequate and inferior. I had to borrow clothes from my friends to go out with her because I only had one decent suit. My car had been repossessed so she let me use her Packard station wagon. I rarely paid for anything. Everywhere we went, whether it was a restaurant or a hotel, the charges were always taken care of ahead of time. It was obviously done to prevent embarrassing me, but I still felt humiliated and cheap.

"I was vulnerable and allowed myself to be influenced by her strong personality. I had no job, no money, and became completely dependent on her. Eventually, I developed a real sense of guilt and shame. And after a while it got to a point where I just wanted out.

"When the selective service was implemented in America, I prayed that I would be the first to be called up. But when the numbers were announced I was among the highest. Months away from any chance of being drafted.

"My parents eventually became aware of my affair with Clare and were very upset when they heard that she was married and five years older than I, so they decided to do something about it. Through a friend, they arranged for me to meet a colonel in the Army Signal Corp. So on December 7, 1940, I went out to Governors Island and met a Colonel Dix, who then introduced me to a colonel in the Army Air Corp. I'd indicated a preference to that branch of the service. It didn't take much of a sales pitch for them to convince me that the army needed me. After a short discussion, I was wedged in the backseat of a staff car between two portly colonels and driven to the recruiting station on Whitehall Street in the city. Before I knew what had happened I'd raised my hand and was sworn into the United States Army. I had great hopes of being sent to some faraway place like the Philippines. But no such luck. I was given three day's leave and told to report to Mitchell Field on Long Island for basic training. The base was only an hour and a half drive from home.

"Soon after I arrived at Mitchell Field, I knew I'd made a grave mistake by enlisting. The demeaning and pointless work details I was ordered to perform were ridiculous. The only way out of a bad situation, I realized, was to get a commission. And that's what I did.

"I saw little of Clare while I was confined to the base during basic training. She, too, made it more difficult by moving to Lake Saranac to be near her husband, who had tuberculosis.

"In December 1941, my prayers were answered. I received orders to report to Maxwell Field in Alabama to start pilot training. Clare's husband died two months later, while I was in primary flight training in Florida. She secluded herself for a few months, but I did get to see her when I finished flying school in July of last year. The last time I saw her was when I was stationed at Pocatello, Idaho. I got a three-day pass and flew to Arizona. She had bought a ranch near Tucson. Her doctor thought she may have contracted tuberculosis and suggested that she move to a drier climate for a year or two.

"Clare and I had been going together for over two years and I knew that I would soon be heading overseas. She was no longer married and I felt obligated to propose marriage. I was no longer unemployed. I was making a fair wage-nothing compared to her income, but it was respectable. So I asked her to marry me. I must admit the ranch may have influenced me. It was very impressive. It had been owned formerly by a movie star. But, fortunately, she said no. And frankly, I was relieved. She said she had just lost one husband and was not about to marry one that was going off to war."

It was Mary's turn to become jealous. And that she did with a vengeful and uncontrollable fury. She stood before Bill in her night-gown with her arms folded defensively across her breasts glaring at him. Regardless of what he said, she wouldn't believe him or forgive him. Her rage continued and they became involved in a bitter quarrel. It reached a climax when she said, "Mr. Chalmers is right about you. You plan to leave me and go back to that frightful woman in America. You don't love me. You just want to make love to me and leave. You bastard . . . you . . . you . . . Oh, you bloody bastard."

His reaction was one of anger and indignation. He went into the bathroom and when he finished dressing, he came back and stood before her. Mary backed away, fearful when she saw the rage in his eyes. He tried to control his temper, but in an outburst of anger, shout-ed at her, "I'm going back to Bassingbourn. You're the most unreason-able and distrustful person I've ever met. I tried to be honest with you and what do you do? You turn on me like I'm some depraved, con-temptible jerk who has absolutely no feelings at all."

He grabbed his trench coat, picked up his kit bag, and shouted, "Goodbye!" He walked down the hall and opened the door to the lobby, hesitated, turned around, and looked back. She was standing by her door in her robe and he could hear her sobbing. Bill turned to leave but stopped and, holding onto the door, thought, "She has every right to mistrust me. I really haven't been honest with her."

Again he glanced back at her standing there looking so alone and defenseless. He just couldn't leave her. He went back and took her in his arms.

Her sobbing intensified and she held him tightly saying, "I'm sorry, Bill. Please come in and let's talk."

After much forgiveness on both sides, they got into bed and made love tenderly and with a sensitivity that shattered any doubts about their love for each other. Bill thought lovemaking always seemed better after an argument-and the more intense the quarrel, the better the loving.

Mary said it was difficult to control her emotions and temperament when her love for someone was at stake. She admitted to being jealous and shamefully suspicious, but she couldn't conceal her feelings. She just had to speak her mind. It was, she said, the Irish in her that caused her at times to get things off her chest by shouting like a fishmonger's wife.

They did agree later that it was right to share their pasts and to be honest with each other. They promised never to quarrel or question one another again. However, there were moments when he'd become sullen and silently jealous. But these thoughts passed quickly, overcome by his love for her.

Sunday was a quiet and relaxing day with no regrets and no mention of past affairs. They walked in Regent Park, went to the cinema, and had supper at the local pub. Then it was back to the war for him.

Mary, after seeing Bill off, was once again back in her flat thinking about her confession to Bill and his to her. She worried that Bill might change his mind about her when he got back to Bassingbourn. Because of her affair with Georges, she thought he might not want to see her again. Mary sobbed softly, tears rolling down her cheeks. "If he thinks it was wrong of me to live with Georges, what will he do when I tell him I'm illegitimate and I don't know who my father is? If Bill knew of some of the awful things that have happened to me, he'd certainly leave me." Early memories of her childhood flashed through her mind: those horrible incidents she experienced while trying to hide and get away from her mother.

As a child, she had a part in a film about a man and his mistress. The story made an intriguing impression on her. She often fantasized how wonderful it might be to become a mistress to a rich and handsome man, one who'd take her away from her mother and care for her. But as she matured, her dream changed to one of marriage and family. When Mary met and fell in love with Georges, she hoped that she'd found the man she'd marry and spend the rest of her live with. Unfortunately, that wasn't to be, but she continued to live with him because she dreaded the thought of living alone. Perhaps her childhood dream had surfaced and influenced her affair with Georges.

The war helped to make such relationships morally justifiable. Life was fragile, particularly in London where the philosophy of "live for today, for tomorrow may never come" became an acceptable standard, not just for Mary, but for many other people as well. War seemed to have a way of changing the morals and standards that people normally lived by. However, the war brought Bill to her and with him was a far greater desire to capture every ounce of love and happiness that time would allow by experiencing the ultimate thrill and excitement of giving herself completely to him without worrying about marriage or tomorrow. Physical love seemed much more passionate, intense, and meaningful under the threat of losing the one she loves.

There was some consolation in knowing that had she been living as part of a normal family she may not have met Bill. Living alone certainly created the perfect circumstances and an ideal situation for a budding romance, particularly for one as passionate as theirs.

Chapter 16

There was no activity until June 11, Bill's birthday, and it seemed that everyone wanted to celebrate it with him-including the Luftwaffe. Their target was Bremen, but when they got there, the city was completely obscured by clouds. Instead of dropping their bombs indiscriminately, they elected to bomb secondary targets, which were several German airfields. The combat wings separated from the larger formation and sought out their assigned targets. It was a stupid and ill-advised decision and the Germans took full advantage of the mistake. The Ninety-first was greeted by the most decorated and dedicated German pilots in the Luftwaffe, "Goering's Own," with their distinctive yellow-nosed FW-190s. The full Gruppe, in flights of eight, made one direct attack then disappeared, perhaps to find a more receptive target. Weyland's combat wing maintained a tight and defensive formation and suffered no losses. However, the Luftwaffe succeeded in finding easier prey, and there was no elation in the Eighth that night: Eight B-17s and their crews were lost on the raid.

Two hours after Bill landed he was in London on his way to meet Mary at work. There he met Mr. Chalmers for the first time. Although courteous, her employer didn't appear to be overly friendly. He was another of Mary's devoted protectors.

When Bill arrived, Mr. Chalmers was complaining about the two-hour lunch Mary had taken. Bill later learned that she'd spent the time looking all over London for a tan cloth wristwatch strap. Bill had mentioned some time ago that he'd like one to replace his badly worn one. She finally found a suitable replacement and happily gave it to him for his birthday.

Chalmers gave Mary the rest of the day off after hearing it was Bill's birthday. They left his showroom and walked down Regent Street. Mary needed a new pair of shoes and, with Mr. Chalmers's help, had finally accumulated enough coupons. They tried several shops but found nothing to Mary's liking. They window-shopped through Burlington Arcade, stopping at all the jewelry shops because Mary had a fascination for diamonds. She liked to look, but when Bill suggested getting her something, even though he couldn't afford it.

"Absolutely not," she replied.

They turned up Savile Row where Bill stopped to admire a pair of brown English brogues in one of the men's stores. Mary pulled Bill toward the entrance and said, "Let's have a butcher's look."

"What's a butcher's look?"

"It's cockney. It means a quick look," explained Mary.

"Okay, but that's all it's going to be-a quick look."

The shop was home to a famous English bootmaker, where all the shoes were made to order. The pair in the window had been ordered but never claimed and they happened to be Bill's size. At four guineas, Mary said they were a terrific buy. So Bill, not Mary, got a new pair of shoes.

They crossed over to New Bond Street, continuing along, window gazing. There were still some lovely clothes available in London if one had the scarce ration coupons to buy them.

They passed an American officer talking to an attractive but heavily made-up and extravagantly dressed young woman. When they passed the couple, Bill said, "Wow, what a looker!"

Mary looked up at Bill, eyes flashing, "Well, if you like that sort of person, you're welcome to her. I'm sure she's 'on the game.' Didn't you know Bond Street is famous for its prostitutes? I'm surprised that you think she's attractive."

"Well, I'd say she's not bad, prostitute or not. Boy, what a body!"

"All right, Mr. Leftenant, you have had it. I'm sure she'd prefer you to that American. Why don't you try it and you'll never make love to me again."

"Come on, babe. I was just kidding. You know I wouldn't want anyone but you."

She replied crossly, "You'd better not. I'm serious. If you're ever unfaithful to me I'll chop it off."

Bill looked at her, smiled, and said, "I believe you would."

They walked in silence to Oxford Street and got on a bus to Ivor Court. When they got into Mary's flat, she kicked off her shoes, threw her jacket on the bed, slipped out of her skirt, and said, "Last one in the tub is a rotten tomato. Isn't that what they say in America?"

"No, it's a rotten egg and you're on," he replied as he struggled hurriedly to undress.

Mary got to the bathroom first. When he arrived, she was bending over the tub adjusting the water temperature. He came up behind her and embraced her, reaching around to caress her breasts and press his body against hers. She straightened and he let her turn to face him while holding her close. He kissed her deeply and she threw her arms around his neck returning the kiss passionately.

He grasped her waist and lifted her up onto the lavatory while she held him in a heated embrace and wrapped her legs around his waist. Fully aroused, he eased her off the wash stand and settled her down onto him. As he penetrated her, she opened her eyes wide, drew her head back, and asked, "What made you so randy? Was it that woman on Bond Street?"

He murmured breathlessly, "Hell, no. It was you leaning over the tub."

"Well, whatever. Just remember what I said about lopping it off if you are ever unfaithful to me. So if you really love me, you may carry on, ol' bean."

She crushed her mouth against his and clung to him. Locked in a frantic embrace, he carried her out of the bathroom but never quite made it to her bed. When Bill climaxed, he was so weakened by his explosive orgasm and the exertion of holding her that he collapsed to the floor with her in his arms. When he recovered, they got into the tub and washed and caressed one another until the water became tepid. They vigorously rubbed each other dry with a large bath towel, got into bed, and after a short nap made love again.

That night they went to Rules for dinner. Although Mary was five years younger than Bill, she was much more sophisticated than he. For a woman with a limited wardrobe, she made exceptionally good use of the few clothes she owned. In addition to her fresh and clean appearance, she always looked particularly well-groomed. She had exquisite taste and excellent dress sense. Her early training as an actress gave her the sexual grace of a much more mature woman. When entering a restaurant, she attracted the attention of women as well as men. The ma´tre d' would usually hurry to her, bow, and welcome her with a big smile. Patrons would stop talking to watch her move across the room to a table. Bill would follow, feeling proud and smug. If the menu were in French, she'd interpret it for him and select the wine. She had a fair knowledge of French wines and would normally choose a good, but inexpensive, one.

While they were having dinner, a British army major came into the restaurant. Bill followed Mary's glance as she watched him. The woman who accompanied him was exceptionally beautiful and looked familiar. The major looked at them, stared for an instant, and when Mary smiled demurely, he nodded slightly. He held the chair for his companion and when she was seated, he bent down and said something to her. She turned and looked at Mary and Bill and responded affirmatively. When he started toward them, Bill looked at Mary. Her face reflected uneasiness.

He walked directly up to their table, smiled stiffly, and said, "Mary Carlton, how good to see you."

Mary quickly regained her composure and said, "Hello, Jack. How are you?"

He did not look at or acknowledge Bill.

"Jack, I'd like you to meet Leftenant Weyland." She turned to Bill and said, "Bill, this is Major Profumo."

Bill stood and held out his hand. Ah, so this is the guy. He remembered the autographed picture he'd seen on his first visit to Mary's flat.

The major looked at Bill, took his hand weakly, and said, "Pleasure, leftenant."

He immediately turned to Mary to resume their conversation without any attempt to include Bill. After a short exchange of pleasantries, he returned to his table and his beautiful companion.

Bill looked at Mary and said sarcastically, "Who was that character?"

"Oh, he's not a bad sort. Actually, when you get to know him, he's quite nice."

"Well, I think he's a pompous snob. But I certainly admire his taste in women. Who's the gal? She's beautiful."

"That's Valerie Hobson, the actress. I'm sure you've seen her in films. She's beautiful and a lovely person.

"Yes. I do recognize her now. Looks more beautiful offscreen than she does on. But I still think he's a snob. Where did you meet him?"

"I told you about my job at The Cabaret. I met him while I was working there. He was, and still is I'm certain, a member of Parliament representing Kettering. MPs, like everyone else, were called up to duty in the armed forces but continue to serve in Parliament. He was a captain then and came to the club quite frequently, usually with a beautiful girl. I had a sanctuary, a small alcove, at the club where I stayed when I wasn't peddling my wares. Quite often, he'd leave his table, come over, and buy a pack of cigarettes from me. He was charming and we'd talk for several minutes. He would always compliment me in a flirtatious way and would then return to his companion. I liked him. I thought he was handsome and I enjoyed talking to him.

"One night after work, Muriel asked me to go out with her. I was usually too tired and seldom went out after work, but she insisted. A friend of Werner Schmit was in town and Muriel wanted me to join them for breakfast. He and Muriel were dating at the time. I agreed and we went out to a private club that was open all night. Werner was a gentleman but his friend turned out to be a complete bore. I got very upset at some of the crude remarks he made but endured his bad manners because of Muriel. About an hour after we arrived at the club, Jack Profumo came in and went to the bar. He looked upset. I watched him and finally excused myself and joined him at the bar. He had a misunderstanding with his family and had been out drinking most of the night. I went back to Muriel and her friends and told them that I'd met a friend and was joining him. I sat with Jack and we talked and a short time later we left the club. It was about six in the morning. I found a cab and dropped him off at his flat. We dated a few times after that, but that was the extent of our relationship." She searched Bill's eyes and found only concern, but no resentment.

After dinner, they went to the Astor and shortly after they arrived, Bob Hope and his entourage entered the club and settled at a large table. He and his group had been touring the English bases, entertaining the troops. Bill was feeling exceptionally good after sharing a bottle of wine with Mary and a half bottle of scotch with no one.

He said to Mary, "I missed his show at Bassingbourn. I think I'll go over and say hello."

Mary didn't think it was a good idea. But he persisted and finally got up and walked over to Hope's table.

He got there and just managed a "Hi . . ."

Bob Hope looked up angrily and said, "Beat it, Bud."

Bill turned red and started to say something, but closed his mouth and walked slowly back to Mary.

She looked at him when he sat down and said, "What's the matter, Bill. You look like you've lost your best friend."

"I can't believe that guy. He told me to beat it."

Mary replied, "He's probably quite tired. He does three or four shows a day."

"Yeah. I guess you're right, but for now he has definitely lost one fan," Bill said bitterly.

BOMBER PILOT

A pretty young woman from Hope's group came over a little later and asked Bill if he would trade short snorters. Short snorters were a strip of foreign paper money glued together that air crew picked up in the different countries they visited. When Bill agreed, she sat down and joined them. It was obvious that the young woman's visit was an effort to apologize for Hope's rudeness. Later, others from the group joined their table when Hope left the club, and it turned out to be a pleasant evening.

That evening they returned to Mary's flat and, after more conventional and tender loving, Bill fell asleep beside her with one arm stretched across her back. She lay on her stomach, naked, half covered with the sheet, unable to sleep. She thought about the prostitute they saw on Bond Street and wondered what it would be like to be one. The possibilities she faced were certainly there considering the sordid environment she endured during her childhood, her mother's loose morals, and the frightening close calls she experienced, particularly running away to evade her mother's wrath. It wouldn't have taken much to push her over the edge. She was sure that some girls would have become prostitutes under similar circumstances. Fortunately, she had the strength of character and determination to resist. Unquestionably, someone-probably that guardian angel she'd once mentioned to Bill-was watching over her.

She recalled a night Muriel had encouraged her to go out with a man for money. An attractive tall Englishman and a frequent patron to the club had become enamored with Mary. Not a usual occurrence, but he was much more persistent than the average admirer and constantly courted her. Mary refused his invitation, but after a while she began to look forward to seeing him and enjoyed their flirtatious encounters. His name was Ian Matterson and, except for his yellow teeth and the spaces between them, he was pleasant, personable, and quite wealthy. It became obvious that he not only wanted to date Mary, but was most anxious to bed her. Initially, his advances were innocent, but they became more provocative and Mary had no doubt about his intentions. She consistently refused to date him, but he continued to pressure her.

Most of the girls at the club, along with Mr. Murray, were protective of Mary because of her age. However, there were several, and later that included Muriel, who tried to encourage her to date customers. They bragged about the favors they received and about the money they got from their admirers. A couple of the girls teased her about being so pure, calling her "Miss Prissy" or "Goody Two Shoes." But Mary wasn't ready to venture into a sexual relationship because of the experiences she suffered as a child.

Matterson's arrival at the club occurred shortly after Muriel and Mary had returned from a trip to Paris, where they spent the little savings they had. The two were broke, but continued to spend their earnings extravagantly on expensive clothes. They were behind in their rent and needed twenty pounds. So when Mary told Muriel that Ian had propositioned her, Muriel suggested that she go out with him. Muriel was aware of the fascination he had for Mary. To Muriel, the solution was simply a matter of accepting Ian's offer and taking the money. Since they'd been together, Muriel had a strong influence over her young friend and Mary trusted her. She found it hard to refuse her.

Muriel said to Mary, "Don't be a silly girl. Go out with him. He's not going to hurt you. And if he does want to sleep with you, what's the harm? He's rich and he'll give you anything you want. He'll certainly give you enough money to pay our rent. You like him and besides, it's about time you had a little loving. Mr. Murray will never know."

After much persuasion, Mary finally relented.

The night Mary agreed to go out with Matterson, she fortified herself with several glasses of champagne, which she wasn't accustomed to, hoping it would reinforce her courage. She left the club early, feeling a little woozy, but felt confident she could handle the situation. She'd managed well with men at the club and there was no reason to believe she couldn't take care of herself. He was waiting for her in his new automobile. Mary got in the car and when he drove off, she started to shake. She desperately wanted him to stop the car and let her out. Her mind flashed back to the night in the car with Mavis and the two men.

Matterson said he wanted to show her his flat, where his man had set up a light supper and chilled a bottle of champagne. She thought about the hurt and shame she felt when her mother had forced her to get in bed with her so-called uncle. The nausea started to build and she became lightheaded. She simply couldn't believe that she was going to let this man maul her. When he smiled at her, she saw nothing but ugly yellow teeth. Mary could feel the bitter taste of bile rising in her throat. Whether it was the champagne, the motion of the car, or the thought of his intentions, she could not restrain herself. She felt the fluids erupt in her stomach, rise to her throat, and before she could turn away, she retched. The vomit struck the dashboard, the plush upholstery and his pants and shoes. When the retching stopped she screamed, "Stop! Stop the car! Let me out. Let me out!"

Astonished, he quickly pulled the car over to the curb and shouted, "Damn, look what you bloody well did to my car!"

She pushed open the door and fled, running down the street until she found a taxi. What a horrid experience. Her first attempt at being a femme fatale came to an abrupt and sickening end. After that, Mr. Matterson was rarely seen at the club and when he was, he brought his own cigarettes and Mary never went near his table.

The degrading thought of being a prostitute frightened her and she struggled to dismiss the horrible possibility. She could've easily fallen prey to the seduction of men's lasciviousness, as others would have under similar conditions. How a woman could give her body to different men and become a human repository for their lust was beyond her comprehension.

The memory of Matterson still lingered and she deliberately didn't turn over when Bill stirred. Lying on her stomach with her face turned away from him, she pretended to be asleep. The dreadful experiences slowly faded as he tightened his arm around her. He moved closer, pushed her hair off her shoulders, and kissed the nape of her neck, his tongue seductively caressing her skin. She remained still, trying to control the arousal in her loins. He straddled her, bent over, and continued kissing her, slowly moving his mouth down her backbone, kissing her.

She tightened her stomach muscles, forcing herself to lie still. He moved down over her buttocks, lingering there tracing little circles on her skin with his tongue. She tried to hold her breath, but it became impossible to hold back the sensation that pulsed through her body. Finally, she exhaled deeply, releasing the tension, and cried out, "Oh, darling." She tried to roll over but he held her down. She turned her head, looked at him, and said, "Sweetheart, what do you find so fascinating about my bum?"

He mumbled, "It's the most beautiful ass in the world and I love kissing it."

"Well, don't get carried away," she replied.

Bill spread her legs, knelt between them, and raised her hips up off the bed. He stroked her for several minutes until she begged him to enter her. When he did, she moaned, climaxing almost immediately. He held her hips tightly, moving energetically until he flowed into her. He rolled off of her and when she turned to face him he wrapped his arms around her and kissed her lips, eyes, and face repeatedly.

When he stopped, Mary said, "Bill, what is this compulsion you have for trying all these unusual positions while making love?"

He responded, "Oh, I understand there are many more ways and I intend to try them all."

She said, "Well have at it, darling, but promise me you'll not try making love while hanging from the chandelier."

Thank God she waited for Bill. The thought of sex with anyone else sent despair and shame shivering through her body.

Chapter 17

The Ninety-first went back to Bremen on Sunday, June 13. The weather was good and the bombing was excellent. Andy Wieneth was out of the hospital and back flying copilot. When given a choice by the squadron ops officer, he elected to fly his first mission after being released from the hospital with Bill.

The Germans tried to conceal the target by setting down a smoke screen, but wind direction changed and the ground was plainly visible. However, they did send up a formidable flak barrage, followed by fighters that attacked the formation just prior to bomb release. Their tactic caused the bombers to separate slightly, and a B-17 slid across and under the Eager Beaver just as Woody released the bombs. One of the weapons struck and completely severed the right horizontal stabilizer of the plane beneath them. Lloyd saw it happen and reported that the plane was still flying and it looked as if they would make it back. To Bill's relief, the pilot, Captain Chuck Weitzenfeld, got the plane back to Bassingbourn with just half a tail stabilizer-another testimonial to be added to the legend and durability of the Flying Fortress, to say nothing of the pilot's skill.

A diversion by the Fourth Combat Wing drew most of the German fighters away from the First Combat Wing. The Ninety-first had little opposition. However, the Ninety-fifth Bomb Group lost ten of their bombers on the mission. General Forrest, leading the Fourth Wing, was killed, the first Eighth Air Force general officer to become a casualty. The Ninety-fourth Bomb Group, also in the Fourth Combat Wing, lost six B-17s just off the English coast near Norfolk. When the English coastline was sighted, most gunners would download their guns. On this occasion, the Germans, in their night fighter version of the JU-88, followed the bombers unobserved and caught them by surprise. With the bomber's guns inoperative, the Luftwaffe had a field day with little or no opposition. A total of twenty-six Forts and their crews were lost that day. After only nine missions, half of the original crews were lost in the Ninety-fourth and Ninety-fifth Bomb Groups.

A mission to Le Mans on Monday was scrubbed. The Americans tried again on Tuesday, but were recalled shortly after they reached the coast of France because the target was completely obscured by clouds. On their way back, the Ninety-first was attacked by a dozen enemy fighters and as a result they all got credit for the sortie.

Colonel Wray, the original group commander of the Ninety-first Bomb Group, left at the end of May for reassignment to Molesworth as the commanding officer of the newly formed Second Combat Wing. Lieutenant Colonel Clement Wursbach was assigned as the group commander in June. Wursbach was said to be an outstanding pilot, but as a military commander he was not in the same class as Colonel Wray. Everyone left Wray's spirited briefings before a mission with a strong sense of duty and determination. Conversely, Wursbach left the briefing to his operations officer while he sat and watched. This was an essential part of the mission and the group needed someone on the stage who could motivate and fire up the crews. Unfortunately, Wursbach wasn't the type.

A commander's ability to lead is often reflected in the discipline of his organization. If an airman believes he doesn't have to conform to established military standards and follow orders on the ground, it's a good possibility that he'll ignore them in the air. The deterioration of military discipline may start on the ground, but when it reaches air operations it can be disastrous. The first indication of a lack of air discipline is reflected in the number of air aborts. The decision to abort a mission is left entirely to the pilot, and he does it in good conscience, knowing the lives of his crew depend on him. However, there are some pilots who love to fly but can't tolerate being shot at. Other fully qualified pilots preferred to fly as copilots to avoid the responsibilities of being an aircraft commander under combat conditions. Fortunately, there were not many of them. Instead of sending them back to Training Command in the U.S. and replacing them with the pilots there who desperately wanted combat duty, their commanders let them stay on. These types wanted to bathe in the glamour and glory of being where the action was, but not in it. If you had to be in a war, the Eighth Air Force in England, with easy access to London, was the place to be.

Some of the not-so-eager combat pilots were assigned as permanent copilots or to duties in the squadron where they could pick and fly the easier missions. Others continued to fly but aborted missions on the slightest provocation. Such action endangered the bomber formation by reducing the firepower, making it more vulnerable when facing the enemy. The loss of the one B-17 reduced the effectiveness of the combat box concept.

A short time after the change of commanders, Bill noticed that two or three, and sometimes as many as four, B-17s from the Ninety-first were turning back on each raid and the effect was beginning to show in the number of losses. It was apparent that each abort should be thoroughly reviewed and the pilot questioned to determine if he had a legitimate reason for turning back. However, the squadron commanders were reluctant to press the matter and the new group commander did not force them or spell it out in a written directive. Colonel Curtis LeMay, the commander of the 305th Bomb Group, one of the original units in the UK, had no problems with excessive aborts.

When he first arrived with his unit in England, he told his crews they were not to fly across the channel if anything on their plane was inoperative. "Don't try to be heroes. Abort," he'd said. On their first two missions, a large number of crews turned back with one malfunction or another. When on the next mission an exceptionally large number aborted, LeMay told his bomber crews, "I told you I'd court-martial you guys if you tried to be heroes, but now I'll court-martial the first guy who turns back without a damn good reason."

Bill was proud of his record. The only time the Eager Beaver had turned back before reaching the target he was able to make a successful alternate attack on a German airfield. On one mission, Lloyd cut his oxygen hose when he was getting into the ball turret-a legitimate reason to abort. However, Lloyd told Jim and Ray, the waist gunners, not to tell the pilot. They handed him down several ten-minute portable oxygen bottles and he flew the entire mission at twenty-one thousand feet on just sixty minutes of oxygen. Bill was unaware of the problem until they landed and he was told about the ruptured line so he could enter it in the Form-1 as a discrepancy.

One reason Bill and his crew wanted to avoid an abort was an unofficial rivalry Bill had with Harry Lay. Harry was a real gung-ho type who was assigned to the squadron at the same time as Weyland's crew. Each was determined to finish his tour before the other. Harry wanted to be a fighter pilot and as soon as he completed his missions he was anxious to go back to the States and get checked out in fighters. He was about 5' 10", slender with rugged good-looking facial features. He had an engine fire shortly after takeoff on one mission and had to abort. As a result, Bill had one more mission to his credit.

Since there was no activity for the balance of the week and nothing planned for the weekend, Bill left Friday afternoon for London. Mary wasn't home when he arrived, but the concierge let him in to her flat. He dropped his kit bag and helped himself to the scotch from her cabinet. Impatient to get to London, he hadn't showered before leaving Bassingbourn and he decided to bathe and change while waiting for Mary. He took off his tunic, went into the bathroom, turned the tap on in the tub, got undressed, and stepped into the tub. He lay back in the warm water sipping his drink and thinking how wonderful life was. He dozed, awakening when he heard Mary come in.

She peeked in on him with a cheery, "Hello. Well, what have we here? Adonis lying there without his nickers for all the world to see."

"Hi babe. Gosh, I must've fallen asleep. The water's cold. Would you mind running a little hot water into the tub for me?"

"Certainly, my lord," she said mimicking an upper-class English maid as she kissed him and reached over to turn on the faucet. "Do you want me to wash your back?"

They had a mutual agreement: I'll wash yours if you wash mine.

"Would you? I didn't bathe before I left the base. Couldn't wait to get to London and you."

"All right, master. Your every wish is my command. Let me get my coat off."

She returned in her slip and turned the bathroom light off so the room was dimly lit by the hall light. She picked up the soap and face-cloth, knelt down, and washed his back. That done, she looked down at his levitating penis.

"Well, what about my little old padasha. Looks like he needs some care and attention, too."

She soaped his partial erection down, stroking it affectionately. When he became erect, she rinsed away the soap, bent over, and kissed it lovingly, saying, "It's mine, all mine." She teased the head several times with the pad of her thumb and looked up at him with those big, beautiful, innocent eyes. "Bill, dear, you do look rather uncomfortable. Do lie back and relax while I indulge myself. I promise to be gentle."

As uninhibited and intimate as they were during sex, they were never crude or uncouth. They never used any of the four-letter words associated with sex. They reacted to subtle hints passed to each other by body language to enhance their enjoyment of physical love. The slightest pressure on his shoulders while lying between her thighs kissing her breasts would be an invitation to move down to the sweet taste and smell of her. They respected each other's privacy and never trespassed on one another when the bathroom was being used for purposes other than sex.

There was a modesty about Mary that was very becoming and ladylike. She did not like to undress completely in Bill's presence and preferred sex in subdued lighting. But on the other hand, she could be, and was at times, a wanton little vixen.

Mary never before felt so libidinous and openly eager to share with Bill the variety and joy of sex. She was surprised and later embarrassed by her passionate outbursts made during their heated lovemaking. Exploration of each other's body gave them a new and exhilarating meaning of physical intimacy.

They never found it a problem to entertain each other. A film usually gave them some diversion from their lovemaking and togetherness. There wasn't much talk about the future. They were living pretty much for today and making every minute count. Mary would occasionally mention her dream of a small house with a fireplace, a proper kitchen, and a dog. She wanted a place where she could cook fine meals and cuddle up by the fire when it was cold. She never specifically mentioned Bill in her fantasy, but he felt sure that he was a part of it.

They never discussed the possibility of pregnancy and were certainly not innocent of the fact that something might happen as a result of their complete and reckless abandonment toward sex. They took no precautionary measures, wanting nothing to inhibit or hinder their sexual appetites. Marriage was more of an understanding than a spoken vow. A waiting period of three months was required before an American could marry a British subject. Although Bill hadn't applied, there was no question in his mind that he would marry Mary when he finished his missions.

Mary made no demands and was completely unselfish in her love toward him. He realized this and loved her more for it. He settled any doubts or misgivings he had about his feelings for Clare. His love for Mary was deep-rooted, fired by an intense passion that was matched equally by hers.

They spent two glorious days and sensual nights in London together. He left Sunday afternoon when told by squadron ops that the group had been alerted for a maximum effort on Monday. Mary went to Kings Cross Station to see him off. While they were waiting on the platform, a distinguished-looking man in civilian clothes, accompanied by a young girl, walked up to the first-class compartment next to Bill's. As the man held the carriage door for the girl, he turned and looked at the young American officer and his beautiful companion. His friendly smile suddenly disappeared when his eyes met Mary's. He turned quickly and followed the girl into the compartment. His reaction puzzled Mary because she thought he looked familiar. But when she tried to place him, the train started to move and her mind was distracted when Bill took her in his arms and kissed her warmly.

In the taxi on her way back to Ivor Court, it suddenly dawned on Mary who the man was. Not too long after starting to work at The Cabaret, Mr. Murray asked her if she'd join a gentleman at his table. That request surprised Mary because she'd been told when she started working there that she could not sit with club patrons. However, Mr. Murray made exceptions when the person was someone important or an exceptionally good customer.

She'd heard the manager mention the name Sir James, but when she got to the table the man stood and greeted her warmly. He introduced himself, "I'm James Brixton. Thank you for coming. I know sitting with patrons is frowned upon, but I'm delighted that you could join me." He held a chair for her and when she was seated, he sat down, took her hand, and said, "Please call me James, and I shall call you Mary."

He was about fifty, ancient by Mary's standards, but very pleasant and charming. He was handsome in an aristocratic way and obviously well-bred. Mary sat with him for almost an hour, sipping a glass of champagne and chatting away merrily. She responded to his many questions, most of which were directed at her and her job at the club. She finally excused herself by saying, "I've enjoyed talking to you, sir." She just couldn't call him by his first name, "But I must get back to work. Thank you. Please excuse me."

He stood up, took her hand, held it longer than necessary, then raised it as though he intended to kiss it. When he finally released her hand, he took a £100 note from his wallet and placed it on her tray. In return, he took just a single pack of cigarettes and said, "Thank you very much. You are a delightful young woman and I have enjoyed talking to you. I look forward to seeing you again. Perhaps you'll have dinner with me one evening and we can have a longer chat."

Mary was shocked by the tip he left on her tray. Large tips were not uncommon, but £100 was a small fortune. When she refused to accept it, he said, "Please, I insist that you have it."

She left him and went on with her routine. By the end of the evening, she forgot about Mr. Brixton but not the tip.

At eleven o'clock the following morning, her mother entered her room and said, "There's a gentleman here to see you."

Mary was still in bed and had been eating a jelly tart. She couldn't imagine anyone calling on her. She quickly shoved the last bite in her mouth and pushed the plate under the bed, ran her fingers through her hair, and modestly covered herself just as her mother ushered the man into her room. Mary almost choked on the remains of the tart when she saw that it was Mr. Brixton. He looked uncomfortable and irritated at Mary's mother standing by the door. He seemed embarrassed, and "Jolly well he should be calling on a girl at this hour," thought Mary.

"Good morning, Mary," he said quietly after a moment's hesitation. "I was in the neighborhood and thought I'd pop by and tell you how very much I enjoyed talking to . . ."

He stopped in mid-sentence and looked sternly at Mary's mother, who glared back at him, then left the room. He continued, "You must forgive me for barging in like this, but when you told me where you lived I assumed that you lived . . . " He paused again. Perhaps he was going to say "alone," but decided against it. Apparently, after their meeting the previous night, he had every intention to ask her to become his mistress. But now, seeing this girl-child with jam on her cheeks and looking much younger than her seventeen years, he couldn't believe she was the same person. She sat in bed with no makeup, her mouth open, staring at him with those huge innocent eyes. He stood stiffly, obviously agitated, carefully scrutinizing her and coming to the conclusion that the woman he was with last night was really just a child living with her mother. After an awkward, one-sided conversation, he excused himself and left hurriedly.

After a subdued, "Goodbye, sir," Mary jumped out of bed, ran to her window, and watched him get into a chauffeured town car. He was seldom seen at the club thereafter, and when he was, he didn't invite Mary to join him at his table. She didn't tell Mr. Murray about his visit to her house. She did, however, learn later that Brixton was a knighted member of Parliament.

Mary wondered whether the young girl with him at the rail station was his daughter. Or perhaps he had found a young mistress after all.

Chapter 18

The mission scheduled for Monday, June, 21, 1943, would be the first American raid into the heart of the German Ruhr valley. A large chemical plant at Huls was the primary target. Heretofore, cities of the Ruhr valley were bombed only by the RAF at night. After being all tensed up and eager to go, the mission was scrubbed just prior to take-off. Another tweak at the crew's nerves. On Monday afternoon, orders came down from Bomber Command at High Wycombe changing the mission on Tuesday from Huls to Villa Coublay in France. Weyland's crew wasn't scheduled to fly this one. They'd flown every scheduled mission since his first on May 4 and were ordered to stand down. To say the least, the crew was upset because the mission looked like a milk run. Further, the mission would allow Lay to draw even with Bill on the mission tally.

That night, Bill talked to Mary on a pay phone as long as his coins held out, had a couple of drinks, and then went to bed. Much to his surprise, he was awakened by Fred at three o'clock in the morning and told to report to the briefing room at four.

When he got to the briefing room and didn't see his crew there, he remained in the back of the room. The formation of aircraft for the planned mission was displayed on a blackboard. The names of the pilots scheduled to fly were printed in the outline of B-17s stenciled on the board. Weyland's name was not shown. He assumed that he wasn't going on the sortie but wondered, nonetheless, why he'd been summoned.

After the crews settled in their seats, Lieutenant McFarland, the assistant operations officer, came back and said to Bill, "Clyde wants you to fly with Carroll today. This is Johnny's last mission and you'll be taking over his flight."

Bill, surprised to learn that he was being promoted to flight leader, replied, "Okay," then added, "Thanks, Mac."

Bill went forward and joined Carroll's crew. Johnny looked up and grinned at Bill, then moved over so he could sit beside him.

When the curtain parted, Weyland saw that the mission had been changed back to Huls. He still didn't have an inkling of the reason he was being asked to fly. He accepted the change without question and was pleased about becoming a flight leader.

On the way to their Seventeen, Johnny said to Bill, "I see Mac talked you into taking his place. I guess he changed his mind when the order came down last night to change the mission back to Huls." When he got no response from Bill, he added, "You know, Bill, I've made it this far with my own crew, except for Frank my first copilot, and we're damn well going to make it back from this one."

Bill finally responded, "Johnny, I'd like nothing better than to fly with you on your last mission; and more than that, I'll be damn happy to make it back with you. We'll let Mac wait for the next milk run, but I'll be damned," he added with determination, "if he'll ever bump a copilot of mine to fly an easy raid."

The raid would be the biggest to date for the American bomber force: 235 Flying Fortresses would participate. Clear weather over the continent was reported, but murky weather covered England and the bombers had some difficulty assembling into their combat formations. As they approached the coast of Holland, their contrails were clearly visible and abundantly spectacular, giving the Germans fair warning that the Yanks were coming. Carroll's tail gunner reported that four Forts from the

Ninety-first had turned back during the flight over the North Sea. The flak was unmerciful all the way to the target and the fighter attacks were vicious. Again, Bill thought how miserable it was to fly copilot, watching everything without that feeling of being a part of the action.

The Ninety-first, in the first combat wing, was leading the formation. Carroll was leading the low flight in the lead group.

The German Ruhr was nicknamed "Happy Valley," and Bill could see the irony of it as they were met by one flak barrage after another when they crossed into the industrial heartland of Germany. The visibility became restricted because of dense contrails, and the heavy flak was so close he could hear the explosions. Normally, when the formation neared the IP and the flak was that intense, the enemy fighters would slack off. Not today. They were making savage attacks in the midst of the bursting flak.

The navigators in the high and low flights followed the planned flight course to the target so they were capable of taking over the lead if necessary. For better viewing, Carroll's navigator, Lieutenant Brown, had been following the course of the formation from the bombardier's position. Before they reached the IP, he switched positions with the bombardier, Lieutenant Bamber, so he could make the bomb run. Just as Bamber changed places with Brown and settled down over the bomb sight, a 20-mm round from an FW-190 making a head-on attack burst through the nose of their aircraft.

Seconds later came Brown's shocked voice, "Johnny, Bambie's hit!"

"How bad?"

There was a slight delay and then Brown said, "He's dead, Johnny. He was hit in the head."

Carroll cried out, "Oh, God, no!" He took his hands off the control column, tore his oxygen mask off, and put his face in his hands.

Bill grabbed the yoke, took control of the aircraft, and said calmly, "I've got it, Johnny. Put your mask back on."

Carroll sat there, making no effort to take the control column or put his mask back on.

"Put your mask back on, damn it!" Bill shouted.

Carroll stared at Weyland in disbelief, and Bill had to reach over, grab the mask, and push it up against Carroll's face until the pilot finally got the mask back on. Carroll then slumped down in his seat and stared at his hands, making no attempt to fly the plane. Brown got the bombs out, closed the doors, and told the pilots he had put Bamber in the crawlway and covered him up. Had the shell hit the plane ten seconds sooner, Brown would've been hit. Bamber was hit in the forehead and died instantly when the 20-mm slug tore off the top of his head. What a strange thing fate is. Until that point, that was the first and only bullet to hit their Seventeen.

"Why? Why in God's name did it have to happen to Bamber on our last mission?" said Carroll. He mumbled something else into his mask and stared down into the hatch between the pilots where Bamber lay in the crawl space.

There was no letup on the way back. The Germans threw up everything they had at the American formation. The battle was one of the most bitter Bill had encountered and he was thankful Johnny had let him fly the aircraft. Flying the Fort was so much better than just sitting and waiting for something to happen. Carroll said nothing on the trip back. He just sat looking numb and dismal.

After Bill landed the plane, Carroll got out of the left seat, put his hand on Bill's shoulder, and said, "I'm glad you came along, Bill. Thanks for getting us back."

He then stepped down through the hatch and helped Brown carry Bamber off the plane.

Bill remained in his seat and waited until they'd put the body in the ambulance. He didn't want to see Bamber. He wasn't sure what his reaction would be and he didn't want anything to distract him from his determination to keep flying and fighting.

Sixteen Forts were lost on the raid-four from the Ninety-first. Two more of Bill's classmates were missing in action. Of the seven B-17s the 401st deployed, only Carroll's and Lay's aircraft reached the target and got back to Bassingbourn. Another black day for the 401st Bomb Squadron.

BOMBER PILOT

On numerous occasions before the Huls mission, Carroll had talked about how he was going to tear the field up with the damnedest buzz job ever when his crew completed their tour. However, all that was forgotten-even the promise he made that he'd be on his way home the day after he finished his twenty-fifth mission. He hung around the squadron for three weeks, not attempting to process out or make arrangements to go home. The squadron adjutant finally cleared the base for him and took him to the port.

Carroll had been with his crew all through training, and they'd flown every one of their combat missions together. He became too fond of them. Losing Lieutenant Bamber at the end really tore him apart. Before he left, Bill saw Johnny almost every day and tried to talk to him, but nothing seemed to interest him. Bill reasoned that there was probably a motive behind his probing and it was as much for his benefit and comfort as it was for Carroll.

Bill's first thought was to isolate himself emotionally from his crew, but there simply was no way he could alienate himself from them. After all they had been through, it would be impossible to break the bond they had forged together. Bill had been with the guys in his crew since the beginning. He knew all their wives' and children's names, where they were from, and their hopes and dreams. Losing one of his men would be difficult and it would be impossible to shut out the feelings of loss and grief if one of his men were killed.

As he pondered Johnny's dilemma, he realized how difficult it would be for Mary if he was shot down or killed, and short of not seeing her again, there was no way to spare her the grief that would follow. For an instant, Bill thought about not seeing Mary, but quickly rejected the idea. He loved her and needed her too much and he believed she felt the same about him.

There was no activity for Weyland and his crew for the next seven days. Four missions were scheduled after the Huls raid but three were scrubbed, and 401st Squadron didn't participate in a sortie to St. Nazaire. Because of scheduled activity and cancellations, Bill hadn't been able to go to London to see Mary.

On June 29, the group went to Tricqueville, a German airfield in France. Shortly after takeoff, a fuel line ruptured on their Fort causing an engine fire. The quick reaction of Weyland and his copilot, Lieutenant Dennis Frank, the pilot Bill flew his first mission with, had the engine shut down and the fire out before they reached an altitude of one thousand feet. Bill called the tower and asked if there was a spare B-17 available. The group would normally set up two spares, loaded with bombs and ammo, ready to go in the event a crew had a mechanical problem during engine start. When the tower said there was, Bill told them he was coming back to switch planes. He alerted the crew to be ready. "We missed the mission to France yesterday, and I'll be damned if we're going to miss this one. So let's make the changeover fast. Be sure to take all your gear with you."

After landing, Bill quickly taxied next to the spare B-17 on the hard-stand and he had the two outboard engines running on the spare bomber minutes after he reached the cockpit. He checked with the crew and found they were all aboard. He immediately released the brakes on the all-clear from the crew chief. He had Lieutenant Frank start the two inboard engines as the Fort rolled out of the dispersal area, "We'll make our preflight check while we're taxiing," Bill told Frank.

They had all four engines running when the Seventeen reached the ramp. To accomplish the required preflight checklist, they alternately increased the two outboard and then the inboard engines to full power to make magneto checks and run the props through the full-pitch cycle. The power produced during the checks was far in excess of normal taxi speed and when they rolled down the ramp past the tower the Fort was going 45 MPH.

Major Clyde Guilford was on the catwalk in the front of the tower and said to the group commander standing next to him, "There goes Weyland's crew. Talk about eager beavers. You won't find a crew more eager than that one."

Bill barely slowed the Fort down as he took the two ninety-degree turns onto the runway. They just completed the pre-takeoff checklist and Weyland had the throttles full forward when they reached the centerline of the runway. They caught up with the formation as it started across the channel. He couldn't join his group in the lead wing, so he slid into an empty slot in the second wing. He approached cautiously since American gunners were known to shoot at strange B-17s. The Germans had repaired and made airworthy several Seventeens that had crash-landed in enemy territory. There were plenty of parts available from the bombers that were forced down. On one occasion, a German crew flying a recovered Fortress joined the bomber formation and played havoc, shooting down two B-17s before the Americans realized what had happened. The bomber crews were not about to let that happen again.

The mission was aborted over France because of weather, but the crew got credit for it. Weyland's crew was happy about that, particularly after missing the mission to St. Nazaire the day before.

On Friday, the mission to Le Mans was canceled but rescheduled for Saturday and then again to Sunday, which meant no weekend with Mary again. Weekends meant nothing to the American bomber force. Saturday and Sunday were like any other day. If the weather was good, they'd fly.

Eighth Air Force bombers got their mission to Le Mans on Monday, the Fourth of July. The most disturbing and horrifying accident happened shortly after takeoff. As they were climbing out, Bill watched a flight of B-17s forming up ahead and above them when suddenly one of the planes exploded for no apparent reason. It completely disintegrated in the sky-thousands of pieces falling earthward amid smoke and fire. Bill had seen a number of aircraft shot down in flames, some with the wings torn off. But never before had he been so affected as he was when this plane was blown apart, killing ten men who had no possible chance of survival. Bill found it impossible to block the picture out of his mind.

Weyland's crew had flown eleven missions and he had flown thirteen. He promised them he'd fly two extra missions, so they'd all finish together. He then planned to take a short leave, go home and see his family, tell Clare about Mary, and return to England. He hoped that he could come back to the Ninety-first as an operations officer, or perhaps later get a squadron and continue to fly, as the squadron commanders did, every fourth mission. He was anxious for the war to end, but as long as there had to be a war, he wanted to stay in England and continue to fly missions.

The past two months had been the most exciting and frightening-but satisfying-time in his life. And to have a beautiful, passionate, and wonderful person like Mary to share it with him was more than he could ever want.

Bill hadn't told Clare about Mary but continued to write her, although much less frequently. He felt sure the tone of his letters reflected to some extent his change of heart, but if they did she gave no hint of it. He didn't particularly like the deception he was living, but on the other hand he just couldn't write to Clare and tell her the truth. He'd seen the horrible reaction a few friends had after receiving "Dear John" letters and he wasn't about to be the writer of one. If it had to be done, it was going to be face-to-face. At the rate he was going, he'd finish his twenty-five missions in two months. He would then go back and tell her.

Looking back over the past eighteen months, he realized how his life had changed and how little he'd seen of Clare since the war began. He was home with his parents that Sunday, December 7, 1941, on a weekend pass when the Japanese bombed Pearl Harbor. He returned immediately to his base at Windsor Locks, Connecticut, as all servicemen were directed to do. That evening, the three squadrons in his group were dispersed to different airfields in New England. His unit, the Sixty-fourth Pursuit Squadron, went to Logan Field near Boston. The 110-mile move was made at night under secret orders in a blacked-out train. The train was shunted off on a siding at almost every station to let the scheduled ones go by and it took them all night to reach their destination. The priority movement of troops hadn't been a serious consideration in America at that time.

Ten hours later, they reached their destination at Revere Beach where they were bedded down in a dance hall that was closed for the season. It served as a temporary billet for the airmen. Bill had no sooner settled in when he was awakened and told there was a phone call for him. It was Clare, and knowing her tenacity and the friends she had in high places, he wasn't surprised. So much for military secrecy. The country was at war and she, like many others, was anxious to know what the army had planned to do with him.

At that moment, he hadn't the slightest idea of what his future would be, but it was just a matter of days until he received his orders to report to Maxwell Field in Alabama for preflight training as an aviation cadet. What a magnificent day that was. His impossible dream had become a reality and everything else, even Clare, became less important.

While he was in primary flight training at Carlstrom Field in Florida, Clare called to tell Bill that her husband had died. She took his death hard, even though they'd been separated for the past two years and he'd been hospitalized in a sanitarium for more than a year. She said she had to sort out her feelings and stay at Lake Saranac for a while. Later, she would let him know what she planned to do.

Bill saw Clare in New York during a short leave between basic and advanced flight training, and again when he completed his flight training at the end of July 1942. The next and last time he saw her was the previous January. She'd moved to Tucson, as suggested by her doctor. She had bought the ranch.

He was amazed when her foreman dropped him in front of a magnificent home on a hill overlooking Tucson. It was a modern, one-story, Spanish adobe, with all the modern conveniences and was fully equipped with a small herd of cattle, a dozen beautiful horses, a foreman, and two cowhands. It was most impressive.

During flight training, there was little time to think about anything except flying. The fear of being "washed out" in pilot training, and later the thought of being a career copilot, kept him in a constant state of competitiveness. Now, seeing her in these affluent surroundings quickly brought back his taste for the good life. This, as well as knowing he was going overseas and thinking she expected it, prompted a marriage proposal. He was surprised when she said no. She felt it was no great hardship to wait until he came back or, if necessary, until the end of the war.

He now realized he wasn't in love with her when he proposed. Nonetheless, he felt he'd made a commitment to her. It was also possible that she didn't want to marry him, wanting only to possess him as her lover and escort. But whatever the attraction he had for her then, it was nothing compared to the feelings he had for Mary. There comes a revelation in everyone's life when true love, as opposed to physical attraction, is felt for the first time. Bill Weyland was truly in love

Chapter 19

After the July 4th mission to Le Mans, Bill found that nothing was scheduled for Tuesday and got clearance from his squadron commander to go to London. While at Bassingbourn, the only time he could get Mary and the thoughts of their lovemaking off his mind was when he was in the cockpit. So when there were no planned missions, Bill felt there was really no need to hang around the base when he could be in London with Mary. So off he went that Monday afternoon in anticipation of a delightful evening. He arrived before she did. As expected, a supply of scotch and seltzer water was on the end table waiting for him. It was a little before five o'clock, so he decided to wait awhile before having a drink. He'd tried to moderate his alcohol consumption knowing the effect it had on Mary when he drank too much.

Shortly after five, Mary rushed into the flat and into his arms. They clung to each other until she pushed him away saying, "I've got to bathe, Bill. Why don't you have a drink. I'll be ready in a jiffy. What shall we do tonight? I don't particularly care to stay out too late. Tomorrow is a workday for me."

"That's okay with me. Let's go to Siro's for spaghetti. We can catch a movie if you like. The sooner to bed the better I like it."

"You know, you really do have a one-track mind. But it sounds fine to me. Did you fly today? I haven't heard the news. What's happening in the world?"

"Yeah, we had an easy run into France to celebrate the Fourth of July. They got us up at three o'clock, but held us on the ground until seven before we could take off."

"Well, you must be tired, darling, so we'll get to bed early and get a good night's sleep," she said as she disappeared into the bathroom.
Bill poured himself a drink, went into the bathroom, dropped the toilet seat, and sat down. Mary looked at him shyly and said, "Bill please don't sit there and watch. You know it embarrasses me."

"Sorry, baby. Was I staring? I didn't mean to. I just love watching you bathe." When she started to reply, he interrupted her and said, "Let me wash your back. I promise to behave." He had become aroused watching her and decided to do something about it.

She shook her head and said, "Well, all right, Bill. But no hanky-panky."

"Okay. Let me put my drink down." He left the bathroom and was back in less than a minute wearing only his shorts and said, "Move down and let me in." He kicked off his shorts and stepped into the tub.

Without a trace of anger she said, "Bill, I said no." Nonetheless, she moved forward and let him slide in behind her.

Bill washed her back then reached around and soaped her gently, paying particular attention to her breasts and the area between her legs.

"Bill, you devil. You do remember promising me that you were just going to wash my back?" There was no conviction in her voice since she felt him hard against her back. "All right, you stinker," she relented, "help me turn around. What is the saying? If you can't prevent being seduced, just lie back and enjoy it."

He replied, "Well, that's not exactly right, but it'll do." She did, and thoroughly enjoyed it.

After dinner at Siro's, they went to the local cinema and saw The Man in Grey. It was a good English mystery. Mary remarked as they

214

left, "That's the first time I've seen that fellow, James Mason. He certainly played the part of the beastly villain very well."

"Yeah, he and Margaret Lockwood were a real nasty pair," replied Bill.

"Well I liked the film. Steward Granger has been one of my favorites. Well, with one exception."

"Who's that?"

"You, of course. But then, you're more the Gary Cooper type."

"Is that bad?"

"No, not really. I'll settle for him most anytime."

After the short walk back to Mary's flat, they were soon cuddled up in her bed. Bill had been talking about his home and family.

When he stopped, there was a prolonged silence and finally Mary said, "Bill, I told you that I didn't know my father. My mother never spoke about him. She just told me that he died before I was born. I accepted that and never thought too much about it until I was sixteen. Until that time, my surname had been Chambers-the same as my brothers, Harry and Fred. That was the family name, and I never questioned it until I realized later that I couldn't possibly have the same surname as my half brothers, not if we had the same mother but a different father. When you're young, you simply accept your parentage. I did."

Bill said nothing waiting for Mary to continue. She hesitated, took a deep breath, and went on.

"Shortly after I started my job as a cigarette girl, my mother woke me one morning. She stood at the foot of my bed staring strangely at me for several minutes. I knew she'd been drinking because she swayed slightly and had to hold on to the brass foot rail of my bed. When she drank, I could see that mean and malicious look in her eyes, and I knew something bad was about to happen. She finally said, 'Your name isn't Chambers. It's Carlton. Your mother's name was Carlton. I didn't give birth to you. You were born on the seventh of October.' Until that time we celebrated my birthday on the first of October. Then she told me that my mother wasn't married."

Mary stopped and then continued in a soft voice. "She stared at me in a strange, spiteful way and said . . . she said . . . I . . . I was a bastard. I looked at her in shock. I didn't know whether I was dreaming or she was joking. I just couldn't believe or understand what she was saying. When I finally realized she was serious, I said, 'What do you mean my name isn't Chambers? How can I be someone else? It can't be true. You're my mother.' "

"She replied, 'Well it's true. Your name is Carlton and you better start using it, for all the good it'll do you.'

"I was stunned, frantic, and on the verge of hysterics. I pleaded with her, 'Please, mother, tell me who I am. Who was my mother?'

"She told me, 'I'm the only mother you've had. I've raised you, fed and clothed you, given you a good home and the best of everything. I educated and brought you up to be a respectable young woman.' She stopped, the intense hate so apparent in her eyes, then continued, 'I had such wonderful plans for you. A lot you've given me in return, working in that awful nightclub. Is that what you want to do for the rest of your life?'

"She wouldn't tell me anything about my mother or father and told me to forget about who my real parents were. She walked out of my room and never mentioned it again. She did, however, have my name changed.

"I sat there after she left, clutching the blanket around me, shivering and sobbing my heart out. I just couldn't believe that she could be so cruel. Because, as difficult as she was and as badly as she treated me, I still thought of her as my mother. Strangely enough, I still do. I guess I loved her. Then suddenly to be told she wasn't my mother and wouldn't tell me who was, I was numb, devastated, and felt completely empty, unwanted, and ashamed. It is such a horrid feeling knowing that you are not part of a family and you are completely alone."

She stopped, trying to erase the memory before continuing. "I somehow overcame the hurt and tried to put it aside. Each time I recalled the incident, I'd dismiss it by saying to myself, 'I'll worry about it tomorrow.' I promised myself that one day I'd have my own family and that would make everything all right.

"When I was about ten years old, I overheard my mother and my half sister Lillian talking. Lillian said to my mother, 'Does she know that she has blue blood in her?' My mother replied, 'No and I'll never tell her.' At the time I didn't understand what they meant and never really thought anything more about it."

Mary sat forward and rubbed her eyes with the back of her hands. Her eyes were dry, but the anguish was clearly visible in them. Bill felt her tremble slightly in his arms.

"So, Bill, what do you think of me now? I'm illegitimate, and I don't know who my real parents were."

When he didn't answer immediately, she pushed away, and turned to look at him. His eyes met hers and he took her hand.

"What do you expect me to say? I love you. Why should that change the way I feel about you? It wasn't your fault that your mother and father weren't married. I'm sure one day you'll find they were very much in love and something happened that prevented them from marrying. They must've been fine people to have given life to a person as wonderful as you."

Mary threw her arms around Bill's neck and hugged and kissed him countless times and said, "Oh, I've been so afraid to tell you. I was positive that you'd stop loving me and I'd never see you again. Oh, darling, I'm so happy. I know now you do truly love me and will never leave me. I love you so much."

"I think I love you more because of what you told me. You've had such a hellish life. I want to try to make it up to you in some way."

"Well, you have, Bill. Just hold me tight." He held her close until she fell asleep.

It would be fifteen years before Mary learned of her mother, Doris Carlton's, tragic love affair with Captain Frank Anderson.

Bill called operations on Tuesday afternoon and learned that no missions were scheduled for Wednesday. He decided to spend another night with Mary. He realized it wasn't the right thing to do, but the temptation was too great. His pressing need to be with her was influencing his judgment. This, coupled with the relaxed discipline under their new commander, provided the opportunity and he took advantage of it.

When Bill returned to the base on Wednesday afternoon, he found that they'd flown an unscheduled training mission. He was reprimanded for being absent and was confined to the base for three weeks. He had no quarrel with disciplinary action and no one to blame but himself. Yet, he knew he'd have to find a way to be with Mary. Her letters alone would not be enough. He normally received two or three letters from Mary during the week, the first written minutes after he left her. They were the most beautiful, passionate letters, filled with endearing phases of how she worshiped him and how wonderful it was to love him. Her written words were much more explicit than the ones she spoke. But her letters wouldn't suffice.

Weyland prayed for a lot of flying activity to keep him occupied. Only when flying-and especially when facing the enemy-did he not think about making love to Mary. However, the only activity for the week was a cancellation on Thursday and another air abort in an attempt to bomb the Folke Wolfe plant at Villa Coublay on Saturday. Aside from that, the week was gloomy and lonely.

Bill called Mary when he learned a dance was planned for the following Tuesday night at the officer's club. He told her he'd arranged for her to stay at the Red Cross women's quarters if she could stay overnight. Mary happily agreed and told him she'd take Wednesday off and leave for Bassingbourn on Tuesday after work.

They met as planned at the main gate and Bill took Mary to the Red Cross quarters and waited while she bathed and changed. In that brief period, she became friendly with an American girl named Lois. It was amazing how easily she met people and became comfortable with them.

Bill and Mary left the Red Cross quarters and just before entering the club, Mary said to him, "You won't believe anything you hear about me, will you, Bill?"

"No. Why should I?"

She answered, "Oh, you know what they say about English girls."

He didn't reply, but wondered why she wanted to warn him. He knew a lot of Americans considered English girls easy. Mary had told him about dating an aide to General Eisenhower before she met him. Aside from that, she hadn't mentioned any other relationships with Americans. It bothered him and remained one of those nagging little mental barbs that can cause green monsters to thrive.

They joined Woody, Joe, and two other officers from the squadron and their dates, two local girls, and two who were from London. Mary was already acquainted with Joe and Woody and was warmly welcomed at their table. Although her poise and genteel manner set her apart from the other Englishwomen, she was so unpretentious and friendly that even they were soon captivated by her charm. The evening progressed with much laughter and fun even though no one was drinking a great deal because a mission was planned for the following day.

Dave Eanes, the squadron operations officer, asked Mary to dance and shortly after he brought her back to the table Clyde came over and asked her if she would dance with him. Woody's date, Gwynne, a girl from London, was not very pretty, but had a terrific body so Bill asked her to dance and she accepted. As they got up to dance, Bill glanced across the room and saw Mary look at him oddly. When she and Clyde danced by them, Mary glared at him openly and Bill wondered why. When the music stopped and they returned to the table, Clyde held Mary's chair, but she remained standing. She thanked him and when he left she picked up her purse, said she was leaving, bade everyone good night, gave Gwynne a scathing look, and walked away.

Bill sat there completely dumbfounded. He shook his head, looked at Woody, and said, "What the hell's wrong now?" Then, realizing she was serious, he went after her and caught up to her as she leaving the club.

He took her arm and stopped her, saying, "Why are you leaving like this? Did Clyde say something to you?"

She wrenched her arm free, glared at him, and said, "Don't you dare talk to me. I saw the way you were looking at that girl you were dancing with."

He tried to explain, "Look, I was just dancing, the same as you were. I..."

"That's different. The only reason I danced with Clyde was to see if I could get him to revoke your three-week restriction. And what do you do the minute my back is turned? You grab that dreadful girl just because she has a sexy body. She's not a nice girl. How could you do such an awful thing to me?"

"I'm sorry. I just didn't think you would mind."

"Well, you know now, and I'm going back to London."

"How? There are no trains or buses running at this time of night."

"I don't care, I'm going even if I have to walk," she replied angrily as she pulled away from him.

He stood, completely frustrated, realizing there was some truth in what she said. However, he quickly discarded the idea as ridiculous and lost his temper, "Okay, damn it, go. Go back to London," he shouted, taking all the change out of his pocket and throwing it away. "Now you'll damn well have to walk!"

She walked away from him while he deliberated whether to go after her or back to the club. Soon after she disappeared in the darkness, he heard her cry out. He grudgingly followed and found her trying to get over a railed fence. He picked her up and lifted her over the fence. He set her down not too gently and she lost her balance and fell backward.

"Now look what you've done. My stockings are ruined."

He vaulted over the fence to help her up. And as he did, she swung out with her fists, hitting him repeatedly. He told her to stop and when she wouldn't, he pushed her away and she fell back down on her bottom again.

She sat staring angrily up at him, "You brute. How dare you! You hit me!"

"I didn't. I just gave you a little shove."

She began to cry. He stood watching her. Finally, he knelt down to help her up and as he did she put her arms around his neck and sobbed. He picked her up and she nestled her face into the hollow of his neck, sighing softly. He carried her across the field to his quarters, put her down, and said, "Let's go to my room."

The pilot's house was quiet. The others were either asleep or at the club. They undressed and got into his small bed. It was a small cot the size of a hospital bed and it squeaked. Their lascivious proximity was perfect for the little bed and each time it squeaked, he grimaced and she giggled.

Afterward, Bill held her close but couldn't stop thinking about the remark she made before they entered the club. "What did you mean when you said I shouldn't listen to what anyone said about you."

She said, "Oh, that. It's really not important, Bill. I don't know why I said it."

"Well, you must have had a reason. Did you know other Americans?

"I told you about Tex Lee. I liked him and we had several dates before he went to North Africa. I met a couple of other Americans that I didn't particularly like. You know the type: conceited, huge egos. I remember one saying to me, 'See these silver wings? Well, that means that I might not be around too long. So I really don't have much time. Let's not waste it on preliminaries and I promise you by morning you won't regret it.' I was with Dorothy at the Deanery. I borrowed ten shillings from her, gave it to him, and told him to take a taxi to Bond Street where there were lots of girls who would be happy to oblige him.

"You know, Bill, that's why I got so upset with you when we first met and you said you were going to take care of the Germans. Remember? I know now that you had too much to drink, and it's not like you to say things like that. But it reminded me of the cocky Americans I had met and I might not have been very nice to some of them."

"Yes, I remember you were skeptical about me then."

Mary was silent for some time, but before they fell asleep, she said seriously, "Did you know that Clyde has smelly feet?"

"No, I never noticed."

"Well, he does. Maybe I've just got a sensitive nose. And you know what? He told me you can come to see me in London this weekend if there are no scheduled missions."

"Gosh, that's great. You know, you not only have a very sensitive nose but you are a conniving, cunning, little hussy."

She laughed, "He really does have smelly feet."

With that, they fell asleep huddled together, as Mary would say, "bums to bellies." A perfect fit and as snug as two spoons placed side by side.

He was awakened by a discreet knock on the door and a lot of commotion in the building. "Briefing at six o'clock, sir," Fred called out from the hall.

Mary awakened, startled, "What's happening?"

"It's the mission they mentioned last night. I've got to go, but you stay in bed and I'll get you some tea and biscuits."

He washed, dressed, and went down to the kitchen where Fred had water boiling. When he got back, Mary was dressed and waiting for him. He gave her a big mug of tea and said, "Wait until it's light out before you leave. Everyone should be gone by then. Go to the club and I'll have Lois meet you there for breakfast. I'll see you when I get back." He kissed her and left.

It was July 14-Bastille Day in France-and the Ninety-first was going Amiens to help the French celebrate.

After the briefing, Bill stopped by the officer's mess and saw Mary entertaining the Red Cross girls at their table. She told him she would stay with them until he got back. She didn't seem to be overly concerned about the mission, or so it seemed, and in a way he was glad. He certainly didn't want an emotional scene. She waved to him as he left and called out, "Good luck, Bill."

He cycled hurriedly to the personal equipment shack and caught up with his crew as they were loading their gear on the truck that would take them out to the hardstand.

As they taxied down the ramp to take off, Bill saw Mary standing up on the catwalk in front of the control tower with the Red Cross girls, Clyde, and the rest of the brass waiting for the takeoff. He slid open his side window and waved, and she waved back. As he passed them, he wondered what her true feelings were. They never talked about the danger he faced or the possibility that one day he might not return from a raid. He knew that she, as most English people did, felt strong-ly about the war and defeating Germany. He thought about the night he and Mary were walking home from the cinema. It was just after the pubs had closed. When they passed the Boston Arms on the corner of Balcombe Street, there was a group of elderly women gathered on the sidewalk in front of the pub. They were dancing in a circle lifting their skirts up and singing "Knees up, Knees up, Oh, Knees up, Mother Brown . . ." Then they raised their fists, shouting and jeering Hitler, and daring "Jerry" to come back and bomb them. This was the spirit that lived in England and brought them through the Blitz, particularly in the East End where the devastation was massive.

The way Mary felt, or perhaps the way she hid her true feelings even in the most unguarded moments, meant so much to him. They knew what the odds were. One crew in twenty in his squadron had fin-ished twenty-five missions. And that was not without the one fatality in Carroll's crew. It was much easier to face the perilous odds without being reminded of them. Every minute he spent with Mary was won-derful and because of the danger, their passion was more intense and exciting. They relished every minute together and lived life to its fullest. To have someone so lovely, passionate, and understanding to share these exciting days with him was something he would never forget.

It was a beautiful clear day. Bill turned the plane over to his new copilot, Lieutenant Louis Bianchi, and sat back daydreaming. Just before reaching the target a flight of ME-109s suddenly came out of the sun and flashed through the formation before any of the gunners had a chance to fire. They disappeared as suddenly as they arrived. The tar-get was well defined in the clean air and the bombing results proved to be outstanding. On the way back, American Thunderbolts, P-47s, met the bombers to cover their withdrawal. This was their first mission where they appeared in any great strength and probably their first encounter with the Luftwaffe. A few enemy aircraft managed to get through to attack the bombers, but for the most part they became involved with American fighters in a hotly pursued dogfight.

When Bill landed and pulled into the hardstand, Mary was waiting in a jeep with Dave Eanes. He shut down, hurriedly filled out Form 1, got out of his seat, and dropped down through the forward hatch. His crew gave him a hard time as he left the plane, but he didn't mind a bit. Mary's face brightened with a welcoming smile and when he came up to her, she got out of the jeep, and hugged him modestly, saying softly, "Hello, my darling."

He pushed her away gently knowing the guys in his crew were watching him and he'd have a hard time living it down. He got in the passenger's seat and lifted Mary up onto his lap.

Dave asked, "How did it go, Bill?"

"Not bad. Not bad at all."

When Dave sensed that neither of his passengers wanted to talk, he accepted it and drove them back to Operations in silence. They appeared to be completely satisfied being close to each other. Words didn't seem necessary. That evening Bill took Mary to Royston, where she boarded the train for London. He returned to the base and the war.

Chapter 20

In the fifteen missions Bill had flown, he'd been assigned eleven different copilots. He didn't complain about it initially because he expected Hal to return to duty. Later, he began to realize that the practice could become a problem. Some of the young inexperienced pilots were assigned to Bill just prior to the mission briefing. After one flight with Bill, they were turned over to another crew and sometimes assigned to another squadron. A copilot is essential to the survival of the aircraft and its crew, particularly in an emergency. He had to respond quickly in an emergency, not only on orders from the pilot, but on his own initiative. Most importantly, he must be capable of getting the crew and the plane back if the pilot is disabled. According to Eighth Air Force statistics, a pilot's chances of being hit were three times greater than any other crew member. The frontal assault, most commonly used by the German pilots, was made primarily to kill the bomber pilot.

With the safety of his crew in mind, Bill told Eanes that if Hal DeBolt was not coming back he wanted a permanently assigned copilot. Lieutenant Louis Bianchi had flown with Bill on two previous missions, and Eanes promised he'd assign Louis to Weyland's crew permanently. Bianchi was a young second lieutenant from San Luis Obispo,

California, fresh out of flying school with less than one hundred hours in B-17s. He was a quiet slender guy who was about 5' 6" tall and weighed no more than 130 pounds-the perfect size for fighters. At times, a Flying Fortress behaves as its name implies and requires a good deal of physical strength to fly her. Bill had concerns about Louis's ability to handle the plane under extreme conditions, such as flying in formation over an extended period of time with an engine out or with a damaged control surface. Regardless of his concerns about Bianchi, the kid was eager and the crew liked him, and Bill didn't have the heart to turn him down. Weyland hoped his decision wouldn't come back to haunt him.

A mission to Vitry was scrubbed on Thursday and Friday, and the raid on Saturday to Hanover was recalled over Germany due to weather. Some aircraft did, however, bomb secondary targets. Light flak and meager fighter attacks were encountered. The mission on Sunday to Kassel was also scrubbed. It wasn't a very successful week.

After a mission was scrubbed, most men were left with mixed feelings. The tension built up during the process of preparing for the flight and when it was canceled, there was an immediate feeling of relief, but soon after, disappointment set in and they wished they'd gone.

Six long tedious days were spent staring across the flight line at the soggy English weather. Finally, on Friday evening, orders came down alerting the group for a mission the following day and when the airmen saw the target, they were pleasantly surprised. It was near a small town called Heroya on the coast of Norway. Rumor had it that the Germans were carrying on some experimental work there on a secret weapon of mass destruction. The crews were told only that it was an important target calling for precision bombing. It was the longest mission flown so far, twelve hundred miles round-trip and all over water.

Lieutenant McFarland had scheduled himself to fly copilot with Weyland's crew. When Bill saw that Bianchi was not scheduled to fly, he told McFarland he could go with them as an observer, but Bianchi was going as their copilot. He wasn't going to have his newly assigned copilot bumped from what seemed to be an easy raid. After offering a lame excuse, Mac agreed when he realized Bill wasn't about to change his mind. McFarland picked the easy missions to fly, but he also picked the pilot whom he considered the best in the squadron to fly with. It was a back-handed compliment when Mac scheduled himself to fly with a particular crew, but to Bill it was still a cowardly act.

The mission to Norway turned out to be a long easy one, but it was the beginning of what later would be known as "Blitz Week." On Sunday, the Eighth went to Hamburg following the RAF, which had bombed the city the night before in one of its massive raids. When the Americans arrived, the entire city appeared to be on fire. Smoke covered the area making bombing extremely difficult. The Luftwaffe came out in force to meet the American formations, and the fighting was fierce and continued from their arrival at the German border all the way back to the North Sea. The group lost only one B-17 and had several damaged, but eighteen aircraft from other groups failed to return.

The Eighth Air Force went back to Hamburg on Monday, again following an RAF night raid. A heavy overcast made assembly a hazardous affair. Flying in and out of clouds at 27,500 feet, Bill was leading the second element in the high flight in the high group. Just before reaching the enemy coast, a runaway propeller on the number four engine forced him to shut it down. Fully loaded and at that altitude, it was impossible to keep up with the formation. Bill wanted to press on, but realized that would be foolish and unfair to his crew. It was their first abort. He knew it had to happen sooner or later, but he hated the thought of missing the sortie.

He alerted his crew and motioned to his wingman that he was turning back. As he made the 180-degree turn, he looked to his left and saw Lieutenant Wieneth turning with him. When he rolled out of the turn, he saw Lieutenant Arp pulling up in position on his right wing. There wasn't much he could do without breaking radio silence, but he couldn't imagine why they had also aborted. A short time later, Jim McBride called from the tail and said that another B-17 with a tail number of 5427 had joined them in the slot. That would be a Fort from the 324th Bomb Squadron. Bill wondered what was going on. The weather was rotten and he guessed they simply decided to stay with him and there wasn't a hell of lot he could do about it.

When they got back, he found that eight other B-17s aborted, making a total of twelve aircraft from the Ninety-first Bomb Group. Just six aircraft in the group went on to bomb Hamburg. Of those, one was shot down and another with severe battle damage had to ditch in the North Sea. Not a very good day for the Ninety-first, and Bill blamed himself for not pressing on, but he knew if he had there would have probably been more than two planes missing in action. It was their first abort in seventeen sorties-and what a disaster it was.

When Bill asked Andy at the debriefing what had happened, Wieneth replied, "I couldn't get more than thirty inches of manifold pressure on number three engine and had a hard time keeping up with you. I was thinking about turning back just before you did. So when you aborted, I decided to go back with you. I couldn't have made it to the target."

Weyland agreed. Then he asked Arp why he aborted. Arp replied, "When I saw you guys turning back I thought it was a recall." There were no repercussions, but Bill still felt bad about it.

It was later learned that the combined raids of the RAF and the Eighth Air Force on Hamburg on July 25-26 were, until that time, the most devastating of the war. The massive bombing, primarily by the British, caused an intense firestorm and it was estimated that fifty thousand German lives were lost. That number was slightly less than the total number of English lives lost during the fall of 1940 and winter of 1941 during the German Blitz of London. After hearing the death toll, Bill knew that their bombs hadn't been dropped with practiced accuracy over Hamburg, and for the first time he realized that their bombs were killing civilians. That reality hit him, and he reasoned that whatever the Germans had done, this wasn't right. No one could escape the guilt and shame caused by the war. He hadn't really thought much about the damage their bombs were causing. He found some consolation in the fact that he didn't take part in the bombing of Hamburg on the second day.

BOMBER PILOT

Most crew members felt they were fighting Hitler and everything he stood for, and if they were told that their bombs were killing women and children, they would disagree vehemently. Fighting the war from between twenty thousand and thirty thousand feet was impersonal. There they were matching their skill and courage against the Luftwaffe. Only an occasional glimpse of the enemy in the cockpit of an attacking fighter screaming through the formation personalized the war to most bomber crews. The designated targets of the American bombers were military objectives, isolated and attacked by using precise aiming points. The Norden bombsight was considered the best in the world and the bombs were not dropped indiscriminately. It wasn't difficult for the crews to convince themselves that they were doing the right thing. They were fighting a madman who was causing much suffering and destruction in the world. It was evident in London in the bombed-out buildings and the homeless people sleeping in the Underground. The atrocities occurring in Europe were more than enough to provide the incentive and determination for the bomber crews to fight on without remorse.

Bill was a fatalist and felt certain he would survive the war. When flak suits were issued and the crews were told to wear them with steel helmets, he wouldn't. He wore the same clothes on every mission: leather jacket, turtleneck sweater, pink slacks, and jodhpur boots. He wore only his parachute harness and threw the pack in the crawl space when he climbed aboard. He felt that if Lloyd couldn't wear a chute in the ball turret, he wouldn't wear one either. Besides, it was uncomfortable.

Weyland did not consider himself a lover of war. He did, however, love flying and the challenge of combat. The fear and exhilaration a combat mission generated was beyond belief. After it passed, there was nothing to compare to the sensation of being so completely alive. This absolute high came as they were letting down in sight of the English coast when returning from a raid. He wanted to shout with joy, "I made it back and I'm alive and the guys with me are okay. And Mary, so beautiful, loving, and provocatively passionate is waiting for me. God, how lucky can a guy be!"

Harry Lay and McFarland got their promotions to captain that Tuesday. Clyde told Bill that he'd withdrawn his recommendation for promotion to captain the day he missed the practice mission, but said he'd put it back in and it should come through in a couple of weeks. Bill was disappointed, but he didn't regret the extra night he had spent with Mary.

On Wednesday, the Eighth Air Force set off to Kassel on their deepest penetration of Germany. Adverse weather over the target area forced them to look for secondary targets that were even more difficult to bomb. They encountered about one hundred ME-109s, some of which were firing rockets into the formation. It was a harrowing raid that made the crews feel good about getting back, but not about the effectiveness of their effort.

On Thursday, Clyde flew as Bill's copilot, the procedure used when the 401st Squadron was leading the air division. The target was Kiel. Bombing results were excellent and Joe was cited for his outstanding navigation in leading the formation. As they crossed the enemy coast, Joe missed his landfall by a few miles, and to be sure they flew the exact planned course to the target, he called for a slight S turn. Joe thought he had goofed, but when they got back he was complimented on the correction he made. They said it was an excellent decision on his part since it gave the spread groups time to close up into a formidable combat formation before entering enemy territory.

They encountered minimal opposition from enemy aircraft, but the flak was heavy. After leaving the coast of Germany on the way back, two twin-engine ME-110s followed the formation out over the North Sea. They flew ahead and to the right of the bombers just out of gun range. Every gunner in the formation had his eyes glued on the two German planes, hoping they would attack. About fifteen minutes out, one fighter finally broke off and turned into the formation for a head-on attack. Bill could picture the German pilot raising his right hand in a salute, saying, "Hiel, Hitler," instead of a more appropriate, "Hail, Mary" before turning into the formation. The anxious American gunners held their fire patiently until the fighter got in range of the bomber formation. When it did, over one hundred guns fired simultaneously and thousands of fifty-caliber rounds converged on the fighter en masse, completely disintegrating the German plane. There was no lack of courage on the part of the German pilot. However, the other pilot decided to turn away without attacking, knowing there would be no witness to question his lack of courage.

On Friday, the forecast was for excellent weather over Germany, and that meant another attempt on Kassel. The bomber force was scheduled to get American fighter cover. The rumor was that the commanding general of the fighter command was relieved of duty and his replacement, Major General William Kepner, was more eager to have his pilots tangle with the Luftwaffe. Some of the P-47 units had been rigged for external fuel tanks and could now take the bombers a short distance into Belgium and, hopefully, meet them coming back out. When this announcement was made at the briefing, the room erupted in boisterous cheers. Until that time there had been little to cheer about. The American bomber crews weren't complimentary toward their "Little Friends" and would quickly voice their opinion about their lack of combat in the war to date. In truth, they realized that the American fighter pilots were anxious to tangle with the Luftwaffe, even though it was their former CO, General Hunter, who was cautious. Conversely, the Germans had no intention of attacking the American fighters and would avoid a fight with them if at all possible. Their sole purpose was to stop the bombers.

Bill was leading the low flight of his group in the third and last wing of the bomber formation. The German pilots patiently waited until the American fighters turned back just beyond Brussels. Some of the FW-190s had their wing tips painted blue so they'd resemble the wings of P-47s. For a time, there was a slight hesitation on the part of the American gunners to fire at them. That soon ended when they saw their wing cannons flashing in their direction. The lead wing was taking a hell of a beating, but they pressed on.

The weather forecast was accurate. Visibility was unlimited and, after passing the industrial Ruhr, the countryside of Germany looked peaceful and serene. There wasn't much flak after they passed the Ruhr and the Luftwaffe attacks had diminished. They were probably on the ground refueling. As they approached the city of Kassel on the Weser River, Bill watched the lead wing turn on the IP and head northwest to the target. According to the intelligence types, the American bomber force would receive the least amount of flak on that approach. As the lead group started their bomb run, a massive barrage of flak was sent up to meet them. The sky above the city became a huge angry black cloud. There must have been several hundred guns firing at them. Bill couldn't imagine how the wing could survive such deadly fire, but out they came, visible now as they were making their turn to the west and away from the target. There were a few holes in the formation, but he marveled at the tenacity and courage of his comrades. Close behind them was the second wing ready to meet the same ravaging flak. For a time, the visual image seen through Bill's windshield was so astonishingly dramatic that he felt like a spectator and not a participant. It was like watching a motion picture.

The second wing got through much like the first. As the third wing turned to make their run, Bill cursed the intelligence people. He said a little prayer and told his crew to "hang in." He thought about Woody leaning over his bombsight looking directly into the upcoming flak with nothing between him but clear plastic and of Lloyd in his turret hanging from the belly of the plane. At least in the cockpit there were a couple of layers of sheet metal beneath him. He knew his crew was as frightened as he was, but not one word betrayed their fear, except for an occasional, "Oh, boy! That was close. Too damn close!" The angry black clouds with their orange centers were breaking all around them.

Some were so close the explosions could be heard over the roar of the engines. The exploding shrapnel sounded like someone was lashing the plane with a huge chain. The crew felt greater fear and vulnerability when the bomb bay doors were open exposing the naked bombs. Taking a hit among the armed bombs brought horrible thoughts to their minds. Woody had the doors open and the excruciatingly slow countdown began. Finally, he called "Bombs away," and all the men silently breathed a deep sigh of relief. They managed to get through. The group looked good and as far as Bill could see they all made it.

It later dawned on Bill why this mission seemed so different. As they approached the target, the German fighters had left them and it was a beautiful clear day. Kassel, a picturesque city on the bend of the Weser River, looked peaceful and serene. To have it erupt so quickly and violently, and with such fury, made it ironic and surreal.

The mission was seven hours long and as soon as Bill shut down the engines on the dispersal pad the hatches flew open, the crew jumped from the plane, and hurried to the grassy spot beside the hardstand where they collapsed. Bill watched them from the cockpit and when he finished filling out Form 1, he slowly climbed down, walked over, and dropped down in the grass beside them.

They'd flown six missions in seven days, and it was beginning to show on their faces. They just lay down on the grass and stared up at the sky. No one spoke and that was not like the crew he knew. They were always joking, kidding each other, or just horsing around, particularly after a raid. But not this time.

At the debriefing, Clyde came over and sat at their table. He looked at them for several minutes, got up, and said, "Bill, I'm putting you and your crew on R and R for seven days. I'll set up the reservations for Wednesday of next week. I don't think there'll be much activity before then."

Bill hadn't thought about R and R, and his crew hadn't mentioned it. He was sure that they had thought about it, particularly after hearing from other crews about the good times they had at the rest hotels. Crews with less time and fewer missions had gone on R and R. He just assumed they all felt as he did-that they'd take the leave when they finished their tour.

He looked at his crew and saw the tension leave their faces, and said to his CO, "Okay, boss. You got a deal."

When they finished debriefing, he told Woody, Joe, and Louis he was going to London on Saturday morning, but would be back on Monday to go to Bournemouth with them.

In the weeks prior to Blitz Week, the Eighth Air Force had acquired several more B-17 groups. Each of the four original groups picked up two new groups, giving the Eighth Air Force an armada of four wings, or twelve groups. The wing integrity of the formation was maintained with its three groups of fifty-four B-17s. They started the week with 330 B-17s. When it was over, that force was reduced to just two hundred effective aircraft. One hundred B-17s and ninety crews were lost. Nine hundred men were missing, KIA, MIA, or wounded. Half of the total remaining number of Fortresses suffered battle damage from enemy action. The Combat Crew Replacement Center would have to come up with the equivalent of nine squadrons, or ninety replacement crews, to cover their losses.

There had been constant pressure on the Eighth Air Force by RAF Bomber Command to join them in night bombing of Germany ever since the Americans arrived in England in the summer of 1942. The RAF had convinced Britain's prime minister, Winston Churchill, that night bombing was the only solution to the air war against Germany, and he was putting pressure on president Franklin Roosevelt to have the Eighth Air Force join the RAF in night raids. The American aircrews weren't trained, nor were the B-17s equipped, to fly night missions. General Ira Eaker, commanding general of the Eighth Air Force, knew that if they were forced to fly at night, their losses would triple.

In the fall of 1942, before the Americans had a chance to start their bombing campaign in earnest, the priorities switched from England to North Africa. Part of the bomber force was sent to North Africa in November 1942 to support the American invasion, delaying the bomber buildup in England. At that time, the pressure intensified on General Eaker to give up daylight bombing. Many air force generals, including General Henry "Hap" Arnold, were ready to concede to the British.

At the time of the Casablanca conference in January 1943, General Arnold, commanding general of the U.S. Army Air Force, who accompanied Roosevelt, asked General Eaker to meet him in North Africa. On Eaker's arrival, he was met by General Arnold, who said, "I've got bad news for you, son. Prime Minister Churchill has talked President Roosevelt into having the Eighth Air Force discontinue daylight bombing and join the British in their night effort. If you want to continue daylight bombing you've got to convince the prime minister. I'll get an appointment for you. I know he'll see you 'cause I heard him tell the president he has a high regard for you. If you can't get him to change his mind, we're sunk."

General Eaker met Churchill the next day and began by saying, "I've set down the reasons I believe we should continue daylight bombing on one page. All I ask is that you read it."

Of the essential points that Eaker made, the one that seemed to interest Churchill most was, "With the RAF bombing the Germans by night and the Americans by day we would cause the German civilian population such hardships that Hitler's war effort would be seriously undermined."

Churchill perused the sheet of paper further and quietly kept repeating the phrase, "bombing around the clock." That one point of Eaker's, more than any other argument, saved the daylight bombing strategy-and perhaps thousands of American lives.

General Eaker won his point and got his bombers by February 1943. Initially, however, he couldn't strike targets in Germany with any consistency because of the foul winter weather, excessive losses, and shortages of spare parts, replacement aircraft, and air crews.

Blitz Week had ended. It was the most intensive period of operations for the Eighth Air Force since their arrival in England less than a year ago. Nonetheless, bombing results in May, June, and July weren't impressive. With the heavy losses and bad weather preventing precision bombing, doubts arose in Bomber Command. Luftwaffe opposition had increased threefold by moving fighter units from the Russian front and Sardinia to western Europe. Six units were added and the fighter strength of ME-109s and FW-190s rose from 270 to 630 in June and July, with plans to add more Luftwaffe Gruppes.

Eighth Air Force planners thought they could outwit the enemy by feints, diversions, and divided missions. However, the German controllers weren't easily fooled. Americans overestimated the effectiveness of their defensive firepower, and accepted the outrageous claims by the aircrews on the number of enemy aircraft shot down. Poor judgment and errors on the part of those planning raids also caused greater losses. The general impression and theory that the German fighter force could be defeated by the massive firepower of the Fortress formations was proving to be not only questionable but erroneous. Shooting down enemy fighters was much more difficult than initially believed. The losses in the new B-17 groups were far in excess of those planned or considered. But these initial battles kindled a fierce sense of pride and regardless of the losses the commanders and the aircrews of the Eighth were determined to go it alone.

Chapter 21

Saturday, July 31, was payday. Had it not been payday Bill would've gone to London on Friday after the raid to Kassel. When paid, he would settle all his debts-money he borrowed from the crew. Then for the first two weeks, he and Mary would really live it up-fine dining at Scots, Hacketts, or Simpsons, and then on to the Astor or Embassy Clubs. By the middle of the month, their lifestyle changed drastically back to their little Greek restaurant where they could get chicken, spaghetti, and a carafe of wine for ten shillings. Or they'd eat in a pub or at Mary's. Mary loved good food and Bill thoroughly enjoyed watching her eat. It wasn't only because of the wartime short-ages that she was enthusiastic about food. Most girls that Bill had dated believed that it was proper to leave some food on their plate. Not Mary. She ate every last morsel and then helped herself to Bill's dinner. It was not that she ate faster, but more efficiently. She used both hands as Europeans do, while he awkwardly changed hands to use his knife. One night at Scots, the headwaiter came to their table and whispered to Mary, "Mademoiselle, homard!" They were scarce and hardly ever found on menus. Bill sat, completely enraptured, watching her devour the lobster. She picked every last morsel of flesh from the body cavity and sucked each leg dry.

After getting his pay and settling his debts, Bill took off on a wild cycle ride for Royston railroad station looking forward to an extravagant and marvelous evening with Mary. He stowed his bicycle and anxiously waited for the train to London. He thought about another amazing English virtue: being able to abandon your unlocked bicycle and find it there when you returned.

The journey to London was a time for calm recollection, to look back on the action of the past few days, and forward to the thrill of seeing Mary. Trains became an important part of his life. He was either on his way to see Mary or had just left her. It was a quiet tranquil time between combat and love. During the past week, with a mixture of fear and excitement, there had been little time to think of anything but surviving the raids.

For nearly an hour Bill would sit back, smoke, and relax in a comfortable first-class compartment and gaze at the English countryside. It wasn't quite the England he had envisioned. The once lovely parks and athletic fields were now a patchwork of scrubby victory gardens. Nearer to London, the train passed the dreary row houses with their tiny gardens and corrugated metal bomb shelters, and he'd wonder about the people living there, their fears, anxieties, and passions. From the train, the suburbs appeared drab and dismal. Here the real hardships of wartime shortages were apparent. Except for the people living in the Underground, Bill rarely came in contact with the suffering most English people endured during the war. Although the austere living conditions were evident during that short interval between Bassingbourn and London, it was forgotten the moment he reached Mary's cozy little flat. She had a way of glamorizing and sanctifying their space.

When the train approached the city, past the factories and warehouses, he'd be standing, trench coat on, kit bag over his shoulder, anxiously waiting to get off. As the train pulled into Kings Cross Station he'd pull the sash window down and look out to see if Mary was waiting on the platform. Occasionally, she met him at the rail station, but more often, he'd jump off the train before it stopped and head for Ivor

Court. One of the many things he liked about England was that you could jump on or off a moving train or bus without someone shouting at you. He'd dash through the station to the Underground, where usually a train would be waiting to take him to Baker Street. Up three steps at a time and out of the tube station to Marlebone Road. By the time he turned the corner at Baker Street onto Park Road, his momentum would pick up to a fast trot. The people he'd pass would either smile or look aghast.

When Mary was home, as she was today, she'd buzz the front door open and they'd meet in the hall in a crush of bodies. If she wasn't there, the concierge would let him in. Inevitably, the moment he got in and sat down the phone would ring with a cheerful, "Hello, darling. I'll be home in a jiffy." When she arrived it would be a time for wonderful love, happiness, leisure, and a kind of togetherness that he had never before experienced.

This morning, shortly after Bill arrived, he sat at her small dining table savoring one of Mary's fabulous English breakfasts. She sat across from him attentively watching him devour his food. He looked at her, caught her expression, and said, "Why so pensive?"

"Oh, I don't know. Just thinking how nice it would be if every morning could be like this. I love to watch you. The way you eat. The funny things you do, like eating toast and jam with your eggs."

"What's wrong with that?"

"Nothing, really, but I like to eat my toast and jam after I finish my eggs."

"Big deal. But you're right. So I'll have some more toast and jam now that I've finished my eggs."

Mary smiled and got up to make more toast and to refill his coffee cup.

Bill wiped his mouth with his napkin and said, "Clyde scheduled my crew for R and R next week, starting on Wednesday. Made reservations for us at the rest home, the Standbridge Earls Hotel in Bournemouth. I hadn't thought much about taking R and R, but the guys are all for it."

"Oh, that sounds wonderful, Bill. You'll adore Bournemouth. I was there on holiday before the war. Perhaps I can get a few days off and join you."

He shook his head, "I decided not to go. My crew can go, but I'm staying here. You probably wouldn't be able to stay in the hotel with me if you did come down, so I'm not going."

"You should go. It'll be good for you."

"No. I'll tell Clyde when I get back to Bassingbourn on Monday. I don't think he'll object. The guys in my crew will understand if I don't go with them. I want to stay here and be with you. That's if you want me." And before she could reply, he added with a knowing smile, "Well . . . we can have breakfast like this every morning and perhaps a little loving as well-at least for seven days anyway."

"Oh, Bill, you know I do. It'll be wonderful. Poor Mr. Chalmers, with you in town all week, I don't think he'll get much work out of me. But I'm sure he'll understand. Oh, I do hope so, because it's going to be marvelous. A bit like one long weekend." She threw her arms around Bill and hugged and kissed him and after a pensive hesitation added, "I know I'm being selfish, darling. Really, shouldn't you be with Joe and Woody? I'm sure they're looking forward to you all being together at the rest hotel."

Avoiding the suggestion, Bill replied, "Speaking of the weekend, Dave Eames invited us to a party. He met a very gracious woman at an embassy party last week, and she invited Dave to a cocktail party tonight and suggested he bring along some of his friends. I have her address here somewhere." He pulled a scrap of paper out his pocket. "Here it is. Damn it, I don't know her name but she lives in Mayfair at 600 Park Lane, Apartment 4C. What do you think? Would you like to go?"

Mary responded, "Yes, I'd like to, Bill." The address sounded familiar to her, but she couldn't place a name to it.

That afternoon they walked along Oxford Street to North Audley Street where Bill stopped in the post exchange to get cigarettes, his ration of candy for Mary's butcher, and a bottle of fragrance for her. On the way back to her flat, they stopped at the food market in Selfridge's and used Mary's few remaining ration coupons.

Back in the flat, they napped. Mary was a fanatic about her rest. Particularly when she planned to go out in the evening, she'd insist on taking "a little lie down." She claimed it was the best possible way to prevent wrinkles and have nice clear eyes. Why a girl of twenty-one would worry about wrinkles was more than he could comprehend. But he welcomed a nap with Mary and was usually handsomely rewarded.

Bill was ready at five o'clock all bathed and dressed. Mary sat at her dressing table in her slip applying makeup. It amused him to see her meticulously applying mascara and lip rouge to a perfect face that had scant, if any, need for it. She'd been trained in the application of cosmetics as a young actress and now she wouldn't go out without it. She said she felt naked. It transformed her into a different person, and he wasn't quite sure which he preferred. In the morning, he'd wake before her and relish those moments lying there watching her while she slept. Without makeup she looked like a beautiful, innocent, and defenseless child-so naive and virtuous-and he would be overcome by a strange feeling of guilt after a night of making arduous love to her. He knew that someday someone would put to words and music the way he felt watching Mary in the morning. With her makeup expertly applied, she became a glamorous and sophisticated young woman, one whom he couldn't wait to bed.

When finished, she skillfully slid her black silk dress over her head without disturbing a hair and said, "Viola," did a pirouette, and then a soft-shoe shuffle toward the door as though she was exiting the stage in a vaudeville act.

They left Ivor Court, crossed over to Park Street, and caught a bus to Marble Arch. From there it was a short walk to the stately apartment block on Park Lane. In the foyer, they were accosted by a formidable-looking doorman.

In responding to his "May I help you?" Bill replied, "I'm Lieutenant Weyland and this is Miss Carlton. Captain Eames invited us to a cocktail party in apartment 4C and I have forgotten the host's name. Would you mind calling up and announcing us?"

He looked hostilely at Bill, then turned to Mary, who returned his look with a charmingly disarming smile and said, "Please."

The man's face softened and lost its pretentiousness, "Yes, miss, I'll call up to Miss Lamond. Please wait here."

He motioned to a love seat in the lobby and walked over to the house phone.

Mary took Bill's arm and said quietly, "I know this woman. I met her some time ago. She's very beautiful. Please don't flirt with her."

He looked at Mary with mock surprise at her sudden show of vulnerability, "Don't be a silly girl. Of course I won't."

She replied with a hint of skepticism, "Well, you know how jealous I can get. So please don't play up to her and make me feel . . ." she stopped and added, "Sorry, I didn't mean . . ."

"Don't worry, I'm not going to do anything to hurt you. If you'd rather not go, that's okay with me."

The doorman returned, "Miss Lamond is expecting you. I'll take you up. Please follow me."

They crossed the lobby to the elevator and the doorman took them up to the fourth floor. He watched them as they walked down the spacious corridor to 4C.

The door opened and a smartly dressed maid welcomed them, "Come in, please. Let me take your hat, sir, and your gloves, mademoiselle. I'll tell Miss Lamond you're here."

While they waited, Bill thought he should reassure Mary that she had nothing to worry about. But when he looked at her, she had fully regained her composure and returned his look with one of confidence and self-assurance.

A tall and exceptionally attractive brunette walked up to them. She hardly glanced at Bill, but appeared pleasantly surprised to see Mary, "Darling, Miss Carlton, correct? How very nice to see you again."

She turned to Bill and said, "Leuitenant Weyland, hello. You're David's friend, right? Good of you to come."

Before Bill could respond, she took Mary's arm and led them into a large magnificently furnished reception room done in what Bill thought was a French provincial decor. They circled a group of about twenty people, several of whom she introduced. The maid offered them champagne, which Mary accepted, and then moved away with the host. Bill asked if he might have a whiskey and water. While he waited, Dave Eames came over.

"Hey, Bill, glad you could make it. Not many of our types here," he said as he looked around the room. "But it's a great party. What do you think of Arlene? Quite a gal, isn't she?" Before Bill could reply, Dave asked, "Where's Mary? I thought I saw you come in with her."

"She's with Miss Lamond. Oh, is that Arlene?" Dave nodded.

Bill said, "Yes, she is very attractive." Bill wouldn't call her beautiful, but she certainly was a strikingly handsome woman and had a magnificent body. "I think Mary has met her before."

Mary eventually joined them. She said hello to Dave and met his date, Helen, a pert, radiant, redheaded, Irish girl. A short time later, Miss Lamond came over to them and asked Bill if she could borrow Mary for a few minutes.

Bill didn't see much of Mary for the rest of the evening and spent most of the time talking to Eames and two RAF officers. The Britishers were from a Pathfinder wing stationed next to Bassingbourn. The four pilots immediately fell into a deep discussion over the merits of night versus daylight bombing. Bill admired RAF pilots, remembering how much he wanted to become one. The Pathfinders were a special breed. They would fly to the target area ahead of the RAF bomber stream, circle there, and advise the incoming bombers when to drop their bombs. It took a lot of guts to hang around the bombing objective. Bill, for one, couldn't get away quickly enough after bomb release. When offered, Bill accepted an invitation to fly with them on a night mission.

Eames said, "You'll have to wait until you finish your tour before you can, Bill."

"That's okay, I should finish in a couple of weeks."

"I hope so. But don't jinx yourself," replied Eames.

The minute Bill said it, he realized Eames was right. It was considered bad luck to make any specific plans before you finished your twenty-five missions. The words had just slipped out. Finally joining them, Mary caught the drift of the conversation and asked Bill, "You're not serious about flying with the RAF, are you?"

Fortunately, Helen and the RAF wives returned at that point to join them, so Bill did not have to reply.

The party began breaking up so he took Mary's arm and said, "Let's go." He shook hands with the RAF officers saying, "Look forward to seeing you all again."

They found their host, thanked her, and said good night. She shook Bill's hand, kissed Mary's cheek, and said, "Please phone me, Mary, and we'll have lunch. And don't forget what I told you, darling."

Outside on Park Lane, Bill asked, "What did she mean when she said not to forget what she told you?"

Mary replied, "I'll tell you later. Let's go to Armands in Knightsbridge and get a bite to eat. I'm starving. It's not that far. We can walk,"

Bill said, "I don't know what you were worried about. It seemed to me that the Lamond woman was more interested in you than me. In fact, I don't think she said more than a half dozen words to me the whole evening."

"Yes, I know. That was silly of me." And then as if to change the subject, "Let's cut across the park."

He talked about the people he met at the party, but Mary had little to say during their walk to the restaurant.

When they were seated at Armands and the waiter had opened a bottle of red wine and half filled their glasses, Mary took a sip and said, "All right, I'll tell you what Arlene Lamond had to say. But please don't get cross with me." She took another sip of wine and continued. "I met her over a year ago when I was going with Georges. It was at a party given by a Greek friend of his. She was, and I believe still is, General DeGaulle's mistress. He was in London at the time, but not with her that night. They were seldom seen in public together. As you know, he went to North Africa to join the Free French in January after the American invasion. She was very friendly that night, and we talked to some extent . . . nothing that I remember of any importance, mainly just gossip.

"Several weeks later, Georges and I were invited to her apartment for dinner. From the photos in her home, it was apparent she and the general were more than just good friends. Again, she was very amiable and for some reason seemed to take a special interest in my well-being, discreetly delving into my background. She was rather effusive and quite gregarious. Frankly, I was flattered that she liked me. She's a glamorous and elegant woman. That was about it and I had completely forgotten about her until tonight."

Mary stopped while the waiter set down two plates of steaming cannelloni. He refilled their glasses, smiled when Mary thanked him, and left their table. After several generous mouthfuls of the stuffed crepes, Mary continued, "Tonight, she was gracious and friendly as she had been before. She led me into her bedroom and invited me to sit down beside her at her desk. She said she'd heard that I had left Georges, and she wanted to know who you were and if I was serious about you. I told her I was very serious and very much in love with you. And when she asked me, I told her as far as I knew you weren't rich. She then said that I was a foolish girl. I was surprised at that and said, 'I'm sorry, I don't understand what you mean.' She ignored my question and ask me pointedly, 'Why did you leave Georges Lavanas? He was an exceptionally fine man from a very wealthy and prominent Greek family. He obviously adored you. He would've taken good care of you and you'd never had to worry about anything . . . ever.'

"I must have appeared angry, but before I could answer her, she raised her hand, stopped me, and said, 'Please, darling don't be angry. I'm very fond of you and I'd like to help you.' She reached into her desk and pulled out a large folder and continued by saying, 'Here, let me show you something.' She took out several documents. I didn't know what they were, but they looked important. She told me about the arrangement she had with the general and went on to say that it was important to have an understanding with a man that you were involved with-a secure financial agreement that'll take care of you for the rest of your life. A flat, clothes, and jewelry were all very fine and every woman needs beautiful things, but it's more important to have investments and securities that will guarantee a secure and comfortable future. She told me about her investments, which I didn't understand. Then she went on to say that I should seriously consider my future and not let my heart blind me to the realities of life. She said..." Mary stopped suddenly and looked at Bill for his reaction.

He was silent for some time, then looked up at her and said, "Well, that was quite an evening you had. For someone you met only twice, she seemed to take a personal interest in your welfare. It was sound advice, and I can't find fault with any of it, except that she forgot to mention marriage. That's a pretty long-lasting and secure arrangement."

"I know. And that's why I would never take her advice. I really can't tell you why she singled me out as a person who needed such advice."

"Well, I'm sure she felt you were wrong to break off the relationship you had with Lavanas. Perhaps one day you'll regret it."

"Oh, Bill, how can you say such a thing? I love you and I want to be with you as long as you'll have me. I want nothing more. Please let's talk about something else. I've had enough advice for one evening."

After a subdued and quiet dinner, they left the restaurant and took a taxi back to Ivor Court. Their somber moods continued even after they got in bed. But once Bill felt the warm closeness of her body, he became aroused and quickly forgot about any differences they had.

Mary wasn't ready to make love after their unsettling discussion. She just wouldn't cooperate. She was lying on her back holding her nightgown down with her arms at her sides. Bill wasn't sure whether she was serious or faking it. He persisted and finally pushed her gown up, but she held it down to cover her face. When he tried to kiss her through the thin gown, she turned her face away. He moved down to her neck and shoulders kissing her incessantly. She cupped her hands over her breasts, but he removed one without too much resistance and kissed her tenderly. He lingered there kissing each breast. She trembled with excitement when his tongue touched her, but she held her legs tightly together and moved her hands down to cover herself.

He loved to make love to her while she played the reluctant partner. He moved his lips down to her stomach and when she removed her hands and spread her legs slightly he knelt between them and moved his mouth down to the junction of her thighs. After hesitating there he continued to move down her limbs kissing the soft smooth flesh of her inner thighs. Her body tingled with expectancy until his tongue found the place where she loved to be touched. He lingered there teasingly until she pleaded with him to enter her. When he joined with her, their mating left them ecstatically satisfied, and then, locked in each other's arms, they slept contentedly.

Bill was an unselfish lover. If it took Mary longer to reach an orgasm, he made sure she came before he did or that they came together. Foreplay was an essential part of their sexual compatibility and he enjoyed his role as a lover who shared and gave her as much pleasure as he received. To him, the most satisfying and joyful time during their lovemaking was the moment Mary climaxed. The thrill and satisfaction he received was beyond any experience he'd ever had.

Mary's body fascinated him. It was a beautiful magnificently proportioned body and one that exuded sexuality. All his senses were attuned to her. He enjoyed watching her sleep in the semidarkness of her room, lying there uncovered and unclothed. Her breathing, sighs, and sounds of passion murmured in response to their lovemaking thrilled and excited him. He loved the velvety feel of her smooth flawless skin and the clean fresh smell of her body with the rarest hint of her fragrance, Je Revien, that seemed to surround but never touch her. Most of all, he loved the moist natural perfumed taste of her.

Mary woke a short time later and now she became the aggressor, wanting to revive her passion while Bill seemed content to sleep. She was a paradox of virtues: one moment modest and demure, the next wildly amorous and wanton. She reached around and held him, slowly massaging his member back to life. When he rolled over on his back, she moved over and straddled his chest. Kneeling over him, she lowered first one breast then the other to his mouth. When satisfied that he was fully awake and ready to receive her, she moved down and mounted him. Mary sat upright, arching her back and forcing him deep inside her, momentarily holding him down and motionless, wanting him to feel that he'd become an inseparable part of her. After releasing him, she moved slowly at first, relishing the power and joy of being in control and giving him the ultimate pleasure. His hardness, coupled with her mounting passion, compelled her to move faster. He found it impossible to lie back passively while she forced herself down onto him. He reached up, held her, and moved with her in a frenzied rhythm until both, drenched in perspiration, climaxed. They remained immobile, holding each other tightly, their groins and mouths locked firmly together. After the erotic spasms of their orgasmic coupling receded, a sudden feeling of despair and loneliness seized her and she held him tightly until the sensation passed.

Mary finally released Bill when she felt his grip slacken and carefully moved off of him realizing that he was completely exhausted. He turned onto his side and brought his legs up in a fetal position. She listened as his breathing deepened, certain that the fear, anxiety, and tension of the past week had finally left him and he'd rest peacefully. Mary snuggled up against his back, wrapped her arms around him and held him close, so full of love and happiness, she was too excited to sleep.

Mary thought about her conversation with Arlene Lamond and wondered how anyone could possibly think about financial security in exchange for love. Ironically, thoughts of her affair with Georges entered her mind and she wondered if she had stayed with him, would she have become like Arlene? Mary couldn't believe that she could ever be so materialistic and insensitive. Georges was obviously wealthy, but he never disclosed how much money he had and it never occurred to her to ask. It was not unusual to overhear his colleagues boasting about the money they were making. But Georges never joined in those discussions and became uncomfortable when his friends brought up the subject of money. He seemed more concerned about the lives of the men sailing in his ship. During that time, the German submarines were taking a heavy toll on Allied shipping.

Georges rarely talked about his family in Greece, but it was obvious that he was well-bred. He was a patient and decent man. Most notable to Mary was the considerate way he treated the people who worked for him.

Mary never asked Georges for money and when her meager savings ran out, spending money would mysteriously appear in her purse. He was generous and received enormous pleasure in giving her expensive gifts. It was difficult for her, a young girl of nineteen who loved beautiful things, to refuse him. But despite her aversion to accepting money from him, she enjoyed the comfortable lifestyle he provided. She had no worries, anxieties, or fears. Life couldn't have been better.

Mary's social life with Georges was limited to his circle of friends, most of whom, although married, were living in London with their English mistresses. The women generally accepted the fact that the men would leave them and return to their families in Greece when the war ended. They knew, however, that when the men left, their mistresses would receive a generous financial settlement that would provide a comfortable living for the rest of their lives.

Georges was the first man in Mary's life and she was very much in love with him. He loved her and cared for her in a way that no other person had. She was lavishly supported. For her part, she returned his generosity with affection, gratitude, and adoration. However, as their affair matured and there was no mention of marriage, Mary came to realize that Georges, like the others, would eventually leave her. Although she loved him and wanted to stay with him, she knew in her heart it wasn't the kind of relationship she was seeking.

During the war, this was particularly true during the Blitz, people didn't think a great deal about the future. They lived for the present and each day grasped every bit of fulfillment they could. Initially, living with Georges was wonderfully romantic. They dined out most evenings, danced at their favorite nightspots, and gambled at the casinos or the races. Aside from Mary's part-time work as a Red Cross volunteer, there was little for her to do when Georges was working. For the most part, her leisure time and lack of purpose became boring and pointless. She began to develop a sense of guilt and a loss of self-esteem, realizing she was idling her life away. She even began to question the feelings, attraction, and infatuation she had for Georges. At times, her frustration caused an occasional argument and she became difficult, taking her anger out on Georges. However, he was forgiving and understanding and rarely displayed annoyance when she had one of her temper tantrums.

One night while they were dancing at Coconut Grove, Mary left Georges on the dance floor over some insignificant disagreement. She walked out of the club and went back to their apartment. When she arrived, she discovered that she had no key and had to wait for him in the lobby. He arrived about thirty minutes later and, for the first time, she sensed an anger in him she'd never seen before. Although he was restrained, she knew he was upset. He quietly told her that she must never leave him like that again. Mary realized it was a foolish and childish thing to do and apologized. He was a proud man and she had embarrassed him in the presence of his friends. Later that evening, he suggested that it would be better if she had her own flat where she could come and go as she pleased. It was their first real quarrel, but it ultimately led to their breakup.

Together, they found and furnished an attractive flat for Mary on Queensway, a short distance from his apartment. Georges told her she was free to live there as long as she wanted without any obligation or commitment to him. Initially, she welcomed the privacy and freedom of her new flat, but soon realized it was wrong and spent a great deal of time agonizing over their relationship.

While living with Georges, she didn't consider their relationship immoral or improper and never considered herself his mistress. She loved him and they lived together. It was that simple. However, living separately from him was quite different. Mary soon realized she was now a kept woman. The reality consumed her and more than ever she was determined to leave him, even though it meant returning to a lonely, dismal, and austere life.

Her love for him made her decision all the more difficult. And although he wouldn't marry her, she knew he loved her. Her leaving would hurt him deeply. However, in the end, her strength of character prevailed and she left him.

It was a difficult time for her. She found a small flat off Bayswater Road and managed to get by with her small savings and the money she received from pawning some of her jewelry. Mary realized she had to find a job and support herself. Going back to work at The Cabaret was out of the question. The club's atmosphere and the nighttime work no longer appealed to her.

Mary remembered a man she'd met at The Cabaret. He was in the clothing business and he'd told her if she ever wanted a job modeling he would help her. His name was Benny Newman. He was a short plump Jewish man. He'd always treated her respectfully and never made any indiscreet or overt advances toward her. She decided to ask him to help her find a job.

They met for dinner and Newman agreed to help Mary. However, he thought it might take a little time to find her a good position. In the meantime, he suggested that she move in with him so he could take care of her. Now that Mary was older and more experienced, she realized his intentions toward her were more carnal than paternal. She told him tactfully that she wasn't ready to become involved in another relationship. She only wanted to get a job and live on her own for awhile. He was disappointed, but he was a gentleman and accepted her decision. The following day, Newman called to tell Mary he had made an appointment for her with Mr. Chalmers. Her starting salary was only five guineas a week and for the first several months it was difficult getting by.

As a child actress, Mary made a considerable amount of money. By English law, her mother was required to put her daughter's earnings in a trust to be held for her until she reached age twenty-one. When Mary came of age in October 1942, she asked her mother for the money. Her mother refused, saying the amount of money was barely enough to compensate for the expenses she had incurred raising and supporting

Mary. As distasteful as it was, Mary threatened legal action if her mother did not give her the money she was entitled to. Fearful of being brought to court, Mary's mother finally conceded and gave her daughter a sum of money that was far less than she had earned. It was enough, however, for Mary to buy the lease and furnish her flat at Ivor Court. Mary put the little remaining money in a post-office account to supplement her wages from Mr. Chalmers.

Mary realized that being a mistress to a rich man would have been easy if she had been willing to sacrifice her principles and dreams. Thank God she had the determination and willpower to keep her hopes alive. She met Bill, they loved each other, and one day he'd fulfill her lifelong dream of marriage and family.

Chapter 22

Bill returned to Bassingbourn Sunday evening. The mission to Villa Coublay was canceled on Tuesday and that afternoon he signed out for a seven-day leave. Joe and Woody were not too upset when Bill told them he planned to stay in London.

Woody said, "Hell, I don't blame you. I'm sure you'll have a very restful and relaxing time in London. Give Mary my regards."

"I'm sorry I'm not going down with you guys. I just want to spend the time with Mary." A week away from her would be a complete waste of time. But being with her for a whole week would be the closest thing to complete fulfillment.

Mary was excited about their week together. Bill had just been paid, so they planned to enjoy London in grand style. The first night they had a fine dinner at Scott's and went on to the Embassy Club where they left after one dance, both desperately anxious to get back to Mary's flat and into bed. The second night was no different. After a light supper in the intimate surroundings of The Deanery, a small club behind the Dorchester, they were home before eight and passionately entangled in bed. They gave up after that and resigned to stay home and make love at their leisure. Dorothy came to their aid and gave Mary the most precious gift imaginable-food stamps. Mary greedily accepted them and miraculously found two filets of sole, two thick lamb chops and a small chicken. By using Bill's liquor ration at Mary's wine merchant, they were able to dine in luxury for three nights. As much as Mary enjoyed people, being alone with Bill was blissfully appealing. They seemed to know intuitively that it was important to spend every possible minute together. Her flat became their haven, an intimate place to be alone, and where, at the slightest inclination, they could make love until they were exhausted. Although they made love passionately and tenderly, there was a feeling of intensity and anxiety that caused them to silently hold each other long after climaxing.

Bill had always been an early riser and the many early morning briefings at Bassingbourn made it habitual. He found it difficult to sleep beyond five A.M. Instead of lying next to Mary, awake and wanting her, he'd get out of bed, slip quietly out of her flat, cross over to Regents Park, and walk the many winding paths around Boating Lake. He enjoyed the early morning mist and the stillness of the park just before sunup. He would return from his walk after about forty minutes and quietly bathe and shave before waking Mary with a steaming cup of tea. After sipping her tea, she would set the cup down, throw off the covers, stretch out her arms, and say, "I want you to bring tea to me every morning and then make love to me. Oh, I love you so much. Hold me, darling."

Her beautiful exposed breasts and inviting gesture always brought a prompt tightness in his groin and he would quickly shed his shorts, get into bed, and wrap his arms around her warm, desirable body. Making love to Mary in the morning was, to him, the ultimate pleasure. She smelled clean and fresh and during their lovemaking, she purred like a kitten.

After making love, there was a great rush to get Mary bathed, dressed, and off to work. Fortunately, Mr. Chalmers proved to be a fine gentleman who forgave her late morning arrivals, long lunches, and early departures. In fact, he was quite generous. During the week, he took Mary and Bill to lunch twice, paid the bill, and left them together in their own world.

On Thursday, Mary's char, Mrs. Beasley, came to tidy up her flat. She was a stout, cheerful woman who, along with many others, adored Mary. This morning, she arrived after Mary left for work and before Bill went out. She insisted that Bill join her for a "cup of," which she made before starting her chores. Bill sat and chatted with her, enjoying her cockney accent and sense of humor.

"We were bombed out of our 'ome just before Christmas 1940 by the bloody Hun. Me daughter, Alice, and I 'ave been living with me sister, Abby, in Southwark since then. It's a bit snug, but we manage quite well. Better off than most. 'arry been with Monty in North Africa for eighteen months. I 'eard they're in Sicily now, ready to 'op over to Italy. Been a long time.

I pray for him every night," she told Bill.

"I certainly admire your attitude and spirit, Mrs. Beasley. I just wonder how we Americans back home would stand up to the horrors of war like you all have here in England," Bill responded.

"I'm sure you Yanks would 'andle it as well as we 'ave," she replied.

When the tea was finished she rinsed off the cups and saucers and put them back in Mary's cupboard. "Best get on with it. I've two more flats to do. Tell Mary I dropped her linen off at the laundry," she said, as she began to remake the bed.

Like most Londoners of her class, she accepted the shortages and hardships of the war with a spirited determination. Her attitude made Bill feel humble and fortunate to be among the courageous people of England.

While Mary was at work, Bill wandered around London. He fell in love with the city and its people. To him, it was the most fascinating city in the world. The English people were the most courteous, pleasant, and pluckiest he had ever encountered. They represented all the strength, courage, and determination of their great leader, Winston Churchill. Rarely did Bill enter a pub without a friendly greeting like, " 'Ere, 'ave one with me," or "Good show, Yank, give Jerry the what for."

Mary taught Bill how to get around by bus and on the Underground. As much as he enjoyed talking to the cockney cab drivers, he loved riding atop the buses and got accustomed to the long queues at the bus stops. Most of all, he relished being with Mary and listening to her talk about the city she loved. They might be headed in one direction when she'd suddenly stop, grab his arm, turn him around, and say, "There's a number 73 bus, let's catch it to Harrods." And off she'd run to catch the bus that was pulling away from the curb, twenty yards away.

Mary's breeding and self-assurance with people was natural and spontaneous. Whether they were humble or illustrious, she treated them all with the same easy friendliness. Mrs. Beasley, who idolized Mary and refused any compensation for the many additional chores she performed, was typical of the generosity of Mary's friends. Her kindness and courtesy toward older people was sincere and unpretentious. Bill watched with admiration when she stood aside to help an elderly woman board a bus or get up and let an elderly man have her seat on the bus.

Her manners were impeccable. "Thank you" and "please" were the most frequently used words in her vocabulary. However difficult and uncaring her mother was, she couldn't be faulted for Mary's upbringing. Her personality was contagious and seemed to bring the best and warmest response from everyone they met. She never hesitated to ask favors and rarely took "no" for an answer. She was frank, outspoken, and often appeared tactless in preference to being hypocritical. However, there were some of the female gender who found her charm, openness, and comeliness difficult to match and this generally erupted in jealousy.

Mary had a marvelous sense of humor and loved good jokes, particularly those on the racy side. She could be risqué, but never vulgar and was completely turned off by crude or obscene remarks. She did, however, enjoy shocking people, particularly Americans, with such expressions as "keep your pecker up," a common English phrase that refers to one's spirit.

BOMBER PILOT

Bill took advantage of Regents Park's lush grass and aesthetic shrubs, trees, and flowers while Mary was at work. The war seemed far away from where he sat feeding the numerous species of ducks and geese. The weather in August could be marvelous, but not always. He'd start out in the morning on a clear, sunny day and by lunchtime he could be shivering in the shelter of a tree from the cold rain. He no longer found it amusing when he saw an Englishman carrying an umbrella on a sunny day.

Just down the road from Mary's flat was Lords Cricket Grounds in St. John's Woods. One day, Bill walked there, sat in a sparsely occupied viewing stand, drank tea, and tried desperately to understand what was going on. The small group of spectators would suddenly break out in cheers that he couldn't relate to the action on the field. Although it seemed quite tame and monotonous, he enjoyed sitting and watching the fans as well as the players.

The bombing of London had all but stopped by day and only occasionally occurred at night. A few daring bombers might appear, which would cause many to flee to shelters. Mary and Bill would sit or lie in her darkened flat, listening to the sirens and the antiaircraft guns and sometimes hear and feel the vibration from the bomb blasts. Bill was amazed at the number of people still living in the Underground shelters. Some had lost their homes and others wouldn't feel safe living anywhere else.

While alone in London and away from combat, Bill often thought of his family, particularly of his mother, and he would become homesick. He knew they worried about him, even though he tried to dispel their fears in his letters. The American bombing effort at that time had captured newspaper headlines. Even though an attempt was made to minimize the losses, it was difficult to conceal the truth and the controversy over daylight bombing.

Bill told his mother about Mary and she seemed to be happy that he found someone she considered more suitable than Clare. He felt sure that word had reached Clare through his letters to his family, although Clare never mentioned it in her letters. Bill told his mother that at last he had found someone who could cook almost as well as she could. He promised to go home when he finished his tour, but told her he wanted to come back to England.

During the week, Mary had accepted an invitation to Sunday lunch at Carlotta Oppenheimer's home in Buckinghamshire. Mary told Bill she accepted the invitation because she knew he'd enjoy going and meeting this unusual and gracious lady.

Mary first met Carlotta Oppenheimer while dating Major Ernest Lee. Carlotta had invited four members of General Eisenhower's staff to Sunday dinner and Major Lee asked Mary to accompany him. Since then, Mary had been to her home in Gerrards Cross and when Carlotta was in London they occasionally got together for lunch or tea.

Carlotta's late husband was the founder and owner of the Oppenheimer diamond mines in South Africa, reputed to be the largest in the world. Carlotta's sons were now managing the mines while their mother devoted her time to the war effort. Shortly after the war started, Mrs. Oppenheimer began a custom of inviting members of the military to her home for Sunday afternoon dinner. She'd entertained thousands and had a guest list that included an assortment of nationalities and ranks, from privates to generals.

At exactly eleven o'clock, Mary's buzzer sounded and they went out to the foyer to meet Carlotta's chauffeur. He was dressed in a brown uniform and black puttees. He stepped forward, cap in hand. "Good morning, Miss Carlton, leuitenant, sir. Are you ready?" he said, as he held the rear car door open.

After acknowledging his greeting and introducing Bill, Mary stepped in the car. Bill stood admiring the gleaming bronze Rolls-Royce, "Boy, what a beauty!" he exclaimed.

The chauffeur smiled and replied, "Yes, sir. She is that."

"What model Rolls . . . Rolls-Royce is it? Looks brand new. England can't still be manufacturing automobiles?"

"No, sir. This is a Phantom III. The car is five years old and has been driven 42,000 miles."

"Well, she certainly looks new to me. Looks like you take good care of her."

"Thank you. Mrs. Oppenheimer also has a 1927 Phantom I, an open touring car, and it still looks like the day it was delivered. The madam routinely inspects her cars-checks under the bonnet and gets down in the pit to look underneath. Won't stand for a spot of oil or grease. Very strict about her cars, she is."

"It's a magnificent auto and I'm sure you're mighty proud of the way she looks," Bill responded as he followed Mary into the back seat. The interior was so spacious he could almost stand up. It was beautifully finished in glossy walnut, cream-colored leather, beige silk and deep plush carpeting. It was the ultimate in comfort and luxury. They slithered down in the soft cool seat, looked at each other, and grinned. The car started, the engine barely audible in the rear, and silently slipped away from the curb.

The day was overcast, the sky slate colored and dismal, but it didn't detract from the wonderful feeling of grandeur that surrounded them. Bill sat up straight, while Mary rested her head on his shoulder and wrapped her arms tightly around his.

They drove out through Paddington and North Kensington and on to Westway. After leaving the built-up area of London, they passed RAF Station Northolt, an airfield familiar to Bill. Then on through the quaint and picturesque village of Denham, where Mary did film work in the Arthur Rank Studios. Bill had never seen this part of the London suburbs and was completely enraptured. It was quite different from the region he was familiar with when coming into London from the north. It was more like the England he envisioned. When Bill asked about a partially damaged church, the chauffeur responded enthusiastically and from then on carried on a running commentary, describing points of interest along their route. Bill unintentionally pulled away from Mary and leaned forward for a better view and to hear the chauffeur.

A strange sensation of hurt and envy clouded Mary's thoughts when he moved away from her. She had felt so good and secure and didn't want to share Bill with anyone. The loneliness that she had known so many times flooded back through her. She wondered why such unpleasant thoughts often gripped her when she should be happy. She forced the gloom away and told herself she was silly-Bill loved her and would never leave her.

Gerrards Cross was truly a delightful and quaint English village with small individual shops set along the high street.

Bill said, "We've got to come out here, Mary, and spend some time wandering around. It's perfect. Just the way I've always imagined an English village. I bet we could find a small, cozy inn. Wouldn't it be great? Look at that little tearoom. It reminds me of the one we went to back in April. Remember? My introduction to afternoon tea."

"Yes, I remember. I'd love to come here and we will. I'll find a place where we can stay." Mary stopped and then went on, "There are so many wonderful things we can do together. When you finish your missions, I promise I'll take time off and we'll go any place you like."

He smiled at her. "Okay, Mary. You've got yourself a date."

They drove through the village and out along a narrow road lined with hedgerows on both sides. Bill became a little apprehensive at the speed of the car. The road didn't seem wide enough for two cars to pass and hedges hid anything that might be approaching around the many blind curves. To make matters worse, they were driving on the wrong side of the road. Mary didn't seem a bit concerned, but Bill, not easily frightened, was worried.

As they turned through two stone pillars and onto a tree-lined drive, Bill noticed the brass name plate, Lantern Cottage, on the open wrought-iron gates. They stopped on the circular drive in front of a large, two-story, red-brick, gabled mansion with numerous dormers and chimneys spread over a considerable area.

The front door of the house opened and they were greeted by a middle-aged bald-headed man dressed in dark trousers, a striped vest, white shirt, and black tie. He approached them and said, "Miss Carlton, how good to see you. It's been some time."

Mary replied, "Thank you, Charles. It's good to see you. This is

BOMBER PILOT

Lieutenant Weyland."

"Welcome to Lantern Cottage, leuitenant. Come in, please."

He stepped aside and Mary led Bill into an entryway of black-and-white marble. She turned left into a reception room where they were met by a tall, slender, and exceptionally handsome woman. Bill's first impression of this elegant lady perfectly fit his image of what a grand dame would look like. Her gray hair was bobbed short and set in tight waves, flapper style. Her bright red lipstick and a touch of rouge on each cheek accentuated her stark white powdered face. She wore an ankle-length, loose-fitted, floral chiffon dress, complete with a long string of large pearls. Everything about her was reminiscent of the twenties.

She put an arm around Mary. "My dear, how good of you to come. And this must be Bill. Hello and welcome." She released Mary and took Bill's hand in both of hers.

"Yes, this is Bill, Carlotta. Bill, Carlotta Oppenheimer."

"It's a pleasure to meet you, Mrs. Oppenheimer, and thanks for inviting us. I thoroughly enjoyed the drive out in your magnificent car and your chauffeur's knowledge of the area made the trip very interesting. It's beautiful and just the way I pictured England."

"Yes, it is lovely, particularly this time of year. Please call me Carlotta, and I shall call you Bill. Mary has told me so much about you I feel that I know you quite well."

A maid arrived at Mrs. Oppenheimer's side, and was told to bring a glass of wine and a whiskey and water.

She let them into the room, where they met an elderly and distinguished-looking gentleman, probably in his early seventies, with gray hair and mustache, obviously in good health, tall, and immaculately dressed. They were then introduced to a British brigadier and a colonel and their wives and two American colonels. When their drinks arrived, Bill eagerly accepted his as he was not as self-confident as Mary was in such a group. The warm scotch was most welcome.

The two Americans immediately surrounded Mary, separating her from Bill. When he looked at her pleadingly, she smiled and returned his look as if to say, "Sorry, old bean, but can I help it if I'm so much in demand." The elderly man walked to Bill, took his arm, and led him off to a bow window that overlooked the magnificent gardens. His name was Alexander Moulton. He was a member of Parliament who lived near Carlotta.

"What a pleasant surprise and a marvelous opportunity for me to meet and talk to a young American flyer," he said to Bill. "I'm very interested in your daylight bombing endeavor. In fact, we were discussing it the other day in the House. So please don't be offended if I pry a bit."

From that point on, Bill was monopolized by the Englishman, but he thoroughly enjoyed their discussion.

After Bill's second scotch, he became completely at ease and comfortable as he chatted with his new friend. Diana Fairmount, wife of the brigadier, joined them and fell easily into their discussion. She was quite attractive, but very English-precise and direct-and although she was somewhat superior, Bill thought she was very charming. She made several interesting and intelligent observations about England's most popular topic, the war with Germany.

She remarked, "At the rate our chaps are moving toward Messina it shouldn't be long before Sicily falls. But you must admit the Germans have put up a remarkable resistance there."

The Allied armies from North Africa had landed on Sicily on July 10, the British Eighth Army on east coast and the American Seventh Army on the south. The Allied armies met five days later and were moving toward their final assault on Messina in preparation for the invasion of Italy. Mussolini had been deposed and his military forces were shattered and on the verge of capitulation. However, the German forces were putting up a stiff resistance. They had successfully withdrawn most of their troops to Italy where they were prepared to defend the country fiercely.

Just before two o'clock, Carlotta led her guests into a spacious dining room. Mary was seated between the brigadier and one of the American colonels while Bill sat between the two Englishwomen. When they were seated and the wine poured, Mr. Moulton looked at his hostess and said, "Carlotta, may I?"

She responded, "Why, of course, Alex dear. Please do."

He stood, raised his glass, and said, "I would like to toast all the brave young American airmen and our own gallant lads in the RAF who fly courageously over Germany by day and night to bring the war home to Hitler, Goering, and their lot. I salute you. God bless you and protect you." He looked directly at Bill and raised his glass.

The guests followed suit. Bill reached for his glass, stopped halfway, and looked, embarrassed, at Mary. She held her glass out to him in a toast and smiled. The tension Bill felt broke when the brigadier said, "Here, here." Then everyone began talking.

Bill had never before seen a dinner table so superbly set. The china, crystal, and silverware sparkled on a heavily starched white table linen. He looked at the cutlery in front of him and wondered how he could possibly use all of it. It brought to mind what his mother once said, "When in doubt, always start from the outside and work in." That was fine advice, but what about the silver utensils above his plate? He'd follow Mary's lead.

After two strong whiskeys and two glasses of wine, Bill was completely relaxed and talked eagerly with his two charming dinner companions, while across the table, Mary chatted easily and enthusiastically with her two dinner partners. Bill occasionally caught parts of their conversation and heard her say, "Well, I certainly don't agree with that," or "In my opinion, we should have..." She was completely at ease and could hold her own with anyone regardless of their intellect or station.

It was an excellent dinner: soup, fish, salad, dessert, and cheese supplementing a delicious leg of lamb. Bill thoroughly enjoyed the food and the interesting conversation, wondering why he had initially felt so unsure in the presence of such pleasant people.

After coffee in the drawing room, Mrs. Oppenheimer led her guests on a tour of the house and gardens. Her home was filled with priceless artifacts, paintings, and antiques. The gardens were spectacular. There were eight of them symmetrically divided into thirty square meters, each enclosed in a solid twelve-foot-high brick wall. Mrs. Oppenheimer told Bill that before the war each garden contained a specific species of flower. Now only the rose garden remained intact, and it was magnificent. The others had been turned into vegetable gardens in support of the war effort.

The group was led by Carlotta, who used her silver knobbed cane as a pointer to identify the variety of fruit trees in the well-cared-for orchard. The earlier overcast turned to broken clouds on numerous occasions revealing an elusive sun. The tour ended on a patio off the solarium where talk continued until teatime. When tea was served, Bill was surprised to find himself eating several delicious pastries.

Shortly after six, the party broke up and Mary and Bill were placed once again in the capable and congenial care of Carlotta's chauffeur, who returned them to Ivor Court. There, they thanked him graciously and bid him goodnight.

The week slipped by so quickly it was almost impossible to believe he had to return to Bassingbourn on Tuesday. They went to Quo Vadis in Soho Monday night for dinner and then to the Astor. But there Bill became moody and despondent when he thought about Dopey, Norm, and others who were no longer around. On base, he spent most of his time with his crew. Because of the unusually high turnover rate, he wasn't too enthusiastic about making new friends among the officers in his squadron. His crew provided all the companionship he needed. He'd either finish with his crew or they'd all go down together. He'd completed twenty missions and was eager to get back to the base and get on with it. When away from the base, he had no time for anyone but Mary, so in a short time, the loss of his friends and his affair with Mary had changed his relationships and social activities considerably.

When Mary sensed Bill's mood they left the club and went back to her flat, where she quickly cleared his mind of all thoughts but those of warm affection and heated passion

Chapter 23

When Weyland got back to Bassingbourn on Tuesday, there was much talk about a mission to Schweinfurt, Germany, that was scheduled to go that day but had been scrubbed. He was told that the mission was to be flown by the largest number of B-17s ever assembled and strike targets deep in Germany. Bill hadn't missed the big one. He knew the raid would be rescheduled. Nothing was scheduled for Wednesday but that night they were alerted for a mission on Thursday.

The evening before a raid Bill usually cycled out to the hardstand, talked to Joe Blaylock for half an hour or so, and left when he was satisfied his plane was ready to go. That routine came to an end after his sixteenth mission when he became a flight leader. The Eager Beaver was configured with two fifty-caliber machine guns in the nose, which meant a bombsight couldn't be mounted on the pedestal. Weyland could've requested a modification and had their plane converted, but after discussing it with his crew, he decided to fly a plane that had a bombsight installed. As a result, he didn't normally know his aircraft assignment until the morning briefing. The Eager Beaver had been a fine aircraft. Weyland and his crew had flown sixteen accredited sorties in her without an abort, and that was somewhat of a record for a B-17.

He did have some misgivings about changing planes. But his fatalistic attitude overcame any superstition he might have about using any Seventeen assigned to his crew.

He did, however, continue to visit his enlisted crew the night before a planned sortie. He usually found them at the armament shop cleaning and checking their guns and the linkage in the ammunition belts. Ever since their first mission together not one gun had malfunctioned. That could've been a hard, if not deadly, lesson to learn, but it was a lasting one for his crew. The guns had to be absolutely clean and dry. At high altitudes, the least bit of moisture or grease would cause the guns to freeze and jam. A small burr on the ammo belt could also cause a stoppage.

Bill usually took a lot of verbal joshing from his enlisted crew members. He felt that this was their way of showing their respect for him. They made him the target of their jokes, and they had a bagful. He looked forward to these meetings, and as hard as he tried to out-gun them, he never could. Regardless of what preplanned witticism he came up with about any member of his crew, they always managed to trump him. They were at their best the night before a raid.

Next, he would stop by to see Joe and Woody. They were usually together in Joe's room, as though they expected him to stop by and talk. In most cases, no one knew where the target for the next day would be, but they'd sit and speculate, helping each other to ease the jitters. Woody, the pessimist, was always vocal about their next mission.

"It's going to be a rough one tomorrow. Believe me," Woody would say. "Hey, man, I'm scared to death of those fighters and that flak."

Woody was the type of guy who would openly admit that combat scared the hell out of him. After the first few missions with him, his actions seemed to contradict his words. He was probably less afraid than any member of the crew. Unlike most men, he overcame his fear by speaking openly about it, but never voiced any unwillingness or hesitation to fly. Once the action started, Woody was a fighting terror. It was a kind of bravado in reverse. Where most air crew members would cover their true feelings with boast and bluster, Woody did the opposite.

BOMBER PILOT

On the other hand, Joe showed little emotion. He quietly went about his job and did it exceptionally well. Woody told Bill after the second mission that he noticed Joe wouldn't fire the fifty-caliber machine gun assigned to him in the nose compartment. When Woody asked Joe why, he replied that it was against his principles to try to kill anyone.

When Bill asked Woody about losing the gun and its firepower, Woody responded, "I like nothing better than having both guns to myself. We'll take care of the front of the plane for you, Bill, so don't worry."

And they did. Woody had two confirmed kills to his credit. Joe simply didn't like war and wanted no part of the killing, but that didn't prevent him from doing his job. He took the one position in the crew where he could make his contribution without violating his principles. Bill had a great deal of admiration for his crew, but he probably respected Joe the most.

After leaving Joe and Woody, Bill might stop by the copilot's house next to his quarters. He'd usually find the copilots gathered in one room and they always seemed to be in a lively discussion about their pilot's flying ability. The conversation would change on Bill's arrival, but from what he heard, some of it was not too flattering to some of the pilots in the squadron. It amazed Bill. If they didn't like or respect their pilot, why the hell did they fly with him? Then again, there was not much they could do about it. Some, however, managed to move up to become aircraft commanders. They were a peculiar lot, but Bill admired them. Someone had to do the job and as far as he was concerned, being a copilot was the worst position in the crew.

He'd find Louis among them and wonder what Bianchi had to say about him. Inasmuch as most of them had flown with Weyland, he reckoned they all had an opportunity to voice their opinion of his flying ability. He felt that Louis was the loyal type. Bianchi was a shy lad and it was hard to reach him, as much as Bill tried to draw him out. The army missed its mark on him. He should've been put in fighters. But he was eager and the crew liked him. Bill had a feeling that Bianchi, as small as he was, could probably handle any situation if the need arose.

Bill's preflight ritual continued even though most planned missions were scrubbed. He believed it served a purpose and, regardless of the few concessions he had made, he wasn't going to stop for fear of jinxing himself and his crew.

He'd finish the day back in his room, setting out his clothes and shoes, toes always pointing outward. Doing everything the same way gave him a strong feeling of equanimity and optimism. Was it being superstitious? Probably, and if so, what the hell. If it had been a charm so far, why change? He'd then fall asleep almost immediately, thinking not of the mission tomorrow but of Mary. He never had any problem sleeping. In fact, one day he fell asleep on a mission over France. There was no activity, so Weyland let a classmate fly the plane. Bill dozed off and was awakened suddenly when two ME-109s sped out of the sun and through the formation.

To Bill, sleep was a precious commodity to be used sparingly and only when necessary. When he indulged, he made the most of it. The mental and physical fatigue after a mission was so complete and satisfying that sleep came quickly. That feeling of being so completely alive provided the perfect antidote against any nightmares about combat. And as far as he could tell, his crew had no sleeping problems either.

The best sleep of all, however, came from his love for Mary. She was an active and demanding sex partner. After strenuous lovemaking, he would fall into a deep languid sleep from a most sensual and deliciously sated exhaustion. He slept so soundly that he woke one night to find Mary astride him.

He admittedly lacked willpower when it came to Mary and grabbed every opportunity to be with her. The lack of discipline in the group gave him the freedom to come and go as he pleased. As long as he was available to fly, no one placed any restrictions on him. However, his responsibility as a combat pilot came first. He never let his affair with Mary interfere. He never missed a combat mission or let his affair affect his ability to perform his duties.

BOMBER PILOT

On Thursday, the Forts went to Gelsenkirchen, another deep penetration into the Ruhr valley and one that was purported to be exceptionally rough. Weyland's crew was flying Johnny Carroll's old plane, the Bad Egg, and Bill was leading the low flight. About halfway across the North Sea, Jim called from the tail, "Lieutenant Lockhart is aborting." Lockhart was leading the second element in Weyland's flight. A few minutes later, from McBride came the word that Lieutenant Wieneth was turning back, too. That left Lieutenant Arp alone in the second element. It was just his third mission as first pilot and Bill was concerned about his lack of experience.

"Jim, keep an eye on Arp. Let me know if he moves down in the slot."

"Will do, sir. Right now, he's trying to tack on to Lieutenant Heller's wing."

Bill looked out to his right but couldn't see Arp. He hoped Arp would move up to the lead flight where he could fill in a slot vacated by another group abort. Before they reached the coast of Holland, the crew reported that five more Forts in the Ninety-first had aborted. That left the group with just eleven of eighteen aircraft.

"The group is really going to hell," Bill said to himself and then to the crew, "We'll be sitting ducks up here if we run into any opposition. So let's be alive back there and keep your eyes open. No sack time for the next ninety minutes. Okay?"

"Got ya, boss," came the reply in unison.

Friendly fighters brought the formation over Holland, but the minute they left, the Luftwaffe picked up the bombers. Weyland's position in the high group and with the second wing was a reasonably good spot. However, the weather was foul and the few aircraft in the group's high flight were forced to fly in the base of the clouds.

McBride called again, "Lieutenant Arp's having trouble staying with the flight. He's all over the . . . damn . . . Okay, he just made a 180 and is heading for the deck." That left Bill with half a flight, but he was relieved to hear Arp had turned back. Alone in the second element was no place for a young, inexperienced pilot.

The lead wing was taking the brunt of the German attack. Bill saw several Forts go down. The intensity of the attack continued as the fighters flashed through the formation in flights of two and four aircraft. The bomber formation had almost come apart and was the most ragged and spread out mess Bill had seen. The Germans seemed more determined than ever to break it up and pick off their targets one at a time and it was beginning to look like they might succeed.

The lead group was forced to reduce their speed due to the number of disabled planes. Their prop wash could be felt by the second wing closing in on them. This, coupled with the rough air and the vibration caused by swinging turrets and continuous firing, made it almost impossible to keep the aircraft in level flight. The supercharger on number three engine started to over speed and Bill was forced to retard the throttle, which dropped the manifold pressure to eighteen inches on that engine. Fortunately, the formation had slowed to 140 MPH and Bill had no trouble keeping up. He got the power up on number four engine, set the throttles, and used both hands on the control column to keep his position by raising and lowering the nose slightly.

Bill was surprised when Joe called, "IP coming up, sixty seconds," realizing they had been fighting off the German attacks for over half an hour. When they turned onto the IP and the enemy fighter attacks diminished, they were met by a ferocious flak barrage. Just as Weyland rolled out of his turn over the IP and leveled the wings, a tremendous jolt seemed to stop his Seventeen in flight, followed instantly by a violent muffled explosion to his right. He turned quickly to see the cowling and sheet metal being stripped off the number four engine and part of the wing. He quickly glanced at the instruments and saw the oil pressure on that engine drop precipitously. He immediately retarded the throttle and mixture control and hit the feathering button to number four as the oil pressure dropped through 25 PSI. He watched anxiously for the propeller to feather. It slowed, then coughed several times, but continued to rotate. Oil and fuel flowed out over the wing from ruptured lines. He opened the cowl flaps and told Bianchi to shut the fuel off and release CO_2 to number four.

Bianchi did as ordered, then turned to watch the engine. The prop wouldn't feather and fuel continued to flow over the wing, but there was no fire. Bianchi looked back at Bill and shook his head.

Bill rolled in all the trim he could to compensate for the loss of power, but still had to retard the throttles on number one and two engines to keep control of the plane.

"Push the feathering button in again and hold it down," he shouted.

The propeller continued to turn. Bianchi held the feathering button in and stared at the engine. "Damn thing won't feather. But the fuel flow has stopped."

"Okay, Louis. I guess we'll just have to fight her all the way."

He called to the bombardier, "I got it, Woody. Drop your load on Strickland."

Under normal conditions, the bombardier would take control of the aircraft at the IP and fly the plane by centering the PDI to the target. It wasn't possible with the excessive trim problem. Now Woodward would salvo his bombs on the group bombardier in the lead plane while Bill fought to keep the plane straight and level. When they began to fall back behind the lead flight, he pushed the power full forward on the two good engines and applied all the pressure he could on the control column to hold the Fort level. The drag caused by the rotating prop on number four just about canceled out the power on one good engine. It became impossible to hold his position in the formation, so Bill signaled to Lieutenant Wilson, flying on his left wing, that he was dropping down. He eased the control column forward and descended beneath the two Forts left in his flight.

He dropped below and behind them and called his crew, "Okay, guys. I'm going to try and make it to the target with the group. After that, it looks like we'll be on our own. If we can't keep up, I'm going to take her down."

They fell behind his group and Bill watched the two aircraft left in his flight come together. It looked like Wilson was in trouble or taking excessive evasive action and his wingman, Heller, was trying to stay with him when their planes collided. Heller was pulling up and over-shot Wilson, who was descending. Their wings overlapped and Heller's number one engine chewed off about a third of the trailing edge of Wilson's right wing.

Bill sat mesmerized, watching this frantic scene unfold before him. He became so engrossed that he almost forgot his own problems. The collision of the two planes occurred just as both planes released their bombs over the target. For what seemed like several minutes, both B-17s flew on, seemingly without difficulty as though nothing had happened. But in a matter of seconds, Heller's left wing burst into flames and the plane fell off to the left in a steep diving turn. Bill lost sight of Heller's plane as it dropped beneath him, but heard Jim McGovern calling out the chutes he could count coming out of the disabled Fort.

Wilson's plane continued to fly erratically indicating a serious control problem. While watching this melodrama in the few short seconds it took, Bill labored physically with the controls and mentally with his own situation. He found it difficult to dismiss the feeling that if he hadn't left his flight, he could've prevented the collision. Wilson was the more experienced pilot and had he held his position, Heller could have taken up a position on his wing.

Bill's thoughts were forced back to the condition of his aircraft when Woody called, "Bomb doors closed. Let's get the hell out of here, Bill."

He pushed any guilt about the other two crews from his mind and tried to concentrate on his own predicament. This was decision time. The wing behind them had changed course before reaching the IP and was no longer in sight. He looked ahead. The lead wing was involved in another savage air battle with German fighters.

He pressed the call button on his intercom, "We can't keep up with our group and there's nothing behind us to join up with. We're heading for the deck. Maybe we can get down before those fighters up ahead see us. Joe, give me the shortest and most direct heading to the coast."

BOMBER PILOT

Weyland pushed the nose of his plane down and left the throttles set forward. The air speed increased until the needle was pegged against the red line. He was forced to retard the throttles and slow the bomber down to stop the violent vibration of the number four engine. Fortunately, there was no sign of fire and the flow of fuel from the failed engine had stopped. He dropped down to treetop level and called the crew.

"Stay alert, you guys. We're crippled and we can expect trouble. Dump any excess weight-everything except guns and ammo. Lloyd, get out of the turret." Then to the radio operator, "Jim, put out a distress call on MF/DF and open the pulse on IFF. Maybe some of our little friends are about. Get a hold of MLS and keep them informed of our position. Joe, keep Cobb advised on our position."

They weren't within range of friendly fighters, but maybe the main locator station could pick them up on radar and track them. There was a good possibility that-Bill wasn't ready to get overly optimistic-someone out there could pick them up, but hopefully not the Germans.

Bill's greatest concern was the vibrating engine tearing away and taking part of the wing with it. They crossed the Rhine and flew parallel with it until they reached Nijmegen, where he turned west and hedgehopped over the fields and hedgerows of Holland. They were too low to bail out and Bill alerted the crew. "I might have to set her down, so be prepared for a crash landing. Remember your positions. Woody, don't forget the bombsight. And Jim, get rid of those classified radio frequencies."

The classified communications codes were printed on rice paper and it was the radio operator's responsibility to destroy them by eating them. The bombardier could destroy the bombsight by a self-destruct mechanism or, if necessary, with his forty-five-caliber pistol.

He had Louis run through the checklist several times to be sure nothing would be left to chance in the event they had to set the plane down. He concentrated on the route ahead of him, looking for large level areas. As quickly as he passed one he had another in mind, knowing that if he had to put it down, he'd have but a few short minutes to pick the best landing area. At that low altitude and without a super-charger, the manifold pressure on the number three engine increased and gave them a little better air speed. Bill optimistically thought they might make it back.

Then came the dreaded call, "Fighters, five o'clock!" cried McBride.

Bill heard Bayne's turret hum as it rotated and he called, "How many? What are they?"

Jim came back, "Two. Twin engines. Could be 110s or 210s."

Bayne hurriedly cut in, "They're ME-110's. Two of them. And they're coming in high at five o'clock."

"Okay, you guys let me know when they get in range and I'll try to skid her into them. I'm going to get down on the deck. Hold your fire until they're in range. Lloyd, stay out of the ball turret. You can't do any good down there. We're too low. Use Cobb's fifty in radio."

A few minutes later, Bill heard the rattle of the turret.

Bayne shouted, "Now!"

Weyland eased the pressure off the left rudder pedal and the air-craft sideslipped to the right with the help of full power from the two port-side engines. He pushed the nose down until he was only twenty or thirty feet above the ground. The guns were roaring.

"One's hit!" Ray called from his right-side waist position.

"Damn right. We got one!" said Jim from the tail.

Bill looked up just in time to see two twin-engine fighters flash by above him. He saw smoke streaming from one. He couldn't believe that the Germans had missed.

"Pilot to crew. Did we take any hits? Anyone hurt?"

"We took a couple in the vertical stabilizer," shouted McBride from his tail position. "I can see the sky through it. I'm okay."

"Okay here in the waist."

"All right in radio," Cobb reported.

"Bayne, can you see any damage to the vertical stabilizer? I felt no impact on the rudder. It feels okay."

"I can see some torn sheet metal sticking out of the stabilizer about halfway up. Otherwise most of it's still there." Scurlock then went on to say, "We got one. They're splitting up and one's trailing a lot of black smoke. Looks like he's heading for the barn."

"All right. Keep me informed, Bayne. You've got the best shot at them."

"Yeah, Bayne," retorted Woody from the nose. "See if you can coax one of them around front, so I can get a shot at him."

"Let's hope they're both hightailing it," Bill replied.

"Here he comes. Ten o'clock high!" called Bayne.

Bill looked up to his left and there it was: a dark gray, twin-engine night fighter bearing down on them from about two miles out. He knew he had to turn into the ME-110. But that was going to be damn hard with the two good engines on that side.

He looked at Louis and said, "When I drop the left wing, you get on the left rudder and help me turn her."

When he heard Bayne's turret let go a short burst, he pushed the left wing down and stood on the left rudder. The Fort turned grudgingly. He also heard Woody's gun blasting away from the bombardier's position. That helped, knowing that he had his sights on the German. The airspeed fell below a hundred, and Bill glanced up quickly to see the fighter's wing cannons blasting directly at him. Two shells tore through the Fort's left wing and he felt the buffeting control surfaces as the plane was about to stall. Just as he released the pressure on the control column and the left rudder, the fighter sailed over the top of them. There was no more power available, so Bill pushed the nose down further and held her just a few feet off the ground, thinking if it was going to stall they'd only have a few feet to fall. He thought about dumping some flaps, but that would only increase the drag. He watched hopelessly as the airspeed fluctuated between eighty and ninety mph and then slowly built back up to ninety-five.

"Where is he, Bayne?"

"Out about two thousand yards at four o'clock and starting to turn."

Bill thought he wouldn't have any trouble turning into him coming in on that side.

"Okay, Bayne, let me know when he's in range. Anyone hit?"

"Negative," came an anxious reply from the rear.

"Picked up two more holes in the waist just aft of McGovern. Close, just a little too close for comfort," said Gillet.

Bill quickly checked the engine instrument on the number three engine. It was putting out, but not the emergency power he needed, even at that altitude. There was something more than a supercharger problem with that engine.

He called the engineer, "Bayne, what's the damage to the left wing?"

"Ripped a couple of holes outboard of number one. I don't see any fuel coming out."

"Where is he now?"

"Coming in high about three o'clock," Ray cut in.

Weyland looked to his right and Bianchi ducked so he could see.

"All right, I see him. Let's see if we can get the son-of-a-bitch this time!"

The plane shook with the vibration of short bursts from the Fort's guns. Bill let the plane skid around to the right.

"He's pulling up! He's turning away!" shouted Bayne excitedly.

"Was he hit?" called Woody.

"No. I don't think so. But he's turning away," said Bayne.

"Good. Damn good. Keep your eyes open. He may come back. We're not out of it yet. He might have some buddies on the way to take over," said Bill anxiously.

He wondered why the German broke off the attack when it seemed to be a certain kill for him. The odds were too great against the Fort surviving another attack. Maybe his guns jammed. But certainly not all four of them. Whatever happened, it was a godsend to Bill. He hauled his window back and let the slipstream suck the stink of cordite, sweat, and fear out of the cockpit. He scanned the engine instruments. The two engines were still putting out, but their cylinder head temperature was pegged in the red. Number three was just holding its own without producing a hell of a lot of thrust and number four was vibrating like mad. How the engine was still attached to the wing was a mystery to him. Most of the cowling had been torn away and several cylinders had blown out of the engine frame. But, from what they could see, there was no fuel leaking.

He got the airspeed up to 105 MPH, but the force needed to hold her straight and level was beginning to take its toll. Louis noticed it and got hold of the control column and helped ease the strain.

Bill called down to Joe, "How are you doing down there?"

"Okay. Coast should be coming up in about twelve minutes."

The pilot eased the power off a little on the two good engines and that helped to reduce the force needed on the control column. He was anxious to get away from this hostile land but realized he had a long way to go.

Occasionally, some light flak would arch up at them, but because of their low altitude most of it fell behind.

The coast finally slipped slowly by beneath them.

"The hook of Holland, gents," Joe announced. "About one hundred miles to the coast of England."

"Praise the Lord," came Woody's response.

"England," Bill murmured. "If I can just make it to England. God, there are hundreds of airfields there. Good old England, how I love you." He couldn't stop thinking about that pilot in the ME-110. "Why did he break off when he had us cold?"

"I'm going to try and make it across the pond. But there's a good possibility we may have to ditch. Check your Mae West and remember your crash position and get out fast when she stops. I'll hit the alarm. Two-minute drill. That's all we'll have before she sinks. Bayne'll release the starboard raft. McGovern, you back him up and Ray, you get the port raft out and Lloyd will back you. Any questions?"

They all responded in the negative, "Hold your positions until we get a little further away from the coast. I'll let you know when to start back to radio." If they had to ditch, everyone except the pilot and copilot would squeeze into the radio room.

When they were about ten minutes past the coast of Holland, the plane's airspeed had increased another five knots, so Bill eased the plane up at the rate of about twenty to thirty feet per minute. Slowly, he got her up to three hundred feet thinking if they had to ditch, they'd have a little more time to prepare. He switched his junction box to command and heard Cobb talking to a cheerful Englishman.

"We paint you! Yes. Lovely, see you fine. Hang in there, old chap. Air Sea Rescue has been alerted and they're on their way to intercept you. Bloody good show, old boy."

"Roger that, sir. Y'all keep talking and we'll keep this old gal flying and we'll make it back."

Bill looked at Bianchi and, as serious as the situation was, he had to grin over Cobb's southern accent and the Englishman's calm confident voice. Bill realized that the Germans were probably listening in on their transmissions as well; however, there was no alternative but to transmit in the clear. If he had to ditch, he hoped the RAF would reach them first.

Weyland had a hard time convincing himself that they could make it across the North Sea. He was prepared to ditch the Seventeen, but he was determined to get as close to England as possible. To compensate for the windmilling propeller, he kept emergency power on the three engines even though the cylinder head temperature was well into the red.

When he estimated he was halfway across, he slowed the plane down as much as he dared to ease the vibration and the stress on the good engines.

He called to the crew, "Okay, men, throw out everything we don't need: guns, flak suits. I mean every damn thing that's not bolted down. If we get our weight down, we just might make it. Bayne, you keep your turret guns, just in case. The rest, overboard."

He began to feel a little more confident and dismissed the idea of ditching and concentrated on getting to the coast of England.

Woody, with his excellent eyes, was the first to see the English coast-and what a magnificent sight it was. The loss of fuel from the wing tanks and the overworked engines now appeared to be the most crucial problem, but if he had to set the bomber down there were a lot of fields in England.

They finally crossed the English coast north of Harwich. The old gal was still flying and lady luck was up there with them. Bill had nursed her up a few hundred feet more, and he now felt confident that he could make it back to Bassingbourn. If not, he had enough altitude to bail out the crew and set the Fort down in any available field. He decided to press on. Joe kept Bill aware of their position and called out the miles to go. Finally, there was that old black hardtop, Bassingborn, straight ahead. The relief glowed in Bill's face as he heard his crew shouting and cheering over the rumbling engine noise.

He set her down gently and taxied to their hangar. What a joy it was to pull the throttles back and shut down those engines that had served him so well. He cut the switches and turned to Louis with a big grin and an audible sigh of relief.

Louis said, "Good show, Bill," and Bayne grabbed the pilot's right shoulder and squeezed it hard.

They learned at debriefing that Wilson's crew, as well as Heller's, didn't survive the midair collision. Of the six B-17s the 401st dispatched on the mission, Weyland's was the only aircraft in his squadron to reach the target area and return to base. Three had aborted and two failed to return. Lieutenant Arp got credit for the mission because he aborted over enemy territory. The 323rd Squadron also lost two aircraft. Only six of the ten aircraft went on to what they believed to be the target. It wasn't a successful day for the Ninety-first. The discipline was going to hell in the group and the losses were increasing at a disastrous rate. The outlook was getting grim for Bill and his crew. With just four missions to go and six to finish up his crew, Bill, for the first time, was beginning to wonder whether they would make it.

Eighth Air Force lost twenty-five of the 330 bombers dispatched on the raid to Gelsenkirchen. Only two groups reached the designated area and there clouds and smoke obscured the target resulting in a futile bombing attempt.

WILLIAM WHEELER

The weather improved that weekend and the crews were told to stand by for a max effort, a strong indication they were getting ready for a big one. If the rumors continued, it would no longer be a secret to anyone by the time they actually flew the mission. Bill didn't get to London that weekend.

On Sunday, they flew an easy raid to Flushing on the coast of Holland. On Monday, with Clyde, their squadron CO, flying with them, Weyland's crew led the wing to Le Bourget. Bill insisted that Bianchi ride as an observer on the raid into France since it was considered a milk run. Guilford agreed. Because the Ninety-first was leading the wing, the group navigator and bombardier, Lieutenants Williams and Strickland, were put aboard Bill's plane. Woody and Joe flew with another crew, to their obvious displeasure. However, the mission results were excellent and they all got another sortie behind them.

When Bill heard they were alerted for a mission on Tuesday, he called Mary. He didn't get to see her over the weekend because of a scrubbed mission on Saturday and the raid to Flushing on Sunday. He told her he would try to get to London Tuesday evening.

Mary asked Bill if it would be all right to accept a dinner engagement the following night.

"Yes. I'm sure I'll be able to get in to see you then. Where?"

"Mrs. Freeman, a woman I occasionally model for. She's anxious to meet you and would like to have us over for dinner."

"Sounds great. I'll see you tomorrow. Love you."

"I love you, Bill. Be careful, darling."

Chapter 24

Bill was awakened at 0300 hours on Tuesday, August 17, 1943, and told that the briefing would begin at 0400 hours. His bed was in the middle of his room and he got out of it as he always did-on the left side. He washed, shaved, and dressed in his pink trousers, turtleneck sweater, that Clare had knitted for him, raunchy garrison cap, and worn leather jacket. He slipped into his loafers instead of the jodhpur boots that he usually wore. The loafers were more comfortable inside his sheepskin flying boots.

As he cycled to the mess hall in a heavy mist, he was overcome by a strange feeling of despair and loneliness, but it passed quickly when he walked into the noisy dining room. "Today's mission is probably the one they canceled last week," he thought. He walked over and sat down at a table with his crew for breakfast and Joe confirmed his hunch.

"It's Schweinfurt, Bill," Joe whispered, "Williams, the group navigator, told me a few minutes ago."

Woody shook his head and responded cynically, "Bill, I sure don't like this one bit. Is it really necessary? After the screw up over Gelsenkirchen, we'll never make it back. You know we're living on borrowed time. We replaced six crews in the 401st and since then we've lost six crews." He stopped and tried to look serious, then continued,

"Maybe I should have a talk with the chaplain to see if I'm mentally and spiritually up to it. Would you mind if I skipped this one, Bill?"

Bill replied with the slightest hint of a grin, "Come on, Woody, you wouldn't want to miss this one. This is the big one. Just think, after this sortie you'll only have three more to go. Besides, Joe will miss you up there in the nose. What's he gonna do with all that extra space?"

Joe and Woody were both over six feet tall and each weighed more than two hundred pounds. When they put on all the gear the government issued, including flak vests and steel helmets, it was hard to understand how they could breathe in the small confines of the nose compartment. In addition, Woody always took twice the normal load of ammunition with him.

In the briefing room, Bill noticed a certain tension among the other crews that he'd not experienced before. It wasn't the usual noisy bunch of guys standing in small groups, talking loudly and horsing around. They were all settled, sitting down, quietly waiting for the briefing to start. Apparently, the word was out, and when the curtains parted, confirmation of the target was met with a subdued and nervous reaction, not the usual chorus of loud moans and groans. Bill's reaction was no different, but what impressed him most was the length of the red ribbon. Until that moment, he had no idea where Schweinfurt was.

"Damn! All that way! Whattayouthink, Joe? Woody?"

Joe's response was the understatement of the war, "It's a long way, Bill."

"This is absolutely ridiculous, Bill," said Woody. "How the hell do they expect us to get there and back? It's impossible, right Louis?"

Bianchi said, "Oh, I don't know, Woody. I think we can do it. How about it, Bill?"

"We damn well better," was Bill's quiet response.

Weyland couldn't believe the number of aircraft involved in the mission: sixteen groups, nearly four hundred B-17s. Just a few months prior, the Eighth had to scramble to get seventy-two Forts up for one mission. Just two weeks ago, one hundred Forts and crews were lost during Blitz Week. He wondered where all the young men and new

Fortresses were coming from. That day was the birth of the legend that would later be known as the Mighty Eighth, made possible by the vast potential and the inconceivable warmaking capability of the United States. It was one year to the day on August 17, 1942, that the Eighth flew its first mission over Europe with a grand total of eighteen Flying Fortresses.

The mission called for the main force of 230 B-17s, designated as the First Air Division, to bomb the ball bearing factories at Schweinfurt, while a second force of 146 bombers of the Third Air Division would bomb the ME-109 factories at Regensburg. The Ninety-first Bomb Group would lead the First Air Division. Weyland's flight, the 401st Squadron, would become part of the 101st Composite Group flying in the high group position in the lead combat wing. There he would lead the low flight in the composite group. It would be a maximum effort and all available crews and aircraft would participate.

The mission as planned-and this was emphasized as the most important aspect of the operation-called for the 146 B-17s of the Third Air Division to take off first, bomb Regensburg, then continue on to, and land at, bases in North Africa instead of returning to the United Kingdom. It would be the first of several shuttle missions the Eighth would fly. The one redeeming and favorable part of the mission that Bill liked was that their formation would follow the Regensburg force, crossing the Belgium coast just ten minutes later. The first formation in would probably take the brunt of the German opposition. Inasmuch as the main objective was to destroy the ball bearing works, getting the First Air Division to the target intact was of singular importance.

Getting back from the target would be a different story. By the time the Schweinfurt force was withdrawing, the Luftwaffe would have alerted all its fighter units and have them refueled and waiting for the bombers' return, while the Regensburg's groups, if the secrecy of the mission held, would fly on to Africa. The returning Schweinfurt groups would then be on the receiving end of a fierce German attack. But Bill still preferred that. He would rather fight his way out than in.

Just before leaving the briefing, McFarland told Bill he would be taking a war correspondent along on the raid.

Bill wasn't happy about the added responsibility of a passenger, but agreed saying, "I hope we can find some room for him. I'm sure the crew will load up every bit of extra space with ammo on this one."

"He's Tex McCrary, an AP photographer. He's flown on several raids with us. I told him you were the best pilot in the group, so take good care of him."

"I'll try. I'm sure he'll get some good pictures today."

The crew rode out to the hardstand together. There was a good deal of horsing around on the way out, but some of it was a little too forced. They were flying Our Gang, a 324th Squadron aircraft. The Bad Egg ended up in the hangar after the Gelsenkirchen raid and wasn't available. There were fourteen 20-mm shell holes in the bomber and the windmilling prop had caused major structural damage to the wing.

Takeoff was scheduled for 0615 hours. They completed their pre-flight checklist and just before engine start, Tex McCrary arrived in a staff car and climbed aboard. He came up to the cockpit and introduced himself.

Bill shook his hand and said, "I'm not going to say I'm happy to have you aboard 'cause I think you're making one hell of a mistake. But it's your call. Where would you like to ride, the nose or radio?"

"I'd like to try the nose. Last time, on the Huls raid, I was in the radio compartment and got some good pictures of the action behind the formation. This time, I'd like to see what's up ahead."

"Okay with me, but I think you might have a little trouble finding some space down there. Got two pretty big guys in the nose and I'm sure Woody has loaded it down with ammo."

They heard Woody from below, "Hey, Joe, we got a hotshot pho-tographer flying with us today. We'll let the fighters come in real close so he can get some good pictures. Gotta have something to show our kids when they ask, 'What did you do in the war, Daddy?' "

The pilot grinned and said, "Don't mind him. He won't let any fighters within a thousand yards of us."

On orders from the tower, they cranked engines and finally got the go-ahead to taxi. They had just gotten out of the dispersal area and onto the taxiway when the tower told them to hold.

They held for about twenty minutes and were then released to roll again. Weyland's Seventeen was first in line and about halfway down the ramp he was told again by the tower to hold. Four minutes later the controller called, "Cut your engines, but hold your crew positions. Anticipate a thirty-minute delay. Maintain radio contact. Acknowledge."

"Roger tower. Baker zero six niner. Shutting down. Standing by."

Woody grumbled over the intercom, "Goddamn it, I hope they don't scrub this one now. We're flying in a good position. I'd like to get this one behind me."

Hearing for the first time such a positive statement from Woody, the pilot transmitted to his crew, "You guys hear that? Sounds like Woody's finally coming around. He'll probably sign up for another twenty-five."

"No chance, Bill. I just want to get this one behind us. Sweating it out on the ground is for the birds."

"I agree. If this raid goes as planned it might not be too bad. But the longer they delay, the rougher it's going to be. So let's hope they get this show on the road, pronto," replied Bill.

They sat in silence. Occasionally, Jim McGovern or Jim McBride, the rear gunners, would make some caustic remark about the delay. The sun was up and it was trying to burn through the fog. The tension was beginning to build. The restlessness was heard over the intercom. A mike button would be depressed and the only sound heard was clothes rustling or a crewman's breathing. Waiting was far worse than any torture contrived by man. Bill wondered whether the brass at headquarters fully realized what they were putting the crews through.

Finally the tower called and said, "Baker zero six niner, you are cleared to start engines. Hold your position until advised to taxi."

Bill rogered in response to the tower's message and went through the starting procedure again with Louis. When he had all four engines running he was told by the tower to proceed to the active runway. He released the brakes and started to roll again. The sound of nearly one hundred 1,200-horsepower Wright Cyclone engines rumbled through the English countryside. As they jockeyed in position, line astern with their squealing brakes, it again reminded Bill of a herd of elephants moving out trunk-to-tail.

Just before they reached the final turn unto the runway, the tower called, "Hold your position Baker zero six niner."

"Oh no. Not again," Bill mumbled.

Then from the tower, "Takeoff will be delayed indefinitely. You may shut down your engines and deplane. But stand by your aircraft. Ops will be along to brief you on the delay."

It was now 0730 hours, and Bill wondered if the Third Air Division had gotten off and what the problem was at Bomber Command. They shut down and while Louis was running through the checklist, a staff car pulled up in front of their Fort. Tex McCrary, the correspondent, moved out from under the nose and got in the car. He didn't turn or wave so it was assumed that he would be back. Just as Bill dropped out of the forward hatch, Dave Eames drove up in a jeep. Bill walked over and got in the passenger seat and said, "What's the latest, Dave?"

"It's going to be at least a one-hour delay. They don't want to release the fighters because of the fog. If the fog doesn't burn off, they'll have trouble recovering them."

Bill turned, looked down the runway, and said, "Not that bad here. Got over a mile visibility and the clouds don't look much over a few hundred feet thick."

Eames responded, "The bases to the east are much worse off. They're down to less than a half mile."

"Did the Third Air Division get off on time?"

"No. They took off at 0715, over an hour later than scheduled. They couldn't hold them back any longer because the division had to get to North Africa before dark. The raid was going to be rough enough without the added risk of trying to find and land at strange airfields after dark. But keep that info to yourself, Bill. We were told not to tell our crews about the change in the mission plan. It's going to be a lot rougher without the Third just ahead of you."

"You can say that again. That was the only good thing I liked about this mission."

Weyland got out of the jeep and Eames said, "Take it easy. See you later."

"Sure hope so. See you." Bill walked over to his crew lounging on the grass smoking.

Woody looked up, "What's the scoop, Bill?"

"Delay for at least another hour."

"Balls. Is this going to be another screw up? We've never had a delay this long. They'll probably cancel the damn raid and that's okay with me," said Woody.

"Eames said they're holding us up because the fighters may have trouble getting back down in this fog."

Bayne Scurlock said, "Hell it doesn't look that bad here. Besides, what good will the fighters do? We'll be on our own most of the way."

"Yeah, they sure haven't been much good to us so far," said Jim McGovern with much cynicism.

"Okay, guys. Let's just relax," ordered Bill. "They'll probably cancel before long."

Two and a half hours later, McFarland drove up and said, "Takeoff is scheduled for 1115. You all set, Bill?"

"Yup. We'll be ready." He got up and walked toward the Fort.

The rest of the crew pulled each other up off the grass. There was a lot of grumbling and McBride said, "Damn, I'm hungry. It's been seven hours since breakfast. Wonder what they're having for chow tonight?"

When the crew climbed back onboard, they rechecked all their equipment and the pilots completed the checklist. The tower called and confirmed the takeoff time. Bill had the four engines turning over and was ready to roll at 1112 hours.

"Tower to Baker zero six niner, clear to Runway 33 and hold."

Weyland's crew was scheduled to take off first because they had to climb higher and join up with the two flights that would form the 101st

Composite Group. He rolled Our Gang to the left side of the runway, stood on the brakes, advanced the throttles, and released the trembling Fort when the tower cleared them for takeoff.

When Louis called, "Wheels up," Bill checked the clock on the instrument panel and it read 1118 hours. They climbed through the thin layer of clouds and broke out in a beautiful, clear sky. Bill circled the field in a gentle left turn while his flight formed. He then turned to the heading Joe gave him. As they were climbing toward their rendezvous, he remembered his passenger and called down to the nose, "Woody is Tex on board?"

"No, not here. There wasn't a hell of a lot of room down here. He's probably back in the radio compartment."

"No, not back here," replied Cobb.

"Not in the waist either," called Ray Gillet.

"Well, I guess he decided to take a rain check on this one," Bill told his crew. "Eames told me that his boss at AP and the brass at Bomber Command headquarters didn't want him to go."

"I don't blame him a bit, Bill. I wish I had a buddy down in High Wycombe to tell me, I didn't have to go," responded Woody sarcastically.

Bill checked his wingmen. On his right wing, Buster Peek, a classmate of his, was flying the Eager Beaver. Peek had some bad luck and ditched on his way over from the States and again on the Huls raid. Andy Wieneth, now an aircraft commander with a new crew, was on Weyland's left wing. Bill called McBride, the tail gunner, and asked him to report on his second element.

"They look great, lieutenant, all tucked in nice and tight."

Lockhart was leading the second element and his two wingmen were Lieutenant Arp and Flight Officer Pitts. Bill settled back to have his last cigarette before going on oxygen, thinking it would be more than four hours before the next one. He wondered what Bomber Command's reasoning was in letting the Schweinfurt mission go after a five-hour delay. The delay negated the surprise of shuttling the Third Air Division to Africa. According to Bill's calculations, they would be crossing the Dutch coast three and half hours after the Regensburg force, not ten minutes as originally planned. If the secrecy of the shuttle mission prevailed, the Germans would have every fighter alerted and ready to meet them coming back. About the time they'd realized that the bombers were not coming back, the German radar would be tracking a larger bomber force out over the North Sea heading toward der Fatherland. The Luftwaffe would be all refueled, rearmed, and ready to intercept the American bomber formation with the largest fighter force Hitler had ever assembled.

The decision to release the Schweinfurt force was made by Brigadier General Fred Anderson of Bomber Command. He'd just recently assumed the command position, but had practically no combat experience. However, General Eaker, his superior, certainly the best qualified and experienced general officer in the Eighth, decided not to interfere with Anderson's decision. He believed a commander should have the authority to make the command decision. So he remained silent.

Bombing the ball bearing factories in Germany had been an obsession with air force planners for months. Now that they had the number of bombers necessary to carry out this mission, the only obstacle would be the weather over the target. Precision bombing was necessary to ensure complete destruction of the factory. The loss of this vital industry, they believed, would cripple Germany and end the war in a short time.

When a promising high pressure weather system finally settled over Europe, the mission was laid on. However, the English weather wouldn't cooperate. Dense fog settled over most of eastern England and caused great anxiety among the Eighth Air Force planners.

Colonel LeMay's bomber formation, the Third Air Division, took off for Regensburg an hour and a half late, but only after he convinced the powers-that-be that his pilots were capable of taking off in limited visibility. However, no assurance was made by the commander of the Schweinfurt force, even though their pilots were as qualified. Hence, the five-hour delay. But instead of canceling the mission, General Anderson ordered the bomber force off after major changes were made to the initial plan. One of the most serious miscalculations he made was believing that the friendly fighters could be turned around after escorting the Regensburg force in time to cover the Schweinfurt bombers.

He further reasoned that when the Germans found that the Regensburg force had gone on to Africa, they would disperse their fighter units and send them back to their home bases. Accordingly, the Schweinfurt force would receive little opposition on their entry into Germany. In both cases, he would be deadly wrong and the error in judgment would prove disastrous. It was later learned that General Eaker couldn't help feeling some uneasiness when he heard that General Anderson had ordered the bombers off. But Eaker had said nothing.

Bill joined up with the other two composite squadrons and eased his flight into position below and to the left of the lead flight. He was flying from the right seat for a better view of the lead squadron above and to his right. The 101st Composite Group was staggered above the Ninety-first Bomb Group, which was leading the Schweinfurt force.

The flight across the North Sea and over the Rhine Estuary was uneventful. Reports were received from different crew positions on seeing friendly Spitfires above the formation.

As they crossed over Holland and into Belgium, the groups started to let down. Cobb told Bill he'd just received word over HF that the formation was letting down two thousand feet because of the high clouds ahead and the possibility of the formation flying into them. Weyland looked at the clouds, but from his position in the high group, it looked like the clouds would be well above them. The decision to fly at a lower altitude was made by Colonel William Gross, the First Task Force Commander flying in the lead B-17 with the Ninety-first commander, Colonel Wurzbach. That would drop Bill's group down to nineteen thousand feet and the low group to seventeen thousand feet-an altitude at which the German 88-mm flak guns were deadly accurate.

It was also the most effective altitude for the ME-109. Above twenty-one thousand feet, the 109 was not too maneuverable. It was another change that Bill was not happy about. Colonel Wray, their former group commander, now at Bomber Command, specifically told Colonel Gross during the briefing to keep the formation above nineteen thousand feet. It seemed that every change made to the original mission plan favored the enemy. Bill was beginning to have bad feelings about this bombing venture.

As they leveled off at lower altitude just south of Antwerp, the expected flak came up with vengeful determination. Jim McBride reported that Lockhart was having trouble. McBride speculated that Lockhart had been hit by flak. Some of it was very close. Bill asked Jim to keep him informed and within a few minutes McBride called to say that Lockhart was dropping down and back and one of his wingmen was turning back, but the other was staying with him. The pilot said aloud but without benefit of the intercom, "Damn. Not again. Up here with only half a flight."

Lloyd Thomas called from his turret and said that it looked like Lockhart was trying to join the Ninety-first below them and his other wingman had also turned back.

Woody was the first to see the unfriendly fighters above and ahead of the bombers. The German pilots came in and just before they got within range of the American guns, they turned 180 degrees and flew east and about fifteen hundred feet above and ahead of the formation. The American fighter reported by McBride had just joined the formation. They were flying above and to the rear of the bombers. There were some reported dogfights to the south, but for the most part the bomber formation, along with the American and German fighters, all seemed to be heading peacefully east toward the same destination. Then came those dreaded words, "Bandits, twelve o'clock high!"

There, straight ahead and slightly higher, were eight ME-109s heading for the lead flight in the composite group. Somewhat lower were thirty to forty enemy fighters turning toward the lead group below the composite group.

McBride called from the tail, "Our fighters are turning back. They're heading for home."

The Luftwaffe appeared to know the exact range of the American fighters. It was a frustrating and agonizing time for the American fighter pilots, but a desperate one for the bomber crews.

There were sharp bursts of fire coming from the nose. Woody was quickly sending out his signal to Jerry, "Beware! Our guns are ready and waiting for you!"

In the first attack, three Forts in the lead wing went down. The first was from the Ninety-first. The bomber spun out of the formation, made two rapid turns, and then came apart. Lloyd reported seeing only two chutes. The other two B-17s were from the 381st Bomb Group, the low group in the lead wing. Both went down in flames. The composite group survived the first attack as the formation crossed into German air space near Eupen.

Ahead Bill could see flight after flight of German fighters climbing above them. Never before had he seen so many. They were stepped up in groups of twelve to sixteen aircraft. He estimated more than a hundred fighters and each time he looked ahead, more specks materialized into planes. He prayed, "God, help us."

The flak became more intense and at one point Bill felt the Fortress buck and heard the clank of steel against the plane's skin. He got a negative response from his crew when he asked if anyone was hit. Although the plane continued its normal flight, he was sure that they'd taken on additional weight in the form of shrapnel.

The second attack was massive. An estimated sixty to seventy aircraft were stepped up in a long stream, heading for the lead wing, while a phalanx of sixteen enemy fighters flying in four-finger formation were setting up for a frontal attack on the composite group. In the past, these attacks were usually made by two or four German fighters. Never had Bill seen the Luftwaffe attack in such overwhelming force. He thought, "God, how can they miss?"

The towering cumulus clouds to the north and south of the formation gave Bill the impression of being enclosed in a huge ravine. As he watched the mass of fighters bearing down on them he couldn't help but recall that famous line of Alfred Tennyson's, "Into the valley of the death rode the six hundred . . .," and his admiration for those brave horsemen on reading those words as a young boy.

The composite group leader descended abruptly at the first flashes of cannon fire erupting from the oncoming FW-190s. Bill promptly punched the yoke forward in hot pursuit. He quickly glanced at his wingmen and saw them hanging in there, dangerously close. The Germans came in firing point-blank at the plodding Forts, then rolled, twisted, and screamed down through the formation.

A bomber pilot doesn't have a lot of options. He can take evasive action, but if it's too violent he may endanger other planes in the formation. His responsibility is to fly the mission as directed and he is the only one in the crew who can deviate from it. He must set the example through leadership, courage, and duty. Fortunately, Bill had a crew that more than matched his courage, for never once in the missions they had flown did any crew member suggest that they turn back. He heard his crew calling out incoming fighters, their voices a mixture of excitement and fear as the enemy closed in with maddening speed and firepower.

Some came so close it was impossible to believe that they hadn't intended to crash head-on. Earlier in their tour, Bill had to caution the crew if their chatter on the intercom got out of hand. Not now. His crew had developed into an effective fighting unit. They were so intent on downing the enemy fighters that hardly any sound came from their parched throats. But as soon as the enemy fighters shot past and there was a lull in the fighting, they'd erupted in shouts and cheers, particularly when a German went down in flames. Behind him, he heard Scurlock break out in a wild rebel yell.

It was impossible to believe that they survived the second onslaught of cannon fire unscathed. But four Forts in the lead wing were not so fortunate. Two more B-17s went out of control from the low group, the 381st, one with a huge flame streaming from its left wing, the other headed straight toward earth. Bill saw the lead plane in the low squadron in the Ninety-first take a deadly hit. Its number three engine burst into flames, exploded, and tumbled over the wing, hitting the stabilizer and tearing it off. The B-17 flopped over on its back and headed straight down engulfed in flames.

In the composite group, the right wingman in the lead squadron dropped down and turned abruptly to the left in a maddening maneuver directly in front of Bill's flight. Bill pulled up sharply and as the troubled B-17 slipped under Wieneth's plane, a stream of bodies bailed out in the midst of the formation.

A few minutes later another mass of German fighters was setting up for a frontal assault on the American formation. While the main Luftwaffe force descended, leveled off, and headed for the Ninety-first, about two dozen fighters held their altitude in preparation for another attack on the composite group. The Germans' main objective was to destroy the lead group and they seemed fanatically determined to blast them out of the sky. Bill looked on in amazement as the enemy fighters mauled the Forts leading the formation. He felt a great sense of pride and admiration watching his group beneath him flying straight into the fury of the attack. It was the lead pilot's duty to press on and to keep the formation on course to the target. The only other person in the formation who had the authority to alter the bomber's course was Colonel Gross, the task force commander, flying in the lead plane. Otherwise, it was the lead pilot, whether he was a lieutenant or a colonel, who had to grit his teeth and press on. That courage was passed down to the other group and squadron leaders and the aircraft commanders. There were some, but not many, who would turn back under such circumstances. Fortunately, they were not placed in a position to lead.

Weyland became so engrossed in the scene beneath him that for a moment he forgot the fight raging about him. The spell was broken when he looked up to see eight gray ME-09s directly ahead bearing down on his flight. They were echeloned off in two flights of four, one slightly above the other, and when in range, they blasted away directly at Weyland and his flight. Although it seemed an eternity, it was just a matter of seconds from the time they started firing until they did a split S and dove swiftly beneath the American formation. Bill marveled at the fact that he was alive and unhurt. Instinctively, he turned quickly to his wingmen. Peek was there hanging in tightly on his right wing and as he turned to the left, his port wing rose abruptly and a huge orange flame blotted out the sky in a silent explosion. He was certain that they were hit, but when he forced the wing down, he saw the wing on Wieneth's plane separate from a fuselage engulfed in flames. He shouted to his crew, "Watch for chutes!" But there were none.

With only his and Peek's B-17 left in the flight, Bill knew the enemy fighters would concentrate on them. He closed as near as he dared to the lead squadron, but it still left him and Peek pretty much on their own. Some of the German fighters were circling back through the formation. He could hear Jim McBride in the tail calling out fighters attacking from the rear. The main German force, however, was still building up in front of the American bomber formation. And that was the action that Bill was most concerned about. There seemed to be no end to the Luftwaffe fighters climbing to gain enough altitude prior to making their frontal assaults.

The next attack, as Bill expected, was directed at his meager flight. As they came in range he pushed the control column forward and watched helplessly as the Germans' cannons blasted away at them. Again, they flashed past and the same incredible feeling flooded through him. It was inconceivable that they had missed again. But they hadn't.

Lloyd calmly announced, "Fire in number two engine."

Bill turned instantly to the left but could see no fire. He quickly checked the engine instruments and saw the manifold and oil pressure on number two engine fluctuate and start to decrease. "Check number two, Louis!" he shouted.

He hadn't noticed, but when the fighting got intense, Bianchi had lowered his seat as far as it would go. As small as he was, not much more than the top of his helmet was visible above the side window and he couldn't clearly see the inboard engine on that side.

Bianchi quickly toggled his seat up and looked out the window and said, "Yeah, fire coming out of the bottom cowling."

Bill reached over with his right hand and hit the fuel shutoff switch, then with his left hand opened the cowl flap, and punched the feathering button on number two engine in rapid succession. When he released his grip on the control column, the left wing went down abruptly. He kicked full right rudder and gripped the column with his right hand, but was unable to keep the bomber from slipping off to the left. He then turned the fire extinguisher selector to the left inboard engine with his right hand and immediately pulled the handle discharging the CO_2 into the burning engine. With both hands back on the yoke, he was able to bring the wing up. He then rolled in full right rudder on the trim wheel.

When the aircraft didn't respond to the rudder trim, he shouted, "Full right aileron trim, Louis!"

The aileron trim control was on the pilot's side. It helped, but it still required considerable pressure on the yoke to keep the aircraft level. Flying the Seventeen from the right seat had its disadvantages and Bill wondered whether he'd done the right thing.

"Is the fire out?"

Bianchi watched the engine intently then turned to the pilot, "No! No, it's not!"

Both Lloyd and McGovern confirmed that the fire was streaming out beyond the trailing edge of the wing.

"Help me keep the left wing up and I'll put another charge of CO_2 in her, Louis. The damn fire should go out."

The cockpit suddenly filled with smoke and the pilot was forced to crack the side window. When the smoke cleared he saw that they'd slipped further to the left. He looked up and saw Peek trying to stay with him and he waved Buster off.

Scurlock shouted, "Fire in the bomb bay!"

Bill turned and looked back through the top turret and saw smoke streaming out of the frame around the forward hatch to the bomb bay.

He immediately called the radio operator and ordered him, "Cobb, grab a fire extinguisher and get in the bomb bay and put the fire out."

BOMBER PILOT

The fire had spread from the engine to the wing root and into the fuselage. And much worse into the bomb bay loaded with live bombs and oxygen tanks.

It was extremely difficult trying to keep the aircraft from turning to the left. He had full right trim rolled in. The vertical stabilizer had apparently been hit or the control cables to the rudder were damaged and he had to struggle to keep the bomber in a controlled spiral as it headed earthward. He just couldn't compensate for the lost power on number two engine.

Cobb called from the bomb bay, "Can't get at the fire. The bombs are in the way."

"Okay, Jim get out of there, we'll open the doors and get rid of the bombs." And then to the bombardier, "Woody as soon as Jim is clear, salvo the bombs."

"Clear!" shouted Cobb.

Followed immediately by, "Bombs away!"

Scurlock shouted again, "Lieutenant, the plane's on fire!"

"Hold on, Bayne." Bill ordered, "Close the doors, Woody. Try again Jim!"

Minutes later Cobb called, "Still can't put the damn fire out...not with this hand extinguisher."

"Keep at it Jim. Give him a hand Ray."

The draft created when the bomb bay doors were opened caused the fire to intensify. But when Weyland closed the side window, the cockpit immediately filled with smoke completely obstructing his vision. He was forced to leave the window cracked to clear the smoke from the cockpit.

"Bandits! Five o'clock level!" shouted McGovern. Two ME-109s were coming in from the rear.

Bill shoved the control column forward and retarded the throttles forcing the bomber into a steep dive. He dropped about a thousand feet and pulled back sharply on the column in an attempt to evade the fighters and blow out the fire. As he pulled up and added power, the plane started a violent roll to the left. He eased the power off on the two starboard engines and pushed the nose down sharply to stop the

Fort from rolling over. It took all his strength to keep the aircraft in a controlled descending left turn.

The ME-109's following them down had to pull up and turn away abruptly to avoid crashing into the bomber, when Weyland jerked the Fort up. The plane shook violently from either cannon hits or prop wash. He watched the two fighters come together out ahead of the bomber.

Bill called Cobb. "Jim! How you doing?"

"We've used all the hand extinguishers and it's still burning like hell."

"Bayne, grab an extinguisher and see if you can help Jim."

Scurlock reached down from his top turret position and snapped up the portable extinguisher and opened the hatch to the bomb bay. But he was forced back through the turret into the cockpit by the intense heat. The flight engineer stood behind the pilot and grabbed his shoulder and pointed to the fire blazing in the bomb bay shouting, "SIR, THE FIRE IS OUT OF CONTROL!"

Bill looked back, saw the intense flames in the bomb bay and knew he had to abandon their Seventeen.

"Okay, guys, stand by to bail out. Jim, get out of the bomb bay. Woody, open the doors."

Bill looked up and saw that the two ME-109s were well out ahead of them beginning an aggressive turn for a final frontal attack on the burning Fortress.

He hauled back on the throttles and shoved the nose down and said as calmly as he could, "All right! Everyone out and good luck." He hit the alarm bell and told Gillet, "Be sure you and Jim get Lloyd out of the ball turret." Then to the bombardier, "Woody, you and Joe, get the hell out. Now!"

Bayne standing behind the pilot hesitated a moment and said something to him that Bill didn't understand, then jumped down to the crawl space beneath the cockpit. Seconds later, Weyland felt the frigid air gush through the cockpit as Scurlock jettisoned the forward hatch and heard his rebel yell as he dove out of the bomber. Woody popped his head up between the pilot's seats, ripped his oxygen mask off and shouted, "Don't try to stay with her, Bill. Get out!"

Bill mouthed an okay and then Woody push Joe out the forward hatch and follow him.

Weyland watched the fighters at a slightly higher level heading straight at him. He prayed to God that they would survive this attack, hopefully the last.

McGovern called and said, "Lloyd's out. We're leaving. See you, lieutenant."

Bill turned to his copilot, "Get out and hand me up my chute."

Weyland used an English parachute and just wore the harness. He left the clip-on chest pack in the crawl space. Bianchi got down and handed up the chute and when Bill reached for it, releasing the pressure on the control column, the plane turned precipitously to the left in a steep vertical bank. He dropped the chute pack in his lap and grabbed the yoke with both hands desperately trying to bring the left wing up.

For a few hectic seconds panic seized him. Could he get his chute on and get out of the burning plane? He forced the fear from his mind and tried to account for his crew. All the guys forward had left and McGovern confirmed that he, Gillet, Thomas and Cobb were leaving through the rear cargo door but he hadn't heard from Jim McBride in the tail.

He called over the intercom, "Pilot to tail gunner. Bail out! Bail out! McBride, do you read?"

When he got no response from the tail position after repeated calls, it suddenly dawned on him, "If McBride's gone, he's not going answer me."

As Bill struggled to clip on his chest pack, he stared helplessly at the two German fighters now well within firing range. He saw the wingman's cannons flashing, but saw nothing from the lead fighter. "Probably out of ammo," Bill thought, "but leading his wingman in for the kill." When the Fort slid off in a diving turn, Weyland yanked back on the yoke with such force that the nose rose abruptly. The lead ME-109 dove sharply to his right to avoid hitting the bomber.

But his wingman was so intent on blasting the Fortress out of the sky that he crashed into the raised right wingtip of the bomber as he tried to pull up and away to the left. Bill felt the force of the impact through the control column as it was wrenched from his hands and watched in stark amazement as the fighter burst into flames. Peripherally, he saw the ME-109 roll over sharply and watched the pilot tumble out and float way from the burning fighter. He quickly pushed aside his concern for the German's fate to return to his own adversity and failed to see if the pilot's chute opened. The fighter tore off about six feet of the bomber's right wingtip and the damage further aggravated the bomber's stability.

While fighting to keep the plane in a steep, controlled descending turn, Bill managed to get one hook of the chute pack clamped to his harness, but couldn't fasten the other one. He could only use his left hand, and then only for a matter of seconds, since he needed both hands and all his strength to keep the plane from going into a spin. His oxygen hose and the throat mike cord got in the way and he just couldn't clamp the chute on. He was suddenly seized by a surge of hopelessness and resignation and fought desperately to force the feeling from his mind. On the verge of losing control, he realized that his life would depend on a strong instinct to survive.

After several failed attempts, he decided to bail out with the one hook holding the chest pack. He released his seat belt, stripped away the oxygen mask and throat mike, reached over and held down the pilot's control column with his right hand and got out of the copilot's seat. Bill stood for a moment between the seats reaching over with both hands trying to force the wing up. When he failed, he let go of the yoke, knowing he had to get out immediately before the bomber went completely out of control. Instinctively, he turned to leave the cockpit as he had been trained to exit the aircraft in an emergency. He bent down and crawled through the top turret and instantly realized his mistake. The flames from the bomb bay seared his face. It was like sticking his head in the open door of a blast furnace. The pain was excruciating and he quickly backed out. The smell of his singed hair and the pain of his burned skin was incidental compared to the fear that raged through him.

Confused, he had no alternative but to retreat to the cockpit. He turned and tried to stand, but the G forces on his body as the Seventeen headed earthward made it almost impossible. He grasped the backs of the pilots' seats and tried to pull himself upright. When he saw the horizon disappear in the windshield, he reached forward and grabbed the pilot's control column with both hands in an attempt to level the wings and pull the nose up.

Intuitively, he felt he had to get back in the pilot's seat to stop the bomber from going into an uncontrollable spin. But the force of gravity held him down and he couldn't pull himself up into his seat. Whether it was his effort in trying to stabilize the bomber or God's will, the Fort seemed to hesitate before rolling over. In those few precious seconds, Bill looked down between the seats and saw the open forward hatch. A voice within him shouted, "Get out! Get out now!" He let go of the control column, unknowingly clamped the other hook of the parachute pack to his chest harness, and dove for the opening. His shoulder hit the side of the hatch just as the Fort rolled over. He was thrown against the top side of the crawl space. Looking up at the open hatch, he tried to raise his arms and pull himself up to it as the bomber headed earthward in an inverted dive. The force of the turning plane pinned Bill helplessly upside down in the crawl space.

As the Seventeen continued its slow roll, Bill managed to grab the sides of the forward hatch and pull himself up toward the opening by planting his feet against the top of the crawl space. He got his head and left shoulder out of the hatch and into the slipstream. The rush of air tore off his helmet and as he turned his head, he was momentarily blinded by an intense orange burst of fire that was followed immediately by a muffled explosion. He caught a fleeting glance of the left wing breaking away from the fuselage. The plane's violent reaction to its lost wing hurled Bill into space. His last thoughts were of Mary and the agonizing despair he felt, knowing he wouldn't be with her tonight.

Chapter 25

A disturbing and unusual feeling gripped Mary. She became lightheaded and her hand shook as she reached for a coat. Fearful of falling, she grabbed the back of a chair until the sensation passed. The clock on the wall read twenty-five minutes past two. The feeling startled her because she hadn't experienced anything like it in quite some time, not since she had suffered somewhat similar fainting spells while working as a wartime conscript in a munitions factory. At that time, a physician advised her that she had a mild form of anemia and should be excused from the type of work she was performing, which involved standing on cement floors for hours assembling small widgets. The same weakness flowed through her. She stood still for several minutes gripping the chair, trying to calm herself.

Mr. Chalmers pushed the door open and looked into the dressing room, somewhat annoyed. "Come along Miss Carlton," he called. "We can't keep these lovely people waiting."

Mary looked up. "I'll be right there."

He started to leave, stopped and turned, and looked at her again. When he saw her concerned look, he said, "Mary, are you all right? You don't look well."

She replied, "Yes, I'm fine. Just give me a minute." She reached for the beige belted coat on the rack.

"Not that one, Miss Carlton," he admonished, "the dark green coat. Are you sure you're all right?"

"Yes, Mr. Chalmers."

He left and she put the coat on, checked herself in the mirror, fluffed her hair, and walked into the showroom. There were two buyers from Yeagers and three others whom she didn't recognize. She walked the length of the room and back, stopping in front of each buyer so they could better examine the coat. Mr. Chalmers walked over to her, hitched the shoulders of the coat, and smoothed it down on her back.

He patted her gently on the shoulder when the buyers nodded, "Thank you, Miss Carlton. Now, may we see the beige one?"

Bill was suddenly overcome by a strange sensation of emptiness, apprehension, and depression as he fell through space and away from the burning bomber. The sudden contrast between the muted sound of air rushing past him and the terrifying pandemonium of the fire and the roaring engines filled him with despair-and yet a sense of relief. Bill fought to clear his mind of a temporary state of shock in which he couldn't remember how he had gotten out of the dying Fortress.

He remembered that they'd descended several thousand feet after being hit by cannon fire, but in his desperate flight from the pilot's compartment he failed to check the altimeter and had no idea how high above the ground he was. He was determined to free-fall as far as he dared in hopes of evading capture. After what seemed like an infinitely long time, he pulled the rip cord and felt his chute pop open, jerking him upward.

He looked down on the spectacular panoramic view of the German countryside. It was a clear, magnificent day with unlimited visibility. He saw a large river, obviously the Rhine, and his first thought was that the river would separate him from his crew. He thought they would be on the near side, while his trajectory would put him on the other bank since they left the plane before he did.

Bill was much higher than he thought and realized that he had opened his chute too soon. From his height, he could see seven or eight fires on the ground, which he assumed were burning bombers. He began to swing precariously in his parachute and wondered whether he had properly fastened it.

Now the fear of falling out of his harness consumed him. He looked up at the canopy and was tempted to pull on the shroud lines in an effort to stop the swaying and control his descent. But as he glanced around, the fear of falling out of his chute was quickly replaced by a far more frightening sight. Not more than a mile away, he saw an ME-109 bearing down on him. He was terrified by the shocking realization that after his desperate escape from the bomber he was going to be shot while hanging helplessly from a parachute. The German pilot approached within a hundred yards, banked sharply, circled Bill once, and raised his arm in what could have been a salute, and flew away.

Relief flowed through Bill and he wondered if that was the pilot who led his wingman in for the final attack on their Fortress. He and his wingman, if the latter survived, would share the kill of the American bomber. The Luftwaffe credited the German pilots with four kills when they shot down a four-engine aircraft.

Bill's gratitude toward the German pilot diminished his fear and he regained a measure of self-confidence. His thoughts turned to evading capture.

Weyland had prepared himself, as most airmen did, with a plan of what he'd do if he ever had to bail out. However, his actions to this point were more a reaction to his survival instinct. As he approached the ground, he thought, "I must evade, get away, find someone to help me." Even though he knew he was coming down inside Germany and the prospect of getting away was extremely remote, he knew that he must try.

He landed in the backyard of a house in a small village. The moment he hit the ground, he pressed the release button on his chest pack and slipped out of his harness as the chute collapsed. Suddenly, a young boy appeared at the side of the house motioning to Bill. The boy then turned and ran back around the corner of the building. Bill assumed that the boy wanted to help and followed him around to the front of the house. There, hurrying into the front yard, were two German soldiers in uniforms of the Volkstrum with their rifles pointed at him. His hopes of evading and getting back to England crumbled. One of the Homeguard was an older man in his sixties who was breathing heavily, apparently after he had run some distance to get to the American. The other was a pimply-faced teenager.

The older man gestured toward Bill to get his hands up and said, "Komen sie."

Bill walked out ahead of them to the narrow road that led down to the village. Several people had gathered and they followed him and the soldiers down the road. One person shouted something at Weyland and several others joined in. Although he couldn't understand them, he sensed the anger in their remarks. He heard someone approach him rapidly from the rear, felt two blows to his back, and heard someone spit. Bill turned to face his assailant, an old man, who immediately retreated. The older guard jabbed Bill in the chest with his rifle and motioned him forward. As Bill started walking, he heard a rifle bolt slide back and forward, chambering a round. He looked up to the sky, said a silent prayer, and waited, expecting any minute to feel the impact of bullets striking him in the back. But none came.

Recently, an imbecilic B-17 crew calling themselves "Murder, Inc." had been shot down. A picture of the crew with the insidious name lettered on the back of their flight jackets was seen in most German newspapers. As a result, Weyland was concerned about the angry crowd gathering around him.

They continued down the street to the center of the village and there he was met by another group of people. The guards directed him into a beer garden behind a restaurant where he stood surrounded by more than twenty people-most of whom were very angry women.

The older guard left. A woman then pushed her way through the group. She came up to Bill and asked in excellent English, "Why do you come and bomb the German people? What have we done to America to make you bomb us?"

Bill wanted to say, "What about Warsaw, Rotterdam, London, and Coventry?" but remained silent.

The harassment continued and the tension built. The picture in an English newspaper of an RAF bomber crew who had been hanged in a square in Cologne flashed through Bill's mind. The younger guard stepped away from him and the group of women moved closer. The idea of striking a woman was repugnant to Bill, but if need be he was ready to defend himself. Their jeers and shouts intensified as they screamed and spat at him. Just as they appeared on the verge of grabbing him, a car stopped abruptly and a German in a Luftwaffe uniform got out, shouted, and pushed his way through the crowd. The driver of the car joined him and they took Bill and shoved him into the car and drove away.

He was taken across the river to the local police station in the city of St. Goar and put in a dungeon-type cell in the basement of the building. He was given a sausage sandwich on dark bread and a cup of water. No attempt was made to talk or to interrogate him. The guard slammed the cell door closed and left. Bill was finally alone. He stood for a moment holding the barred door, then turned and sat on the edge of the iron cot. He bent over and put his head in his hands. He was overwhelmed with feelings of despair and remorse. He wondered if his crew had survived. They were so close to finishing and so eager to go home. Why this time? He blamed himself. He had let them all, including Mary, down. Incriminating thoughts and accusations flooded through his mind.

It had been sixteen hours since Bill had eaten and he was hungry, but he couldn't stomach more than a few bites of the sandwich. He finally fell asleep after much soul-searching, thinking of Mary, and agonizing over the fact that he would probably not be with her again for a long time-if ever. He was awakened during the night by rats scrambling across his chest to get to the remains of the sandwich. The scary instant was no doubt a wretched preview of horrors that faced him.

Mary got through the afternoon in a lethargic stupor, modeling sixteen new patterns. After the buyers left, she slumped down on a chair and sat wondering what had come over her. She thought about Bill and wondered if he was all right. Could anything have happened to him? No, she felt certain that he was fine.

"Ere, dearie, 'ave a cup 'o. You don't look too well."

Mary looked up and saw Mae, the seamstress, smiling down at her and holding a cup of steaming tea out to her.

"Ta, Mae. Just what I need. Thank you very much."

Mr. Chalmers came in and said, "It's half past four, Mary. Why don't you run along home. I'll be locking up soon. Are you seeing your Yank tonight?"

"Yes, we're going to Mrs. Freeman's for dinner."

"Lovely. Give him my regards and say hello to Free for me. I haven't seen her in quite some time. Off you go now."

"Thank you, Mr. Chalmers. Good night. See you in the morning."

Mary left the showroom, walked down Oxford to the wine and spirits shop at the corner of Holles Street, and purchased a half bottle of whiskey for Bill. She then walked to the bus stop and caught a Number 159 and arrived home at five o'clock. She wondered whether Bill was on his way to London. She knew he was flying today, and if he'd been on a mission, he normally returned by mid-afternoon. She would soon know. If he was late, he'd call from Bassingbourn.

She still felt rather languid. Sitting in her lounge chair, she kicked off her shoes thinking, "I should get into the tub and be ready when Bill arrives." Then she thought, "Maybe I'll wait and he can wash my back."

Mary couldn't shake the odd sensation she felt in the pit of her stomach that had persisted since she became faint earlier in the afternoon. She sat daydreaming, thinking how wonderful it would be to see Bill again. It had been seven days since they were together, but it seemed like months, especially after being with him every day for a week. Well, they would make up for it with many more days and nights together.

At 5:45, Mary decided to get ready because they were expected at

Mrs. Freeman's at seven. She got up, shook off her melancholy mood, turned on the bath water, and undressed. As she lay back in the warm water, she again experienced the feeling of despair. She couldn't understand the anxiety that persisted in her mind.

She became anxious and distraught. She wondered what could be keeping Bill. He'd been very punctual lately, knowing how she hated to be kept waiting. She decided to give him another ten minutes, then call Bassingbourn. He must be on his way.

At 6:45, Mary got through to Clyde Guilford. He sounded a little stilted and after a polite greeting, he said, "Mary, Bill didn't get back from the raid today. But he still might make it. That's why I haven't called you."

Mary gripped the phone, unable to respond for a moment. Finally, in a trembling voice, she replied, "Oh, Clyde, are you sure?" After a pause and a deep breath, she said flippantly, "He wouldn't go to that extreme to stand me up, would he now?"

"He'd be a damn fool if he did, Mary. We had more than a five-hour delay getting off this morning. They took off a little over seven hours ago. So there's a possibility that he's still flying. Buster Peek was on Bill's wing and he saw Bill get hit. Peek said he tried to stay with him, but Bill waved him off. Buster said Bill's Seventeen went down in a steep diving turn with the left wing on fire. Apparently, Bill was trying to put the fire out. Buster's crew counted six chutes before losing sight of them. You know, Mary, if anyone can make it back, Bill can. I'll call you when I have something solid, okay?"

"Please call me as soon as you know, Clyde, and thank you. I know he'll get back."

Mary hung up the phone and sat staring at the wall. She was completely numb. She just wasn't going to believe that Bill wouldn't be with her tonight. Although she knew what the odds were and that one day he might not return, she wouldn't accept it. Not Bill.

Forty-five minutes later, the shrieking telephone snapped Mary out of her trance. She grabbed it quickly, "Hello . . . Clyde?"

"Hi, Mary. It doesn't look like Bill is going to make it back. It's been more than eight hours now. RAF Air-Sea Rescue has nothing on him.

They picked up Lockhart and his crew in the channel. He was leading the second element in Bill's flight. All the other bases in the UK have been checked as well. He went down over Germany, so his chances of evading are not very good, unless he managed to get the Seventeen back over France before he bailed out. It was a tough mission. We lost sixty aircraft. If he's captured and held as a POW, he'll come back. It's a tough break, Mary. He was so close to finishing. I'll let you know if I hear anything at all, but I'm sure he's okay."

"Thanks, Clyde. I've got to hang up. Goodbye."

She completely broke down and cried until she became nauseous and had to rush to the bathroom. After some time, she remembered that she must call Mrs. Freeman and break the dinner engagement. She splashed her face with cold water and dried her tears. Mrs. Freeman insisted that she come over and they would have dinner together and talk. With some difficulty, Mary convinced her that she would be all right and said she wanted to stay by the phone in the event someone called with news of Bill.

Later, realizing she might do something dreadful if she didn't talk to someone, Mary called Dorothy. By the time she arrived, Mary had pulled herself together. Dorothy's calm and gentle presence helped to soothe the devastation Mary felt.

Dorothy sat with her arms around Mary for some time and when she felt her relax, she asked, "Have you had anything to eat?"

Mary replied, "Not since this morning. Oh, Dorothy, I don't think I'll ever eat again. If anything has happened to Bill, I'll just die. I love him so. I don't want to live without him."

With a subdued but determined voice, Dorothy answered, "Mary, you'll do just as thousands of other women are doing. You will continue to eat, sleep, and work, and he'll come back to you. He'll come back when all the other men do, when this bloody war is over."

"But Dorothy, I don't know if he's alive."

"He is, Mary. I know he is. Now let's get something to eat."

Mary finished dressing, freshened up, and they walked to the local pub on the corner of Park and Baker Streets. Dorothy ordered a double whiskey for Mary and made her drink it. Then she ordered soup and a beer and kidney pie and persuaded Mary to eat most of it.

There were three American officers at the bar and one of them stood with his back to bar trying to get Mary's attention. When she didn't respond, he walked over, pulled up a chair and sat down next to their table, and said, "Hi."

Mary turned and said coldly, "Do you mind?"

Dorothy added, "Please leave us alone, leuitenant!"

He replied, "Well, you two lovely ladies looked kind of lonely sitting over here and I thought I might join you."

Mary looked at his tunic and saw that he was not wearing the silver wings of an airman. She stood up and pointed to his chest and cried, "Get away from me. You're just a ground officer. You're not a flyer. My boyfriend was shot down today flying over Germany. Go away!" She sat down shocked and embarrassed at her outburst and covered her face with her hands.

The officer turned away, red faced, walked past his friends and out of the side of his mouth said, "Let's get the hell out of here."

Mary turned to Dorothy, "I'm sorry. I didn't mean to scream at him. I just lost control of myself." She turned and looked at the patrons seated near them. She tried to smile at them and said quietly, "I'm sorry."

One middle-aged woman whom Mary knew was sitting at the table next to them and said, "He'll come back, Mary. Just you wait and see."

The woman next to her said with a scowl, "The nerve of that bloody Yank."

Chapter 26

Mary got through the next few days in a bewildered and tormented state. She clung to her daily routine, but didn't feel truly in control. Mr. Chalmers was very helpful. He kept her busy, encouraged her to smile, and offered his fatherly advice on every possible occasion. Dorothy, too, helped her through those first few dreadful days. The days turned to weeks and although the hurt remained, she began to feel whole again. Weeks went by without news about Bill. She contacted his squadron several times, only to learn that his promotion to captain came through.

Mary had wired Bill's mother the day after he was shot down, thinking it might help her to know that the men in Bill's squadron felt sure that he got out of the plane and was alive. His mother wrote back to thank her and said the only information she had received was a telegram from the War Department stating he was missing in action.

Six weeks after Bill was shot down, Mary woke one morning feeling nauseous and wondered whether she was having a recurrence of the problem she had on that horrible day, August 17. After her morning tea, the feeling subsided and she forgot about it. The next day, and for several days after, it occurred again. She thought she was coming down with the flu, so she went to her doctor, who examined her, smiled and said, "The nausea you feel when you get up is morning sickness.

You're pregnant."

She looked at him in shock. Her mouth fell open and she placed both hands on her stomach. She was, for once in her life, at a loss for words. She sat numb, staring at the doctor.

He said, "There's nothing to worry about. Women are having babies all the time."

Mary finally said, "Yes, of course, you're right. Silly of me to feel this way. I just didn't think it could happen to me."

"You should have no problem. You're a healthy young woman. Come back to see me in a month."

Mary got up and said, "All right. Thank you very much." She left his office rather shaky, but managed to get to the bus stop. On the bus, she sat back and thought, "I'm going to have Bill's baby. Isn't it wonderful!" But by the time she got off the bus and back in her flat, she was terrified. "What if Bill isn't alive? What if he doesn't want me or doesn't come back to me? How can I support a baby? Will Mr. Chalmers let me keep my job? I won't be able to model his coats. How can I care for a baby if I'm working? What am I going to do?" The doubts kept mounting. "Maybe my mother will help me so I can keep the baby and when Bill gets back, he and I will be married. But what if Bill won't marry me? And if he does, will he still love me or will he despise me for making him marry me? Oh, dear God. Please help me."

After a great deal of deliberation and torment, she decided to call her mother. She got no further than, "Mother I need your help. I'm pregnant."

Her mother's reaction was quick and vehement. "I told you you'd come crawling back, begging me to take you in. And now you want me to support your little bastard? Who's the father? That bloody Yank? What did he do, leave you and go back to America?"

Mary tried to stop her, saying, "Please, Mother, let me explain."

But her mother refused to listen and hung up.

Mary carried her burden alone for two days and finally decided the only possible solution to her problem was to get an abortion. She remembered that one of the girls at the Cabaret had become pregnant and had an abortion.

That night, she called Mr. Murray and he told her that the g Susan, no longer worked at the club, but he had her phone number aı gave it to Mary. Mary phoned Susan and she agreed to take Mary to tł woman who had performed her abortion.

The following day, Mary called in sick and drew £10 out of her posł office account. Susan took Mary to a shabby flat on Wilcox Road in the East End. Susan insisted that the woman was a trained nurse who had performed many such operations. Mary was frightened to death and her fear was compounded after meeting the woman and seeing the miserable state of her home. Susan reassured her, saying that it was a simple procedure and Mary would feel much better when it was over. Terrified and trembling with shame, Mary consented.

The woman brought out a basin of hot water and a bar of carbolic soap, spread a towel on the kitchen table, and said to Mary, "Take your panties off and get up on the table." Quaking with fear, Mary looked to Susan, who nodded.

"Up you go, dearie, and spread your legs. It won't take but a minute," the woman urged.

Mary did as she was told, got on the table, and squeezed her eyes shut. She felt the woman insert a thin medal rod into her vagina, force it up into her uterus, and withdraw it. Mary smothered her screams by clamping her hands over her mouth, biting into her palms until she tasted blood. The excruciating pain was unbearable.

The woman made several more probes and finally said, "All right, dearie. It's over now. Just lay back and rest while I wash up a bit."

Mary felt hot water being poured over her and the sting of the strong soap. She lay on the table for several more minutes before she felt she had the strength to sit up.

Susan put an arm around her and said, "Now that wasn't too bad, was it?"

When Mary looked down and saw a wire coat hanger among the bloody towels, she almost vomited when she realized that it was the instrument the woman had used to abort her baby. She got to her feet

Soon Mary sat holding a mug of hot tea between her hands, letting the warmth penetrate her hands and into her body. She finally got control of herself, thanked the woman, and asked if she would telephone Mr. Chalmers. He arrived a short time later, got Mary into a cab, and after a few brief responses from her he realized what had happened. He gave the cab driver an address in Chelsea and took her to a small nursing station, one of many dispensaries set up during the bombing of London. The doctor quickly assessed the situation, got Mary into surgery, and performed a D and C on her. He told her she had contracted peritonitis from the botched abortion and she'd have to stay in the hospital until the infection was cleared up.

She responded nervously, "Oh, no. I can't do that. I must get back to my job."

"I'm afraid not, young woman It will take at least three to four days to clear up the infection and until it is you must stay in hospital."

He turned to Mr. Chalmers who responded, "Of course. You'll stay here until you're well, Miss Carlton. We can manage very well without you for a few days. I won't hear one more word about it. All right?"

Mary was so weak, she did not have the strength to argue and said, "Thank you, Mr. Chalmers. I'll stay here for a day or so if you think it's all right."

"You'll stay as long as the good doctor wants you to and don't worry about anything. I'll take care of everything."

He bent down and kissed her forehead and patted her hand. He took the doctor aside and spoke to him. After a brief conversation, Mr. Chalmers looked back at Mary, smiled, and left.

The sedative the doctor gave Mary soon forced her eyes closed and she fell into a troubled sleep. She was awakened several hours later by voices and heard a woman say, "Who's that in Recovery?"

The second woman's voice responded, "Oh, just some little tramp. Got herself in trouble with a Yank and found some butcher to give her an abortion. It wasn't done properly and we had to clean up the mess. She's just a little whore, if you ask me."

The first one replied, "Right, that ought to teach her to stay away from the bloody Yanks. The lot of them are no damn good. And I should know."

Mary lay with tears streaming down her face thinking, "How could they say such horrible things about me? I loved Bill so much and I know it wasn't wrong the way we felt about each other. I know it was wrong to have the abortion and God will punish me for doing such a dreadful thing. But they have no right to say such horrid things about me. How could I have kept the baby?"

Mary remained in the hospital for four days. Mr. Chalmers or his wife Paula came by each day to see her. Mr. Chalmers paid all the medical bills and picked up Mary on the day she was discharged and brought her back to her flat. When he dropped her off she hugged him and thanked him profusely.

He blushed, made an endearing remark in Yiddish, and pushed her away saying, "Off you go, girlie. Take tomorrow off and rest. I'll have Paula bring something around to eat. See you Thursday."

She watched him get into the taxi, and then went into the lobby of her apartment block. She retrieved her mail from the letter box and proceeded to walk down the hall to her flat. She shuffled through the few letters and stopped suddenly halfway to her flat. Her hand shook as she held a strange-looking letter addressed to her with "Kriegsgeniengenpost" printed in black letters across the top. She knew it was from Bill. She turned the letter over and on the back next to the word, "Absender" was printed "Lieutenant William H. Weyland, Number 2180." Yes, it was from Bill! She rushed to her door and after several attempts, finally unlocked it, rushed in, and fell into her chair. She held the letter up staring at it and with shaking hands.

She unfolded the letter and there were several phrases cut out of it. But at last she knew Bill was alive! Her heart thumped in her chest as she read,

My darling Mary,

I never thought I would end up here. But I'm okay. Got the whole crew out safely and I'm with Joe, Woody, and Bianchi. Saw most of the other guys in my crew but they were sent [the next few lines were cut out]. It's not too bad here. We get enough to eat and the huts [cut out]. Have met quite a few friends here and so many others that I know. It's like old home week. I miss you terribly, Mary. I just cannot understand why it had to happen to me. I wanted so much to be with you the night of August 17. I should have made it back and blame myself because I didn't. But, darling, God only knows how long I'll be here and if I'll ever get back to see you. It's not fair for you to wait for me. So please don't feel you must. Find someone else. You're much too good for me. Just remember that I love you and I always will.

She crushed the letter to her heart, tears flowing down her cheeks, and said aloud, "Oh, Bill, my love, thank God you're alive. I know in my heart that you'll come back to me and I'll wait-no matter how long it takes."

Epilogue

Captain Bill Weyland, along with eight thousand American airmen and several thousand Allied prisoners of war, was liberated by General George Patton on April 29, 1945, at a POW camp near Moosburg, Germany. Bill was evacuated by air on May 13, 1945, to Camp Lucky Strike near Le Havre, France. The camp was designated to process former prisoners of war and return them to United States military control. There he was deloused, fed, issued a clean uniform, and dismissed. He left with a friend the following morning for Paris, where they got a flight to Northolt, the RAF airbase near London.

Mary and Bill's initial meeting that evening was somewhat awkward, but that feeling was soon ended when they embraced. They were married five days later on May 19, 1945. A gracious hotel manger, touched by their story, gave them one of the royal suites at Dorchester. There they had a lavish wedding reception and a wonderful four-day honeymoon. Dorothy and Stephanos completed their wedding day by hosting a marvelous dinner party for them at the Embassy Club. All was accomplished with little or no planning-just a lot of extraordinary good luck.

Mary's mother refused to meet Bill and took no interest in their wedding. But Mary's many friends made their wedding, although spontaneous, a remarkably wonderful event.